Six-Gun Two-Step

by

William C. Duncan

PublishAmerica
Baltimore

ISBN: 1-4241-8609-9
PUBLISHED BY PUBLISHAMERICA, LLLP
www.publishamerica.com
Baltimore

Printed in the United States of America

Dedicated to my mother and my father.

Chapter 1

It was sometime past midnight when Sandy Polarski felt she just couldn't wait anymore and found herself, shaking and sort of sick, knocking on Bam and Susie's side door.

The neighborhood creeped her out more than a little and it was cold. The drive in from Fairview Park had taken only fifteen minutes because nobody much was out and about. The streets were icy and gusts of arctic air whipped the bitter Cleveland night. Dirty frozen snow coated lawns and sidewalks. The sky sat low and dark, clotted with dense clouds which covered the moon and threatened further misery. But February was usually like that.

Sandy wanted to come down earlier but Suse told her this afternoon that there would be no point until at least ten o'clock.

There was nothing to come down for until Susie got her order filled.

Sandy glanced back down the driveway. The muted sound of rock and roll drifted through the night, closed up inside one of the run-down turn of the century houses closely packed on their tiny lots.

Aerosmith? A few lights were still on in the neighborhood and a little traffic noise filtered over from Bridge Avenue. There were gangs here, and who knew who else, and Sandy wanted to get in the house, get her stuff, maybe get a little high with Susie, and get back home to her warm suburban apartment.

She knocked again, not too loudly, not wanting to attract attention from the next-door neighbor's dark house looming only fifteen feet away on the other side of the driveway. She could go up on the front porch and ring the doorbell, but Bam had a policy: if you come here to buy shit, you go to the side door and knock. People hanging around on the front porch attracted attention. They'd moved six times in the three years Sandy had known them, edging around the West Side, never staying long enough in any rental to draw suspicion from the neighbors and get a dime dropped on them.

Where were they? There were a few lights on inside. Maybe upstairs getting high with the TV on, not able to hear the knocks? Were they asleep? Sandy had never known Susie to go to bed before three in the morning, but who knew? They hadn't answered the phone all evening, but that could mean that they had scored and weren't taking calls until they were good and ready. Sandy's own six-year-old daughter and four-year-old son were in bed and she knew she had to get back home because one of these nights she was going to overstay her absence and one of her neighbors would drop a dime on her. Then no more public assistance, she could lose the kids to her ex, and she didn't want to think about that.

She was freezing her ass off despite her down coat and so she reached out and gently tried the doorknob. It was unlocked. Sandy knew that walking unannounced into a drug dealer's house was a good way to get shot, but she was on a mission and she had customers of her own who were counting on her. Why in the world would Bam leave the door unlocked? Were they expecting her? She eased the door open and stepped inside. A blast of warm air hit her; it had to be eighty degrees in there.

She closed the door and leaned back against it, listening. Ahead, the stairs ran down into the basement and a faint light was on back there somewhere. Sandy turned right up four steps into the kitchen and looked around. The kitchen was, as usual, a mess, and the sink was full of days old dirty dishes. The battered ancient refrigerator hummed in its corner. Filthy plates and the remains of Chinese takeout food cartons covered the table. She walked through and into the living room.

"Susie?" she said, not too loudly. "It's me. Are you there?"

The house was quiet. The living room drapes were closed, the broken down couch covered with a brown bedspread, paperback books lay about. Hot rod magazines lay in a pile on the floor. Bam never left any signs of dealing on the first floor, where somebody coming to the front door or looking through a window could see them.

Had they gone out for some reason? Why would they do that and leave the door unlocked? Sandy headed for the stairs to the second floor.

"Suse? Bam? It's Sandy."

No sounds, no TV. For some reason Sandy felt the fine hairs on her arms and the back of her neck suddenly stand straight up and she wanted to run. That was silly, she thought, *I'm always nervous when I come here,* and she went upstairs, her steps quiet on the worn carpeting.

On the second floor landing Bam and Susie had created a sort of parlor with a loveseat, and chair and a coffee table. This was where they did the transactions, with the product appearing like a birthday present from its hiding place in one of the two bedrooms and being parceled out to the visitor. On the table was a mirror with a razor blade and two thin ten inch lines of white powder on it. A small mechanical scale sat beside it, and a box of plastic sandwich bags.

"Susie?"

Sandy went to the doorway of the darkened room where she knew they slept. Was someone in bed? Sandy needed light because she was feeling another trickle of fear and the darkness definitely wasn't helping. She flicked on the switch next to the door and a sixty watt bulb in a bedside lamp lit the room.

Susie was on her back on the bed wearing panties and a white T-shirt. Her left arm was tied off above the elbow with a thin leather belt and a hypodermic syringe dangled like an obscene bauble from the vein below it. Her dark hair fanned out on the pillow. Her eyes were closed, her mouth a relaxed straight line and she looked very pale. Sandy stepped forward and touched her forehead, then recoiled because she was so cool to her touch. She felt her neck, then shook her shoulder. Then she realized Susie was gone and never coming back.

Sandy stepped backward and her mouth dropped open but nothing came out. She ran into the wall behind her and her knees gave out for a second. She turned and walked onto the landing.

Then she noticed the two bags of white powder on the floor between the table and the loveseat. It looked like two ounces of product, which was exactly what Sandy had come for. She snatched them up and stuffed them in her coat pocket, functioning but stunned, a woman on a mission. She headed back downstairs, wanting to get out of the house as quickly as possible. She half-fell down the stairs and hurried through the house to the side door and it occurred to her to wonder again where Bam was. Taking a chance, she looked down the steps into the moldy unfinished basement. There, in the half light of dim bulb hanging from the low ceiling, surprise number two awaited her.

Sprawled on his back on the dank basement floor was a large man wearing jeans and nothing else, with Bam's signature red dragon tattoo on his right bicep. His head was shattered, his features unrecognizable, a balloon of blood and tissue on the floor beyond him. Near his right hand was a large silver revolver.

Sandy couldn't get out of the place fast enough. Her car was on the street two doors down and she didn't care whether she was acting suspicious or not when she tore off down the street.

Chapter 2

Timmy Thomas finally reached Sandy at home at eleven in the morning. It was Saturday and he was plenty ticked off, but trying his level best to be diplomatic because, hey, he was counting on her to come through even though it looked like she was screwing things up so far.

"Sandy. What's up? Did it happen?"

"Uhhh, well, I don't know what to tell you," she said, and right away Timmy knew something wasn't right, so he chose his words carefully.

"I waited up pretty late for you. I was hoping to see you. Did you, uh, see your, uh, friends?"

He waited a beat or two and thought about the ounce of coke he'd been counting on getting last night, and how Bobby was ticked off too, and Glendy and her friends. They'd sat around Timmy's Lakewood apartment until two waiting for a call, a rare night off for Glendy and a bunch of people out there with dollars in their hands looking for their Friday night nose candy. Their cell phones rang for hours, customers looking to score. They drank a bunch of wine and smoked a few joints, Bobby snorted some meth, and they watched a movie, *Napoleon Dynamite*, which was funny as hell but didn't keep the aggravation from seeping in. Finally Bobby couldn't sit still anymore and took off with one of Glendy's work friends, another dancer named June. Timmy and Glendy eventually crashed and she was gone when he dragged himself out of bed at ten. When somebody drops the ball, especially on a weekend, lots of people wind up disappointed.

Sandy half laughed and then choked, which Timmy found odd under the circumstances. "Oh yeah, I saw them," she said, and Timmy could hear the frayed edge of her self-control letting go. "I think we can do something," she said, now sounding a little desperate, like she was sort of pleading with him. He thought about this.

"What is up with you?" he asked.

"I'm okay, I'm okay," she insisted. "Some things are a little, uh, screwed up for me, but we can get together. Usual place? Noon?"

Timmy did not want to get mixed up in whatever her personal issues were. He didn't think meeting her would be risky because they hadn't said anything on the phone which could be construed as criminal. She was a dingaling but she could get product and her contacts were usually dependable. He decided to play it out but do it cautiously.

"Okay, noon," he said and hung up.

Tim sat for a few minutes thinking about the call. If she had gotten popped by the law she could be drawing him into a setup. But if he didn't go see her he had no chance of scoring an ounce of coke today, he would have a dismal Saturday night, Glendy would be pissed off and difficult, Bobby would be out of luck, too, and their customers would be bitching. He prided himself on coming through; it was what he did. And he stood to make over seven hundred bucks on the deal. A fifteen hundred dollar ounce of cocaine yielded thirty grams. Good quality coke, like what Sandy had been providing, could easily take four grams of cut. If he and Bobby each took two uncut grams for themselves, they'd have thirty grams to sell at one hundred dollars per gram. They'd split the fifteen hundred dollar profit fifty-fifty, as always. A no-brainer.

Timmy yawned and got up off the sofa. His Clifton Avenue apartment was on the third floor of a brick four story 1920s building, overlooking the street. A one bedroom, one bath place here was affordable on his pay, but just barely. He worked on the loading dock of a department store at nearby Great Northern Mall. If things ever got tighter there, he'd either be forced to move to Birdtown or to

Cleveland. He counted on his blond good looks and drug connections to keep girls like Glendy around. He had a year of community college but at the age of twenty-eight he had absolutely no ambition outside of his current lifestyle, unlike the rest of his family.

He wanted to get high, deal and get laid. Bobby had wrestled in high school and did part-time security work for rock concerts. He liked trouble, was bigger and burlier, and that's what made them such good partners: they complemented each other. Timmy believed his personal strength was finesse.

He flicked off the thirty-two inch plasma screen he had bought last year with the profits from a particularly good couple of weeks and stripped off his shorts and got into the shower, blasting his mind and body clean. His head was clearing progressively as he brushed his teeth, pulled on jeans and a polo shirt and heated up some instant coffee and a bagel for a quick fuel injection. He needed to feel solid and alert to do this deal. New Balance cross trainers and a brown leather bomber jacket and he was out the door with a six pack of Miller Lite in hand. One more precaution to take.

He knocked on the aged wooden door across the hall from his own, paused, and heard Albert shuffling across the room. When the fifty-year-old school bus driver answered, Timmy was all smiles.

"Albert, my friend, I would really like to use your car for a few minutes, okay? Mine's been acting up a little and I don't want to get stranded." And he waited.

Albert was bony and a couple of inches shorter than Timmy's five feet nine inches.

His beaky nose was all red veins, his thinning hair awry and his blue eyes peered out from under hooded lids in an attitude of permanent disconnection. Albert didn't care about why Tim wanted to borrow his car yet again, but he did want the six-pack.

Timmy's own car was a red Mustang and everybody who knew him knew it when they saw it. His brother Wade said it was "arrest me red." This was an advantage sometimes because Timmy could fly below people's radar simply by borrowing Albert's seedy gray Ford Focus, and he did it frequently. Albert was home most of the time and only used his car for commuting to work and shopping. Albert got free beer and Tim got stealth and both were happy.

11

The sun was actually out, which was a miracle for a Saturday in Cleveland in February. The temperature was edging up a little, pushing the freezing mark and turning the frozen landscape slushy.

There were lots of people on the roads, a typical Lakewood Saturday.

Shoppers, parents ferrying kids to ballet and tae kwon do, people hustling to restaurant and retail jobs. Tim drove through the grid of streets to Madison Avenue, checked by traffic lights and semi-skilled weekend drivers in salt-encrusted cars. Madison boasted the greatest concentration of bars in the United States and Tim had been in most of them. Small neighborhood establishments, they hosted various softball, bowling, and darts teams and were open and active at this time of day. They and their parking lots provided cover and anonymity for activities like Tim's.

He liked Lakewood a lot because of the dense population and abundance of young women. On any early weekday morning you could cruise down Clifton and see dozens of twenty-something clerks and secretaries waiting patiently for buses to take them downtown to their office jobs. In the evenings they hung out at the trendier watering holes where they often outnumbered the available men.

The downside was that the Lakewood cops were tough, alert and well-funded. Cleveland was like the Wild West by comparison, and the Lakewood PD worked overtime keeping Cleveland crime on the other side of West 117th Street. So Tim was fifteen minutes early, driving his borrowed car, and circling the block around Petrie's Tavern looking for cop presence or anything out of the ordinary.

He found a parking spot on the other side of the street a few doors down from Petrie's and edged in. He watched cars grind by in the frozen muck that plastered the street, first deposited in December and showing no real signs of leaving anytime soon. The sun reflected off the road salt smeared on the windshield, but Timmy had a clear view of the front door of the bar and the parking lot next door.

He didn't spot any loitering strangers, and the police patrol car that crunched by after a few minutes actually reassured him. The middle aged cop inside looked bored.

Sandy's small Toyota pulled into the parking lot a few minutes past noon, late as usual. She hopped out, short and bulky in a red down winter coat, her dishwater blond hair stuck up under an Indians baseball cap, large sunglasses masking her face. She glanced quickly around, didn't spot him, and went into the bar. This was odd; they usually just got together in her car. Maybe she didn't want to wait in the cold. Timmy climbed out of the Focus, waited for traffic to clear and strolled across the street.

Petrie's was dark and close, and old neighborhood bar in an old neighborhood, dark with age and smoke. A young woman tended bar and a couple of guys in plaid shirts and jeans played darts. A senior citizen in a grimy pullover sweater nursed his shot and beer at the bar and didn't look up when Tim entered. The dart guys were laughing and discussing each other's lack of darting ability. Sandy was turning from the bar with a squat glass of ice and amber liquid in her hand. She saw Tim and walked to the nearest booth and slid in, facing the rear of the room. Tim followed and sat across from her.

She downed her drink in three quick swallows as he looked at her.

The tension was obvious in her face and her eyes behind the sunglasses jumped back and forth between him and everything else in the room. She tried a half smile but the effect fell flat and came out more like a grimace.

"Hey, Timmy. How are you doing?"

"How are you doing? You look like crap," he said. "You're worrying me. What the hell is wrong with you? Take off those shades. You trying to be Jane Bond?"

She looked down and back again, tried the smile again but it wasn't any better.

"I need another drink."

She jumped up and went up to the bar, where the girl threw together what looked like a seven and seven and traded it to Sandy for a couple of bucks. She came back and sat down again and took off the sunglasses. Now Tim could see that her eyes were very red.

Her nose was running a little and she sniffed to restrain it. She was having a hard time keeping her anxiety in check.

"We can do this thing. I just need a couple of drinks to chill out. Okay? Are you gonna have something?"

"Sure," he said. He got up and ordered a Coke from the thin brunette, tipping her a buck. She liked that and she smiled at him with her eyes and not just her lips. It never hurt to cultivate new friends.

13

The dart guys started laughing again, loudly, and drinking beer. They weren't paying any attention to them. The old guy was mumbling a little.

The temperature, moderated by the cold air brought in by Sandy and Tim, started rising and Tim suddenly relaxed. He realized he'd been holding his shoulders stiffly, as if anticipating a blow. He worked his head around on his neck to loosen it and sat back down in the booth. This was going to happen and whatever was wrong with Sandy wasn't going to mess it up.

His mind drifted forward to the evening. Glendy would be working and that was too bad, but he could get together with Bobby and get high. They could divide up the coke, adding the cut and parceling it out into little gram envelopes. Then they could start shopping it around to the customers. They'd probably be up at that lawyer's place on the Gold Coast, looking through his floor to ceiling windows out at the lake and the lit up skyline of Cleveland a few miles east from fifteen stories up and drinking good wine while the lawyer's friends came by and scored their blow, sampling it with them. That was always a good time and they met people with serious bucks and sometimes some interesting women. Later, maybe around one in the morning, he could go downtown to the Mad Pony on St. Clair and wait around for Glendy to get off work, and they could go back to his place and get into his stash from the deal and party. Tomorrow was Sunday so they could sleep all day if they felt like it.

He smiled at Sandy and relented. "So what's wrong? Your kids okay?"

He was surprised when her composure almost fell apart completely. She jerked in her seat and looked like she was going to cry.

"Something happened. I wasn't going to tell you. I was just going to say that I gotta find a new source because the old one won't work anymore. I gotta talk to somebody about this. This is bad."

She wasn't loud but he looked around to see if they were attracting attention. Enclosed by the booth's walls, they were invisible to the other patrons and the bartender had disappeared.

"What are you talking about? You got the stuff, right?"

She nodded several times. "Yes. I've got it. But my guys are, uh, they're not gonna be doing this anymore." She looked at him and for the first time she held his eyes. "They're dead."

He didn't absorb this for a second or two. "What do you mean, they're dead? And keep your voice down, okay?"

She was more in control now, the burden shared. She lowered her voice a little and went on.

"I went down there last night and the door wasn't locked and I went in. They were dead in there. I don't know what happened. She was dead in bed and I think she OD'ed. He was in the basement and maybe he shot himself." She looked hard at him and swallowed down her drink.

Timmy blinked and just stared at her for a moment. "You're sure, right?"

"Hell yeah I'm sure!" she hissed. "I about peed myself. I got out of there as fast as I could."

"But you got the stuff, right?"

She smirked and shook her head. "Timmy, man, yes, I got the stuff."

Tim sat back and considered this. He had met Susie and Bam once at Sandy's place and he had driven her down to their house another time. They were alarming people, living farther out on the edge than he was, in a place that invited disaster. He had been right about that.

Bam was a big dangerous looking guy with an unkempt goatee and a shock of thick black hair with a lot of tattoos. He had an intimidating presence and Timmy had no interest in hanging around with him, so he was relieved rather than insulted when they told Sandy to leave him in the car that one time he'd taken her down there to score. They were both a few years older than Timmy was, and at home in the low income, mean streets of the near West Side.

Susie was pretty and kind of sexy but had a hard edge that put Timmy off.

Sandy had told him they both got after her one time when she was down there getting high with them, pulling her clothes off and touching her, kissing her and laughing. She had put an end to it before more happened, she said. But the word was that they were into this sort of thing and pulled it on people who hung out down there. Timmy had been happy to leave them to Sandy. As long as she went down there and did the scoring, he could deal in the suburbs and hang out with Glendy and the other young hotties when they came home from working downtown.

"Let's get out of here. Let's go out to your car," he said, and Sandy nodded.

Once inside the Toyota she started driving around Lakewood in a random pattern. She reached under her seat as she drove and handed him a rolled up plastic bag of white crystalline powder. He opened it and smelled the clean chemical scent and dipped his small penknife blade inside, scooping up a little coke. He dipped his head below the dashboard and snorted it up his right nostril, then did it again in his left. He sat back, exhaled and watched cars and people glide by.

"Do you want some?" he asked her.

She shook her head. "No, I'm good" she said. The smell of the coke yielded to sensation and he felt it spreading into his brain, euphoria accelerating through his neurons in a rush of light.

"That's pretty good," he said.

They drove a little more and he fished the fifteen hundred dollars from his front pocket, a roll of hundreds and twenties.

"Weight looks good, too. Did you check it?" He tucked the bag into his inside jacket pocket and slipped the money into her outstretched hand. She nodded and they headed back to Madison Avenue and Petrie's. Timmy was buzzed, excited, and his thoughts began to race.

"How did you get this if they were dead?"

She looked straight ahead at traffic. "It was sitting there. They must have weighed it out for me before...whatever happened to them."

"Hmm," he said. "It was just sitting around? You should give me a discount." He smiled broadly at her but she only looked blankly at him, then back at the street. Petrie's was coming up. "Is this on the news? Does anybody know?"

She shook her head. "I didn't hear anything about it. I was up all night and watched the news. I don't think anybody knows yet."

She stopped in front of Petrie's and Timmy hopped out onto the sidewalk. It was 12:45 in the afternoon and the sun was even brighter than before. He put on his Ray Bans and scanned the street. There were a lot of "for sale" signs in front of the nearby buildings, and many of the people on the street appeared to be Middle Eastern. Lakewood's population was changing. Change was in the air, he decided.

"Thanks. I'll be talking to you." He smiled, and shut the door.

Sandy glanced at him, nodded, and wheeled back into the street and was gone.

Chapter 3

Wade Alan Thomas III worked his way across the linoleum floor, alternately throwing right and left kicks at the big stuffed vinyl pad held by another seven-year-old. The twenty children in the Saturday afternoon tae kwon do class at Master Kim's reached the far wall, then headed back again. They were thirty minutes into a forty-five minute class and showed no signs of running out of steam yet.

Wade's father sat on a folding chair in a group of parents at the front of the room watching the proceedings. Tae kwon do and other martial arts had been around when he was Little Wade's age twenty-eight years ago, but he'd never been very interested. He liked team sports better and played some baseball and basketball, and later was a running back on the Rocky River High School football team. Soccer hadn't become big yet in that era, but he probably would have liked that, too. Little Wade liked the individual sports best.

The room was warm and the storefront window was opaque with condensation. The other parents, two dads and three moms, either looked on as the kids practiced or quietly read magazines, waiting out the class period. Two parents, a man and a woman, were outside in the cold talking on cell phones. Wade II could make them out through the window, pacing back and forth as they talked, their breath visible, their cells huddled to their ears. Master Kim had a sign on the wall saying "No cell phone conversations please," and Wade had seen him ask a woman to leave once when she had answered the tinny musical ring tones of her phone while in the studio. It had played something classical, he didn't know what, and that was an improvement over some of the ring tones he had heard.

His own mobile phone simply rang discretely.

He liked Little Wade being in tae kwon do because it had helped him to be more confident. His younger brother had been an individualist like his son, interested in solitary pursuits to the exclusion of team activities. Tim liked art and reading but had never gotten involved in any sports at all and had drifted. Wade wanted his son to have the benefit of acquired self-discipline because there was so much that could go wrong for a kid these days without it.

Wade glanced at himself in the mirrored wall next to him. A six-footer like his father had been, he was lean and dark-haired, clean-shaven and recently barbered. He was wearing L.L. Bean Gumshoe Boots and a flannel shirt with his Levi's cords. A dark green Bean Adirondack Barn Coat hung over the back of his chair. His stainless Rolex Submariner peeked out of his shirt cuff. His blue eyes stared levelly back at him. He looked like a successful man, and he was.

Fourteen years out of Ohio State with a business degree and five years post-MBA from Cleveland State, he'd parlayed a couple of entry level sales jobs into a sales manager position at an office equipment firm operating out of Cleveland and into all of Ohio, Michigan and Indiana. They had diversified into computer systems and custom software for business clients and had grossed $22 million in sales the previous year. Wade was overseeing notebook sales and applications for the company with eight reps under him, and reporting to the director of sales. His boss had intimated to him that there was a bump upstairs coming for himself; they were looking for a new V.P. of sales. If Ralph was promoted it meant that Wade or one of two other sales managers were in line for his job, and Ralph sharing this bit of intelligence with him meant that he was looking good for the spot.

Wade had a long range plan, and it included getting the top sales management slot and then, at some point when Ralph moved up further or moved on, the V.P. job. If that opportunity did not present itself he would fish around for another company but he did not really want to leave H.B. Conlin. They had been good to him and he had reciprocated, and they had grown together. There were more or less recurring feelers out from other companies with a national and even international presence who were interested in a possible acquisition, but old man Conlin and the board of directors were happy with the company's growth and performance, unusual in Cleveland's difficult economic climate. They were not inclined at present to sell out and lose control of their enterprise. Wade felt pretty sure that their run would continue the way it had been for the next few years; they were gaining a larger market share.

He had nailed down $172,000 last year and this year, with bonuses, had the potential to be even better. When he and Amanda had bought the house in Westlake four years ago there had been some trepidation about affording it, but no more.

Finally the class ended and the kids morphed from disciplined mini-warriors into what they really were, which was noisy and hungry.

Little Wade sat and put on his socks and shoes and shrugged into his bulky winter coat, a smaller version of his father, dark-haired and even featured.

"Dad, can we go to the movies today? Can we go to Jax's Deli first, though, then to the movies? I'm starving. I want to see that *Supercross* movie. Can we?"

Wade took his hand and they walked out into the strip mall parking lot, plowed out and passable but now showing signs of turning into slush as the sun worked on the piles of dirty snow that ringed it.

"We've got to go home. I've got to go to Grandma's today. Do you want to go? I'm not sure what Mom's got going on, so maybe she can take you to Jax's. Maybe we can hit the movies tomorrow."

They reached the Boxster and Wade unlocked it, savoring once again the fact of his possession of it. He had rewarded himself with it in November, when the year's totals were coming in, taking out a four-year lease. It was dark blue, a joint statement of his affluence and his personal taste. It advertised him as someone who was doing well, performing and succeeding in life, and his co-workers admired it when he wheeled into the company lot.

"What's the rating on that movie?"

Little Wade hopped into the snug passenger seat and slammed the door much too hard for his father's liking, not for the first time.

Wade winced and the boy rolled his eyes.

"I think it's PG-13," he told his dad.

"Uh-huh. And you're seven. How do you figure that's going to work?"

He fired up the car and the throaty rumble put a smile on his face.

He backed out and thumped it into first, cutting across the lot and out into the road.

"Dad, you know how all that stuff works. That's just a guideline. I can watch it. Only disturbed kids can't see it if they aren't thirteen."

Wade shot him a look, shook his head in surrender and laughed.

Wade sailed up Detroit Road, goosing the Porsche through the moderate traffic. It handled like a tight little rocket ship, agile and solid. Driving it was most of the pleasure of having it. Amanda had even approved of it, never begrudging him his financial success.

Truth be told, she got a charge out of riding in it, too.

They cruised through Rocky River and into Westlake, angling over from Clague Road onto Hilliard Boulevard and heading west. Their subdivision was announced by a substantial entryway that was planted with flowering shrubs, dormant now in the winter cold. They coasted through the winding streets past large homes on roomy lots.

A very few for sale signs dotted the properties; most people living here were in solid jobs requiring minimal relocations. Wade's immediate neighbors included an anesthesiologist, an attorney and several people, like himself, in business.

He pulled into his driveway which curved to the side-facing three car garage on their three sided brick colonial. The garage door glided up at the press of the remote button and Wade pulled in alongside Amanda's Jeep Grand Cherokee. The third garage space was cluttered with bicycles, picnic coolers and boating accessories and a work bench stretched along the back wall. They climbed out and went up the three steps and into the warmth of the back hall, walking through to the kitchen. Amanda was at the stove stirring a large stainless steel pot.

She was wearing her nurse's uniform, an official looking white smock with her nametag and hospital ID and her nursing school pin over a flowered top and pants. Thick white socks and comfortable clogs completed the ensemble. She gazed at him over the center island, the hanging cooking utensils only partially blocking his view of her.

Her dark red hair set off her green eyes and he had one of those unexpected and startling moments when her beauty touched him like physical contact.

"I'm making soup," she announced. The aroma of chicken and vegetables simmering densely together suffused the kitchen, and Wade's stomach growled.

"I got called in to work. I've got to do a three to eleven. Sorry!"

She worked in critical care at St. John West Shore Hospital, which was less than ten minutes away. She worked part-time, usually twenty hours a week or less, which allowed her to be available for Little Wade. But she also picked up shifts as a substitute at times, which paid time and a half or better.

She was a skilled RN with ten years of experience. They had met at Ohio State when Wade was a senior and she was sophomore who had just gained admission to the very competitive nursing school there. They had gone out a couple times, introduced by friends who knew her from her hometown of Youngstown and Wade from business school, but not much came of it at first. He graduated and they stayed in touch, friends with an edge of something deeper, and he found himself looking her up when he went back to Columbus on a visit. He started going down just to see her then, and it grew into a physical and emotional bond. She took a job in Cleveland when she graduated, at odds with her parents' preference that she return to Youngstown, and he proposed six months later. A year later they married and Little Wade came along a while after that.

"Okay," he said. "I've got to go to my mom's and help her with some financial stuff. I'll take him with me."

Little Wade was already out of the kitchen and up the curved stairway leading to the four bedroom second floor. His room with its own bathroom was there and Wade heard his TV come on, some Saturday afternoon science-fiction thing. Wade walked into the foyer and picked up the mail from the small table there, where Amanda had left it. A couple of bills, some credit card offers and his copy of *Golf* Digest. Nothing unexpected, everything as it should be. He went back to Amanda in the spacious kitchen with its floral wallpaper, cherry cabinets and solid surface counters, dripping a little melting snow on the hardwood floor, and nuzzled his wife's neck.

A little later he was back in Rocky River at his mother's house, a somewhat downsized and older version of his home. It was the house that he, his brother and their younger sister had grown up in, a comfortable middle-class place in a quiet and established neighborhood. Now Dad was six years gone, Timmy was nearby in Lakewood and Allison was in grad school over at Kent State, working on an anthropology master's and hoping to go further in the world-class program there. She anticipated an academic career, possibly including forensic consulting work. She and Wade had been always been close despite their twelve-year age difference. They shared a curious nature and an intellectual drive, and valued ambition and success much as their father had. Allie loved the academic world and thrived in the competitive atmosphere at Kent, much as Wade had at Ohio State and Cleveland State. She had dated as much as anyone in her crowd but there was no one serious in the picture right now and she was focused on completing her degree and getting into the doctoral program, which seemed pretty likely. She'd made herself indispensable to the department head as a teaching and research assistant.

Wade liked going to his mother's home for a lot of reasons, and fortunately so did Little Wade. Grandma loved him wildly and always had some special toy for him which she had picked up while shopping, anticipating his next visit. He was her only grandchild and had only been a year old when her husband had died. She'd been a young widow and was active in various clubs and groups, and did volunteer work for the American Heart Association, but seeing Little Wade was the high point of her schedule. She maintained a bedroom for him so that he'd feel at home when Wade and Amanda took a rare getaway or allowed themselves a late night out and it included his favorite books and posters on the walls, and a favorite teddy bear on permanent loan. Harriet Thomas was a doting grandparent who read to her grandson, sang to him and liked to have him around. It helped that Little Wade was usually agreeable and was himself a loving person. He even liked Grandma's bridge playing lady friends, and helped with refreshments when they were over.

Wade felt comfortable in his childhood home and felt his father's presence acutely. Wade Thomas senior had done well in the life insurance business and had been a firm and steady hand during his eldest son's growth, a trait Wade II tried to repeat with his own child.

The house was much as it had been when he was alive, although Harriet had relented after a year of mourning and allowed Wade to remove his father's clothing from the closets and donate them to charity. The furniture, the draperies, the dinnerware and the fifteen-year-old TV were all the same as they'd been when Wade's father was alive. His easy chair still faced the TV in the family room, and Wade never sat in it without silently asking his father's permission.

His mother was active and competent but her husband had handled all the financial aspects of their marriage and so she was somewhat at sea when faced with proceeding in life alone. Wade made it a point to look into her routine monetary affairs, making sure her investments were doing well and balancing her checkbook, which was why he was there today. He sat at the kitchen table, fresh chocolate chip cookies cooling on the stove and Little Wade playing on the floor with Grandma's cat, the impossibly large and lugubrious Benny, a gray calico. Full of Amanda's wonderful homemade soup, he scanned the checkbook register with the practiced eye of an MBA and was a taken a little off guard by a payment to a bank that he did not recognize and had not anticipated.

"Mom, what's this $355 check to Ohio Trust Bank?"

Harriet came around the table behind him and looked over his shoulder at the entry.

"Oh, that was for Tim's car," she said.

She walked back to the stove and began transferring cookies from the baking sheet to a plate. Wade looked at her, late middle-aged, dark-haired, attractive still, and entirely too indulgent with her second son. She had co-signed a car loan for him over Wade's objections.

Tim had been enamored for some time with the idea of owning a Mustang, and when he found out that Wade had lined up a Porsche he became determined to make it happen somehow. Unfortunately, his income and credit history did not allow him to get a loan and he had complained repeatedly to their mother about the situation, which was not going to improve any time soon and which he was helpless to change, he said. Predictably, she intervened, once again saving him from himself and assuming co-responsibility for the deal by adding her signature to the bank note.

"He missed a payment?" Wade asked.

Harriet looked at him steadily, smiling, and said, "Well, he was doing very nicely with it but something came up and I had to help. I did co-sign, you know."

"Yes, I do know, and that's the problem," muttered Wade. His mother put the plate of cookies down beside him while he considered the fact that his brother had a $20,000 Redfire Clearcoat Metallic Mustang V6 Deluxe Coupe that his mother was now paying for on a fixed income.

Tim's effort to pay for the car himself had lasted three months.

Chapter 4

There was nothing going on down on Bam and Susie's street when Tim cruised it in the dim afternoon sunshine. A few people were around, a kid bundled up like the Michelin Tire guy made a futile effort to get his sled moving in the corrugated frozen muck of a front yard, but only a couple of cars were moving on the street. There was no yellow crime scene tape, no cops, nothing to suggest that there were dead drug dealers in the shabby two-story house with brown wood siding and its windows blanked out with curtains.

He circled the block twice, noticed an old van parked near the corner which could have been a police stakeout, and didn't slow down or rubber neck too much because, hey, he was just an innocent guy who happened to be driving around, not somebody with thirty grams of fresh cocaine in his jacket. Then he headed back to Lakewood to get the car back to Albert.

Of course he called Bobby right away when he got home; it would have seemed odd if he hadn't because Bobby was expecting him to.

Bobby came over right away and they got down to business on Timmy's little electronic scale, weighing out four uncut grams for themselves one at a time, then four grams of manitol for the cut, which they blended into the ounce. Then they weighed out and packaged up the thirty grams they would sell in little waxed envelopes.

Along the way they sampled the uncut product, then the product for sale. They were pretty buzzed by then and they couldn't tell the difference between them.

They called the lawyer on the Gold Coast and he told them to come over around seven so they chilled out and drank a few beers, watching VH1 on the plasma screen and keeping the high going with a small line every once in a while. Timmy kept thinking about the drug dealers' house and what else was may be lying around in there, and how soon somebody else would find out what had happened.

Sandy would probably tell somebody else because she sure didn't keep it to herself when she was with him. And Bam and Susie most likely had other customers sniffing around, looking for their product and wondering what was going on. Would they show up at the house, like Sandy had, or were they more tuned in to the dangers and protocols of dealing to risk that? Timmy decided that it was better to err on the side of irrational thinking when it came to dealers and users. Somebody would be coming around the house if they hadn't already.

The afternoon wore on and he knew he had to act or lose out. He needed to get back down there before someone else did, and he better not wait until it was too late at night because he didn't want to be the only person on the street when he went into the house. He hoped that normal neighborhood traffic would cover his entry, but darkness would be an ally, too.

"Bobby, man, I'm thinking I want to go see Sandy again in a little while. She said she might get some of that good hash we had before."

Bobby stirred himself from his full-body sprawl in the easy chair facing the TV and gazed over at Timmy. High on the coke and beers, it took a few seconds for the words to register.

"Really?" he said. "I didn't know that. That would be cool."

A little taller than Tim and forty pounds heavier, Bobby looked more like somebody the police would take an immediate interest in, with long and thick dark wavy hair and earrings, tattoos peeking out of his collar and sleeves, and a partiality to tattered jeans and black leather. Although he was a Rocky River kid like Tim, and they had known each other since grade school, Bobby liked to project an affinity for the dark side that Tim found unnecessary. It attracted too much attention. Just the same, Bobby's appearance was intimidating enough to cause suburban hipsters to think twice about short changing them or ignoring overdue payments. Timmy fronted product when he had to, and then only to well established customers.

But it was Bobby who made sure everyone was right on schedule.

"Yeah, she said I should cruise by later and check it out. Maybe you can go to the lawyer's and I'll catch up with you there. Take my car. It'll look better than yours in the lot over there and nobody'll pay any attention to it."

Bobby grinned and nodded his head. "Twist my arm." He had an old beater Camaro that was falling apart and he drove Timmy's new Mustang whenever he could.

They went out a little later and got some food at Mickey D's in Timmy's car and then picked up the Camaro at the apartment.

Bobby happily motored off to the lawyer's place at seven, spinning the tires in the muck, and Timmy headed out to the Shoreway and back down to the near West Side.

Still buzzing on the coke, he was excited about what he was about to do. He didn't want to see any dead bodies and he didn't want to get caught in a house with dead bodies, either by the cops or by any dealers who might come by. But he couldn't believe Sandy picked up a bag of coke that was just lying around if there wasn't something else to be found. Maybe they actually had a kilo or something squirreled away in there, and that's why they'd left a weighed-out ounce sitting out.

He pulled into the street at 7:20 and it was already nice and dark.

The shabby van still sat at the corner and Timmy gave it a quick once-over as he went by but it looked empty. He didn't want to circle the block like he had before because he wanted to be as inconspicuous as possible so he pulled right up to the curb a house short of Bam and Susie's. A car drove by, an old guy driving with a ski cap on, paying no attention to him. He looked over at the house where the kid had been trying to sled in the afternoon, but there was nobody in the windows. Casually he got out of the car and walked directly over to Bam and Susie's side door, as he had seen Sandy do once before, and knocked. It was cold, but that was okay because it kept most people indoors and out of his business. He turned the knob with his gloved hand, quickly stepped inside and closed the door behind him.

He was at once immersed in heat and a noticeable bad odor.

Something was dead in there, for sure. His skin turned to gooseflesh and he shivered. He listened carefully for a full minute for any sign that someone else was there. Then he went carefully down the basement, where he could see a light burning, and immediately saw Bam on the concrete floor. He thought for a second about taking the gun, which looked like a nice stainless steel magnum of some sort, but shrugged off the thought. That was stupid. Only an idiot would even touch a gun that had just killed somebody.

Bam looked terrible and Timmy stared at him for a moment, taking in the pulverized skull. His head had exploded. The blood and brains fanned out behind him were black and congealed, and bits of white skull showing through. It looked like somebody had smacked him with a giant hammer. Would you even have time to feel something like that? Or would it be instant oblivion? Timmy was jittery and unsettled, the coke high giving way to a nervous downhill tension. He knew another toot would help him along but he didn't want to waste any time in there at all.

Could there be anything in his pockets? Again Timmy rejected the idea. He'd seen the cop shows and didn't want any particle of himself coming in contact with the body. He pulled himself away from the gruesome sight and headed upstairs. He didn't know the house but the layout was pretty simple, and a couple of lights were on in the kitchen and living room. Either Sandy had turned them on, somebody else had been there or whatever happened to Bam and Susie happened after dusk. He knew Susie was lying around in there someplace and he steeled himself for his first sight of her.

He found the mirror with the lines on it in the upstairs landing and this time he indulged himself, snorting up a long thread of coke quickly. A Goldilocks and the Three Bears comparison occurred to him, which was kind of funny in a sick way. Then he saw Susie in the dim light of the bedroom and it wasn't funny at all. She was blackish looking and her features were swollen, a syringe incongruously hanging from her arm. The smell was worse than it had been with Bam lying on the cold basement floor. His stomach rebelled for the first time and he felt queasy and alarmed. Seeing dead people in a funeral home was never pleasant, but here he was, pulling a B&E in a drug den full of corpses. This was more like a nightmare in a haunted house. He forced himself to focus and covered his face with his gloved hand to filter out some of the smell while he took a few deep breaths. He could taste the death in his mouth.

29

He started looking around the bedroom and immediately found a small plastic bag of white powder in the drawer next to the bed, along with some matches and a blackened spoon. What in the hell had she OD'ed on? He put his face close to the bag and saw that the powder wasn't crystalline and it smelled funny. It looked more like flour than sugar. Another newsflash: it looked like Susie was into heroin. He carefully closed the drawer again.

In the pocket of a jacket thrown casually on the floor he found a roll of money secured with a thick rubber band. Fifteen hundred dollars. He stashed it in his own leather jacket. He worked his way around the room, delicately probing clothing and drawers and then found what looked like about a half a brick of cocaine wrapped in plastic and covered with tape, hidden under clothing on the floor of the closet. One corner of it had been carefully cut open and then sealed again, so it looked like maybe a couple of ounces had been taken from the pound. Timmy's breath caught in his chest and he felt a huge grin begin to form. He had been right! This was what he'd gambled on.

He did the math in a blur and figured he had just copped about $20,000 in product even if he only sold it in ounces. If he took the time to gram it all out, the profit would be much larger. He stuffed the brick inside his jacket and zipped it up to secure it. Time to leave.

"Thanks, Susie," he whispered, looking at her distorted features one last time. He thought, *You don't need it anymore.*

He snorted up the remaining line on the mirror before he quietly made his way back downstairs, checking to make sure he hadn't left wet footprints on the linoleum kitchen floor. He eased open the side door and started outside when a sound brought him up short.

Someone was crunching their way carefully along the sidewalk, just out of sight, coming toward the house.

Timmy's thoughts went into overdrive. If it was somebody coming here they would find him. If he proceeded out of the house and went to his car they would see him. For the first time he noticed the old single car garage standing just behind the house at the end of the driveway. A side door was cracked open, the overhead door invisible and facing onto the alley in back. He darted out of the house and silently closed the door, quickly and quietly moved to the garage and slipped through the door.

An instant later a figure turned from the sidewalk and strode purposefully up to Bam and Susie's side door. From the darkness of the garage Timmy could just make out that it was a short and broad male wearing a full-length leather trench coat. He had a bandana on his head, but beyond that the moonlight and streetlight afforded no details. He looked around and then, tentatively, rapped on the door.

He repeated this a couple of times and then opened it and let himself in. The door quietly eased shut.

Timmy waited a moment and shifted to get a better look back down the driveway and he bumped into a suitcase that had been placed just inside the door. Curious, he squatted for a better look.

Fake Samsonite, cheap and gray, with rusty latches. But heavy nonetheless. He tilted it on its side and popped it open.

In the faint light he clearly saw that the suitcase was packed with bricks of white powder wrapped in plastic. He staggered to his feet, knowing he had to move fast. He closed the suitcase and latched it and cautiously peered down the driveway. The man hadn't come out; he was probably making his own surprising discoveries in there about now.

Timmy hefted the suitcase, which weighed probably twenty pounds, and darted out of the garage and into the alley. It was dark and nobody at all was around. He worked his way several houses down to the end of the block, cut up the side street and back to Bam and Susie's block. He approached the Camaro carefully, popped the trunk and heaved the suitcase inside. He got into the driver's seat, turned the engine over and edged away from the curb, careful not to spin out or race away. This was too good to be true, he thought.

Hector Ortiz heard the car start up and pushed aside the curtain at Susie's bedroom window in time to see the Camaro cruise past.

He memorized the license plate number.

Chapter 5

Wade wheeled the Boxster into the parking lot of the Log Cabin Restaurant on Detroit Road and looked around for Ralph's BMW. He and Amanda were early and they'd arrived first, as usual. Keeping the boss waiting would not be prudent move.

They got their table and settled in to wait. The place was a log structure dating to the 1930s and a very popular destination for business types and singles in the west suburbs. Small, it offered an intimate atmosphere and excellent food, and the waitresses wore outfits that were just tastefully short of politically correct. Wade looked around the crowded room and spotted a couple of people he went to high school with. Not surprising for a Friday night, the place was booked.

"I think I'd like a martini," Amanda said.

She looked wonderful in a pale green cashmere sweater and slacks, her emerald earrings catching the light from the fireplace.

Wade knew she liked Ralph and his wife Amy, and that would make what was essentially a business dinner that much more pleasant.

Amanda was nobody's pushover and would not easily conform to the role of a corporate wife. On the other hand, she was smart, beautiful and outgoing, which made her welcome on everybody's "A" list.

Wade knew they were an attractive couple and were able to move easily in important social circles, which was both fun for them and necessary for Wade's career.

Across the room Amanda spotted her friend Kathleen with her husband and waved. Kathleen was also an RN at West Shore, working in the emergency room where her husband, Brian Pomeroy, was an attending physician. They lived in Bay Village, as did Ralph and Amy. Wade wondered if they knew each other.

Ralph had asked them to dinner earlier in the week and Wade was pleased; this probably meant that his promotion was seriously moving forward. He settled back and ordered a Grey Goose martini with olives for Amanda and a Glenmorangie on the rocks with a twist for himself. They'd had plenty of nights out with Ralph and Amy Goodwin in the past and a few cocktails would be expected. He was scanning the menu when they walked in.

Amy always made a big entrance, which was understandable, since she was five feet eleven inches tall, blond and whip-thin. A former model, she was taller than Ralph by a couple of inches, which was magnified when she wore spike heels, as she did now. Ralph was extremely proud of being married to her. In their early forties, they had two kids in middle school and seemed devoted to each other. Ralph's portly stature belied his quick mind and considerable personal charm. He was quiet, she was ebullient and his dry wit complemented her ready humor.

After the requisite hugging and cheek kissing they all settled in and Ralph and Amy ordered drinks. The menu was wonderful and inventive, with thick Porterhouses, T-bones and filet mignons complemented by creative side dishes, including southern-style greens with bacon, cheesed garlic mashed potatoes, and Waldorf salad. The wine list and dessert tray were generally considered irresistible. Several minutes into the ordering and cocktailing, Ralph decided to spare them all any extended anticipation.

"Wade, I'll put you out of your misery and cut to the chase, I think." He grinned and raised his glass. "I got the word this afternoon from Mr. Conlin himself. I'm the new V.P. of sales, and you are my director of sales for the company. Congratulations."

Wade smiled and raised his glass as well. While not unexpected, it was very good news and was deeply gratifying. This meant that he could more effectively form the company to the image he envisioned, working with Ralph and with his own team of hard-driving sales executives. There would be more money, sure, and that was an important part of it. But now Wade was truly in deep as a major player with the firm and, even in the unlikely event that it didn't work out for him there, he'd carry that cachet wherever he went.

Amanda shrieked joyfully and hugged him and they all toasted each other. Over outstanding meals they discussed their kids and their plans. Ralph told Wade that golf on a regular basis with Mr. Conlin and various board members would be in the cards for them both, as personal relationships at this level were what drove an enterprise like theirs. Amy told Amanda about a charity for hurricane victims on the Gulf Coast she was volunteering with, and asked her if she'd be interested as well. Later Kathleen and Brian Pomeroy came by and introductions were made all around. It turned out that they didn't know Ralph and Amy but lived less than a mile away from them. Chairs were pulled up and they all enjoyed after dinner drinks together. Amy suggested indoor tennis sometime next week for the three women and everyone agreed that sounded great; they'd discuss schedules tomorrow.

They split up around eleven, everyone heading home to relieve the babysitters. Wade and Amanda had planned to leave Little Wade with Grandma for the night, which suited all parties just fine.

They pulled into the garage and, through look and touch, established that the evening was not yet over for them, that they had more to share and to celebrate with each other, and they moved to the master suite upstairs and lit the bedroom fireplace as a fresh, light blanket of snow began to fall outside the window.

Chapter 6

Bobby Fallon hadn't heard from Timmy in days and he wondered what that was all about. Up in the lawyer's very cool apartment on the Gold Coast last weekend everyone had been having a great time listening to music, talking and buying Bobby's grams when Timmy had reached him on his cell. He said something had come up, a family thing, and he wouldn't be coming by after all. He'd catch up with Bobby in a couple of days and they could get even on the coke.

But Bobby knew this was a load of crap because Timmy never had much at all to do with his family, and he sure wasn't going to start on a Saturday night when they had an ounce of blow to unload. Plus Bobby wanted his car back. It wasn't that he didn't like having the Mustang to bomb around in. It was because he didn't trust Timmy to not do something stupid with his Camaro. So they met on Sunday morning, quickly switching cars and going their separate ways.

Timmy hadn't even asked for his cut of the coke profits. And that was really odd.

Then Bobby found out from June, the stripper he had started seeing, that Glendy had called off of work for the past few days, and he knew something was up. So he figured he'd track them down and find out what was going on. He suspected that Timmy had scored some of that good hash from Sandy and he and Glendy were holed up somewhere smoking until they lost track of the outside world.

But he couldn't get them on Timmy's cell; all he could do was leave yet another voice mail. And the Mustang wasn't parked outside his apartment. Bobby cruised past Glendy's apartment on Lake Avenue near W. 105th but her car wasn't around either, and she wasn't picking up her phone. This was getting stranger and stranger, and Bobby was at a loss. Their weekend ritual was set in stone, and if somebody didn't come up with some product soon they'd have a total wipeout for both Friday and Saturday. Then their customers would be pissed, and he wouldn't be getting high, either.

So it came as a great relief when Timmy finally called him on Saturday morning, exactly a week since they had scored the ounce from Sandy, and told him where they were. Bobby threw on his black leather motorcycle jacket and headed out the door. He had a tattoo on his right forearm which said "Always Down, Never Out" in a circle around a grinning skull, and he reminded himself again that he was down for whatever was happening and with that attitude he'd get over on the bad luck, difficult people and unfair circumstances which tended to dog his existence. He was back in the game, Timmy had something for him, and the weekend was about to take off. He shouted a goodbye to his roommate, Spin, an emaciated guy he worked construction with in Cleveland. Spin had a preference for crappy drugs like meth which Bobby only fooled around with when he couldn't get coke. They shared the two bedroom second floor of an old Birdtown house in Lakewood's southeast corner, the poor, close-packed streets named for birds. He hopped in the Camaro at the curb and headed off across Thrush to Quail and up to Madison Avenue, over to 117th and onto I-90 for the trip downtown.

Timmy knew he had to lay low and figure out what the hell he was going to do about his windfall. When he got home the night he went down to Bam and Susie's and hauled the suitcase upstairs he discovered to his amazement that it contained six bricks of compacted white powder wrapped in plastic and sealed with tape. As with the half brick of coke he'd found in the bedroom, one of the bricks had a corner sliced opened and then carefully resealed.

Timmy reopened it and knew at once that this was not coke but heroin.

Suddenly several things made sense. Sandy's runny nose and miserable state were probably due to heroin withdrawal as much as to emotions. There'd been more going on down at Bam and Susie's than he'd been aware of. It looked like Susie had been using and had OD'ed and that maybe Bam had killed himself in anguish after finding her like that. Either that or she got a hot shot from somebody who then shot Bam and staged it to look like a suicide. But why would anybody kill them and then leave all that product and cash around? That didn't make sense. He figured that, after Sandy, he was the only one who had been in the house until the trench coat guy showed up, or all the goodies would have disappeared. And who was the trench coat guy? Timmy decided that at this point it didn't matter because he had the product and the money, nobody else knew about it, and what he needed to do was keep quiet and figure out how to convert the heroin into cash. Just in case somebody knew about Sandy, like the cops or somebody, and she might send them his way, he thought it was a good idea to go to ground with the drugs somewhere other than in his apartment.

He told Glendy about the pound of coke he'd come into possession of, told her he'd gotten it on a front, and said he wanted to find a place to hide out and sell it off. She knew about a pretty cool furnished apartment which a friend had just vacated and Timmy went downtown and grabbed it, paying two months rent up front from the fifteen hundred he'd taken along with the dope. It was a unique and hidden place, a hideaway built during prohibition where high rollers reputedly went with their mistresses for fun and forbidden pleasures. It consisted of a bedroom in a loft, a living area and small kitchen and a bathroom featuring a shower room in black and white tile with two shower heads for large-scale post-coital cleanup. In an alley off of E. 14th Street between Euclid and Prospect, in the Playhouse Square area, the apartment was only accessible by a steel staircase rising from the dank asphalt and trash bins. A lone barred window overlooked the alley. It was a dump and long past its glory days, but it suited his needs exactly.

He settled in with a bag of groceries and his scale and began splitting the coke into ounces, steadily doing small lines as he went.

The suitcase full of heroin was stowed under the bed. He had never had access to anywhere near this much cocaine before and had to remind himself that it wasn't going anywhere and he could take his time with it. He didn't need to do up a whole bunch at once and stop his heart and wind up like Susie. The image of her lying there, turning black and starting to decompose, was enough to keep him in line and he didn't even do enough to get a nosebleed.

He weighed out fourteen ounces; two had disappeared, probably when Sandy showed up. Of the fourteen he broke four down into grams, carefully taking out four grams of powder from each first and adding four grams of cut. The manitol, a white crystalline vitamin used as a baby laxative, was harmless to most people. So when he was done he had ten uncut ounces and one hundred twenty grams.

If he sold it that way he'd clear $27,000. Plus he had sixteen grams for himself, more than half an ounce. He could see himself using more than that but with those uncut ounces sitting around, he knew he had plenty of reserve.

Glendy came by every day and it broke the monotony.

Sometimes she slept over and they lost all track of time. They had sex and did a lot of coke, the sixteen grams quickly dwindling as they snorted it, then free based it and played games with it, rubbing it into sensitive body areas when they were naked in bed.

They used the shower room for fooling around in for a day or so but that got to be too complicated. They drank a lot of wine and ate very little. Glendy, tall and surgically enhanced, was a stunning brunette but after several days of this Timmy noticed that her twenty-two-year-old face had grown gaunt and he supposed he was looking a little worse for wear, too. The mirror confirmed his suspicions and he was surprised to discover that he was unshaven and couldn't quite remember whether he had showered today or yesterday.

TV reception was terrible on the thirteen inch set with a rabbit ears antenna he had brought along and he knew he couldn't just hang out here, calling in sick on his cell every day, and have any kind of life when he was finished with the deal. He needed to move the coke, and he needed to figure out how to move the smack. He needed Bobby for the first part and he wasn't sure what to do about the second. He thought about it as he lay in bed with Glendy, neither of them sleeping, buzzed and agitated and talking all the time, the six kilograms of smack hidden under the bed like burglar.

He called Bobby and told him how to find him.

Chapter 7

The beat up old black Dodge van pulled out behind Bobby as he cruised out of Birdtown. Hector and Jaime had been staking out Bobby's place since early that morning and now something was finally going on. Hector's relief was like clouds lifting from the sky, letting the sun shine through. He had been suffering for days.

Next to him, riding shotgun, little Jaime didn't say a word. Hector had gotten himself into this and Jaime was along to make sure he got out of it again. There would be no excuse for not getting this taken care of.

Hector Ortiz's first mistake was giving so much product to the two Norte dealers, but he wanted to get the project moving. His task was to set up a conduit for selling heroin into the larger community of Cleveland's West Side, and he found that he needed to use Norte contacts to do that. Other homies were covering the Latino neighborhoods, that was not a problem. Cesar had put him in charge of their effort to branch out and sell smack to the Nortes who made up most of the population of the West Side. This was a huge and untapped market which extended beyond the rough and sometimes trendy neighborhoods of Ohio City, Old Brooklyn, Tremont, Edgewater and Cudell. It meant they'd be able to extend out into Lakewood and beyond, where there was more money and the yuppies were using coke and weed in really serious quantities.

Over in the sprawling East Side, with its largely black population, this process had been underway for a long time, and Cesar's crew was working with the established dealers there to politic them into buying their smack from them. This meant that other suppliers were getting annoyed but that was not Hector's department. Their smack was the best in the world and Cesar had a firm grip on the East Side situation.

So Hector, knowing that these particular Norte dealers were doing a lot of business in coke, weed and some meth, some of which he was selling to them, approached them about exploring the world of heroin trafficking. He let them have a few small bags while they got a taste for it and sampled it to their friends. But being new to that game, they of course didn't have the kind of funds needed to buy a good supply of product. So, following the accepted rules in the business, he agreed to front them their first load of smack. They wanted a kilo; Hector insisted they take more. If they were going to do this they had to be serious about it. Thank God he didn't give them the entire ten kilos Cesar had entrusted to him.

Fully aware of the stakes involved, Hector began watching the house from the van parked on the corner right after he brought them the stuff at six o'clock the previous Friday evening. He wanted to make sure they were doing it right and he wanted to be able to intervene if something unexpected went down.

The trouble was, it was cold as hell out there and he couldn't run the engine for heat because all the neighbors would know he was out there. This North American climate was killing him. He'd been in Cleveland for a year but he was a Tegucigalpa marero, born and bred. He didn't know why people chose to live in a place which to him was like the North Pole. He was here because that's where the money and his homies were, and because he'd be instantly arrested in Honduras.

So he climbed into a down sleeping bag, black leather trench coat and all, keeping an eye on the house from the elevated sleeping platform in the back of the van. He kept watch on the front of the house all evening and saw Sandy Polarski pull up in her Toyota after midnight and head down the driveway and out of sight. She came out again a few minutes later, hopped in her car and took off in a hurry. He didn't know Sandy but he made note of her car and license number and reminded himself to tell the dumbass Norte dealers to tell their people to act a little cooler.

Around three in the morning he closed up shop and went home to his house off of Lorain Road near West 25th, where he lived with his mother and five brothers and sisters. As the oldest child at twenty-three and as the breadwinner, Hector had his own bedroom on the first floor, from which he could escape quickly through a rear window into the alley if the cops or immigration showed up. They were all in the country illegally, as were most of their neighbors.

He was up and back on station the next day at ten in the morning but nothing was happening and he didn't expect any action until the evening. He dozed in the sleeping bag, occasionally emerging to urinate in a liter soda bottle he had brought along and sometimes eating candy bars and chips he's picked up at a convenience store.

He drank some beers, too, which turned out to be a bad idea because he found himself startled awake in the early evening when the dark and cold crept in again and realized that he'd fallen deeply asleep for a while in the warmth of the sleeping bag and didn't know what was going on.

There was a new car parked on the street, a beat up Camaro, which he hadn't seen arrive. He thought maybe he heard its door slamming, and that had also awakened him. But nobody was in sight, meaning maybe somebody had just gone up the dealers' driveway. Alert now, Hector pulled himself out of his cocoon and considered his options.

There had been surprisingly little activity at the house and he didn't know why. The dealers should have called their contacts last night and he had expected to see a low profile parade of people coming and going over the last twenty-four hours. So far, only the chick in the Toyota and maybe whoever this Camaro person was had shown up. The chick had a bulky coat and he felt pretty sure she'd carried out some product. But something didn't seem right and he thought maybe he ought to engage in a little direct supervision. If these clowns didn't get going with this, he'd find somebody who would.

He quietly hopped out of the van and slipped his Vietnam era M-16A1 inside his long coat under cover of the side door. He put the sling over his shoulder and gripped the handle through the coat pocket. It was already locked and loaded. Central America was full of military M-16 assault rifles from the United States and the mareros found them easier to get there than handguns. Plus their intimidation effect was right off the scale, and if you needed to do some real shooting they beat just about anything he could think of.

What he found in the house was both a profound shock and deeply disappointing. The two dealers had obviously been dead since yesterday and there was no product around at all. Had the chick whacked them out? But she couldn't have made off with the suitcase full of smack or he would have seen her do it. Had she sent the Camaro guy around to collect the drugs? Where was he? Then Hector heard the car leaving and got a look at it, couldn't see the driver except to note he looked like a male, and got the license number. He also found the dealers' address book, squirreled away in a living room drawer near the phone, as he expected.

Of course he had to explain it to Cesar. Terror was too kind a word for describing how he felt about that. He'd gone to see him in person simply because there was no way he could avoid it. He was a stranger in the United States and he didn't know anyone there outside of his homies in Cleveland. His English was limited and returning to Honduras was out of the question. His kind were arrested on sight if they weren't killed by the Sombra Negra vigilantes and automatically got up to twelve years in a piss hole prison merely for displaying their mara tattoos. Besides, he could not imagine a life outside of his set.

Cesar was of course not pleased but the fact that Hector had the address book probably saved his ass. Cesar gave him Jaime, a small nineteen-year-old with a quiet demeanor and a trail of five tears tattooed down his left cheek to help him track down the people who had been stupid enough to screw around with Mara Salvatrucho 13's property.

They had started out with a high tech approach, using a public library computer to try to track down the license numbers, but they found that they couldn't access that information. If he'd gotten the identification numbers off the dashboards they would have had a better chance. So they put together a plan and started calling the women in the address book. They got Jaime's sixteen-year-old sister to do it because her English was very good. She'd call the women and ask about their Toyota, telling them she was from a car dealer they'd selected from the phone book and was notifying them of a recall. They only managed to reach fifteen of the thirty five numbers they called in the first few days, and only one woman had a Toyota but it wasn't the right one.

Hector was getting very nervous about this and Cesar wasn't happy either. Hector knew that Jaime was also reporting back to Cesar and didn't even want to think about what would happen if they didn't find the chick. All they needed was her phone number and they could get her address from the phone book or online. He was considering running once again when they hit pay dirt.

When they showed up at Sandy's apartment at 7:30 that Saturday morning she'd been asleep, her two kids eating Cheerios on the living room floor and watching cartoons on TV. Fairview Park was a pretty quiet suburb and they'd been quick and quiet going into the building, a brick three story place overlooking the valley of the Cleveland Metropark; no one had seen them. One of the kids answered the door at their knock and went to get the mom, but Hector and Jaime were already inside the door. Jaime started smiling and talking to the kids while Hector went right into the bedroom and put the M-16 in the sleeping woman's face and tapped her on the forehead with it.

"No scream. Don't scare you kids," he said when her eyes popped open. And she didn't. It was the same chick he'd seen outside the dealers' house, small, thin without the bulky coat, washed out blond hair and pale blue eyes. He hauled her out of bed and said, "You maybe have some thing which is ours."

Her eyeballs were huge and darting around and she said, "Okay, okay. Don't hurt my kids."

He let her go to the bathroom while he watched, pointing the big black rifle at her. She kept talking in a low tone, afraid terribly for herself but even more for the children.

"I'm sorry. I didn't know. I'm really sorry. I'll pay you back. Please just be cool and don't hurt us."

Hector watched, listening to Jaime talk to the kids in the next room, joking around with them. He was nervous about being there but things were going well, she was scared out of her mind and she knew what he was talking about. They would be out of here in no time.

"Okay, bitch. We are cool. Where is the stuff?"

"Not here. It's gone. I'll pay you back, I mean it. It's not a problem. I'm really sorry, I didn't know it was your stuff."

Hector considered this. How could six kilos of heroin be gone, and how the hell was she going to pay them back? He studied her and she seemed scared beyond any possible bullshit. He'd done this before and knew scared when he saw it.

"How you gonna pay us back?" he asked.

She looked wildly around, shaking in her sweat pants and T-shirt, reluctant to stare straight at the gun as if that alone could set it off.

"I can get it. What do you need? $3,000? $4,000? It's not a problem, I swear to you."

Hector kept pointing the M-16 at her but suddenly realized, with depressing certainty, that she didn't know about the heroin.

"What you think cost $4,000?" he asked quietly.

"Two ounces of coke, right?" she answered. "I admit it, I took the two ounces. The money's no problem, I swear." She was pleading, sincere.

Hector felt the weight of his dilemma fall back on his head and he sighed and lowered the gun.

"You know a guy with a gray Camaro?" he asked.

So now Sandy was in the back of their van wearing her red down jacket and unlaced Reeboks, glad to have gone with them to get them out of the apartment and away from the kids. She had led them to Bobby's place in Birdtown and they still hadn't told her what they were really after, but she had explained to her children that she would be back soon and they were safe. She would do anything these men wanted to keep them from doing something bad. She couldn't even imagine what they were capable of but she was going to cooperate if it meant she kept her kids and herself alive. Just like Hector and Jaime knew she would.

Chapter 8

Wade unsnapped the canvas cover on his boat and peered into the dark interior. Aside from a residual smell of staleness and a little mold, the boat was intact and buttoned up tight in its storage berth at the Rocky River Yacht Club. He liked to check on it a couple of times during the winter, just to make sure there was no rot setting in on any of the wooden fixtures and that nobody had been using it for partying.

People he knew had opened their boats in the spring to discover empty liquor bottles and used condoms in the cabins which the management could offer no reasonable explanation for. Of course, that was at other marinas, which didn't always maintain the Yacht Club's high standards. The bulky padlock securing the hatch into his cabin was undisturbed. The incongruous name, *Mudpuppy*, stretched across the boat's stern.

He jumped down to the frozen ground and grinned at the attendant. "Got any larger berths available, Nate?" he asked.

The attendant looked at him askance as they walked back to the office through the yard with its rows of drydocked boats sleeping through the winter. "You getting a bigger boat, Mr. Thomas?" he asked.

Wade glanced back at his twenty-six-foot Bayliner and considered that, while it was a nice enough boat and plenty big for most of what he used it for, which was a little family cruising around Lake Erie in the summer, it may not be appropriate for his new status. As the director of sales he would be entertaining larger groups of people as he had many more sales personnel reporting to him, both managers and their teams. Plus, he may find himself wanting to make a serious impression on various vice presidents and board members. The Bayliner's twenty-six feet was a minimum, in his opinion, for comfortable navigation on the lake, which was actually a huge body of water but quite shallow compared to the other Great Lakes. Sudden weather changes could kick up serious waves which could turn a pleasant cruise into a real battering before you could get back to shore.

Something like, say, a thirty or a thirty-two-foot Sea Ray would really be a lot nicer and more impressive, with a comfortable ride, plenty of amenities and lots of power to get back and forth to the islands or back to safe harbor in a hurry. Not cheap, though, that was for sure.

All boats were holes in the water into which you poured money. A new Sea Ray would be really big bucks, but it would pay off in prestige and that would mean more status and influence in business.

He decided to consider it.

Allison was waiting in the Boxster, shuffling through his CDs.

"Don't you have any, like, Kelly Clarkson or something?" Her face was screwed up in dismay at her older brother's lack of contemporary musical appreciation. She sorted through the Miles Davis, Robert Johnson and Mozart discs, disconcerted.

"How about John McLaughlin?" he offered.

"Who?" she asked.

They buzzed up onto Detroit Road and over to Jax's Deli, which was packed with the weekend lunch crowd and they stood in line while the delicious aromas engulfed them. They were actually salivating by the time the got their takeout orders and, loaded down with corned beef on potato pancakes and cheesecake, headed for their mother's place. Wade glanced over at his sister, bouncing along in her seat to something he didn't recognize on the car's Blaupunkt stereo. She looked like their mother when she was younger, he realized, curly blonde hair and dimples, an older Shirley Temple with drive and a yen to learn about what made people tick, the flesh and bones of them. She and Tim had gotten their mother's blondness, while he looked more like their father had.

"How's school?" he asked.

"Great," she said at once. "We're doing some interesting stuff in the lab. Sherds from Medina County."

Wade knew this had something to do with old pots or something but his ignorance of her field rivaled hers for the Mahavishnu Orchestra. It was amazing, really, how close they were despite the differences in their ages and interests.

Amanda and Little Wade were at the mall with Kathleen Pomeroy and her kids. They'd gone over to Harriet's earlier that morning with Wade to hook up with Kathleen and they'd be back for dinner. Wade and Allie tromped into their mother's kitchen and set the food down, barely getting their coats off before digging in.

"Mom, we're back with lunch," Allie called. Harriet Thomas appeared from the living room.

"That Kathleen is so nice," she said, getting silverware and napkins out. "I just do not know how she can work in an emergency room. It must be so hard to see the problems people have." Wade caught the edge of her mood; he knew she was remembering the night those short years ago when his father was rushed to West Shore with his heart attack, startling, terrifying and unexpected. And how he never came home.

"Thank God for Brian and for Kathleen, too," he said.

"Somebody's got to do that work and I'm glad we have people with their smarts and skill to do it."

Allie looked back and forth between them, her mouth full of corned beef, and nodded in agreement. "Where's Tim?" she managed to say.

"Allie, your mouth is pretty full," gently chided her mother, despite the fact that she was twenty-three and lived in Kent, an hour away.

"That's what I come home for," Allison groaned. "I need to be reminded of my perpetual sub-adult status."

Harriet opened her styrofoam container and brought glasses and a carton of lemonade to the table and joined them.

"I talked to him the other day, but he said he had a cold or something." She took a drink of lemonade and smiled at Allie. "He's been pretty busy with his job."

"Hmm," Allie replied. "Maybe I'll give him a call when we're done eating."

Good luck, thought Wade, as Benny the cat slunk into the room, alert to any corned beef escaping from the table. He'd tried to reach his younger brother all week and had left several messages on his cell phone, including one telling him that Allie was going to be around this weekend. He'd gotten no response at all.

Chapter 9

Bobby got Metallica on the radio as he drove downtown, the traffic busy for a Saturday. "Whiskey in a Jar" blasted out of the speakers, a dark homage to disenfranchisement, theft, murder and consequences. Bobby sang along and pounded the steering wheel, oblivious to the black van tailing him into downtown Cleveland.

He cruised off the E. 14th Street ramp and north to Euclid where he made a right. There were several shows playing at the theaters in Playhouse Square, but traffic wasn't busy because there were no matinees this weekend. He found a spot at the curb in front of the Downtown Family Restaurant and hopped out and locked the car.

The black van shot past him without stopping but he was heading into the parking lot next door and didn't see it. He hiked through the lot and turned right into the alley, as directed. He had a clear view back down to E. 14th but Timmy was nowhere in sight. Dark windowless brick hemmed him in on either side.

A door creaked open up a rickety steel staircase, he noticed a small barred window beside it, and Tim's head poked out.

"Up here," he said.

Bobby was impressed with the hideout; he'd had no idea such a place existed downtown. It was a mess but the layout was very cool.

Timmy showed him around and he really liked the shower room.

"This is bitchin', man," he said. "What the hell have you been up to?"

Timmy looked ragged out, his eyes bloodshot. He seemed a little shaky, in fact. They sat in the overstuffed chairs in the shabby living room and Timmy looked at him levelly and told him, "I did a kind of a side deal, man. Something came up and I took it." Then he picked up a shoebox from the floor and put it on the coffee table in front of them.

He opened the lid and Bobby saw a bunch of coke packaged up inside.

"Holy crap!" He was startled but pleased. "How much shit is that?"

"It was fourteen ounces and I broke it down. There's ten ounces uncut and a bunch of grams. I think there's like a hundred ten or so."

Bobby eyed him speculatively and said, "You've been into it pretty good I'll bet."

Timmy laughed and shrugged. "Hell yeah. Who wouldn't? But we've gotta move it now. Enough playing around."

Bobby grinned. "Well yeah, but hold on a second. I gotta do some quality assurance, first, you know?"

Timmy got a mirror off the wall and a razor blade and laid out a couple of thin ten inch lines and they did them up. And then some more. They talked about where the coke came from and Timmy said he'd gotten it on a front from a new contact who wanted to stay anonymous. Bobby was dubious but wasn't going to argue with this kind of windfall no matter where it came from. They opened a bottle of Makers Mark that Timmy had and drank whiskey straight. They talked about Glendy and about her friend June and about how they would get them to shop some of the grams around but they were going to have to work a little harder to move all those ounces. Maybe the lawyer would take a couple. Spin was a screwup but Bobby figured he could unload some grams at the very least, if they could trust him not to do it all up.

So they planned how they'd unload it all, Bobby knowing he'd cut up some ounces into grams, too, and get plenty for himself. They were buzzed pretty good when they figured Bobby should get back to Lakewood and start trying to get hold of the lawyer.

He left the apartment with four ounces in his black leather jacket, feeling remarkably wealthy and fortunate and high. Instead of going back the way he came he walked out of the alley onto E.14th and turned right, then right again onto Euclid. Somebody was standing next to his Camaro and looking in the windows. It was a small guy, probably not a cop, maybe some street asshole screwing around with his car. He walked up quickly, the guy looking the other way and not seeing him until he was twenty feet away.

He turned to him as Bobby approached and he looked like a small blunt looking Mexican with a blue and white bandana on his head and a long black leather trench coat.

"What's up, dude. You need something?" Bobby asked, large and Anglo and cocaine-intense, a tough guy himself and no sucker for any downtown street nonsense.

Hector was surprised to see him; he didn't know where Bobby had gone and they'd been cruising the neighborhood for an hour looking for him. Finally he'd stopped the van just up the street and gone to look in the car, keeping an eye on the parking lot where he assumed Bobby would eventually reappear.

"This you car, man?" he asked.

Bobby wasn't sure what the guy wanted. "Why? Does that mean something to you?"

Hector kept his distance but looked evenly at Bobby and said, "If this you car, man, I want to talk to you."

"Why? You want to buy a Camaro?" Bobby laughed.

"No, man. If this you car, you a guy I been looking for. I want to talk to you."

Bobby considered this and scanned the street quickly, not seeing anybody else around who looked like they were with this guy, only a few people walking around. "Well, talk to me, then," he said.

Hector shook his head and said, "No, I want to talk to you private. Let's go talk in my van," and angled his head toward the black Dodge up the street, beyond the parking lot.

Bobby really grinned at that one. Was this little Mexican trying a street robbery on him? Or maybe it was some sort of drug deal, buying or selling. He couldn't believe it.

"I think not, amigo. Tell me what's on your mind," he said.

Hector saw that gentle persuasion wasn't working. He'd left the M-16 in the van because he didn't want to be lugging it around Euclid Avenue on a Saturday afternoon but he probably wouldn't put it in this guy's face if he had it anyway. It was too public. He knew Jaime had the gun and would shoot this culero if it came to that, but it wouldn't get their heroin back.

He sighed and said, "Okay. Look, chavalo. You were over on West 33rd Place last Saturday night. Yes?" He sounded patient and reasonable.

Bobby was baffled. This guy was wasting his time; he didn't want to be hanging around Euclid Avenue in broad daylight with four ounces of coke on him, and he had places to go.

"Umm, no, I wasn't. I don't think I've ever been on W. 33rd Place." He gave the Mexican a solid five second stare designed to back him off and end this bullshit.

Hector shook his head and seemed disappointed. He gazed up at Bobby again.

"I seen you car over there last Saturday night. I think maybe you have some thing which is mine." He was firm, not threatening yet, but the edge of it was there.

This was going nowhere and Bobby had enough. "Look, man," he said forcefully, "I don't know what the fuck you're talking about. You got the wrong guy. Take a hike."

Hector took a step closer to the big gringo with the long black hair and tattoos and said quietly, "You are making a bad mistake, pendejo. You are fucking around with the wrong people." His voice turned steely and mean. "We want our shit back. I'm gonna give you a phone number. We know where you live, man. Don't be dumb." He stuck out his hand and there was a white business card in it.

Bobby didn't know what ben-day-ho meant but he was pretty sure it wasn't a compliment.

"Fuck you, you ignorant Mexican prick," he snarled. His face went white and he took a step closer to Hector and balled his fists.

Hector stuck the card under Bobby's windshield wiper and abruptly turned and walked away. Bobby followed him for a few steps, pissed off, ready to start swinging. Hector walked quickly to the black van and climbed into the passenger's seat and across to the other side.

The engine roared to life while Bobby stood there.

"Yeah, time to go, Pancho. Get the fuck out of here," he said, wanting to shout but trying not to attract attention.

The side door of the van popped open and Sandy Polarski was thrown face first onto the sidewalk, her forehead taking the part of the impact that she couldn't buffer with her hands. She rolled in pain at Bobby's feet, blood on her face and hands, crying, and he saw another little Mexican with a machine gun grinning at him from inside the van.

"Call us, amigo," the Mexican said, and pulled the door shut. The van took off into traffic and was gone.

Chapter 10

Dr. Brian Pomeroy snapped the latex gloves off of his hands and tossed them into a trash receptacle as he strode out of the cubicle in the emergency room. A ten-year-old girl with a 104 degree fever and bilateral pneumonia sat listlessly on the bed behind him with her mother anxiously hovering over her, a nurse comforting them both.

After washing his hands Brian stepped to the nurses' station and quickly jotted out his notes and gave orders to the charge nurse. The girl had come down with influenza a week before and now was presenting with something not unexpected but definitely more serious. She'd be on her way to the pediatrics unit in moments and Brian was confident that she'd be OK because the parents had gotten her in to see them as soon as they'd noticed her getting worse.

"There's a Mr. Thomas waiting for you, Dr. Pomeroy. He's in the waiting room," said the nurse.

"Great, thanks, Marcia," he said, and headed for the door. He looked out into the waiting area and spotted Wade sitting in a corner among various patients and family members, a *Sports Illustrated* in his hands.

"Be right with you," he mouthed to him, and Wade nodded. His relief was there, had been for an hour, and Brian was past due to leave. He hurried to finish up his notes, dumped his lab coat and shrugged into his brown leather bomber jacket, and headed out.

They had just enough time to get where they were going, do some looking around, and get back to Wade's mother's house to meet their wives.

Brian and Wade hopped into the Boxster and headed out in the late afternoon sunlight up Crocker Road and west on I-90 toward Freeway Marine in Avon Lake.

"How's the hospital business?" Wade asked over the drone of the car.

Brian laughed and shrugged. A little short of six feet tall, Brian was dark-haired with clear blue eyes that seemed made for calming people in distress. His pleasant demeanor and good looks made him popular with the nurses and reassured the patients. Beneath his appearance was a steady and calculating intellect.

"I don't know about the hospital financials. I'm told we're in good shape. They keep paying me." He smiled. "I can tell you that business is booming; this flu has kept us pretty busy all week."

"It's a little late in the season for this much flu, isn't it?" asked Wade, thinking they'd gotten Little Wade a nasal flu vaccination in the fall, but maybe he should look him over when he got home just the same.

"It's gone this way the past few years. We've seen this increase of cases in February and March," said Brian, leaning back in his seat and rubbing his eyes.

Wade looked sideways at him and gauged his mood. "How's Kathleen doing?" he quietly asked.

Brian's wife had been off work for the previous several days, Wade knew, because of a flare up of her lupus. An autoimmune disorder which had developed two years previously, when their daughter Erin was a year old, Kathleen's systemic lupus alternated between remission and recurrence. When it flared she was immobilized with aching muscles and joints and severe skin rashes.

She continued to manage it with non-steroidal anti-inflammatory medications. She wanted to avoid having to become dependent on the immunosuppressive drugs which could leave her vulnerable to infections and long term complications, but the possibility that she could suffer damage to her heart, lungs and other organs was always there. Wade knew that it was burden for Kathleen, a cheerful woman with long dark hair and an terrific grin whose nursing career was devoted to helping others in need. He could only imagine what it meant to Brian, a healer whose inability to repair his wife must have strained his belief in himself and caused him to question the notion of a benign God.

Brian sighed and glanced at his friend. "She's hanging in there. She's better today; she wanted to go shopping with Amanda. I'm hoping this boat will add a little fun to both of our lives."

"She's got to stay out of the sun, though, right?" Wade said.

Brian laughed and said, "So I guess we'll have to get one with a nice big cabin."

Brian and Kathleen had a comfortable home in Bay Village on Lake Erie, a large cottage really, with spectacular views of the lake and the coastline.

"Do you have a dock at your place?" Wade asked.

"There's one there, but it's in need of a lot of work. I suppose it would be nice to keep a boat right there and use it anytime."

Wade nodded enthusiastically. "You bet it would. You'll wind up with all sorts of boat people dropping by in nice weather, including us. Buy lots of beer."

They looped off the freeway and into the access road leading into the parking lot of the huge indoor showroom. Dozens of boats stood in neat rows on trailers in the lot. They climbed out of the Boxster and entered the building and were suddenly in the midst of an even greater display of sleek power cruisers. The boats ranged up into the fifty foot category and Brian was boggled by the beauty and choices on display.

"Where do we start?" he asked Wade. A salesman was striding over, a big grin on his face.

"Well, you've got a lot to choose from. The twenty-five-footers are probably what you need. Of course, you can buy mine." He laughed.

"We'll be looking at those big Sea Rays over there after we do you."

Chapter 11

Bobby drove smoothly out of downtown, keeping his speed steady. He dodged around a little, eyes on his rearview mirror, and picked up the Shoreway going west to keep his route indirect. He didn't see the Mexicans behind him and he wanted to keep it that way.

Sandy sat in his passenger seat, a wad of Kleenex pressed to her forehead, sniffling and grim. He'd picked her up off the sidewalk and gotten her into the Camaro without getting too many raised eyebrows from passers-by. Her cuts looked pretty superficial but she was shaken and fearful.

"What the fuck, Sandy? Who the hell were those guys?"

She shook her head and told him about how they'd gotten into her apartment and woke her up, put the big gun on her and made her take them to Bobby's house.

"It's about Bam and Susie's. But I don't know what they want."

"Who the fuck are Bam and Susie?" Bobby wanted to know.

So she told him that Bam and Susie were her suppliers, only they were dead. It was in the papers last Wednesday, just a small article, two people found dead in a rented house on the near West Side.

Bobby digested that. "That beaner asked me if I was over on W. 33rd Place last Saturday night. He said he saw my car there."

She nodded. "Yeah, Bam and Susie lived there. Looks like they found me somehow so they could find you." Knowing that she'd been there, too, and they must have seen her car as well.

"They're looking for something, probably something somebody took from Bam and Susie's house. You weren't there?"

Bobby drove along Clifton, heading for W. 117th. "Never been near the place," he told her. But the light had gone on, and he remembered who had been driving his car last Saturday night.

They cruised around a little, Sandy wanting to go home to her kids, but Bobby told her they probably ought to try to cool out the Mexicans before they went near their homes again.

They drove to a McDonald's in Fairview Park and Bobby got out his cell and the white card the Mexican had given him, sitting in the parking lot, minivans full of kids all around. The card had a phone number written on one side and "Marabunta" printed in blue on the other. He didn't know what that meant.

"What are you gonna say?" Sandy asked.

He held up his finger, telling her to wait a minute, and tried calling Timmy first, but of course Timmy wasn't answering.

Bobby knew these guys were serious and that Timmy probably had what they were looking for, whatever it was. Probably the fourteen ounces of coke. If it was up to him, they could go piss up a rope because they were a couple of punk ass Mexican gangbangers and he wouldn't ordinarily play their game at all. Screw them. But they knew where he lived and they knew where Sandy and her kids lived, and they seemed willing to hurt people. And, after all, this really wasn't his doing and yet his ass was on the line. He figured he could try some diplomacy. So he dialed their number and hit "send."

Out on I-77, driving south for the hell of it, Hector's extra cell phone jingled, the one he had for short-term contacts and would ditch after a week. He grinned at Jaime sitting next to him, downing a beer, and said, "This will be the Camaro guy."

"Hola, bato," Hector said into the phone, confident it was him.

"Okay, what the hell do you fuckers want?" Bobby said, and he was calm and reasonable.

Hector winked at Jaime, who stared back at him blank faced, letting Hector know not to screw around because they had to get this settled, and quickly.

"Amigo, I think you know what we want. I saw you car at that house."

"Okay, okay, listen. I was not driving my car last Saturday night. That's when you said, right?"

Hector nodded patiently. "Si, yes, last Saturday night. I saw you car there. I know."

"I was not driving my car last Saturday night. But I know who was. Let's not have a big fuckup here. Let me straighten this out."

Hector shot another glance at Jaime and said, "You not driving? Who, then?"

"Let me talk to the guy. I'll get whatever it is from him. If he fucked up it's on him, not me."

"Yes, yes, on him. So you tell me now," said Hector.

"Look, give me a day or so. I will take care of this; I don't appreciate him doing something to get you guys all pissed off at me and this girl. You fucked up her face, you know. That wasn't cool."

Hector laughed at that. "Hey, she rat you out, she tell us where to find you, chavalo. Don't cry about her."

"Okay, give me a day and I'll get this done for you guys. Just be cool and quit fucking around with people until I get this taken care of."

Hector considered this and said, "I got you phone number now on my cell. You leave that thing on so I can call you. You got twenty-four hours, motherfucker. We know where you and this girl and her little kids live. Do not fuck this up. You don't know who we are and you don't wanna know, believe me."

Bobby, thinking he needed to assert a little control, said, "You're a couple of Mexicans who lost something. I'll get it back if this guy has it. Be cool."

"We're not Mexicans, asshole," Hector said, and hung up.

Chapter 12

It was right after Bobby left the hideout, finally really wrung out from days of doing the coke, his insides feeling like ashes and his brain running like an engine which had redlined along time ago, that Timmy considered getting into the smack. The whiskey and wine were no longer making a dent in his agitation and he hadn't been able to sleep in a long time. He needed to level out somehow and he just happened to have a suitcase full of leveler under the bed.

He untaped the corner of the brick that had already been opened and took out a little bit on his coke spoon. Not enough to make him sick or anything. Just enough to try it out and see what all the excitement was about. He sniffed it up his nose.

After a few moments the sensation of warmth and pure bliss came on and it was unlike anything he'd felt before. He sat down on the bed, amazed and delighted, lying back then in total comfort and ease, suddenly in a universe where there was no pain at all. He had transformed from extreme fatigue and nervous irritation to pure joy and comfort in a few heartbeats. He lay there, content for the first time in his life, as time ghosted by on inconsequential wings. After a long time he sat up and did it again, a little more this time, and was struck by nausea. He stumbled to the bathroom and vomited, then slumped in a chair, the TV on, watching nothing, feeling eternity, adrift in profound calm.

Later he did it again, being careful not to use too much, and then tried a little coke with it. He was the Christopher Columbus of narcotics, discovering a wonderful new world of sensations he'd never imagined. When somebody started knocking on the door he looked out and was surprised that night had fallen.

He let Glendy in and she took one look at him and said, "Man, you are so high!"

She went up into the loft bedroom and saw the suitcase open on the bed and the open brick of heroin and said, "Oh, my God. What in the hell have you been up to?" as if it wasn't perfectly clear.

Glenda Jean Willard's family was from West Virginia, her grandfather pulled north up I-77 to work in the Cleveland steel mills in the 1960s like so many others. Now the mills were gone but her family was long settled into the poor West Side, and Glendy had grown up a gangly and streetwise girl, forced to attend the disastrous Cleveland schools, which were ravaged by the effects of federal court ordered busing. Everyone who could have fled to the suburbs and those who were left struggled in a bankrupt and violent system where even the most basic skill levels seemed to elude both the students and the teachers. As soon as she hit sixteen she dropped out of the school system and its incessant crime and squalor and started making it on her own. She kept at a series of low paying part time jobs until she started to fill out a little and discovered dancing. She started in a dive on W. 25th but she was exceptionally good-looking and actually had talent so she got a boob job and applied for work at the Mad Pony on St. Clair downtown, the premier topless club in Cleveland. She was making really good money and moved to the far edge of Cleveland to a respectable apartment on W. 105th and Lake.

She went downtown and danced at night and high rollers and marginal characters of all sorts frequented the place, and Glendy knew about heroin.

She asked him how much he'd been doing and of course he didn't really know. She asked where it came from, this truly huge load of serious narcotics, and he told her the truth. He explained, in slow motion, stopping frequently as he drifted, how he had learned about the dead dealers from Sandy Polarski and had gone down there in the night and found not only the pound of coke but this suitcase full of smack.

She considered all of this and said, "How much is it worth?"

He didn't know for sure but figured maybe somewhere between fifty and a hundred thousand dollars per brick. So they were looking at three hundred to six hundred grand, wholesale.

She did a little coke and started getting her things together for work, putting her costumes into her bag and fixing her face a little.

"I'm putting the suitcase back under the bed. I'll leave out a little stuff for you but don't take any more than that. You could OD."

He looked at her blearily, but her words registered. He remembered what Susie had looked like.

"How are you gonna move this?" she asked.

"I've been thinking about it," he said.

"You've got no contacts for this sort of stuff. We'll have to figure something out. Don't let anybody in here. I'll be back later." Then she smiled and gave him a big kiss, bright red lipstick on his mouth, her blue eyes looking into him.

"This is very cool," she said. "Nice going."

Bobby tried calling him for hours after he took Sandy home and went back to Birdtown. He looked out the windows every once in a while but didn't see the black van or the Mexicans or whatever they were.

Up in his bedroom closet, under a bunch of junk so Spin wouldn't find it, Bobby had a gun and he figured now was a pretty good time to get it out.

It was a Glock 21, a full sized .45 caliber semiautomatic pistol which held thirteen big fat confidence inspiring bullets. He carefully loaded it from the box marked "Federal Premium Hydra-Shok 230 grain Jacketed Hollowpoint," which somebody told him were about as bad as any bullets you could get. He pushed the magazine into the grip until it clicked and racked the slide so he'd have one ready to go if he needed it. Then he decided he didn't like having it ready to go off like that, nothing but the tricky little trigger safety on it, so he dropped the magazine, cleared the chamber, put the bullet back in the magazine and reseated it again. It would take him a second to get a round into the chamber if he needed it, but at least he wasn't going to accidentally blow his ass off. He stuck it in the back of his pants and tried calling Timmy again.

The lawyer was expecting him and so he went out again after dark and drove over to the Gold Coast, careful that he wasn't followed, circling a couple of blocks looking for a tail. He pulled into the parking lot at the high rise apartment building overlooking the lake and the lawyer buzzed him in. They did a quick deal, the lawyer there alone and nervous about taking a full ounce of coke, but barely concealing his excitement about it. Bobby got $2,000 and headed back downtown again.

He tried Timmy's phone once more and knew he wasn't going to reach him that way, so he circled the block at Playhouse Square but all the street parking was filled, the evening performances sold out, so he had to pay to put the car in a nearby lot. He cut down the alley, climbed the stairway and banged on the door. There was a dim light on in there someplace but Bobby got no answer. He kept trying for ten minutes off and on, finally decided he didn't want some cop to find him back there with coke in his pockets and a gun in his pants, and retreated back to his car. He drove over to the Mad Pony and found Glendy's car in the lot so he went back to Playhouse Square, parked again and got a seat at the end of the bar in a pub next to the theaters. He ordered a beer and settled in, going to the restroom occasionally and doing a little blow in the stall.

The theater crowd came and went, he made small talk with the bartender and a couple of middle-aged chicks from Shaker Heights who seemed to think he was exciting and exotic. They flirted around with him, having an adventure with a street-wise younger guy on their big night out, but he had other things on his mind. Even though they weren't bad looking, he kept one eye on his watch while he bantered back and forth with them. When the bar closed and they left, disappointed, he walked outside just in time to see Glendy pull into the alley. He quickly cut across the street and came up behind her on the steps as Timmy opened the door for her.

He came on with a grin but they were startled to see him.

"Hey, what's up, Bobby?" Timmy said, standing aside so they could both come in. Glendy was edgy, Timmy looked like he'd just woken up. They all sat down in the living room and Bobby couldn't read them, there was a lot of body language going on.

"How was work?" he asked Glendy. "June was working, right?"

"Yeah, yeah. She likes you a lot. She was hoping to hear from you today."

63

Timmy wouldn't meet his eyes and looked like he was going to fall asleep.

"Well, something came up for me," Bobby said, and told them about the Mexicans. Straight through, from A to Z, just the facts.

"So, what I wanna know," he continued, "is what you know about this and what you're gonna do about it?"

Timmy and Glendy were staring at him, then looked at each other.

Timmy's head was bobbing around like he was going to nod off but Glendy was wide awake, all focus and energy.

"You've got the phone number for these guys? Do you know who they are?" she asked, and Bobby passed the card over to her.

"What's with him?" he asked, pointing at Timmy.

"He got into some downers. What does 'Marabunta' mean?"

Bobby shook his head, still studying Timmy. "I have no fucking idea. But they were definitely pissed off and they had a fucking machine gun. Is this because of the coke? Did you get the coke from that house? Is that what they're talking about?"

Timmy met his eyes and he nodded in agreement, serious about it. "Yeah. It must have been their coke. What the fuck do we do?"

Then he slumped into the chair and closed his eyes. He looked asleep.

Bobby couldn't believe this. He pulled out one of his ounces and laid three lines on the mirror and did one up.

"Help yourselves. Where's the whiskey?" He got up and went into the kitchen to retrieve it, bringing back glasses and ice.

Glendy was talking quietly to Timmy when he returned. She smiled up at Bobby and quickly did a line. Timmy's eyes were open and he was paying attention but looked like he could fade out again any second.

"We'll call them. We'll make enough selling all this stuff to pay them off. Maybe we can do more business with them," Glendy said.

She sipped her whiskey and bobbed her head up and down. "We'll call them first thing in the morning."

Timmy roused himself and snorted his line. "Yeah, this could even be a good thing. There's no life like the low life. Now we've got a supplier again."

Bobby looked back and forth between them, surprised.

"Hey, you didn't see these guys. These are Latino gangbangers of some kind. They like to mess people up."

Timmy was smiling now, calm and confident, the plan unreeling itself in his mind.

"We need a supplier. The other ones are dead. We move up a notch and get more bulk product and we make more money. It's coming from the same guys."

Glendy nodded enthusiastically. "We'll move this load in no time. We'll pay them off right away." Still smiling that wide red smile.

Bobby thought it over for a minute, his high building, starting to feel good about the idea.

"But what if they come looking for me again before you settle it?"

Timmy reached into his pants pocket and pulled out a key ring.

"This is to my apartment on Clifton," he said, handing it to him.

"Hang out there for a day or two if you want till we get it chilled out. Sandy's never been there; she can't tell them where to find you."

Bobby nodded. "Okay. I better call her and tell her what's going on, too. Hey you almost got us killed, you fuck!" Laughing now, the future looking brighter.

Timmy grinned at him. "Hey, sorry, man. I didn't know, ya know?"

A little while later Bobby left. It was three in the morning, the still of an early Sunday on the streets, and Glendy and Timmy packed up everything they had on hand into Timmy's Mustang and left town.

Chapter 13

His cell phone jingled at nine in the morning as Bobby slept on Timmy's couch in Lakewood. He saw from the caller ID that it was the Mexicans.

"What do you want?" he asked, rolling over and looking at his watch sitting on the end table. "We've got four more hours."

The Mexican laughed softly and said, "Amigo, I say I gonna check up on you. Where you at?"

Bobby came fully awake then. "What do you mean, where am I at? Where are you? Are you at my house?"

"We jus' see you car not home, we kinda wonder," Hector explained.

Bobby picked up his Glock, a reflexive gesture, the gun heavy in his hand.

"Look, pal, stay the fuck away from my house. No, I'm not there and you ain't gonna find me. But I'm working on your problem and everything's looking good."

Hector seemed to consider this for a moment. "Don't you hide from us, we can find you, asshole," he said. "What is good? What you workin' on?"

"I saw the guy you're looking for. He says he took some stuff from that place you said. He's got your number and he knows you want something done by one o'clock and he told me he'd call you."

Bobby heard them talking together, the sounds muffled. Then the Mexican said, "What this guy's name? Where I can find him?"

Bobby laughed then. "Look, buddy, I told you it's under control. You'll hear from this guy. Maybe we can do more business, you know? So don't fuck it up. You'll hear from him by one." And he hung up.

He fell back on the couch again, sleep creeping up on him, but he thought about Spin and decided he should call him. Spin was in bed and not happy to be awakened. "Hey, man, you see anybody out front?" Bobby asked.

"What the hell do you mean? Who's out front?" Spin asked.

Bobby heard him haul himself up and stumble to the front windows.

"There ain't anybody out there. Who you looking for?"

Bobby relaxed a little. "Hey, man, there's a couple of Mexican guys in a black van cruising around, I think they were just there. This is something to do with Timmy, not me. But maybe you should, like, go away for a while. Go to your sister's house or something."

Spin clumped to the bathroom and Bobby heard him taking a piss.

"What the hell, man. Why are these guys looking for Timmy?"

"It's business. Don't worry about it. But until Timmy settles with them, maybe you should go to your sister's."

Spin groaned, "Oh, man, how long is this shit gonna take? I don't wanna go down there. She's got like twenty rug rats running around that place, you can't get any peace and quiet."

"Yeah well, maybe it's a good idea just the same. Just for a day or so, until everything's settled. You hear me?"

Next he called Sandy and she was already wide awake.

"What's going on?" she asked.

Bobby explained that he'd seen Timmy and he had what the Mexicans were looking for.

"He's gonna call them this morning. Don't worry about it."

He could tell she was pacing around. "I haven't slept all night. I've been afraid those guys will come back. I'm thinking of getting out of here. You know, just in case."

"Yeah, that's a good idea. I was gonna suggest it. You got someplace to go?"

"Yeah, yeah," she replied, still upset. "I grew up in Parma, my mom's out there. I can take the kids over for a couple of days. That Timmy's a sneaky dude; I won't be happy till this is all settled."

Bobby turned on the TV, sort of amazed at the brilliant picture on the big plasma screen, clicking through the cable channels for something good.

"Yeah, great, why don't you head out now? Peace of mind, you know? I've got your cell number and you've got mine."

He hung up and settled back into the couch, watching a show about the battle for Baghdad until he dozed again.

At five minutes after one that afternoon he was still in front of the TV, drinking a Miller High Life from Timmy's refrigerator and eating a ham sandwich on rye with Swiss and some good brown mustard when his cell phone went off. Surprised, he saw it was the Mexicans again. He thought about ignoring it but he was curious about what was going on. Maybe it was all settled and they wanted to talk to him about doing more business. So he answered it.

"Okay, you fucker," said Hector, very evil sounding, soft but with steel in his voice. "No more fun. Now we gonna fuck somebody up. You think you can fuck with us? Bad, bad mistake, amigo."

Bobby straightened up and said, "What're you talking about? Didn't he settle it?"

Hector laughed a little but there was nothing funny in it, only grim irony.

"Nobody call us. You invisible friend maybe lost our number, hey? You in trouble now, culero."

Bobby hung up; there was nothing else to be done. He tried Timmy's phone and kept on trying all afternoon but nobody was answering.

Chapter 14

On Thursday Wade had a meeting downtown at Erieview Plaza with a prospective client. The man was fielding a small sales force around Cleveland, selling services for nonprofits, and needed a handful of laptops and specialty software. Ordinarily this could be handled solely by a Conlin salesman or his manager, but the customer was waffling and Wade decided that a visit from the director of sales would demonstrate Conlin's interest in even the smallest client and their commitment to his well being. Plus it was just a short cruise downtown from their corporate headquarters at Rockside Road, so why not make the trip? They closed the deal.

It was late in the afternoon and Wade decided to head home rather than go back to the office. He still hadn't heard from Tim and it was starting to concern him. He ordinarily stayed out of his younger brother's routine but he would be going through Lakewood anyway, so why not stop by? He knew Tim usually got done with work around four and it was half past that.

He pulled into the lot behind Tim's building and didn't see his car. He considered just going home; he knew Amanda was planning something nice for dinner and they had an open house at Little Wade's elementary school that evening. But he was already here and maybe he could leave a note or something.

He was surprised when he pushed the buzzer and a voice came over the intercom.

"Who is it?"

<del><ins>69</ins></del>

It wasn't Tim's voice, but it sounded familiar.

"It's Wade," he said.

The door lock hummed and Wade walked in and headed up the stairs to the third floor. He knocked on Tim's door and it opened and Bobby Fallon was standing there.

"Hey, Wade, how are you doing? Nice suit. Come on in," he said.

Wade walked into the living room which was strewn with beer bottles and empty chip bags. The TV was on softly, some music video playing. Bobby closed the door and locked it and came in behind him.

Wade had known Bobby since his brother had started hanging around with him in elementary school. Wade always felt a little sorry for Bobby, whose father was a landscaper instead of somebody who employed a landscaper, which included a significant percentage of the people in Rocky River. This made him something of a second-class citizen to many of the more self-satisfied kids in town, especially as they entered high school and became more aware of the vagaries of social status. It was as if these upscale kids thought they actually had something to do with their families' financial standing, and Bobby had something to do with his. Nursing a low grade inferiority complex, Bobby had become a little countercultural and one of the town's resident bad boys. He had never gotten into serious trouble that Wade knew of, but the image was there. Of course, the upscale kids were often bad boys too. But they did it more discreetly, disguised in Lacoste knits and neat haircuts, while Bobby looked wild.

Wade hadn't seen him in months and took him in quickly, reluctant to stare. Bobby was about Wade's height but broader, barefoot, wearing black jeans and a red T-shirt from some Florida bar. His colorful tattoos crept out up his neck and down his arms and his dark hair hung heavily on his shoulders.

"Is Tim here?" Wade asked. It looked like Bobby was settled in here, hanging out. Were they roommates now? Bobby shook his head. "No, no he isn't. Hey, have seat, Wade," he said, moving a sweatshirt off the couch. "Have you talked to him?"

They sat and Bobby clicked off the TV.

"No, I haven't talked to him in a couple of weeks, anyway. I thought I'd drop by and see what was going on."

Bobby nodded a few times. "Would you like a beer? He went out of town last weekend. He asked me to watch the place. You haven't heard from him?"

Wade wondered briefly why the place needed watching, but dismissed the thought. "No beer, thanks. I've got to get home soon. No, I haven't talked to him. Where did he go?"

Bobby studied him for a moment and said, "Do you know Glendy? His girlfriend? They went to visit her relatives, I think." He looked away and picked up a beer bottle and took a sip.

"Yes, I met Glendy once. She seemed nice. When will he be back?"

Bobby shook his head and said, "I'm not sure. I haven't heard from him either. Maybe you could ask him to give me a call if you talk to him?"

"Yes, sure. You can't get him on his cell phone?"

"No. You know how Timmy is. He only turns that thing on when he wants to talk to somebody." They both laughed.

Wade asked about Bobby's family and his father, mother and brothers were fine. Bobby asked about Harriet and Allie. Wade knew that Allie had harbored a crush on Bobby from childhood, when he was her older brother's sophisticated friend. Seeing him now, still a nice kid but going nowhere fast, Wade felt relief that Allie rarely saw him anymore. She was on a success track in academia and an entanglement with somebody like Bobby would not be likely to be a positive thing for her.

"They're fine. Our mom keeps busy and Allie's still at Kent in the master's program in anthropology. She was up last weekend but she couldn't reach Tim either. She's doing really well."

Bobby smiled. "Good for her. I'm glad to hear it. Tell her I said 'hi' if you get a chance."

Wade stood and they shook hands and said their goodbyes.

Wade was out the door and rolling toward Westlake as rush hour traffic started to pick up on Clifton. Bobby sipped his beer and watched the cars go by in the street below from the front window, standing back a little in the dimly lit room in case anybody was watching.

Chapter 15

They caught Spin on Friday at a stop sign in the Old Brooklyn neighborhood where his sister lived. He'd gone back to Birdtown to pick up a few things; he didn't know what Bobby was so paranoid about but a quick in and out wasn't going to hurt anything. Of course they already knew his car on sight and were watching for him.

They tailed him out of Lakewood and when he stopped at the stop sign in the close old neighborhood and there were no other cars around they boxed him in, the black van cutting in front and Manuel's old Chevy coming right up on his rear bumper.

Hector jumped out of the driver's seat of the van and Manuel came out too and they rushed up on Spin, trapped behind the wheel and surprised. Hector grabbed the door handle and yanked it open, nobody ever locked their doors although they should, and put the M-16 right in his face. Spin's hands came up and he tried to say something but they grabbed him, Manuel shifting the car into park and turning off the ignition, and hauled him out of there. Holding his arms roughly they hustled him around to the side of the van where Jaime had the door open and they all crowded in.

Inside with the doors closed they beat him for a solid thirty seconds, Hector using the gun butt on his head and back, Jaime and Manuel using bars of soap inside of socks. The inside of the van was just big enough for them to put some reach into their blows.

Then they took duct tape and wrapped his ankles tightly together and secured his hands behind his back.

"Hey, asshole," Hector said. "You mouth and nose all fucked up. I put this tape on you mouth you gonna not breathe. So shut the fuck up."

Manuel went back to the other car where Luis was keeping watch and they all got going again, blood speckling their clothes and their faces.

It was dusk when they pulled up to the storefront on Denison overlooking the freeway, the van turning down the alley behind it.

Jaime hopped out and pushed the button set into the old brick and somebody inside hauled up the corrugated steel delivery door and they drove into the small warehouse section of the building.

They pulled Spin back out of the van and threw him onto the concrete floor. He looked around and saw six Mexicans standing around him wearing baggy clothes, the guy in the leather trench coat with a machine gun, one of the others holding a big black handgun.

They looked angry and excited, their eyes wild, his blood on their hands.

"Okay, asshole, we got you now. We wanna hear some good news. You got some good news for us?" said one of them, a little taller and older than the others and wearing a polo shirt and chinos, not as gangy looking as the others.

Spin groaned and spit out blood and a broken tooth. He couldn't move at all and he thought a couple of ribs were broken.

"What do you guys want? What did I do?" he asked.

The older guy stepped close and said, "You assholes stole our shit, man. Your buddy with the Camaro and the girl. You gotta tell us where they are and where our shit is. Now."

Spin shook his head, sad, knowing this would not work out, knowing these guys were stone killers and he was in trouble, the worst trouble ever of his poor, short life.

"Bobby told me somebody took your stuff. That's all I know. I'll tell you whatever you want but I don't know shit."

The older guy said, "Where is Bobby? Where is the girl, Sandy?"

Spin could only keep shaking his head. "If I knew I'd tell you. I really would. Bobby told me to stay away from the house and I don't know where he is. He didn't tell me. I know Sandy a little but I haven't seen her. I don't know shit."

The guy knelt down beside him and looked into his face, Spin bleeding and crying a little now. The guy had even features, didn't look like a badass, but his eyes were flat and he had those Mexican gang tattoos, thin blue script on his arms and neck.

"Do you have any idea who we are? Did you think maybe nobody would miss all that smack?"

Spin was startled by that. "Smack? What smack? I don't know anything about any smack."

The guy sighed, his patience being tried. "Six kilos of smack, my friend. Bobby took it outta that house on W. 33rd Place. You think nobody gonna pay for that?"

Spin felt lost now, the bad ending coming and he could see it.

Crying, he said, "Bobby said Timmy had to settle something with you guys. It was Timmy's problem, not Bobby's. I don't know anything."

The gangbangers all looked at each other. "The invisible friend," remarked the older one. "Who is Timmy?"

"Timmy Thomas," Spin said.

"Who is that?"

"He deals. He's Bobby's friend, from Rocky River. Bobby told me this is his problem."

The guy stood back up and they talked among themselves, quick Spanish that Spin couldn't follow. The pain from his injuries was very bad, worse than anything he could remember, and for a second he thought maybe he could give them what they wanted and they'd be grateful and help him, alone and hurt on the cold concrete.

"He's blond, wears a brown leather jacket and drives a red Mustang. I don't know where he lives, but he hangs around with Bobby."

They talked some more and glanced at him a few times. Then they wandered to the far end of the room, the guy with the pistol watching him, the rest talking. Then the older guy and three of the others went through a door and he didn't see them anymore. He lay on the floor for awhile, shivering, crying off and on while the two guys he'd been left with sat in chairs and looked blankly at him. They opened beers and began drinking. One of them turned on a radio and Mexican music, bouncy and quick, drifted through the room.

There were several sections of storage shelves lined up but Spin couldn't see anything on them. Some boxes were stacked in a corner and he thought maybe they had drugs stored there. It was a dirty old stockroom or small warehouse, that's all, with a large washtub or sink against one wall. He could see a lavatory next to the tub.

He was numb and starting to think he was home in bed, not on a cold floor and all busted up at all, when the older guy poked his head back into the room and spoke quickly to the two who were watching him.

"Okay, Cesar," said one of them. The older guy left again.

The one with the pistol, a little guy with teardrop tattoos on his cheek, moved his chair up close to Spin and sat down, looking at him and said, "It you bad luck you fuck with us. You know who we are?"

Spin shook his head.

"We MS-13," the guy continued. "We start out in L.A., 1969. Our people leave El Salvador in the war, live in L.A. You know El Salvador? After a while they don' like us in L.A. no more and send us back to El Salvador." He grinned. "We do OK in El Salvador, we get big. We in Honduras, El Salvador, Mexico now. Me, I am from El Salvador like Cesar. Some other homies, they from Honduras. We are marabuntas, you know?"

Spin shook his head. He only vaguely had any idea where El Salvador and Honduras were. Mexico, he understood.

"Marabunta, he is like a red ant, eats everything, takes over everything. We say we are marabunta. Our group, we are mara, each of us is a marero. MS-13 is Mara Salvatrucho 13; we are guys from El Salvador, take over everything. You know what is 13?"

Spin did not know, and said so.

"I tell you inna minute," continued the guy. "They don' like us back home no more either, they kill us, put us in jail. Lots of us come back here now, life is better, we can get more done. You unnerstan'?"

Spin nodded. "Why are you telling me this?" he asked.

The guy gestured to the other one, who put down his beer and came over. The little guy stuck the gun in his belt and they both grabbed Spin by his arms and lifted him off the floor. They dragged him over to the big old industrial sink, the faucets jutting out, and lifted him up and put him inside. Spin was curled in the tub, painfully contorted, and the little guy leaned close.

"I am Jaime. He is Luis. Thirteen means thirteenth letter, M. Some say thirteen is 'mara'. I tell you now a secret, mister stupid Anglo. You fuck with us, you die. 'M' means murder, an' I want you to know this."

Then they turned up the Mexican music really loud and both got machetes from inside the lavatory. Spin watched them coming, their eyes flat and remorseless, and he opened his mouth to scream but they never gave him the chance.

Chapter 16

Wade and Amanda left their health club on Columbia Road on Monday evening and headed to Harriet's to pick up Little Wade.

They enjoyed going to the club together whenever they could, but that wasn't usually how it worked out. There was a children's room, of course, but Little Wade wasn't a big fan for some reason. He preferred to stay home or go to Grandma's. That meant that when Harriet was tied up, Wade and Amanda had to take turns going to the club.

They did different things there, but got some overlap, too. They both did some free weights and used the treadmill. Sometimes they circuit trained on the machines. They liked varying the routine so it didn't become stale. They liked running together, too, but the Northern Ohio winters restricted that a lot, so the treadmills were a necessity. Since most of the other members felt the same way, in the evenings after work people had actually been known to pay off others to get their treadmill time.

Amanda liked the aerobics classes, which Wade had no interest in other than a little chaste eyeballing of the women participants in their spandex outfits, looking as if they had been spray painted nude in bright colors. Nobody did that too overtly, though; it was regarded as bad form. Despite this discretion the club was widely considered something of a meat market and many people Wade and Amanda knew found dates there regularly. But for the Thomases, it was about exercise.

They drove into Rocky River in the Grand Cherokee. As soon as a third family member entered the transportation equation, the Boxster stayed home. It was a blast to drive but could only comfortably hold two people. The snow was melting and they were pleased to see some hint that spring was finally on the horizon. Maybe they'd be able to start on a jogging schedule next week, if the weather reports were right.

Harriet and Little Wade were sitting together on the living room sofa when they came in through the garage. Nobody locked their doors much in the neighborhood and Harriet generally kept the outside door in the attached garage unlocked. There was an open book between them but they seemed to have been caught in mid-conversation, their mouths half open and their faces animated.

"What are you two up to?" Amanda asked.

"Grandma says smoking is okay," Little Wade said seriously, his eyes wide with disbelief.

Harriet shook her head and laughed. "No, I didn't say that." She looked at Amanda. "You know I would not tell him that. What I said was that smoking is not against the law."

Wade and Amanda took their coats off and sat in the easy chairs at each end of the sofa.

"What brought that up?" Wade asked.

His mother gestured toward the picture window and said, "Mr. Hamilton from down the street was walking his dog and smoking a cigarette. I'm sure Marge doesn't allow it in the house. Anyway, Wade was surprised to see him doing it and pointed it out to me."

Wade and Amanda looked at each other and nodded knowingly.

"They put it all in the same category in school these days," she said. "Drugs, alcohol and smoking. They really discourage it all."

Wade shrugged. "Well, I'm sure it's better if the kids are taught that it's all harmful. But there is, or should be, a distinction between things that are illegal and those that aren't."

Little Wade was following this closely and said, "But those things are bad! They aren't good for you!"

Harriet took his hand and said, "Very true. I'm glad you know that and that I don't have to worry about you ever having those kinds of bad habits."

The phone rang in the kitchen and Harriet smiled again at Little Wade and then got up to answer it.

"Are you ready to head out, my friend?" Wade asked his son.

"I guess," he replied. "I have a little homework. I have to find a current event in the paper."

"Did Grandma feed you?" asked Amanda.

"We had macaroni and cheese," said Little Wade.

Amanda grinned at Wade and said, "Your mother deserves a medal for eating more macaroni and cheese than any human should have to bear in the name of pleasing a grandchild."

Harriet came back into the room. "Somebody called looking for Tim. I said he's not here. She sounded like a young Hispanic woman. Who would that be?"

Wade shrugged. "I have no idea. Have you heard from him?"

"Yes, in fact I have. He called me from his cell phone yesterday. He's in New York with his girlfriend. He said he'll be there for a little while and asked me to send him his bill folder."

Wade was puzzled. "What bill folder?" he asked.

"Oh, he has a folder here with his utilities information, rent and so forth. He was paying bills here last month and left it here. I guess he wants to make his payments while he's gone."

That was when he got her to make his car payment, Wade thought.

But he was glad to hear that Tim had made the other payments himself. That was a little encouraging, anyway.

"So you've got an address for him?" he asked.

"Um-hmm," Harriet replied. "Anybody want a piece of cake before you go?"

They passed on the cake and got Little Wade's things together.

Bundling up, they kissed Harriet goodbye and tramped out to the Jeep, loaded up and headed for home.

Harriet straightened up the house a little, putting the boy's toys back in his room. She got into her pajamas and settled in to watch a little TV. At nine o'clock one of her Heart Association friends called and they talked for a while, then she went back to the television until ten-thirty when she began to doze. She roused herself and switched off the TV and went around the living room and kitchen turning off the lights. As almost an afterthought, she flicked shut the deadbolt on the door to the garage. Then she went upstairs to bed.

Outside an older compact sedan cruised past the house for the third time as the lights inside went out one by one. There was no red Mustang in the driveway and the car slowly eased out of the neighborhood, careful to avoid doing anything out of the ordinary.

Chapter 17

Bobby got the call on Tuesday from a guy who knew Spin's family. Someone had found him in a patch of weeds in a dismal corner of the Flats, the old industrial bottoms of the Cuyahoga River Valley between downtown and the near West Side. He was wrapped in a plastic painter's drop cloth. The guy said Spin was almost in pieces, the plastic needed to hold him together. Chopped to pieces.

Bobby knew Spin hadn't been at work on Monday but that wasn't unusual. He went out and got a copy of the paper and there it was in the obituaries. Robert Traczewicz, aged twenty nine, survived by so-and-so. He should have been shocked but instead just felt cold creep up his back. He figured these guys were bad news; this made it clear just how bad they were. And Timmy skipping town had been a giveaway, too. If this was a simple theft of even a pound of coke, it was resolvable, like Glendy said. They could pay for it by selling the coke and still make a little profit. Something more was going on, and whatever it was looked like it was serious enough for Timmy to get out of town and for the Mexicans to come sneaking around and killing the first guy they could get their hands on who may have had something to do with it. This was a message, no doubt about it.

They would kill anybody connected with this thing.

Poor Spin. The guy was an innocent bystander, for Christ's sake. He was sort of a goof but he never hurt anybody. Bobby felt his anger build. What in the world had Timmy done to get them into this mess? Sitting on the couch in Timmy's apartment, he called Sandy Polarski on her cell phone and got her right away.

"How you doing?" he asked.

"I'm good. I haven't heard from those Mexicans at all, and that's okay with me. What's going on?"

"You're still staying at your mother's place, right?"

"Yeah, why?"

"Timmy didn't settle this thing. He left town and I don't know where he is."

"So the Mexicans are still pissed off?"

Bobby decided to tell her straight out. "You can't go back to your place at all. Have somebody get your things. Don't be seen over there, or let your car be seen over there. You know my roommate? They found him dead in the Flats."

Sandy was silent for a moment. When she spoke her voice was unsteady.

"The Mexicans killed your roommate? Is that what you're telling me?"

"I think so. He was chopped up in a plastic sheet. They found his car a block from his sister's place."

"Jesus Christ, Bobby! What the hell did Timmy do?"

He shook his head. "I don't know what he did. This isn't about a little coke, though. I'd bet on that. Do these guys know your last name?"

"Yeah, they looked at my driver's license. Bobby, I'm sorry…I'm pretty sure I mentioned your last name, too."

Bobby swore. "That's fuckin' great. Is Polarski your married name? Or is it the same name your mother's got?"

"It's my married name."

"What address is on your driver's license?"

He heard her rummaging around a moment, then she said, "It's the Fairview address."

"Okay, good. They probably won't know how to find you." He thought, *If they did you'd be dead by now.*

"What the hell are we gonna do?" she asked, the fear really starting to build.

"Well, like I said, don't go back to the apartment. Maybe get rid of your car, too. You might want to think about leaving town."

She was quiet for a while. "I'm so sorry, Bobby. They pointed that gun at me. I thought they were gonna kill my kids."

"Okay. Just stay out of sight and don't give them another chance. Don't say anything to anybody that could attract attention."

They hung up and Bobby considered the situation. They knew his last name. His family lived in Rocky River but they had an unlisted phone number, Bobby's dad not wanting his customers calling the home line all the time. What had the Mexicans gotten out of Spin? He hadn't known where Timmy's place was or where Bobby's family lived, and they hadn't shown up at either place, so that was probably a good sign.

He had sold off most of the coke he'd gotten from Timmy and had some cash, so he drove over to the small used car dealer on W. 117th and found another car, a black Firebird, to replace the Camaro. The dealer would take the trade but basically he was robbing him. Bobby didn't care. He just wanted to unload the car.

He went back to Timmy's apartment and started going through the want ads, looking for a new place to live. As usual, there were plenty of apartments and half houses in Lakewood that were available. He arranged to look at a couple that night, and another two the next day.

He settled on an apartment a few blocks down from Timmy's, right on Clifton. It was a small one bedroom and suited him fine. He got a guy he knew to loan him a van and go with him over to the Birdtown house at night to pick up his things.

Surprisingly there was no sign that the cops had been around at all. They went up to the second floor and quickly got Bobby's belongings and a few pieces of furniture, Bobby touching the Glock in his waistband. He figured the police might want to talk to him but he wasn't planning to be available. Then he moved into the new place and started looking for a new job.

The night he left Timmy's apartment he loaded the flat screen TV and all of Timmy's beer into the Firebird and took it with him. Screw Timmy.

Chapter 18

Hector didn't like the way Cesar had been looking at him since this whole mess began. It was very demeaning to him to be treated like an arrastrado, a nobody, all of a sudden. He had been in the organization since he was fifteen and he had a reputation like Tarzan in Tegucigalpa. He was known as a guy who could get things done and he was fearless with their enemies.

When Cesar had been forced to flee back to the States because the death squad was after him, Hector had helped get him out of the country. And when Cesar was getting set up in Cleveland and needed his right hand chavalos with him, Hector had gladly left his country to join him. Who had Cesar turned to when they got this great new source for heroin, the best anywhere, and decided to build a whole new market among the prosperous gringos of the West Side? Hector, that's who.

But now there were times when he came into the store and found Cesar and little Jaime talking together and they would look at him and shut up. That was disturbing enough. Besides that he suspected they were planning deals that they weren't telling him about at all. He asked Cesar what was going on, what was new, and Cesar told him, "You need to finish up this six kilo thing. Then you can think about what's new."

They had paid their source for the kilos. So they were out a lot of money. True, Hector had managed to move two of the remaining four kilos through a dealer he had developed who was operating out of an antiques shop in Kamms Corners, and that money was in hand.

But the theft had marked him as a screwup, and that was very dangerous. He would have to find a way to recoup the loss. At the very least he would have to punish all the gringos who had stolen from them. They were rich people, and maybe he could get at their assets somehow if he couldn't get the heroin back.

He had found Timmy Thomas's house by searching on the Internet for phone numbers in Rocky River listed under his last name.

They had Jaime's little sister call around, like they did with the Toyota and the women in the address book. There were twenty two Thomases with listed phone numbers in Rocky River. When she called the twelfth one, where the number was listed to "H. Thomas," a woman told her Timmy wasn't there. So that was the place.

They cruised the neighborhood on several nights and on a few afternoons using different cars. It was an upscale kind of place, quiet and established, and they had to work at fitting in. There were some Latino laborers around the town and they dressed in khaki working clothes, so Hector and a couple of others got some, too. Still, guys like them had very little excuse for hanging around out there at night and they had to be careful.

Hector saw the lady who lived in the house twice. One time she was standing on the front porch talking to the mailman. The other time she was sweeping out her garage. There was a small white SUV in the garage but they never saw a Mustang. So after a while Hector decided Timmy wasn't living there, but it looked like his mother was.

Days had passed since they had taken care of the skinny asshole who lived with Bobby Fallon. It had driven Fallon and the woman underground. Nobody was living at the woman's apartment now, and the house the two men had been in was empty as well. Fallon wasn't answering his phone, but the number was still in use. Hector needed to drive the rats out into the open again.

He got hold of a nice gray van and put magnetic rubber signs on both sides which read "Brown Plumbing" with a fake phone number.

He stuck license plates on the front and back which he had stolen from a truck in a downtown parking lot. The van was empty from the front seats back and he put rope and pillowcases and duct tape back there. He got some chloroform and a sponge but he didn't think he'd need it. He also had a toolbox with a few loose tools inside. He drove into Rocky River by himself on a sunny day at ten in the morning and called the Thomas house as he got near.

"Hello?" said a pleasant woman's voice.

"Sorry. Wrong number," Hector said, and hung up.

She was there.

He drove into the street where she lived going slowly, doing a quick scan for nosy neighbors or police. He knew that once he had mamacita, Bobby Fallon would answer his phone pretty damn quick.

And Timmy Thomas would come up with whatever they asked for in order to get his mother back. It always worked in Honduras. Why not here? He backed into the driveway, hopped out and opened the rear doors of the van. He looked like a plumber in his khaki pants and shirt. He had on a brown cotton workingman's jacket that covered the nine millimeter Beretta in his belt. The garage door was closed and five feet from the back of the van; he'd get her out through the garage and nobody would even see it. The tool box in hand, he casually strolled to the front porch and up the steps.

From behind him, a quavering voice said, "Oh oh. Is Harriet having plumbing problems?"

He turned around and two old ladies were standing there looking at him. They were scrawny with frizzy white hair and incongruously dressed in athletic suits, one blue and one red, with reflective blazes and highlights across them. They had on white cross training shoes which made their feet look too big. They were wearing bifocals with clip on sunglasses, which they had flipped up to get a better look at him. Each had on one of those visor things, like a baseball cap without a top. Where had they come from? Before he could answer them the front door opened and Harriet Thomas appeared.

"May I help you?" she asked.

Hector looked back and forth between them for a moment as they expectantly regarded him.

"Is this 1059 Burbank?" he asked, deliberately naming a street nearby.

They all shook their heads vigorously. "No," said Harriet. "I'm sorry. That's two blocks over."

The women all smiled, embarrassed for his error, wanting to be helpful.

"Would you like us to show you the house?" asked one of the old ladies.

"No, no, gracias, I will find. Sorry." Hector came down off the porch, turning his head so they couldn't see any more of his face. He put the tool box quickly in the van, closed it up and got into the drivers seat.

"We thought you had a plumbing problem, Harriet," he heard one of the old ladies say.

He started the van and took off, being careful to go in the direction of the house he'd asked for.

Harriet Thomas said, "You know, he sounded just like that wrong number I had a few minutes ago."

Hector cursed as he drove, keeping his speed steady. He was deep in white suburbia and he had to maintain his composure until he got clear of it. He wanted to pull the magnetic signs off but he waited until he got had been on the freeway long enough to be in Cleveland, then pulled off and did it on a side street. He stripped off his jacket, too, and stashed the pistol in one of the pillow cases. He had a bottle of tequila in the glove compartment and took a long pull on it.

Swearing and raging, he drove to the store on Denison, went into the alley and got out and rang the bell. Luis opened the delivery door and closed it after he drove in.

He hopped out of the van, angry, and walked through the door into the storefront, where Cesar and Jaime sat behind the counter. It was a gift shop, with some hardware and odds and ends for sale that never attracted very much business, on purpose. Hector yanked open the refrigerator and grabbed a Carta Blanca, savagely twisting the top off and gulping down the beer.

"Birria, amigo?" asked Cesar, sarcastically. "What the fuck happened?"

Hector shook his head, mortified by this latest failure. "It went wrong," he finally said.

"Come, let's go in back," said Cesar, and they all went into the storeroom. Cesar walked to the van and opened the side door.

"No lady inside," he observed. "Where is the lady?"

"I was at the door. Neighbors came. I made an excuse and left."

Hector stared at his feet, then finished the beer.

Cesar, Jaime and Luis exchanged glances. "So they saw you, huh?" asked Cesar.

Hector was stopped by this, alarmed for the first time. "Hey, they don't know me. You know, we all look alike to them, right?"

Cesar found the gun in the pillow case as he went through the things Hector had in the back of the van. He checked to see if there was a round in the chamber and then turned to Hector.

"You think they're not going to remember you? You think maybe they'll forget that a Latino came around acting funny? I think you messed up again, Hector. I think you just set us back again. We're not going to be able to get near that place for a while. We're shit out of luck about our money for now."

Hector shook his head emphatically, seeing the gun. "No, no, Cesar. I can get to them."

"I don't think so, bato. This is just too much, I'm afraid."

And he shot Hector between the eyes.

Chapter 19

Wade was at his mother's house looking over her checkbook, performing his monthly oversight for her, when he discovered she had made another payment on the Mustang.

Harriet was out grocery shopping and Wade sat at the sunlit kitchen table, the checkbook and a box of receipts in front of him, an iced tea untouched at his elbow. How had this happened? She had made the payment a couple of days ago, exactly a month after the first one. Hadn't she told him that she'd sent the bill folder to Tim in New York? Wade rubbed his eyes in frustration and then rechecked all of her figures. He reviewed her monthly statements from her savings account as well, then those from her annuity and mutual fund accounts. She had a couple of certificates of deposit which were safe but earning very little. The annuity provided steady income and the mutuals did well but tended to fluctuate quite a bit. The stock market always performed well over time but had been a little flat ever since the post-9/11 recovery.

Many people had shifted stock market money into real estate because of the uncertainty. Now there was concern that the housing bubble would burst, as it surely must in some overpriced markets where average people could no longer afford starter homes. Wade was sure that many real estate investments would continue to do very well but he couldn't convince his mother that it was something she should be involved in. Like many people, and particularly older people, she was influenced by the constant crowing in the news media about the "bubble" and she feared losing money. Of course, it was understandable that people on fixed incomes would fear the loss of their capital. What was less clear to Wade was why his mother was willing to throw it away subsidizing an irresponsible and spendthrift adult child.

He picked up his cell phone and tried to reach Tim on his, but got the voice mail once again. He decided not to leave another message. This was really unacceptable. Tim was eroding their mother's financial security. She was in pretty good shape right now, but a stock market downturn could hurt her monthly cash flow. More than that, it bothered Wade that Tim could be so selfish and indifferent to her well being.

The automatic garage door went up and Wade walked out to help Harriet with the groceries, unloading them from the rear of her white Rav 4.

"I got some nice pork chops at the market. Would you and Amanda like to come over for dinner in the next day or so?"

Wade regarded his mother as they unpacked the bags on the kitchen counter. She was so kind and caring of others, he thought. He couldn't bear the idea of his brother taking advantage of her. Where does concern cross the line into enabling destructive behavior? Probably, he figured, when you pay for an expensive car for somebody who doesn't need it or appreciate it.

"I don't know, Mom," he said. "I'll ask her. By the way, what happened with that Mustang payment?"

She looked at him blankly. "What do you mean?"

"Well, I see that you made another car payment for Tim," he said gently.

She turned back to the groceries. "Oh, that. Yes, he asked me if I could pick it up again for him when he called about the bill folder. I co-signed, Wade, so I'm responsible, too."

"Did he remind you of that?" he asked her.

Her back to him, she replied, "Well, yes, I guess he did. He's busy in New York and he's looking for work. I sent him all the other bills, you know. But he needed help again with the car, so I was glad to do it."

"Mom, it's not good for your finances to be doing this."

She sighed. "I can't not help my child."

Wade was silent, not wanting to provoke her. This was not right and Tim was taking advantage of her. Brother or not, he could not tolerate that.

"I haven't been able to reach him on the phone. Can you give me his address so I can send him a letter?"

She went to the telephone desk in the corner of the kitchen and copied out the address for him.

That evening at home after dinner Wade told Amanda what had been going on with the Mustang. She knew that it bothered Wade considerably, and that it was a symptom of his larger concern both for his widowed mother and for the brother who never seemed to be able to make it on his own. Amanda's own family included a few notorious ne'er-do-wells a generation past who had embarrassed them all and she understood Wade's feelings.

He went into his office and got out the paper with the address on it. He was vaguely familiar with Manhattan from various business trips. This place was somewhere on W. 23rd Street, care of some woman, but he didn't know enough about the area to pinpoint it. That meant Tim was down on the West Side somewhere, maybe just south of the Empire State Building. Was that Midtown or something else? He wasn't sure.

Sitting quietly, a banker's lamp illuminating the dark polished wood of the bookshelves and the mahogany of his desk, Wade used his cell phone to try to reach Tim again. This time he got an answer.

"Hello?" It was Tim's voice.

"Hello, Tim, it's Wade," said his brother, anxious to put his concerns on the table. He heard a series of crackles and buzzes as if there was interference on the line.

"Sorry, Wade, you're breaking up," Tim said, and the line went dead.

Wade sat silently for a moment, a little stunned. He called back and got the voice mail again. He was pretty sure Tim had faked the interference and deliberately hung up on him. Then he was angry.

He turned on his Palm Pilot and looked over his schedule for the next week. He figured he could rearrange a few things after tomorrow and get away. He'd consult with his secretary and with Ralph in the morning and get it worked out. He hadn't taken any time off at all in a while and he felt comfortable telling Ralph that he had to attend to a family matter. It didn't matter either way, really, because he could not let this go on. Tim was way over the line and Wade had to do something about it.

He walked into the family room where Amanda was doing a homework assignment with Little Wade on the carpet, something involving crayons and construction paper and scissors.

"I have to go to New York," he told her. "I'm going to get the car."

Chapter 20

Glendy was a resourceful girl. As soon as she saw the heroin that night in the hideout she began thinking about how they could unload it. Timmy and his pals didn't have the connections to move something that serious.

The first problem would be moving it in Cleveland at all. It would take forever to develop good contacts and even then whoever Timmy had stolen it from would be looking for them. Every time they tried to feel out buyers they'd risk ringing the other guys' alarm bells as well as stumbling over undercover cops. This just wasn't Timmy's field of expertise, but she knew people who could probably help.

After her first set dancing at the Pony that night she went back to the dressing room and got out her cell phone and address book. She was supposed to be throwing on some minimal clothing so she could go back out and work the room, smiling and sitting with the customers and getting them to buy her drinks. But she took a minute to call Gail.

She knew Gail from the Pony. Dancers often circulated through major cities and Gail had been there a couple of months back, a headliner for a week before returning to her home base in New York City. They'd become friends quickly and Gail told her lots of stories about the guys she knew in New York, really high rollers and people with mob connections. She had invited Glendy to visit any time. Men came into the Pony frequently who told her what big time underworld characters they were, but the consensus among the dancers, supported by the bouncers, was that the Cleveland Mafia had gotten hurt pretty badly by the Feds a couple of decades ago and had never recovered. Sure, there were small timers and wannabes who hung around the old Italian neighborhood in Murray Hill, but Glendy was pretty sure they didn't have the juice they claimed to have. Ever since Danny Green and the Irish Mob had it out with the Italians, Green getting blown up and the Italians going to prison, and Green's protégé Kevin McTaggart went away for life for a series of drug related murders, gangsterism in Cleveland had become more of an ethnic affair. The Blacks and the Hispanics were rumored to be running things now, and even the once fearsome motorcycle gangs were much quieter, although rumor had it that they were around. But Glendy wasn't interested in trying to find them, as their reputations preceded them and she assumed they'd be dangerously untrustworthy. And she just didn't know any Black or Hispanic gangsters at all. As a poor white girl from the West Side, she probably wouldn't have trusted them if she did.

Gail was happy to hear from her. Glendy explained that she and her boyfriend were thinking about visiting Manhattan. Like, very soon. Could they stay with her? And Gail said sure, she had lots of room, they'd have blast. And she told her how to get there, Glendy writing it all down carefully. Then the manager came looking for her, telling her she needed to get out front now, and she went back to work.

When Bobby popped up that night when she got back to the downtown apartment and told them about the Mexicans, she knew they needed to be gone as soon as possible. With Bobby getting drinks in the kitchen, she'd briefed Timmy about her plan and told him to keep his mouth shut with Bobby. Timmy was so messed up that he didn't care what they did, as long as somebody besides him figured it out.

They made the nine-hour drive to Manhattan in two shifts. When the sun began to come up that Sunday morning they were a couple of hundred miles from Cleveland in the middle of nowheresville, Pennsylvania, and they found a motel room just off the interstate and crashed. She was beginning to have a hard time keeping him out of the smack. The boy took to it like a fish to water, unfortunately. She had to steer him back to using the coke so he wasn't completely worthless, nodding off and unconscious all the time. She wouldn't touch the heroin herself. She knew several people who had died using it when she was growing up, and that was enough for her.

When he woke up that first morning and wanted to do up some more she had a real heart-to-heart with him, explaining that a junky boyfriend would be useless to her in this endeavor, and that he was going to find himself hooked on this shit in a few days if he kept it up.

They rolled across the George Washington Bridge on Sunday evening, Timmy staying pretty straight and wide awake on coke.

They followed Gail's directions, heading down Route 9A South toward downtown and turning onto W. 14th Street and then following the signs down Hudson Street and into the West Village. New York City was very cool, the lights and the traffic and the sheer multitude of soaring buildings were just amazing. Timmy had been there before, but Glendy had never been far from Cleveland except to visit relatives in West Virginia, and that was a completely different kind of experience. They were very excited.

They called Gail as they pulled up in front of her building and she came down to meet them, a tall beautiful blonde in her early twenties.

They unloaded their few belongings and the suitcase and Gail helped Timmy find a parking spot in a garage she had arranged for them nearby, the guy there wanting two hundred dollars up front for four days. Timmy could barely believe that but paid the man. Then they tramped up five floors in the old apartment building to Gail's two bedroom apartment, and they were afraid to ask what she paid for that. Her roommate Sheree was on the West Coast for another three weeks and they put their things in her bedroom, the suitcase under the bed, and made themselves comfortable.

Chapter 21

Gail went to work at the Promises Gentlemen's Club on Monday afternoon, a regular shift for her. She took two grams of cocaine with her, which was definitely a no-no. Frank, the manager, had a zero tolerance drug policy. Things had been a lot more open a decade ago, when people expected to be able to score coke and weed when they spent an evening out at a strip club, but since Giuliani and the general law and order cleanup of the town, it was no longer a sensible thing to do. And it was good for the owners, too. After all, businessmen, tourists and assorted high rollers spent plenty on watching the girls dance, the lap dances and the drinks and cigars.

Why jeopardize that by encouraging the climate of crime that went along with the drug trade? Guys were flocking to Promises, with its advertised two hundred strippers, twin stages and one hundred foot bar. Things had never been better.

Still, the bouncers and bartenders and dancers were like people anywhere and some of them liked to indulge. So during a break Gail offered a toot to her favorite bartender, Mickey, and he thought it was great stuff. He slipped her a hundred on the spot for the gram. A little later one of the other girls took the other gram off her hands. So Gail made an extra fifty bucks and she passed the rest, a hundred fifty, back to Glendy that evening. Being a good house guest, Glendy handed her back a hundred for her hospitality. And they were off to a mutually satisfying business relationship.

Gail also introduced Glendy and Timmy to a few of the people in her building and around her neighborhood. Inside of three days they had sold twenty five grams and Timmy went back to the garage guy and gave him five hundred bucks for another ten days of rent.

They usually slept late but the traffic noise which was always present, a constant background soundtrack, increased in volume at daybreak and roused them. The hundred-year-old apartment had a living room, a kitchen, a bathroom and the two very small bedrooms.

It turned out Gail and Sheree paid $2,000 a month for it. Timmy learned that this was considered a bargain. His own spacious apartment in Lakewood cost $500 a month. He began to wake up with the sun and sit out on the fire escape drinking good coffee and watching the street below, where dozens of people came and went.

Many of them looked like students or artists in their thrift store clothing, exotic hairstyles and piercings. Bobby would like it here, he thought, and immediately felt bad. He had screwed Bobby and there was no way around that. He would have to do something to make it up to him, whether he forgave him or not.

In their tiny bedroom he would weigh out grams with Glendy on the little electronic scale. Gail knew they had some coke with them, of course, but she had no idea how much. And they didn't tell her about the heroin at all. He broke down two more of the six ounces of coke he'd brought into grams, another sixty grams, and figured they'd probably never have to sell an ounce outright because the grams were selling like hotcakes. He was careful to only give Gail a gram or two now and then to sell because he didn't want her getting caught and he didn't want her to know how much he had. But he told her he'd be interested in talking to the right people, if she came across them, about more business.

He used the heroin only once in the first week they were there. The pull of it was strong and his curiosity told him to find out more, see where it would take him. He understood now why some people loved it more than anything, more than life, even. There was nothing to compare to its soft immersion, its complete release and its bottomless comfort. But he knew that Glendy was right; he had to keep his shit together and organize a way to sell it off. This was his ticket to permanent escape from a life of smalltime criminality. More, it would ensure his rise to financial security and the status that went along with it. He could buy a damn Porsche 911 Turbo if he felt like it, and pull up to his brother at some dreary Cleveland stoplight someday, look over, nod and then blow the doors off of his pissant Boxster.

They had a lot of time on their hands while they nurtured along their contacts and sold grams. New York was lots of fun and they were only using a little coke in the evenings; there was so much to see and do. They left the Mustang in the garage and began taking cabs around the city like everyone else did. The traffic was unbelievable and it was just so much easier to let some guy from Bangladesh or wherever pilot them frantically wherever they felt like going. They hit all the high notes in the first week, first heading into Midtown and standing in line for the Empire State Building. The security was like trying to get on an airplane. They were both awestruck by the views out over Manhattan and they bought cheap mementos at the gift shop. They hung around Times Square, digging the crowds, amazed by the ability of New York pedestrians to blab incessantly on their cell phones while navigating onrushing walls of cars at intersections without fatal injury. The gigantic video screens overlooking Times Square with their perpetually changing ads and graphics created a kaleidoscopic environment that dazzled and amazed their senses. You could get anything here.

They went to the new Hard Rock Café and gawked at Jim Morrison's leather trousers. Then they went to Planet Hollywood and ate overpriced sandwiches while examining space ship props from Star Wars and guns from James Bond movies. They wandered around and worked their way over to 6th Avenue and found Rockefeller Center and all the TV studios and then they discovered 5th Avenue. They spent a day wandering around in Saks and Barneys and all the specialty shops and spent some money on clothes and Timmy bought Glendy some bracelets and necklaces she liked. They found the Museum of Modern Art and stood in line to get in. Timmy loved it but Glendy couldn't understand what a helicopter was doing in an art museum.

The restaurants were great but expensive. They had Thai food and Italian and massive sandwiches at various delis. They bought smoothies from guys in trucks parked at the intersections. They had short order breakfasts at little Greek holes-in-the-wall where they got pancakes faster than at McDonald's and really, really good, excellent even. Timmy couldn't figure out how they did it.

When they got back down to Gail's place late one afternoon they found a guy hanging around in her hallway, some loser they had sold a gram to, and then Timmy got nervous. The guy lived in the building so him being in the hallway was no mystery. He said he wanted another gram and was waiting for them. But Timmy didn't want people staking out the place and told the guy so. It attracted attention.

Worse, he started to worry that one of these people would burgle the place looking for coke and find the suitcase under the bed. They stopped wandering so far from the apartment, although they still went out and explored the nearby neighborhoods. Timmy just made it a point to pop back into the apartment two or three times a day so people would be less inclined to break in.

They wandered around the Village and Soho and Chinatown and Little Italy. Glendy found that the boutiques in Soho had just what she was looking for in the way of fashion and she started haunting them daily. That was okay with Timmy because he could hang out at the apartment or in the cafés in the neighborhood and stay close to his stash. It actually was warming up a little and on some afternoons he could sit drinking coffee out on the sidewalks at the little tables in front of various places and watch the girls and the characters go by.

One day he said, "Hey, do you want to go see Ground Zero?" and Glendy wasn't sure what he meant. He explained that the place where the World Trade Center had stood, where the terrorists had flown the planes into the buildings, was not too far away and maybe they should go look at it.

Glendy wasn't too excited; she thought it was kind of grim and spooky, but she agreed to go with him. They walked the thirty blocks to the site and stood looking through the chain-link fence at the enormous empty space where the towers had stood. It was sad and creepy and awful to think about what had happened there. They walked around the perimeter and Timmy noticed the gray grit and dust pressed into the sidewalk cracks and along the bases of nearby buildings and realized this was what was left of the huge smoking piles of debris and human remains which had buried the area. For a moment he was enraged at the people who had done this to his country. Then he hailed a cab and they hurried back to the West Village to keep an eye on their windfall.

Chapter 22

They dropped by Promises one night as Gail's guests. Everybody was really nice and friendly. Frank, the manager, was pleased to meet Glendy and spent some time talking with her. Timmy didn't mind because this was what Glendy did; he was used to guys approaching her and making a big deal over her, especially in this kind of environment. Frank was telling her how spectacular she was. Timmy had heard it before and he had to agree.

He looked around the place and, frankly, he was impressed. It was a big room done in dark wood with lots of gold colored fixtures and red upholstery, both fabric and leather. Two large stages dominated the space and each had a couple of poles rising from them to the ceiling for the dancers to make use of. Although it was early in the evening both stages had action going on them. A beautiful Asian girl was well into her routine on the nearest stage, already topless and playing to the men sitting up close and fixed on her every movement. Several had bills in their hands, waving them to lure her close so they could put them in her garters or her thong. The music, something upbeat that Timmy didn't recognize, throbbed through the room.

On the far stage a tall blond wearing a feather boa, fishnet stockings and high heels and a scanty sequined outfit strolled indolently out from behind the curtain and began moving to the sounds. The men seated around the stage gradually stopped their conversations and became completely focused on what she was doing.

Timmy turned back to Glendy and the manager, all of them seated along the bar which ran the full length of the room. He heard Frank say, "If you're interested, it would be no problem booking you in here. You've got the look we want."

A bartender approached, a guy in his late twenties with reddish hair and a tough Irish face. He smiled and said, "What'll you have, sir? It's on the house."

Timmy knew about single malts from Wade, although in the past he hadn't had much occasion to be able to afford them.

"I'll have a Glenfiddich on the rocks with a slice of lemon," he said.

Glendy had a white wine and she and Frank continued their conversation, Frank assuring her that she'd make more money than she'd ever seen dancing at Promises and Glendy expressing concern about how much everything cost in New York. Timmy sat back and smiled. Money wouldn't be an issue for long, and Glendy knew it. She was playing with the guy.

Gail appeared from somewhere, already dressed in her costume. She was taller than Timmy now in her four inch heels, wearing dark stockings and a red outfit which barely concealed her body. Timmy was used to seeing her in jeans and a T-shirt, an ordinary though attractive young woman. With her makeup and clothing she had become something different, a sexual thing, a visual stimulus designed to provoke male fantasies and separate men from their money. She put her arm around Timmy as he sat at the bar and kissed his cheek.

"Are they taking care of you?" she asked.

He grinned. "You look great," he said. "You clean up well."

She laughed and poked him in the ribs. "Thanks. What are you drinking?"

"Scotch. Good scotch."

She looked around and beckoned to the bartender. "Let me get you another," she said. "Have you met Mickey?"

The Irish guy came back down the bar and Gail introduced them.

"This is my friend Timmy from Ohio. He and Glendy are staying with me."

The bartender exchanged a look with Gail and put out his hand.

As they shook he said, "Nice to meet you, Timmy. Gail's had nice things to say about you."

After a while Gail went back to work and Timmy and Glendy watched for a while, Glendy appraising the dancers' bodies and routines, Timmy just enjoying himself. They had some nachos and another drink each, the place getting a little busier and more dancers coming on. Gail danced and she was good. In his experienced opinion, her full breasts were natural. Timmy could see how she could headline in other towns.

As they sat talking Gail came back to them and said, "I'm done at ten tonight and so is Mickey. He's coming by. Will you guys be up?"

Of course they would be, and said so. Shortly afterward they thanked Frank and caught a cab back to the apartment and did up a couple of lines and watched some TV until Gail got home.

Chapter 23

They were sitting around the living room at Gail's and drinking wine. Mickey had brought it, a big bottle of Merlot that they'd had at the club. The Rolling Stones were on the stereo, the Sticky Fingers album, thirty-five-year-old kick ass music. Mickey had changed out of his bartender's white shirt and tie and he was wearing some Tommy Bahama-looking tropical thing. Gail was in shorts and a tank top that stopped just below her boobs, her face scrubbed clean of the heavy stripper makeup.

Timmy sat forward and tapped another small mound of cocaine out of a gram envelope and onto the mirror sitting on the coffee table in front of them. He scraped it and chopped it a little with his razor blade and then formed it into four long thin lines. Gail was on Mickey's lap on the couch, sitting next to Timmy, while Glendy perched to his right on the arm.

He held a rolled up hundred dollar bill out to Mickey and said, "Be my guest."

Mickey leaned past Gail and snorted up a line and passed the hundred to her. She stood a little and bent forward, her ass in Mickey's face, and he gave her a light nip with his teeth. She screamed and slapped his shoulder, then grinned and leaned in again and did up her line.

Gail handed the hundred to Glendy and Timmy said, "How long have you two known each other?"

"A couple of years," Gail replied, laughing while Mickey

squeezed her to him. "He's my main man at the club. We take care of each other."

Glendy did a line and so did Timmy and they poured more Merlot.

"So what's going on in Cleveland?" Mickey asked. "Is it a cool place? I've never been."

"It's okay," said Glendy. "We have a good time, you know? It's on the lake and there's parks and stuff. The winters suck."

"You guys been seeing each other long?" Mickey asked. Gail was rubbing his neck and mouthing the words to "Can't You Hear Me Knockin'" as she wiggled on his lap to the beat.

"A year," said Timmy. "Hey, you get free lap dances, huh?"

"Always," Gail said. "Music's good in Cleveland."

"Really?" Mickey asked. "Oh yeah, the Rock and Roll Hall of Fame and all that. I've gotta check that out some time. Hey, man, that's some good coke."

Timmy nodded. "Yeah, it is good. Glad you like it."

Mickey drank a little wine and said, "Gail mentioned you might be in a position to provide some quantity, you know?" And he looked at Timmy seriously, bringing up business for the first time. Timmy shifted in his seat a little and didn't really react, just thought about it for a second or two.

"Yeah, yeah, I'm in that position. You know, depends on what you're looking for, but maybe I can do something for you." He felt Glendy go still next to him, her senses alert, almost as if she were somehow feeling the thoughts circulating between the four of them.

Mickey smiled, a big Irish grin, and said, "I have a very good friend who is looking. It's his deal, you know, handling product, not so much mine."

They all sipped wine and thought about it, going slowly.

"How well do you know this guy?" Timmy finally asked.

"I grew up with the dude. I've known him forever. We both grew up a few blocks from here. He's a cool guy, very well connected. He's a really trustworthy dude."

"Un-huh," Timmy said, and looked at Glendy. They shared some eye signals for a moment and she was nodding at him just a little bit, hardly enough for anyone to pick up on. He looked back at Mickey.

Gail was looking away, minding her own business and pretending she wasn't hearing any of this.

"What's he looking for?" Timmy asked carefully.

Mickey shrugged and said, "Coke, weed, whatever, you know? Whatever's good."

Timmy said, "Coke I've got, and also some whatever. No grass, though."

They all relaxed a little. There it was: Mickey had asked for it and Timmy had said he could do it. Everything else was details.

"Bitch" came on and the coke was kicking in nicely so Timmy laid out more lines while Mickey poured more wine. They were laughing and Gail got up to turn down the stereo a little because it was getting late and she didn't want the neighbors complaining. "Sister Morphine" was playing and it made Timmy think about using a little smack but he didn't do anything about it.

Gail and Mickey started dancing around a little and Timmy said, "What's your friend's name?"

Mickey said, "Joey D.," twirling Gail around, ballroom style.

"Okay," Timmy said. "Bring him around."

On the stereo, Mick Jagger was singing about dead flowers.

Chapter 24

Timmy walked into Promises the next evening and paid the cover charge like anyone else. The place was hopping. There were probably fifty customers sitting around the stages and another thirty or so at the bar.

Gail and another girl were dancing on the near stage, and two other women were on the back one. Spotlights caught the glitter of their costumes and alternated with strobes which turned their movements into stop motion sequences. The air was thick with cigar smoke and the sounds of Nirvana's "Come As You Are."

He went to the bar and Mickey came right over and leaned across to him. "He'll be here pretty soon," he said. "What'll you have?"

"Just a Heineken, thanks."

Timmy sat back and watched the dancers for a while. Some guys were getting lap dances at little side tables overlooking the stages, each sitting unnaturally still as a naked woman gyrated around on top of him, the rules of the house prohibiting touching and the bouncers a persistent low-key presence in the background. Timmy didn't understand the allure of lap dances; all they did was make you want something you just weren't going to get. But he supposed for a guy with nothing to look forward to but the same old hausfrau waiting for him out on Long Island or wherever, it was pretty exotic and worth the expense.

A black woman appeared at his elbow, working the crowd in her lingerie and heels, and touched his arm and smiled at him.

"Hey, baby," she said.

"Hey, yourself. What's going on?"

The woman was very pretty, her hair Afro'ed out, and she sat on the seat next to him and kept her hands lightly on his arms.

"Mind if I sit a little?"

Timmy grinned and said, "Suit yourself. I'm friends with the help here but I'll buy you something. What'll you have?"

She caught Mickey's eye and he brought her non-alcoholic drink of some sort, Timmy laying a ten on the bar.

"I know you're a friend of the help," she said, and she was sweet and deferential to him, not coming on brassy at all. "I'm Tonya. I wanted to talk to you for a second."

"Sure," he said, not sure what this was all about. "What's up?"

She brought her face close to his, still holding on to him gently, and said into his ear, "I heard you're doing a little business. I scored something off Gail the other day. I want to give you the number of a friend in case you're looking to get a little busier, you know?" And she pressed a slip of paper into his hand.

She leaned back and smiled into his eyes. He looked at the paper in the subdued light and there was a name, Leroy, on it, and a phone number. He looked back up at her.

"Okay, thanks. I'm staying on top of things right now, but I'll keep it in mind."

She smiled again and slipped off the seat and ambled away into the crowd. *I'm Mr. Popularity*, Timmy thought.

At that moment a guy pushed past him, turned and looked directly at him.

"Timmy?" he asked.

The guy was had dark hair and big soulful dark eyes, some residual acne speckling his cheeks. He was about Timmy's height and maybe a couple of years younger, wearing a black leather sports jacket and black silk shirt and sharply pressed gray slacks with expensive looking loafers. The top few buttons of the shirt were open and a couple of gold chains dangled in his chest hair.

"Yeah," Timmy said, and stuck out his hand.

They shook, the guy smiling and saying, "I'm Joey. I think Mickey mentioned me, right?" He took the seat the girl had been in a minute before.

"Yeah, yeah, he did. How you doing?"

"Good."

He waved to Mickey, who hurried over and said, "Joey D.! Good to see you, man!" He put a napkin and a scotch on the rocks down in front of him, grinned broadly at Timmy, and hustled away down the bar.

Joey D. sipped his drink and looked appraisingly at Timmy, then said, "Let's cut to the chase. I'm told you got some product for sale."

Timmy nodded. "True. What are you looking for?"

Joey D. glanced around quickly. Nobody could hear them because they could just barely hear each other over the music. He leaned in a little and said, "I could use some blow. Also, I'm looking for whatever's selling, you know?"

Timmy took in a deep breath and finished his Heineken. As he motioned for a bartender he turned in close to the guy and said, "I've got a good supply of coke, mostly grams, not a lot of quantity. But I do have some smack, too."

Joey D. sat back in the seat and his eyebrows went up and Timmy could see the wheels turning.

"No shit," the guy finally said. "That's very interesting."

Timmy's refill came and they nursed their drinks for a few minutes, watching the strippers and listening to the music.

Joey D. said, "I'd like to get a sample of each and see what you've got. Can we do that?"

Timmy had two small plastic bags in his pants pocket, about a half gram of cocaine in one and a half gram of heroin in the other. He palmed them under the bar and passed them across his lap to the guy, who quickly made them disappear into his jacket.

Timmy said, "Do you have a pen?"

He wrote down his cell phone number on a matchbook for the guy, who did the same for him.

Joey D. smiled at him and squeezed his shoulder.

"Very cool, man. I'll check this out and give you a call tomorrow. Thanks."

He slipped off the bar stool and walked out of the club. He had a sort of a strut to his walk and Timmy thought he was probably an arrogant kind of guy on his own time.

Mickey came by after a while and Timmy said, "All ahead full."

Mickey grinned and said, "Phasers on stun, Captain."

Chapter 25

The next morning Timmy and Glendy were sitting at a sidewalk table at a café on Bleeker Street with coffee and croissants in front of them when Timmy's cell went off. The caller ID told him it was Joey D.

He grinned at Glendy and she looked back at him, a little tense, knowing this was it.

"Joey. What it is?" he said.

Joey D. was laughing. "Man, ain't you the shit. You are a serious motherfucker, you know that? You play your cards close to the vest, you know? Where'd you get shit that pure?"

Timmy was momentarily confused. He had no idea how pure the drugs were. The coke was good, he knew, but he had zero previous experience with heroin so he had nothing to compare it to. He played along anyway.

"You know, I had a good source. How'd it test for you?"

Joey was still laughing about it. "Man, the marching powder's good, it's a solid eighty-five percent. But that other shit! Man, that stuff's ninety percent pure. What, are you making the stuff yourself?"

Timmy had done a little research on the Internet on Gail's laptop since he'd been in town and he knew what to expect in terms of the heroin's purity and worth. A lot of heroin was coming from South America these days and purity was in the fifty to sixty percent range, although it could go as high as ninety percent or so but that was very rare. Southwest Asian heroin was generally not as pure. Prices for

110

kilos of South American heroin began at $50,000 and went up from there. Full retail for one kilo of very pure heroin could reach $200,000. Suddenly Timmy found himself in a whole new ball game.

He felt himself break out in a sweat even though it was cool out and a little dirty snow still lingered on the sidewalks. He took a deep breath to calm himself down. Glendy saw his agitation and she was looking alarmed.

"Yeah, that's what I got, too," Timmy said. "I hope you're happy with that."

He smiled over at Glendy, trying to reassure her. He mouthed silently, "This is good news."

"Oh yeah, no complaints from me," Joey D. said. "I'd like to do some business. You really got serious weight with that ninety percent stuff?"

Timmy was nodding. "I can do some weight."

Joey was quiet for a couple of seconds, then he said seriously, "Can you do a key?"

It was Timmy's turn to laugh. "Oh yeah, I can do a key." He thought quickly and then said, "One hundred eighty K."

Joey considered this for a moment. "One seventy-five," he said, and Timmy grinned widely at Glendy.

"Well, okay, but you're sticking me up," he replied.

"Done," said Joey. "When and where?"

"Let me call you back in a few minutes," Timmy said, and the guy agreed.

They sat and considered how to do the deal. They'd been over it before, playing various scenarios out, trying to balance safety with keeping a low profile. They had decided that a quick transfer in public, in a car parked on the street, would be the safest while still keeping the deal out of sight. They went over it again, came up with some guidelines, and figured they'd done all they could and they had better get on with it. Timmy called him back.

"Okay, let's meet on Barrow Street. You know Barrow? You got a car? You pull up in front of the Barrow Deli and I get in. We check out what each of us brought, I leave and you can head straight out and get on the West Side Highway if you want to. Barrow's one way, so we can keep an eye out better. Sound okay?"

Joey D. was quiet for a minute, then he said, "Yeah, sure, that's a good deal. How about tomorrow, ten in the morning? I gotta get the scratch together."

And Timmy agreed.

He and Glendy walked back to the apartment and he explained the entire conversation to her, described the guy, and went over the details again and again. They were flying. Maybe this guy would eventually buy all the smack; he certainly had the connections to do it if he could buy one kilogram. This was finally what they'd been trying to do, and the payoff was beginning.

Back in the bedroom Timmy got out the suitcase and he did up a small snort while Glendy looked on, cutting up some coke on the mirror. They had some wine and coke and Timmy was coasting, the mix of coke and smack just right. Later they made love, getting into each other the way they had when they first met, and like when they first had all the coke in the hideout. They lay tangled in the sheets afterwards and planned what they would do and where they would go when they had moved all the heroin.

Chapter 26

Wade's cab pulled up in front of the West 23rd Street address he had given to the driver and he sat there, a little confused, and looked at the place.

"Is this right?" he finally asked, and the driver, a young African man, assured him that it was.

He paid and climbed out and looked around a little more. The sign said "Promises Gentlemen's Club" above the broad facade. A doorman stood quietly out front dressed in a subdued tuxedo, his broad physique and craggy face encouraging gentlemanly behavior from anyone seeking entry. There were no windows, only the heavy wooden door, which the doorman held open for Wade as he ventured inside.

"Good evening, sir," the doorman said.

A young woman sat inside a sort of teller's window in the small vestibule Wade entered. She was dressed in a dignified cashmere sweater. She smiled and said, "Thirty dollars, please."

He paid her in cash and another door was held open by another burly doorman and Wade walked into the club. The music, muffled by the doors, now rolled over him, some sort of rock song. It was a long, wide room, an enormous bar down one side, everything done in golds and reds and rich dark wood. The lights were low except on the stages, where spotlights held the dancers. Cigar smoke drifted through the air and clusters of men talked together or watched the women.

Wade hadn't been in a strip club since college, and he wasn't completely sure why he was in one now. Several semi-naked strippers danced in the lights and others were walking around in the room, talking to the customers and to each other. Wade had a momentary flash of guilt, wondering what he would say to Amanda about this.

He walked over to the bar and sat down. Well, he knew Tim's lifestyle choices were a little wild, but he hadn't expected this. *I guess you take your friends where you find them*, he thought.

A bartender, another young woman dressed in a white shirt, black tie and black slacks, came over and asked for his order. He thought it best to have a Coke. When she brought it back to him and asked for five dollars, he said to her, "I'm looking for Gail Montgomery. Is she here?"

The bartender quickly looked up and down the room, then smiled at him. "I think she's in back. I'll let her know you're looking for her."

Wade tipped her a couple of bucks.

In the dressing room, a dancer came up to Gail, who was putting on her makeup, and said, "Stacey says there's a tall, dark and handsome type asking for you at the bar. Rolex, looks like a Zegna suit. Go get him, girl."

A few minutes later Wade saw the tall young blond moving across the room in his direction. As she approached he saw that she had him fixed with her big blue eyes and a smile was spreading across her face. She moved right up to him, her largely bare body entering his space, and said, "Hi, I'm Gail. Who might you be?"

Wade resisted confusing impulses to simultaneously pull back from her and to reach out and touch her and simply said, "Hi Gail, I'm Wade Thomas. I'm looking for my brother Tim. I understand he's a friend of yours."

Gail was a little surprised by this. Timmy and Glendy hadn't mentioned a brother showing up. The guy looked like a taller and darker version of Timmy, though. Still, with Timmy being in the line of work he was and all, being careful couldn't hurt.

"Oh, nice to meet you, Wade. When did you get into town?"

"I just got in an hour or so ago. Flew into Newark. I'm staying in Midtown, at the Yorkshire Grand. Have you seen Tim?"

Gail smiled and looked around for a second, then touched his hands with hers and said, "I haven't seen him today, but I'm sure I will pretty soon. You know, maybe tomorrow. Can I give him a message or something?"

Wade shrugged and decided the girl was holding out on him a little, not sure about him. That was okay; she probably had Tim's best interests at heart.

He held her hands in his then, smiled warmly back at her, and said, "Sure, you can tell him I'm here for a few days and I need to see him. Is he with Glendy? I'd like to get together with them, maybe buy them dinner, you know?"

Gail was nodding, the guy was nice, pretty cool, even, and she was sure he was legit, but she was still going to be a little cautious.

"Oh yeah, you know Glendy? We danced together in Cleveland last year. Really nice girl. Your brother's such a nice guy, too. I'm gonna let them know you're here. Write down where you're staying."

He got out one of his business cards and jotted down the hotel name and room number and his cell phone, just in case Tim had somehow managed to forget it. He handed it to the girl, smiling some more, letting her know he liked her, doing a little sales job. She took the card and read it, seeing that he really was Wade Thomas and also that he had a big title of some kind and that the card was nice linen stock.

"Okay, Wade," she said. "Thanks. I'll make sure he gets this. I've got to dance now. Will you stay and watch me?" Wade considered that he'd paid thirty-seven dollars already just to get in here and meet her, so he may as well stay a little longer. Strange, but it had never occurred to him that his brother's striking looking girlfriend was anything other than a secretary or a retail clerk or something. Maybe he really was a little naive.

"Yes, I'll stay awhile. Are you a good dancer?" he teased her a little, loosening up.

She grinned at him. "You can be the judge. I think you'll like it just fine. Would you like another drink?"

He said he would and she flagged down the bartender and he got a scotch this time.

Chapter 27

It was 9:55 in the morning and Timmy was standing in a doorway on Barrow Street, watching traffic roll past and keeping an eye on the Barrow Deli's entrance, which was a few doors down on the same side he was on. It was overcast and drizzling a little and he had on a baseball cap pulled down to his eyes.

He had a kilogram of heroin in an oversized gym bag which hung from his shoulder. He figured he may need a good sized bag to hold all the money he'd be getting in a few minutes. He didn't know what kind of car Joey D. would be driving but that was okay, he'd see him when he went by, slowing to the curb.

He was a little put off by Wade showing up in town but he wasn't going to let that throw off his timing or his focus. Gail had come in to the apartment last night excited from having met him and gave Timmy his card. He was staying in Midtown and he wanted to see him. Timmy had no doubt that Wade had found out about the car payments and had come to get the Mustang back.

Gail thought he was a rich and handsome guy and she asked a lot of questions about him. Timmy didn't burst her balloon by telling her he was a straight and uptight prick who wouldn't give her the time of day if she didn't have something he wanted. He just advised her that, to him, Wade seemed happily married and he wasn't likely to be around long enough for her to get to know him better. Then he went into the bedroom and shut the door before she could ask him again when he was going to call him, and could she maybe go to dinner too, and how she could, like, show him around town maybe. She was telling Glendy that maybe she'd do another week in Cleveland soon as the door closed.

He'd deal with Wade later. Right now he was about to earn $175,000 and he didn't need any distractions.

As he scanned the street yet again a late model white Cadillac coasted past, the wipers slapping, with Joey D. at the wheel and he pulled over to the curb in front of the Barrow Deli. He continued a little further, just enough so they wouldn't be sitting directly in front of the door, and shut off the engine. Timmy stepped out of his doorway and headed for the car.

Across the street, standing in the rain streaked front window of a coffee shop so she had a view of the Deli and the storefronts flanking it, Glendy saw the car ease to the curb and Timmy start toward it. At the same time she saw the fat man who had been leaning against the brickwork of another sheltered doorway beyond Timmy's fold up the newspaper he'd been reading and stuff it in the left pocket of his leather three-quarter length car coat. The guy was dark and greasy looking, with an Elvis-like mop and wraparound shades. He was now watching the Cadillac intently.

Timmy walked around the car into the street, the driver's side against the curb, and opened the passenger door. She saw him bend down and say something to the guy inside, smile, then get in and shut the door. The fat man started moving, stepping briskly out of the doorway and toward the car. He was down the street a little but closing fast. Glendy saw his right hand go into the coat and when it came out, still partially covered, she saw a black gun butt in it.

Her heart accelerated frantically and she quickly moved to the door of the coffee shop and out onto the street. She had a little sequined purse with her and she reached inside for the tiny stainless steel revolver she had hidden there. She sprinted five steps up the sidewalk until she was opposite the car.

"Timmy!" she screamed. "Look out!"

Timmy looked up at her from the front passenger's seat, surprised to see her there on the other side of the street. She saw the driver's startled face beyond Timmy's, his eyes narrowing to something like rage as she stared at him. The fat man had made it to the rear of the car and his head swiveled around, trying to locate the source of the

117

disturbance. Then he saw her and reached out and flung open the rear door on the driver's side, the gun coming up in his hand as he dove into the back seat. He was pointing the gun at Timmy's head.

Timmy heard the rear door open behind and across from him and immediately grabbed the latch and slammed into his door and out onto the street, stumbling, catching himself and running toward her, his gym bag clutched to his chest. The fat man was slow on the uptake and was scrambling to get back out of the car. Joey D. was young and quick and he was out from behind the wheel and after Timmy like a shot.

As Timmy reached her Glendy raised the little revolver in her right hand, thumbed back the hammer and pointed it at Joey D. He either didn't see it or didn't care because he was already across the street and closing fast. She pulled the trigger.

The crack of the .22 round split the air and it missed him, going wide by three feet, smacking off the brick front of the Barrow Deli and spraying little lead fragments across the sidewalk. People in the vicinity ducked and the fat man threw himself into the gutter. Joey D. stopped his headlong rush and his eyes went wide, then he turned and fled back across the street. And into the path of a cab.

It wasn't going very fast, maybe twenty-five miles an hour, but it caught him squarely with a resonant thump and sent him airborne, his arms and legs pinwheeling, and then he came down in a heap on the pavement, the sound like a heavy slap. Timmy turned to look at him and they could both see at once that he was messed up, lying there groaning, his right leg twisted all funny and blood running into the damp street. They looked at each other for an instant, stunned, then turned and ran back up Barrow as fast as they could.

They reached the intersection and turned and slowed their frantic rush, knowing they'd draw attention if they didn't. Glendy still had the little gun palmed in her hand and she put it back in her purse. The adrenaline was still in a full roar through them both and they looked at each other and started to laugh.

They kept walking quickly, cutting around corners and leaving a convoluted trail. Timmy took off his ball cap and stuffed it in his back pocket, trying to alter his appearance. After a couple of more blocks they slowed and Glendy said, "Where in the hell are we gonna go?"

Timmy was heading for the apartment. "We've gotta get our stuff out of Gail's right now, before they get their shit together and come after us."

She knew he was right. "Yeah, we'll have to get the car, too. I can't believe Gail set us up. Do you think she knew?"

Timmy shook his head and the drizzle picked up a notch, misting the streets and driving people into doorways.

"I can't believe that. Mickey, maybe, but I don't think Gail. Where did you come from? Where'd you get that gun?"

Glendy shrugged. "I had a feeling, so I came along. I was watching from the coffee shop. When I saw that fat guy I knew something was wrong."

"I didn't see him very well. I just heard him getting in the car after you yelled. Who the hell was he?"

"Beats me. Some fat Elvis-looking guy, had a black pistol. He pointed it at your head."

Timmy slowed and turned to her. "He was gonna shoot me?"

"I don't know. But they were gonna grab our stuff, that's for sure."

Timmy felt real fear then, and he grabbed her to him and hugged her.

"Thanks, Glenda Jean," he said into her hair. "That was amazing. You were like Calamity Jane or somebody, doing a real standup job. Way better-looking, though."

She pulled back and smiled at him. "Fuck those guys," she said. "They're not ripping me off."

They reached the apartment building and let themselves into the lobby and nobody was around.

"Let me see that gun," Timmy said.

She took it out again and held it in her palm but didn't give it to him.

"I've had it for a while. It just sits in my purse, just in case. It's only a .22, holds five shots."

He looked at it, a tiny stainless gun with an exposed trigger and an inch long barrel.

"So it's got four left? Better keep it handy."

They went up the five flights of stairs and let themselves into the apartment. Gail wasn't home. They threw together their clothes and the stuff they'd bought and grabbed the suitcase and were back out on the street in three minutes. They hiked over to the garage and got the Mustang, didn't bother telling the guy they weren't coming back even though they had another day's rent paid, and cruised out of the neighborhood and started driving uptown.

They drove aimlessly for a while and Timmy said, "Were you really trying to hit Joey D.?"

Glendy looked out the window, watching the people and the traffic, and said, "Yeah, I suppose so."

Timmy shook his head, trying to grasp it. "That took guts, you know? Where'd you learn that?"

Still looking away, she thought for moment and then said, "I've seen people hurt other people before. I decided a long time ago I wasn't going to let anybody hurt me."

Timmy started laughing again. "Fucking Joey D. would have been better off if you'd shot him with that popgun. That cab fucked him up."

They wound around through Midtown and then looped back down and found themselves around Gramercy and pulled up to a small cheap-looking hotel on East 17th between 2nd and 3rd Avenues.

Glendy went in while Timmy sat out front, the engine running. A few minutes later she came out with a keycard in an envelope.

"A hundred twenty-five a night. Parking's another twenty-five. I let them run my credit card but I gave them cash for three days. The garage is across the street."

So they got the car parked and they hauled their belongings over to the hotel and took the elevator to the fourth floor and let themselves into the room. It was an old building and the furnishings were threadbare. They put the security chain on the door and threw the deadbolt and then flopped on the queen bed. After a few minutes Timmy opened the suitcase and helped himself to a snort of heroin, while Glendy looked out the window at the rain.

Chapter 28

That night Timmy was passed out on the bed, his earphones on, and Glendy could just make out the Cowboy Junkies doing "Sweet Jane" on his portable CD player. He'd had enough excitement for one day and had decided he'd earned some serious smack time.

Glendy had gone out and brought back some deli food and some wine a little earlier. Now she sat in front of the TV, the sound off and some talking head earnestly reading the news. She was not ready to call it a day. So she got Timmy's cell phone out and called Gail at Promises.

When Gail finally came to the phone Glendy said, "Do you wanna tell me what the hell that was all about?"

"Glendy!" Gail said, and she sounded happy to hear from her.

"Where are you? What's going on?"

Glendy took a sip of wine while she composed her thoughts. "We had to leave. Do you know what happened today?"

"Well, I heard Joey D. got hit by a car. He's got a concussion and a broken leg and some broken ribs and a ruptured spleen. Mickey's pretty upset. What happened?"

Glendy smiled a little at that. "I've gotta think you didn't know about this, Gail. We're friends, you know? We've always gotten along well, right? You wouldn't do anything rotten to me, would you?"

"No, no, of course not. I'm hurt that you would have to ask. What are you talking about?"

Glendy could hear rock music in the background. Gail must be in the dressing room, she thought. If she was at the bar she wouldn't be able to hear her at all.

"Joey D. tried to rip us off. He brought a big fat guy with a gun when he met Timmy."

She heard Gail gasp and then she was silent. If she was faking it, she was doing a good job.

"Oh, my God, Glendy. I am so, so sorry. I didn't know the guy at all. I've just seen him around with Mickey once or twice. Did they really try to stick Timmy up?"

"Oh yeah, they sure did. But it didn't come off like they planned and Joey D. ran in front of a cab."

Gail was quiet again, then she said, "Mickey asked me if I knew where you were. Do you think Joey D.'s friends are looking for you?"

Glendy laughed ironically. "That would be my guess. That's why we left your place."

"Oh wow, you'd better be careful, Glendy. Joey D.'s supposed to be a connected guy. You know, like with the mob."

"That's not a surprise to me, Gail. That's why we're gone and they're not gonna get another whack at us. So you can tell Mickey thanks a whole fucking lot from us. He was a big help."

"God damn him," Gail said, and her anger sounded genuine. "I'm really sorry, Glendy. Tell Timmy I'm sorry."

They were quiet for a moment and then Gail said, "Hey, did you call Timmy's brother? He could show up here and maybe that's not a good thing, you know?"

Glendy thought about it. "Yeah, you're right. I'd better get hold of him."

Gail said, "Please don't think I had anything to do with this. I'm so pissed at Mickey now I'm shaking. Call me at home tonight, let me know if you got Timmy's brother. I want to help if I can."

"Thanks, hon," Glendy told her, and they said goodbye.

Next she called the Yorkshire Grand Hotel and asked for Wade Thomas's room. He picked up on the second ring.

"Hello?" he said.

"Hi, Wade. This is Glendy Willard. You know, Timmy's friend? We heard you're in town. How are you?"

Wade exhaled and she felt he'd been keyed up, waiting to hear from them. She remembered him as a nice guy, good-looking, a caring older brother. She didn't quite understand Timmy's annoyance with him. It probably had to do with sibling rivalry or something. She figured that Timmy resented Wade's good life and all the stuff he had.

"Well hi, Glendy. It's nice to hear from you. Are you guys in New York?"

"Yes, we are. We've been pretty busy but my friend Gail told us you're here. Can we get together?"

Wade was surprised by this. He'd expected more evasion.

"Yeah, that would be great. Is Tim around?"

"He's not in at the moment," she told him, looking at Timmy's unconscious form on the bed. "But I know he wants to see you. Maybe tomorrow or the next day? Our schedule's a little tight for the next day or so, but I'm sure we can work it out."

"Sure," he said. "Where are you?"

"Well, we're changing locations at the moment. You can reach us on Timmy's cell, okay? Oh, and, Wade, it might be a good idea not to go to the nightclub again. Timmy got into a little argument with somebody there. We wouldn't want you to, you know, catch the tail end of it."

He sounded troubled by that. "What kind of argument? Is everything alright?"

"Oh sure, nothing to worry about. Just a silly thing. My friend Gail enjoyed meeting you."

"She was nice," he said. "I appreciate her letting you know I'm here. So tomorrow, then?"

"Or the next day. Please call us, or we'll call you. Nice talking to you, Wade."

"Thanks, Glendy. I'll wait for your call. Nice talking to you, too."

Then she made the third call. She got out the slip of paper Timmy had brought home from Promises and dialed the number.

After a few rings a deep, quiet voice said, "Hello?"

"Hello," said Glendy. "I'm trying to reach Leroy."

"Who's calling, please?" the man asked.

"I'm calling for Timmy. Tonya at Promises asked us to call you."

"Oh yes," said the man. His voice was resonant, dignified.

"Thank you for calling. This is Leroy. I understand you may be developing some business here, and I was anxious to talk with you."

Glendy thought he didn't sound anxious at all. He sounded perfectly calm and in control. "Yes, that's true," she said. "I can provide you with samples of our products, if you like."

"That would be wonderful. Would it be possible to do that this evening?"

Glendy considered it and decided to go ahead with it. "Well, yes, if you don't mind a trip to Gramercy. I don't know where you're coming from."

"Harlem," he said. "I can meet you in thirty minutes."

"Okay," she said. "I'm five-nine, long brunette hair, wearing blue jeans and a brown suede jacket and carrying a white sequined purse. I'll meet you in the Farmer's Restaurant on East 18th."

"That's fine, I'll be there," Leroy replied. "I'm a black man, six-two, and I'm wearing a dark suit with a gold tie. I'll look forward very much to meeting you. What may I call you?"

"Mary," said Glendy. "I'll see you then."

She quickly set up the little scale and weighed out a gram of heroin, took a gram of cocaine from their stash, and put on her coat and went out the door, leaving Timmy sprawled on the bed.

She walked to the Farmer's Restaurant and got a table near the front. It was a standard New York neighborhood kind of place, small and comfortable, and it wasn't very crowded at nine o'clock at night. She ordered a salad and a Coke from the bored waitress. When she got the Coke a tall black man walked in the door and immediately spotted her.

He walked over and said, "Mary?"

He was in his thirties, athletically built and dressed impeccably in what looked like a black Armani suit and a gold silk tie with an intricate subdued pattern. His shirt was brilliant white and crisply starched and solid gold cuff links winked at his wrists. His watch looked expensive but tasteful, gold with a square black dial on a rich brown calfskin strap. His hair was closely barbered and he wore elegant rimless glasses. He looked like a successful lawyer or businessman. He smiled broadly, quite good-looking and direct.

"Yes," she said. He took her hand and shook it briefly, warmly, then sat across from her.

"Thank you for meeting me, Mary," he said. "I appreciate your coming. Are you eating?"

She told him she'd ordered a salad so he got one as well, with an glass of water.

"You're not what I expected," she told him.

"Delightfully, neither are you," he answered. "I don't always get to conduct business with such pleasant companions. I was hoping tonight would be an exception."

They made a little small talk as they ate. He was a native New Yorker, she was from Ohio. Yes, she liked it here a lot. She told him where she'd been around town. When the check came he took it. She had the drugs in an envelope and she handed it to him as if it were correspondence of some sort. He glanced inside and then put it in his inside jacket pocket.

"What can I offer you for this?" he said.

"Well, two hundred for both should cover it," she replied, and he got out his leather billfold, selected a few bills which he put on top of the check and two hundred dollar bills which he handed directly to her.

"There you are. Thank you very much. I'll get back to you tomorrow and if this merchandise is acceptable I'll be interested in obtaining more. Would that be possible?"

She told him that it would. They left together and he walked to a gray Lexus parked at the curb.

"Thank you again, Mary. We'll talk tomorrow." Then he smiled, got in and drove away.

Glendy was pleased and a little perplexed as she walked back to the hotel. This was more like it, she decided.

Chapter 29

The next morning the sun was streaming into the hotel room with its faded wallpaper and worn furniture and Timmy was wide awake and surprised by what she had done.

"Leroy?" he said. "Fucking Leroy? You called this guy and went out and met him?"

Glendy was in no mood to put up with his nonsense. She was sitting on the bed drying her hair with a towel and wearing nothing, fresh from the shower, and she thought she had done rather well under the circumstances.

"Hey, Timmy. I made two hundred dollars. Also, I set up a good connection. What's the problem?"

Timmy began pacing around the confined room, stepping around the bed and over their clothes and bags which covered the floor.

"You could have gotten ripped off. Or arrested. Or he could have followed you back here."

She turned to him and gave him a level stare.

"None of which happened. Aren't you forgetting who pulled your butt out of the fire yesterday? You were busy in dreamland and I wanted to get this business moving."

He was angry at that. "What, you think I can't do this without you?"

She tossed her hair and shot him a short glance and said, "I think you think you have to be in control. I also think you'd have lost that kilo yesterday, and maybe you would've gotten shot, if I hadn't dealt with it."

On the bedside table, Timmy's cell phone rang. They stopped in mid-argument, frozen for a second, and then Glendy picked up the phone and looked at the caller ID.

"Leroy," she reported.

He looked at her a little longer while the ringing continued, thinking it through.

"Answer it," he finally said.

Glendy flicked the phone open and said, "Good morning."

There was a deep chuckle on the other end. "Good morning, Mary. How are you doing today?"

"Hi, Leroy," she said, and she exchanged a glance with Timmy.

"I'm good. What's new with you?"

Leroy said, "I'm very happy with your products. If you are agreeable, I'd like to discuss further business."

"Hold on a second, okay?" she said, and turned to Timmy again while covering the phone with her hand. "He wants to discuss doing more business."

Timmy nodded. "Okay. Set up a meeting. No deal yet, just a meeting."

She grimaced at him and sighed, shaking her head, but said into the phone, "Great, Leroy. We can meet with you. When would you like to do that?"

"Well, I have an opening in my schedule this afternoon at one. Are you free?"

"Sure. How about Gramercy Park?"

"That sounds fine. Will you be bringing someone else?"

He still sounded composed, a businessman doing what he did best, but there was suspicion in the question. Glendy thought that was a good thing because a cop would have been eager to have her accomplice jump into the net, too. She knew she was right about this; it just felt right.

"I'll have Timmy with me," she said.

"Oh, that's fine," Leroy replied. "I'll look forward to seeing you then."

When she hung up Timmy flared again. "Why did you mention my name?"

"He knows your name already, you dork. Tonya at Promises told him. We meet him at one in Gramercy Park."

Glendy was sullen now, put out with him for his lack of trust in her and his childish display of temper. She got up and went into the bathroom and closed the door.

As they walked to the park that afternoon Timmy was still being difficult.

"So who is this, bad, bad Leroy Brown, baddest man in the whole damn town? First we get the dagos trying to rip us off, now you've got us mixed up with some black gangsta."

He hadn't taken any drugs at all today because he knew she was put out with him. She thought all he wanted to do was get high, which was pretty much the truth, but he wasn't going to admit it to her. So he was a little agitated, his nerves raw from the stress of another impending encounter. They had no drugs with them because Timmy wanted to feel out the situation for himself first.

They were hiking into the park, the sun was out and people were all around. Glendy was sulky and she gave him a disgusted look before she answered him.

"I think you're going to be a little surprised."

They found Leroy sitting on a bench by himself, dressed in a dove gray cashmere overcoat and a beautiful dark blue pinstriped suit with a white shirt, the gold cufflinks and a patterned red tie. He had on black wingtip shoes which were polished to a mirror finish. He stood as they approached and extended his hand to Timmy.

"Hello, I'm Leroy. Very pleased to meet you."

Glendy glanced at Timmy and saw to her satisfaction that he was taken aback.

"Uh, hi," Timmy said, shaking his hand. He felt like Leroy was an adult and he was rather poorly turned out and scruffy adolescent. He looked self-consciously at his scuffed leather bomber jacket.

"Nice to see you again, Mary," Leroy continued, taking her hand as well, and Glendy took off her sunglasses and favored him with the full force of her brilliant blue eyes and wide red smile. Timmy was pissed.

"Shall we sit?" Leroy suggested. They sat on the bench, Glendy between the two men.

"I assume you're Timmy. Tonya spoke of you."

Timmy nodded. "Are you a lawyer or something? You're wearing about three thousand dollars worth of clothes." He was deliberately aggressive, annoyed by the man's smug elegance.

Leroy laughed. "Actually, it's probably more like four thousand dollars. I like to dress well. Also, any policeman can throw on a gangster outfit. Very few can afford to dress like this, and fewer have the style to carry it off."

Glendy was still smiling, which Timmy was finding truly irritating.

"So what can we do for you?" he said impatiently.

"Your product is very good. I'm impressed," said Leroy, and Timmy felt his aggravation subside a little. "I'd like to do business with you, if you're willing."

Timmy and Glendy were both nodding, agreeable. "Sure," he said. "What do you need?"

Leroy shifted on the bench a little and took a note from his pocket.

"My analysis of your products was very favorable," he said, looking at figures on the note. "The cocaine is about eighty percent pure but the heroin is closer to ninety. Very unusual."

Timmy said, "The coke's eighty-five and yeah, the smack's ninety. The very best."

Leroy looked at him and said, "The Dominicans here in New York control most of the heroin trade. They're a violent and possessive bunch, although their product is often pretty good. I'm a businessman and I don't want anything to do with their methods so I like to obtain my supplies elsewhere when I can. That means I'm sometimes forced to get substandard product. Meeting you two is refreshing because you seem like nice people and you have excellent product." He was grinning disarmingly.

Glendy was still smiling. Timmy wanted to get to the point. "So what do you need?" he asked.

"I don't think I've ever seen heroin this pure," continued Leroy. "And I've never seen Afghan heroin this pure. So I'm curious about how much I can get from you. Is this a new source or something? Do you have a regular supply?"

Afghan? Timmy had assumed that the heroin was from South American, especially after Joey D. told him how pure it was. Also, since Bam and Susie seemed to have gotten it from the Mexicans, it made sense that it came from South America.

"Are you sure it's Afghan? Like from Afghanistan?" he asked.

"Oh yes, no doubt about it. The chemical analysis confirms it," said Leroy, holding the note up as if Timmy would be able to decipher it.

"Huh," Timmy replied. "Well, I do have a supply of it. I think I can get you what you need."

A pair of mothers with babies in their strollers walked past them and they fell silent for a moment. When they were gone Timmy continued.

"I can get you a key for a hundred seventy-five. And more after that if you want it."

Leroy nodded and smiled and looked back and forth between them both.

"That sounds fine. Let's talk this evening and confirm a time and place."

They stood and shook hands again and Leroy headed out of the park, erect and with an athletic stride, and Timmy felt his resentment for him return. He and Glendy began walking back to the hotel, passing joggers and idlers and a few homeless looking people.

"Four thousand dollars my ass," he said.

"What's your problem?" she asked him. "The guy's gonna buy our stuff. Don't hate him because he's beautiful."

But Timmy didn't appreciate her humor. "I can't trust anybody after those dagos. I'm gonna call Bobby."

She stopped and turned to him, grabbing his arm. "What? You're gonna bring Bobby here? Why do that? This is going okay."

He was shaking his head. "I need insurance. I can't risk another fuckup. Bobby'll do security for us. I don't want to risk having you covering our asses with that little gun. We need help."

"I don't think we'll need it, Timmy," she said, pleading a little. "This guy's okay."

"And what if it goes bad again? You missed Joey D. by about a block with that gun. Bobby can back us up. He knows how to do it."

She wasn't happy about it. "Bobby's no doubt mad as hell at us."

But Timmy was determined to do it his way.

Chapter 30

Standing around a trash fire on a forty degree, overcast day in Middleburg Heights, Ohio, the laborers were taking a smoke break, bullshitting about the Indians and the Browns and whether all this damn snow was finally going to melt in the next couple of weeks.

Behind them the heavy equipment was still leveling the ground and trucks were coming and going on the construction site, bringing the foundation materials and hauling out debris from the old demolished building they'd torn down.

Bobby was eating a Twinkie and his mouth was full when his cell phone buzzed in the pocket of his black padded Carhartt jacket. His stripped off his heavy gloves and retrieved it and was startled to see Timmy's number on the caller ID.

It had been weeks since Timmy and Glendy had fled, and while Bobby knew he hadn't heard the last of them, actually having that time come around was still a surprise. He pulled his hard hat off his head and turned away from the others so he wouldn't be overheard and then he answered.

Timmy said, "Bobby. It's me." Soft and sort of quiet, as if no time had passed and this were just another conversation between them.

And Bobby felt his anger surge and he couldn't speak for a second. It had been a tough few weeks. Spin's murder weighed on him even though he knew that hadn't been his fault. Christ, he had warned Spin, hadn't he? Timmy had lied about the whole thing, had never come clean about what he was up to. He'd gotten Spin killed and left

Bobby and Sandy Polarski holding the bag. They'd both had to uproot their lives, find new places to live and work. Sandy was gone, moved to Akron, not wanting to be in the same town as the Mexicans and their guns and knives or whatever it was they killed Spin with.

Bobby had changed apartments, cars and jobs but he was still looking over his shoulder all the time. He never went anywhere without the Glock.

"Timmy, you fucker," he finally said. "Where are you?"

Timmy sighed on the phone and he sounded contrite when he said, "We're in New York. Manhattan. How are things there?"

"How the fuck do you think things are, you asshole? What the hell did you do?"

Timmy heard the anger in his voice and said, "Look, I know you're pissed. You have a right to be. What happened with the Mexicans?"

Bobby decided at that moment not to tell him about Spin yet. There'd be time for that when he was in the same room with him.

"I haven't seen the Mexicans. I had to move."

The sound of Timmy's exhale came over the phone and he sounded relieved when he said, "Good, I'm glad you ditched them. What about Sandy?"

"She left town. She was too freaked."

"Yeah, I can't blame her." He was paused for a few seconds and then got to the point.

"Look, Bobby, I'm sorry I cut out. It was the wrong thing to do without explaining it to you. I was freaked, too. Big things are happening here and I can't handle it by myself. I need some help. It'll be worth it big time, I promise you, if you can come here."

Bobby should have been surprised but he wasn't. If he'd thought ahead far enough he could have figured out that anything big enough to cause Timmy to leave town in a hurry would be too big for him to handle by himself in the long run.

"What are we talking about?" Bobby asked.

"I need help closing up some business. If you can get here right away and stay until it's done, it's worth a hundred to you."

For a moment Bobby wasn't sure what he meant. "A hundred?" he finally said. "A hundred what?"

"Thousand," said Timmy.

Bobby suddenly realized that whatever Timmy had gotten mixed up in was truly a major league event. Only high stakes games paid high stakes rewards.

"Okay," he said slowly. "That sounds interesting. How soon?"

"Like, right now," Timmy said, and he was laughing a little relieved that Bobby would do it.

"You mean, like, today?"

"Well, I know you can't be here today unless you get a plane in the next few hours. Tomorrow morning would be alright."

Bobby thought about the gun. "No, I'll drive. This is dangerous, right?" he asked.

"No shit, Sherlock. It could be, I'm hoping it won't be. But why take chances, you know?"

So Timmy told him how to get to the hotel and Bobby wrote it down on a piece of paper he borrowed from another guy at the fire.

When they were done he went and found the foreman, who of course was in the construction trailer out of the weather, and told him he had to leave for the rest of the week because he had a family emergency out of town. The guy was mad and told him he'd fire him if he did that, so Bobby said, "Suit yourself" and walked off the job.

He drove home and packed, gassed up the Firebird and headed out on Interstate 80, the Ohio Turnpike, toward New York City.

Night was coming on and the road was icy in a few spots. It was the time of year when daytime drizzle turned into night time ice, and he had to drive cautiously. He went steadily on, off of the toll portion and into Pennsylvania, traffic thinning out as time passed and he wound up into the hills. He stopped at a rest plaza and got some fast food and a large coffee to keep him alert and motivated.

He hadn't used any coke since he had sold off the rest of the ounces Timmy had given him. His own supply of grams had dwindled during that time and finally one night in a bar in Rocky River he had given away the last of it, about a half gram, to a girl he knew from high school. Naturally, she was thrilled and suggested maybe the two of them should go out to her car and indulge together, but he turned her down. For some reason he wasn't very interested in using now.

He thought maybe Spin's death had changed him somehow but he wasn't sure what that was all about. Of course having the Mexicans after him was part of it, but not all. He felt more serious than he had about things in general. Life wasn't fun and games. He didn't feel the need to rush around, scoring and dealing, looking for action and walking on that edge between safety and the precipice, peeking over and laughing when he came back whole. Spin had gone over that precipice. He would never be here again and his family was still weeping for him, butchered pure and simple for something he had no part in.

Still, if there was anything he might want to gain from such a misadventure beyond some personal insight and growth, a hundred thousand dollars could buy it. He wanted to see Timmy and Glendy and let them know the full extent of what they'd done. And he wanted some compensation for what he'd been through. He didn't think they should have it all for themselves; they owed people.

He played some Green Day and some Stone Temple Pilots as he drove, "Big Bang Baby" keeping him awake as the time rolled past, taking breaks to recycle the coffee at rest stops. Finally he slept for a few hours in a parking lot of one of them, curled up in the back seat of the car, a heavy blanket pulled over him and the Glock close at hand, the sounds of eighteen wheelers coming and going once in a while disturbing his sleep.

Chapter 31

Wade walked around in the lobby of the Yorkshire Grand Hotel and cycled through the gift shop yet again. The pleasant young clerk, a native of Maine, if he remembered correctly, raised an eyebrow discreetly and went back to her magazine. It was his tenth there since he'd arrived the night before last and he'd bought all the newspapers and toothpaste he was likely to need.

Glendy had said they'd call today or tomorrow and today was winding down. Of course, she also suggested that he could call them, but he'd gotten a good feeling from her call and didn't want to press them if he didn't need to. He hoped she'd be an ally and bring Tim around. Yes, he intended to take the Mustang back and drive it home. But more than that he wanted to talk to his brother, to try to bridge the gap that seemed to divide them. He didn't understand why Tim was distant but he wanted to make it better if he could.

Since their father had died and Wade had had to take his place in many areas of their family's life, Tim had been difficult. Of course, they had always had different likes and interests but they had been okay with that, Wade thought.

This was something more, a smoldering resentment of Wade's whole lifestyle, who he was. Tim seemed to be jealous of Wade's family life and his professional accomplishments yet he showed no inclination to establish anything similar for himself. He seemed content to work a menial job and he had decided not to pursue more education, having only a few college credits. He hadn't had a serious girlfriend from a background similar to his own since high school, as far as Wade knew. Glendy seemed nice but now it turned out she was a stripper, for God's sake. He wondered how their mother, or their father, for that matter, would feel about that.

So he didn't want to just seize the car, although of course he'd need to know where it was to even do that. He wanted to reason with his brother, offer his help, talk about his life and his fears and his concerns, help him get back on track. And to tell him that he needed him to be a responsible adult, and that meant pulling his own weight and not taking advantage of their mother's generosity.

He strolled out onto the Avenue of the Americas and watched traffic surging past, night falling and commuters making their laborious way out of Manhattan and back to New Jersey and Long Island and elsewhere. He felt guilty for not being in Cleveland and doing what he was paid handsomely to do, which was directing sales for the H.B. Conlin Company. He also envied the commuters because they were heading home to their houses and their families and Wade missed his.

He had talked to Ralph several times during the past two days, and to his secretary and his sales managers as well, and had good oversight of the major events going on in the business. He used his laptop in his room constantly, thankful for the fairly quick DSL connection, drafting letters, comparing data with the office, and scrutinizing proposals and projections and resumes. So he really was being productive with his time. Still, although Ralph was encouraging and supportive, aware of some vague problem with Wade's younger brother, it wasn't the same as being at the office and in the field with his people. So the guilt was persistent.

The expense was another thing. It was expensive to do nothing but hang around in Midtown Manhattan waiting for Tim to decide to see him. The room and the meals were notoriously costly here and he couldn't help but feel that the money would be better spent in Little Wade's college fund, or, for that matter, on a new boat for the family, or on something else they wanted, and not on this mission to reverse his brother's transgressions.

The doorman tipped his hat to him as he walked back into the hotel; he'd become a familiar sight as he haunted the place, waiting for something to happen. He'd used the exercise room the past two days but he didn't want to wander too far from his room because he feared that Tim would call then and, not being able to reach him or get a quick call back, would rationalize his single call as an adequate effort at contact and stop trying.

He took the elevator to the tenth floor and let himself into his room. It was a king room, expensively appointed and furnished, with a small sitting area and a spacious desk, which was good for the work he'd been doing. He glanced at the phone and noted once again that he had no messages.

He called room service and ordered a Cobb Salad and some Apollinaris water, wanting something light after all his inactivity. Then he got out his cell phone and called Amanda.

"Hi, how's New York?" she answered, seeing that it was him on her caller ID.

"The same," he sighed. "No action. I'm going to give him until tomorrow around midday and then call him again. I don't want to push, you know? But I can't wait around here forever."

He heard her knocking pans around in the kitchen, a familiar sound which immediately made him homesick.

"That's probably a good idea," she agreed. "You don't want to spook him. But you do want to get the car."

"I miss you guys," he told her.

"We miss you too, and I'll let you say hi to Wade in a second," she told him. "You're doing the right thing. Is Ralph still okay with it?"

"Oh yeah, he's being great. And I really am getting a lot done. I've got nothing but time. How about that strip club? Was that the right thing?"

She laughed. "Sure! I'm going to Ladies Night with the girls, though, next chance I get. Deal?"

"We just won't mention it at church," he agreed. "We don't want to shock anyone. Has anybody called?"

"Allie did. I told her what you're doing. She says she won't say anything to your mom until you get back with the car. She feels kind of bad about the whole thing."

"Well, so do I," he said.

"But she agrees with you," Amanda continued.

He was grateful for that. After a minute she put Little Wade on and they talked about tae kwon do and school and Wade promised to bring him something back from his trip. Then he said goodbye to Amanda, told her he loved her, and sat looking out the window, out across the astonishing manmade landscape of Manhattan. Far below in the streets traffic continued to inch along through rush hour gridlock. In a little while there was knock on his door and a waiter brought in his dinner.

Still no call. He ate his salad and watched the news on TV and wanted to be out of there.

Chapter 32

At three in the morning a light rain was falling on East 17th Street and there wasn't much traffic when Bobby found his way to the hotel. He'd slept for a few hours off of the interstate in Pennsylvania but he was blurry and dragged out and the convoluted drive through Manhattan had strained his focus. He was happy to finally see the place.

He pulled up out front and went in, where a half-somnolent night clerk confirmed that Ms. Willard had reserved and prepaid a room for him. He parked his car across the street in the garage and lugged his soft black bag up to his room, put out the "do not disturb" sign, undressed and fell into bed. He slept immediately.

Somebody was pounding on his door and he opened one eye and found the bedside clock radio and discovered that it was seven-thirty. It took him a moment to remember where he was. Then he swung out of bed and went to the door, wearing only his underwear. He had the Glock down by his side as he peered through the peephole and saw Timmy standing in the hall, looking from side to side distractedly. He put the gun under his jeans, lying across the arm of a chair, close at hand but unseen. Then he opened the door.

"Can't you read?" he said.

Timmy walked in quickly and shut the door behind him. He stuck out his hand to Bobby but Bobby turned away, pretending not to see it.

WILLIAM C. DUNCAN

"Glad to see you, man. Sorry to crash in," Timmy said, speaking fast.

Bobby pulled on a pair of sweatpants from his bag and sat down in the chair where his jeans were and said, "Things happen early around here, huh?"

Timmy remained standing and was pacing around a little as he said, "Thanks for coming, Bobby. Really. Things are moving and we're doing something at ten. We've got to plan out how we're gonna do this. How was your trip?" He finally sat on the edge of the bed but he was keyed up, nervous and excited about what was going on, and Bobby saw that it would be up to him to make this happen the right way.

"So tell me what's going on," he said.

Timmy explained about Gail and Promises and Mickey and that he had tried to do a deal with this guy, Joey D., but had walked into a setup and how he'd only gotten out of it because Glendy had followed him there and helped him out.

Bobby interrupted him and said, "Glendy has a gun? She shot at him?"

Timmy grinned and said yes, that was what happened, but it was only dumb luck that it had worked out the way it did and they needed to be more careful. Then he explained about Leroy, leaving out the fact that Glendy had been behind that, too, and said that this guy was very cool, very businesslike, dressed like a straight businessman and talked like he was a Harvard graduate or some damn thing. Glendy trusted him but he wasn't trusting anybody until the deal was behind them.

"How big is this deal? How much product have you got?" Bobby asked.

Timmy had rehearsed for this moment, had planned out what he was going to say. He saw no point in telling Bobby that this was about heroin because Bobby had never had a good opinion of heroin and he didn't want to risk having him walk away from the deal. He was going to let him assume it was about cocaine. He put on a serious face and looked squarely at him.

"It's a big dollar transaction. Over a hundred grand this time, and I'm hoping this guy will do more business with us. I'll give you twenty grand after this one, and when we do it all I'll give you the rest. Sound okay?"

Bobby whistled quietly and shook his head, taking it in.

"Man, you ripped those Mexicans off big time. No wonder they're so pissed."

Timmy leaned forward to Bobby and spread his hands wide.

"Hey, I took this shit out of a garage at a house where the people were dead. The people who owned this stuff had died, man. Anybody would have done the same thing. The cops would have got it or somebody else who just happened to come by. I got lucky. I'm interested in spreading that luck around, and you can have some."

Bobby stood up and looked down at Timmy, fixing him with level stare.

"Spin caught some of your luck, Timmy," he said, and his voice barely contained his anguish and rage. "What's Spin get out of it?"

Timmy was startled and sat back away from him. "What do you mean?" he asked.

"I mean," Bobby said, leaning in closer to him, looming over him, "that the Mexicans got Spin. They caught him and they killed him. In fact, they chopped him up with machetes or some fucking thing."

Timmy turned away, reeling with the impact of the words. Then he looked back up at Bobby, his eyes wide, and said, "Oh, man, how the hell did that happen? When was this?"

Bobby still stood over him, not giving way, confronting Timmy because Spin couldn't, and said, "They must have followed him from our house. His car was found a block from his sister's place in Old Brooklyn. They found Spin a couple of days later in the Flats wrapped up in a plastic tarp. It was a few days after you left town. You could've told us how badly these guys were gonna want to find you."

Timmy's mind raced and he wondered if Spin knew anything personal about him that he could have told the Mexicans.

"But they haven't come after you? You haven't seen them again?"

Bobby stared at him for another few seconds. Timmy suddenly was afraid of Bobby and scared now, at last, of the threat of the Mexicans, feeling it for himself.

Bobby sat down and said with contempt, "They don't know where I am, and if they knew where you or your family were somebody else would probably be dead by now."

Timmy sat for a moment, looking at his hands. Then he raised his eyes to Bobby's unwavering and accusing gaze and said, "I'm sorry. I'm really sorry."

They sat quietly, the traffic noise from the street below drifting up to them, the sunlight penetrating past the buildings and onto the pavement and illuminating the day. After a while Bobby stood again and walked to the window and looked out.

"One other thing I want you to do, Timmy. Two, actually. When this is over you send Spin's family fifty thousand dollars. And you send Sandy twenty thousand. It's the least you can do and it will ease your conscience."

Timmy sat, looking down and nodding, his shoulders slumped.

"Okay," he finally said. "I'll do that."

"Good." Bobby turned back to him. He regarded him for a while, disgusted with him but resolved to see this thing through and get some compensation for himself and for the others who'd been hurt by it.

"I'm willing to make some lemonade with the lemon you laid on me," he finally said. "Now tell me where you're hooking up with Leroy and we'll figure out how to put some security on it."

Chapter 33

At ten in the morning Leroy parked his Lexus in the garage by the Cabrini Medical Center as Timmy had directed when they spoke on the phone at nine-thirty. He walked out front and stood there for a moment, another well-dressed man in a suit with a sizeable salesman's sample case, and waited for his cell to ring. The sample case was made of fake leather, one of those boxy oversized briefcases with a handle of top. Inside the hospital lobby, watching him, Glendy noted that nobody seemed to be with him and nobody was paying any attention to him.

After a minute she called Timmy and said, "Looks good. I don't spot any helpers."

Timmy called Leroy and told him, "Get a cab to Bellevue. Get out there on First Avenue and wait for my call."

Leroy chuckled and said, "I'm traveling kind of heavy to be doing all this running around."

"Bear with me. We'll all be better for it."

So Leroy hailed a cab and Glendy watched him get in and leave. Nobody broke cover and scrambled for a cab to follow him. No cars cruised nonchalantly away from the curb and tailed him.

She called Timmy back and said, "I think he's alone." Then she walked out and caught a cab herself.

A few minutes later Timmy watched Leroy's cab drop him off in front of Bellevue Hospital as he sat in an idling cab, the meter running, and said to the cabby, "I guess my friend isn't coming. Give me another minute and then take me to Lexington and 26th." He watched Leroy standing around with the big sample case and noted that no one had appeared near him and no one was showing any interest in him at all. There was a lot of pedestrian traffic around the hospital, but nobody lingered on the sidewalk. He called Leroy again.

"Okay. Catch another cab to Baruch College, Lexington and 26th, in two minutes."

"That's three blocks away," Leroy said.

"Yeah, I know. There's a coffee shop there, Malcolm's. I'll be inside."

When Timmy got out of his cab at Malcolm's he saw Bobby standing across the street. He went inside with his own large sample case in hand. It was big enough to hold five kilos of coke so he didn't think Bobby would find anything odd about it. The single kilo of heroin bumped around inside as he walked.

He got a small table in the back. Students wandered in and out of the restaurant and the low rumble of their conversations filled the place. He told the waitress, "A coffee, please, cream and sugar. And a blueberry scone."

In a couple of minutes Leroy walked in, spotted him and walked back. He put his sample case down next to Timmy's under the table.

They looked at each other for a few seconds, both calm and intent, and by some mutual unspoken agreement they smiled and relaxed a little more. Nobody was screwing anybody today. They both felt it.

"A coffee, please, dear," Leroy said to the waitress, and she hustled away. "Would you like to see my papers?" he asked.

Timmy leaned over and Leroy flipped open the top of the sample case. Inside were stacks of twenty dollar bills bound with rubber bands. The case was full of them. He looked back up at Leroy.

"One hundred seventy-five stacks of fifty twenties," Leroy said, and snapped the case closed. His coffee came and he added cream and sugar like Timmy had.

"Great minds think alike," Timmy said, nodding at the coffee. He reached down and opened his case. "See what I've got?"

Leroy took an unhurried look into the case, saw the kilo of white powder wrapped in plastic, and nodded.

"Very nice," he said.

They sipped their coffee and Leroy said, "Why all the paranoia?"

"Just being careful. Better safe than sorry."

"That's two clichés in one minute. If you utter another one I'm going to scream," Leroy told him, and then he laughed. "A little bird in the Village told me that the police are asking around about a guy in a brown leather jacket with a tall brunette. Most of the witnesses remembered the brunette. Story is that they took a shot at a member of the Gambino crime family and he ran in front of a cab trying to get away from them. He's laid up in one of these hospitals we've been running around outside of this morning but he isn't saying anything, of course."

Timmy looked steadily at him over the top of his coffee cup.

"Really?" he said.

"So I suspect your paranoia is based upon hard experience. I'd like to continue to do business with you but I'd like to make a suggestion." He gazed at Timmy, his expression expectant behind his rimless glasses.

Timmy shrugged. "Sure. Go ahead." He was eating the scone now, pretending this wasn't the critical juncture of his criminal life, determined to act cool and not run out of the restaurant and back to the hotel so he could count the money. If Leroy could act all detached and relaxed about this, so could he.

Leroy leaned forward, smiled and said, "Get out of this part of town. Get yourself uptown a little and get some nice clothes. Tasteful, you know? You can afford it. I mean no offense but dress your woman up, too. Upgrade your act and don't look like somebody who could be doing what we're doing." He had a little more coffee.

"Doing the taxi run around was smart. Meeting here was smart, too. I look like a doctor or a professor and you look like a student. But hanging around lower Manhattan is going to get you found by the police or by the friends of the guy who got hit by the cab."

Timmy's head bobbed up and down a few times and he said, "Okay, that makes sense. I mean, there's like eight million people living here but I guess it makes sense to be cautious."

"Oh, believe me, it does. Don't go near that strip club again. The Gambinos will find you if you do."

"Yeah, I wasn't planning on it. Thanks for the tip."

145

They waved away the hovering waitress and her coffeepot.

"I'll be calling you in a few days, I think. Is that good with you? We can do this again, or more?" Leroy raised his eyebrows and waited.

"Yeah, sure. Like I said, there's more where this came from. I appreciate the business."

They stood and each took the other's sample case and they walked up front. Timmy paid for both of them because that was only right under the circumstances. They strolled out into the sunlight and Timmy saw Bobby watching them and he nodded and smiled just a little in his direction. He saw Glendy on the sidewalk up from Bobby, pretending to look at a newspaper but keeping an eye on him, too.

He shook hands with Leroy, who grinned and said, "Thanks," and stuck up his arm for a cab. As he disappeared up the street Timmy caught a cab, too. He didn't want to walk anywhere with $175,000 in cash. He saw Glendy and Bobby's cab falling in behind his and they drifted back to the hotel, a happy surreptitious cabal, and went inside to even up and figure out what to do next. They'd pulled off the first big deal.

Chapter 34

At eleven-forty-five that morning Wade was at the desk in his hotel room running sales projections on his laptop, here and there tweaking numbers provided by his managers to conform to his own experience and expectations. He kept glancing at his Rolex. The deadline he'd given himself, noon, was coming up and he would call Timmy then. He preferred not to be pushy but he would make this happen if Timmy wouldn't.

His cell phone jingled and he picked it up and looked at the ID and was surprised to see that it was not Amanda or the office but Tim.

"Hello?" he said, not knowing whether to expect to hear Glendy again. But it was his brother.

"Hi, man," he said and he actually sounded happy to be talking to him.

"Hey, Tim, how are you? It's nice to hear from you."

"Yeah, you too. You're still in New York, right? Glendy told me she talked to you and I wanted to get back to you."

"I'm still here. How about you?"

"Yup, we're here, too. We've been really busy and we're changing locations so I'm sorry I haven't been around. How long are you in town for?"

"Well, sort of as long as it takes for us to get together. I'd like to see you, Tim." And he waited for a brush off or an excuse, anything Tim could come up with to avoid a face-to-face meeting with him.

But, again, he was surprised.

"How about tonight? Can we get together for dinner?" Tim asked.

"Well, sure. That would be great." Could this really be going so well? "Where do you want to meet?"

"You're at the Yorkshire Grand, right? Let's meet in the lobby at seven. We can eat there or figure something out. How's the restaurant there?"

"It's good. Really excellent, actually. Seven is fine. Will Glendy be coming?"

"I'm sure she won't want to miss it. See you then."

"Yes, great. See you."

Wade sat for a moment, pleased but a little uneasy, unsure why Tim would change directions so abruptly. But he decided it was better than more non-cooperation and he would take it.

Timmy and Glendy in the Mustang and Bobby in the Firebird wound through the streets of Manhattan into Midtown and over to 6th Avenue and pulled up in front of the Yorkshire Grand Hotel. Timmy and Glendy got out and trooped inside and up to the front desk where the clerk confirmed their reservation, called in an hour before, for two adjoining rooms for three adults. They ran Glendy's credit card but Timmy paid up front for three days, in cash, almost two thousand dollars, and nobody batted an eye.

They had their cars parked by a valet and a bellman loaded their belongings on a cart but Timmy carried the big suitcase himself and Glendy carried the sample case. They went up to their rooms on the twenty-seventh floor and only spent a little time settling in. Then Timmy and Glendy went back out, leaving Bobby in front of the TV in his room, a room service cheeseburger and a Sam Adams beer in front of him. The big suitcase now had a small luggage lock securing it and so did the sample case. Bobby had $20,000 in cash in his pocket and he would not leave the rooms as long as the other two were out.

They headed over to Fifth Avenue and began shopping. After two hours Timmy had three suits, two Armanis and a Ermenegildo Zegna, and several Zegna ties. He bought some appropriate shirts with the help of the clerk and a some socks and two pairs of Italian shoes.

He needed his clothes immediately and waved a hundred in front of the clerk and he was promised the tailoring would be completed by five.

Glendy bought shoes, pumps that elevated her over Timmy and sandals and some flats, too. She bought a very elegant little black dress and a black Armani pantsuit that was stunning on her. She bought some slacks and silk tops and a sleek fawn colored calfskin jacket. Then they went to Tiffany's and picked out some diamond earrings and a diamond pendant. For a little balance, she added some gold hoop bracelets.

They had to catch a cab to get all of their purchases back to the hotel. A bellman helped them transport everything up to their room.

When Bobby heard them come in he opened the adjoining door and peered in at the boxes and garment bags piled on the bed.

"Man, you buy enough stuff?" he asked. "Is there anything left for the tourists?"

Glendy had been standoffish toward him since that morning, when Timmy had told her what happened to Spin and Bobby had leveled a baleful glare in her direction. She hadn't killed Spin, for God's sake, the Mexicans had. It was terrible and everything but she couldn't do anything about it now. She'd told Bobby she was sorry his friend had died but she didn't think he was happy with her and that made her petulant. But now, with more beautiful clothes and jewelry than she had ever expected to own, she was euphoric.

"Go away for a minute," she told him. "We'll give you a fashion show."

And while Bobby waited in his room they changed into their new clothes, then strolled in and modeled everything for him. After waltzing around once or twice they'd go back into their own room and change, then come back in and do it again. Timmy looked okay, the clothes were great, but Glendy looked spectacular. Of course, she had a lot of experience at this kind of thing, but she usually had fewer clothes on.

They were all laughing and joking and Bobby said, "Hey, if the drug dealing doesn't work out you guys could be underwear models."

At seven they'd decided what they'd wear to dinner and Timmy had on his black Armani with the pale blue chalk stripes and a blue tie while Glendy wore the pantsuit, pumps and the diamonds. Her makeup was subtle and perfect.

"Your brother won't recognize you," Bobby said. "Have fun."

Timmy and Glendy went out and took the elevator down to the lobby while Bobby ordered a filet mignon from room service and a movie on the hotel network.

Chapter 35

Wade didn't see them walk into the lobby and it was as Bobby had predicted: he didn't recognize them. Timmy walked right up to him, Glendy on his arm, and Wade didn't look up from his chair until he cleared his throat. Then it was comical, Timmy thought. Wade actually did a double take before he got hurriedly to his feet and grabbed Timmy's hand.

"Wow!" he said. "Look at you two. I didn't see you come in. You look great!"

And they did. Wade hadn't seen his brother in a suit since their father's funeral six years earlier. And then it hadn't been anything elegant and expensive like this obviously was. And Glendy...well, his brother's girlfriend should probably have been working in Hollywood instead of Cleveland. She looked like she owned the place, and other people in the lobby were noticing her as they stood there.

"Hi, Wade," Timmy said, smiling at him as they shook hands. "You know Glendy, right?"

Wade and Glendy exchanged polite greetings, and she was friendly and smiling, too. Wade had a moment of disorientation.

These were two pleasant and well-to-do twenty-somethings, not his dependent and maladapted little brother and a stripper. He was having a little difficulty reconciling the divergence with what he'd been expecting. And it got better from there.

"So, where are you staying?" he asked.

151

"Right here," Timmy said. "Nice place, isn't it?"

Wade stood there, unable to think of anything appropriate to say for a couple of seconds, and then he came up with, "Uh, yes. It's very nice. When did you get here?"

"This afternoon," Timmy said airily, gazing around the staid and elegant lobby, well dressed guests and uniformed employees bustling about its vast expanse. "We decided to move uptown."

Glendy was regarding Wade speculatively, aware of his confusion. She wanted to ease his concerns and said, "Are we going to eat here? Let's go in and get a table and we can talk some more."

They were seated at an intimate table in the restaurant, which was half full, and the waiter came by for drink orders. Glendy ordered a Cosmopolitan and Timmy said, "What are you having, Wade?"

"I think I'll have a Glenmorangie on the rocks with a twist."

"Is that good? I think I'll have one, too."

Wade regarded Tim as he talked to Glendy about what she was hungry for. He was obviously enjoying the effect they had had on him. It felt something like a childish prank to Wade. *Look at us, guess who we are!* He didn't understand what it was all about.

Their cocktails came and Timmy raised his and said, "To prosperity," and they all drank.

Wade seized the moment. "About that. What's going on with you? Suddenly you leave town and come here and something has apparently changed for you. You certainly look prosperous. What happened?"

Timmy and Glendy were looking at each other and giggling a little.

He turned back to Wade and spoke sincerely. "I've had a business windfall. We came to New York to do some business and it's turned out well."

Wade just stared at him. "Tim," he finally said. "You work on a loading dock. What are you talking about?"

Timmy looked at Glendy again and smiled, letting her know that the story they'd invented was coming, and then he launched into it.

"Stamps, Wade," he explained. "Rare stamps. I've been investing a little in rare stamps for a while and I was lucky enough to come across a large collection in an estate sale a few months ago. The estate was in a hurry to liquidate them and didn't really appreciate what they had. I picked it up cheap and researched it. It was worth a lot."

He paused and sipped his scotch, not looking at him at all.

Glendy was regarding Wade over the rim of her Cosmopolitan. He shifted his gaze to her and she put the glass down and smiled demurely, her eyes wide, looking right at him.

Wade knew his brother had an interest in stamps. He'd had a collection since he was a child and from time to time had mentioned it to him, but Wade knew nothing about the subject. He'd always tried to show the involvement he felt an older brother should, but frankly it wasn't anything that held much allure for him. As with many other likes and dislikes, they didn't share this one. So this was Tim's field of expertise and he had no way to properly evaluate it. It had always seemed more like a hobby; as an investment, it seemed risky and not very likely to yield much. Maybe he'd been wrong and had underestimated the potential.

"You came here to sell the collection?" he asked.

Timmy nodded and smiled at him. "That's right. I just finished the deal. Of course, New York's the place to do something like this. You have to go to the right people to get the right price, eliminate the middlemen. So it's a done deal. I made out very well."

The waiter came back and they ordered, Glendy unsure about what some of the menu items were but the waiter didn't think that was a problem, leaning over her to explain each one in detail. Timmy observed archly that this process took longer than necessary, and that Glendy was aware of it. She rolled her eyes at him, then looked back at the waiter and decided on the shrimp scampi over angel hair pasta. The waiter assured her that she was the most tasteful of women and then took Wade's order for the glazed salmon and Timmy's for the New York strip steak.

When he was gone Wade said, "Huh. Congratulations. So you're well situated now? I mean, financially? Was this a substantial windfall?"

Timmy replied, somewhat smugly, "Pretty substantial, I would say."

Wade shifted around and thought about it, glanced around the room and said, "Well, I kind of hate to bring it up under the circumstances, but what about the Mustang? Mom's been making your payments on it."

Timmy waved a hand dismissively and said, "Of course. Don't worry about it. I intend to pay it off completely now. But to be perfectly honest, Wade, I don't need it here and wondered if you'd consider driving it back home?"

Wade stammered a little at that. "Well, yes, I could do that. It would save me the cost of a return plane ticket. When can we do this?"

Timmy said, "I'm letting a friend use it for another couple of days, but then it's free. I'll call him tonight and try to move it along. I'll give you the payoff on it when you go. I hate to ask you to stay any longer. I know it's inconvenient for you, and expensive. Can I pick up your room until you go? It's the least I can do."

"No, no, that's okay. But the sooner the better. I've got work to do back home, and other things."

Timmy leaned forward to him. "Then let me help out with your costs. It's only fair."

In the end Wade agreed. After all, he wouldn't be here at all if Tim hadn't forced it on him, and his family deserved the money he would be spending hanging around waiting. Timmy was a little pompous but gracious just the same. They enjoyed their meals, had after dinner drinks, and talked about their families and about New York.

They didn't discuss stripping or why Timmy weaseled Harriet into paying for the car in the first place.

They all rode up in the elevator together, Timmy telling Wade that he'd be tied up with more stamp discussions so he wouldn't be around much. He hoped to develop more business, he said, and was meeting different stamp dealers. Wade said okay and even thanked Timmy for dinner, which he'd paid for with twenty dollar bills. Then he got off on the tenth floor and said good night to them.

When the door closed again Glendy said, "You are a smooth liar, sonny. How do I know you don't lie to me?"

He kissed her and said, "I could say the same about you."

She shook her head and replied, "Yeah, but that's your brother. You really put it past him. You were like Leroy's little white cousin."

Timmy sniffed and looked up at the ceiling of the elevator. "He thinks I'm an underachiever. The joke's on him."

Chapter 36

Gail Montgomery had found a plastic bag from Borders Books in her apartment, in Sheree's room, and it had three CDs in it. Since they were hard rock, Green Day and some other stuff, she was pretty sure they were Timmy's, overlooked in the rush to abandon the apartment.

She didn't do anything about it for a day or so; she was busy with work and still pretty upset at Mickey over the ripoff. Of course he claimed he had no idea that Joey D. would try to rob Timmy and Glendy, but she didn't believe him because he kept asking if she knew where they were. He said he wanted to apologize to them, to explain that he was blameless, but she thought he was probably up to no good and she didn't tell him anything about anything. She wasn't speaking to him at all, in fact, and besides that she really didn't know where they'd gone.

But she did know where Timmy's brother probably was. At least, as of a couple of days ago he was at the Yorkshire Grand. She didn't remember the room number he'd written on the card he'd given her to give to Timmy, or his phone number, but she remembered which hotel it was.

And looking him up to return Timmy's CDs seemed like a good thing to do. After all, it was only right, and it sort of made up for the unpleasantness they'd had to put up with. Probably she should go see the guy and give him the CDs. Maybe he'd be glad to see her, too, and they could have lunch or something. But if she was going to do it she ought to get going, she decided, because Timmy said he wasn't going to be in town for very long. She worried that maybe he was already gone.

She had to drop by Promises to pick up some tips Frank was holding for her and so she dressed up a little, because the Yorkshire Grand was a nice place. She walked into the club at eleven in the morning and Mickey was in there, talking to Stacey, and Gail deliberately ignored him. He was watching her but she only acknowledged Stacey, saying hi to her, and put her bulky shoulder bag and the bag with the CDs in it behind the bar while she went up to the office and looked for Frank.

After a minute Stacey left the bar, too, because the place wasn't open yet and she was doing prep work and had to get some supplies from the back. Mickey took that opportunity to come around behind the bar and look at the bags Gail had put there. He opened the Borders bag and recognized the CDs at once because Timmy had shown them to him that night when they were getting high at Gail's apartment. His quickly rummaged through her shoulder bag, too, but there was so much stuff in there that he couldn't possibly check it all out. Then he got back out in front of the bar so he wouldn't get caught.

Thirty seconds later Gail came back into the room, went behind the bar and got her things, and headed for the door.

"Hey, babe, what's going on?" Mickey said.

She paused just long enough to turn and glare at him, said, "Screw you, Mickey," and stalked out into the daylight in her high heeled boots.

Mickey hopped up and followed her to the door and watched as she hailed a cab. As she took off up the street he came outside and got lucky again because there were a couple of more cabs coming by and he waved one down and jumped in and told the guy, "Follow that cab!" just like in the movies.

When they got into Midtown she got out at the Yorkshire Grand Hotel and Mickey held back a minute while she went inside and then he came after her again, keeping her in sight, hanging back so he wouldn't be easily spotted. She walked up to the front desk and was talking to a clerk so Mickey grabbed an easy chair from which he could see what she was doing and snatched up a copy of *USA Today* from a coffee table and pretended to read it, keeping part of his face covered.

The clerk pushed a house phone across the desk toward her and Gail picked up the receiver and dialed. Then she was talking and he saw she was smiling and then laughing a little as she spoke and listened. Then she hung up and started walking toward him, coming toward the expansive furniture group in the middle of the lobby. He kept the newspaper in front of his face and she sat down on a couch twenty-five feet away.

Mickey was afraid she'd recognize his shoes or his pants or something but she seemed preoccupied, fidgeting and looking around the place. He kept getting quick glimpses of her around the paper until he remembered something he'd seen in a movie once, maybe the same one with the cab line in it, and tore out a tiny piece of paper at the center fold. Now he could see her clearly with the paper in front of his face but she couldn't tell he was doing it unless she looked really closely, and she was too busy looking around the place to be likely to do that.

After a few minutes a guy walked up to her, a tall good-looking dude in casual slacks and a polo shirt, and she stood up and smiled at him and then they were both talking at once to each other. Gail was holding the bag with the CDs in it in the guy's direction and he was looking at her and then smiling and nodding his head, taking the bag, touching her shoulder. Mickey could make out part of their conversation and he heard "thanks" and "Timmy" and "Glendy" and "how long?" Then the two of them walked back over to the front desk and Gail used the house phone again but nobody seemed to be answering at the room she called.

Gail and the guy talked a little more to each other, more smiling, Gail gesturing and touching her hair and Mickey could tell she was interested in the guy. Then he touched her shoulder again and they began strolling toward the coffee shop just off the lobby, talking animatedly, and went in and he couldn't see them anymore.

Mickey put down the newspaper and hurried across to the front desk. The clerk raised his eyes to him from whatever he was doing back there and Mickey said, "Is Mr. Tim Thomas registered here?"

The clerk stepped over to a computer terminal and tapped in some information and then watched the screen as the data came up.

"No, sir, sorry, but we don't have a Mr. Tim Thomas registered with us."

Mickey was disappointed and figured he'd misread the whole thing, maybe Gail was just giving some new boyfriend the CDs Timmy had left behind or something. He was about to thank the clerk and turn away when he thought of Glendy. What was her name? Gail had mentioned it several times.

"How about a Ms. Willard?" he asked, and the clerk repeated the procedure with the computer and this time he said, "Yes, sir. We have a Glenda Willard. Is that your party?" He looked up at Mickey expectantly.

Mickey felt an adrenaline rush and said to the guy, "What's the room number?"

The clerk was shaking his head and said, "I'm sorry, sir, but we're not allowed to give out room information. If you would like to use the house phone and ask for Ms. Willard the operator will connect you."

Mickey said no, thanks anyway, and turned away from the desk.

He headed for the door and was reaching for his cell phone as he walked. The doorman ushered him out onto the sidewalk and he kept walking for a block, not wanting to risk having Gail come out and spot him, and then placed a call from the phone's memory. He recognized the voice of Joey D.'s fat friend at once when he answered.

"Yo, Tommy B. This is Mickey from Promises. Guess who I just found?"

Chapter 37

Leroy strolled into the cocktail lounge at the First American Steak House on 8th Avenue and saw Timmy seated at a small round elevated table by the front windows, watching people walking by.

The place wasn't very crowded and Leroy slid onto the stool opposite him and noted the change in his appearance.

"It's always nice to have an influence on people," he said. "Now who's wearing three thousand dollars worth of clothing?"

Timmy smirked a little, looking at him coolly, and said, "When in Rome, dude. It was a good suggestion on your part. You ought to see Glendy."

"Who?" Leroy asked. "Oh, you mean Mary." He laughed. "What are you drinking?"

Timmy picked up his glass and swirled the drink around.

"Glenmorangie."

Leroy gestured to the waitress. "Did you discover that recently, too?"

Timmy said, "I had help." But he didn't elaborate.

Leroy ordered a white wine, something that required an extended discussion with the girl, and then she went to get it.

"So how are you making out with the product?" Timmy asked him.

Leroy sat back and regarded him through the rimless glasses for a moment. The bar began to get a little busier, people coming in after leaving work early, meeting friends. A group of four young women sat down around the little table close by.

159

"Why is that of interest?" Leroy finally asked him.

"You mean, 'mind my own fucking business'?" Timmy said, and laughed. "You are truly a smooth operator, Leroy."

Leroy glanced at the women nearby and spoke quietly. "If it is your business, perhaps you'd like to explain how. You didn't call me just to make sure your customer satisfaction ratings were high."

Timmy nodded and finished his scotch and looked around for the waitress. She was still getting the wine and he looked back at Leroy and smiled.

"I'm wondering whether you are ready yet to do more business."

"So soon?" Leroy said. "Are you anxious?"

"I'm interested. I'd like to give you the opportunity."

The waitress came back and put Leroy's wine glass down on a napkin. Timmy ordered another scotch and she turned to the office girls and began taking their orders. Timmy and Leroy sat quietly watching 8th Avenue until she was gone again and their neighbors were deep in their own conversations.

"Are you implying that someone else may want your product?" Leroy asked.

Of course, this was not so, but it was exactly what Timmy wanted Leroy to believe. He continued to gaze out the window while he said, "I have a good supply of product on hand, but when it's gone I may not have it again any time soon. So I thought I'd offer you first shot at grabbing what I have."

Leroy looked out the window for a while, too. Then he looked back at him and he looked serious for the first time since Timmy had met him.

"Okay," he said. "I'll bite. How much are we talking about?"

Timmy faced him. "Five more of the same."

Leroy sat back again and exhaled. "That's a lot of product. And you're saying that if I don't take it, it could be gone?"

Timmy smiled at him and said, "That's a real possibility."

Leroy considered this for a while. The waitress came back and brought Timmy's refill and a tray full of fruity concoctions for the women next door. They were all talking animatedly at the same time, laughing and gesturing, and Timmy thought it was pretty funny that they had no idea what was happening a few feet away from them.

They'd go home and watch TV and wish their lives had some real excitement, some life, death, big bucks adventure in them, and never know they'd missed it by three feet.

"Do we have a deadline?" Leroy asked.

"I'd like to close it in the next couple of days," Timmy told him.

"That's awfully short notice for that kind of funding."

"I have faith in you, and you know it's an opportunity too good to pass up."

They sipped their drinks and studied each other. Finally Leroy set his wineglass down and leaned toward him.

"Of course a volume price will apply."

Timmy shrugged. "Like what?"

"Eight hundred for the lot," he replied, and sat back again and picked up the wine.

"Eight and a quarter matches what I'm hearing elsewhere, but if you meet it, it's yours."

Leroy grinned then, and Timmy figured out that he had probably been worried he'd want the full hundred seventy-five thousand for each kilogram.

"Done," Leroy said. "Give me until at least tomorrow night, maybe the morning after."

"Okay," Timmy said, and he reached across the table and they shook hands.

They both relaxed and smiled then, and finished their drinks and ordered more. They even moved on to discussing clothing labels and different stores. Timmy admired his watch, a Baume and Mercier, and Leroy told him that too many people automatically assumed they needed a Rolex when in fact there were lots of really fine Swiss brands to choose from, and people with money knew them when they saw them.

The coke Timmy had snorted before the meeting and the scotch created a confident buzz and he found himself grinning at the office girls and thinking, *Hey! I just made a million dollars selling heroin in New York City!* But of course he didn't tell them that.

Chapter 38

Bobby was a little disappointed that he hadn't gotten to see much of Manhattan.

Timmy felt better when Bobby was in his room next door, even when he and Glendy were just hanging around doing nothing. After all, Bobby never walked in unannounced and they had their privacy. Just knowing he was on the other side of the door soothed Timmy's fears. Truth be told, he'd had plenty of those since Joey D. tried to rip him off.

Timmy figured maybe he had a little post traumatic stress or something. After all, somebody had almost shot him. So using a little smack under the circumstances was understandable. Glendy looked miffed whenever he got into it but as soon as it kicked in he didn't much care what she thought, so it was easy to overlook her objections.

They took to hanging around the room a lot because he wanted to stay out of Wade's sight while he plotted the big deal with Leroy. He talked to Wade on the house phone and kept him updated on the plans for the car, and he talked to Leroy on his cell phone and negotiated the logistics of the final transaction. He went down to Wade's room on the tenth floor a couple of times just to keep up appearances, talking about Wade's family. Wade was interested in getting a new boat, and things were going really well for him at work, and Allie looked like a shoo-in for the doctoral program at Kent, and so on. Timmy listened but his mind was always half on the upcoming transaction. Then he'd get to thinking about how wrong the first deal had gone, and he'd get nervous and excuse himself and go back to his room and treat himself to a little heroin. The last time he was in Wade's room he palmed the extra keycard that was in the little envelope on the desk.

When he came back up to his room after that Bobby knocked on the adjoining door and stuck his head in the room. Glendy was downstairs somewhere exploring the hotel. It was just around lunchtime and Bobby was antsy.

"Hey, man, what's going on? I'd like to get a little air, you know?"

Timmy also didn't want Wade spotting Bobby because that would be really hard to explain. He didn't need any complications right now. But when he'd left him Wade was calling his office for an extended conference call, and then he said he'd be calling Amanda, so Timmy figured he'd be tied up for a while.

"Sure," he said to Bobby. "Go out for an hour if you want to. Just don't let Wade see you."

So Bobby left and then Timmy got out the smack.

Bobby walked down 5th Avenue checking out the people and the traffic and the stores, going into a few and looking at the merchandise. He found one of the Lacoste stores and bought himself a couple of shirts with the little crocodiles on them, laughing because these were what the preppies he grew up with wore. He bought food from a street vendor and wandered over to Times Square like Timmy and Glendy had done before him, taking in the sights and watching the continuously shifting images on the giant video screens.

He headed back to the hotel after a while and as he approached he saw Glendy strolling up the sidewalk on the other side of the street. And he saw Leroy sitting on a low wall watching her.

Glendy was heading for the hotel entrance from the north end of 6th Avenue and Bobby was approaching from the west, coming across West 55th Street. Leroy was sitting on a wall in a little courtyard that Glendy had just walked past. Bobby couldn't tell if she had seen him, whether he had turned his head as she went by or what, but he was looking at her now. As she got a little further ahead Leroy hopped up and began following her.

Bobby got across the street as soon as the light changed and came in close behind Leroy, who of course wouldn't know who he was. As

163

Glendy entered the hotel, the doorman opening the door for her, Leroy continued on past, watching her as she disappeared inside. Bobby stayed behind Leroy.

They walked on for another block, past the hotel, and Leroy turned the corner and went around the block and then up 5th Avenue and back to the hotel entrance on that side, Bobby trailing behind, sheltered by the crowds on the street. Leroy stopped for a second and then walked up to the entrance and a doorman opened the door for him and he went into the lobby.

Bobby came in behind him and watched him look around. Glendy was nowhere to be seen. After a minute he walked back out on the 6th Avenue side of the building and turned right, heading north. Bobby came after him, keeping his distance. Leroy continued for a couple of blocks to a parking garage and Bobby saw him go inside. He leaned against a building across the street and after a minute he saw the gray Lexus Glendy had described pull out, Leroy at the wheel. He took off and Bobby lost sight of him in the traffic.

He hurried back to the hotel and caught the elevator up to their floor and let himself into his room. He immediately knocked on the adjoining door and Glendy opened it.

Bobby walked into their room and Timmy was sitting in the easy chair with his headphones on, nodding out. Glendy looked at him appraisingly, then tilted her head at Timmy.

"He keeps getting into downers. I don't know what I'm going to do with him."

Something didn't feel right about it to Bobby but he didn't know what it was. He went over to Timmy and shook his shoulder and Timmy raised his eyes to him and his pupils were huge.

"Back already?" he asked, and except for his eyes he didn't move at all.

Bobby looked back and forth between them. He had a moment of déjà vu and realized this was what it had felt like at the hideout, the night before they skipped town on him.

"What the fuck is going on?" he asked, and his voice was hard.

"What are you talking about?" Glendy replied. She sat on the edge of the bed and crossed her legs, her pose casual.

"I just saw Leroy downstairs. He was following you. He walked around the hotel and came into the lobby, then he took off and got his car out of a garage up the street and split."

There was a flicker of something in Glendy's eyes, fear, it looked like, and she said, "Are you sure it was Leroy? What would he be doing here?"

Timmy had roused himself and was sitting forward, bleary but alarmed by Bobby's news.

"You're sure it was him, man?"

Bobby nodded. "It was him, no doubt about it. I tailed him for a few minutes. He was watching Glendy."

Timmy shook his head from side to side, trying to get a handle on it.

"How would he know we're here? He shouldn't know that." They all looked at each other, trying to make sense of the situation.

"You better call him, man," Bobby said. He sat opposite to Glendy on the bed.

Timmy went to into the bathroom and came out with a little mirror and a gram of coke. He chopped up a small heap of it and laid out three lines and did one up quickly through a rolled up hundred dollar bill. He offered the mirror to Bobby.

"No, thanks, man."

Timmy looked at him and it registered that Bobby hadn't done any coke at all since he'd been here. He passed the mirror to Glendy and she didn't turn it down.

As he felt the cocaine raise his energy level a little he got out his cell phone and dialed Leroy's number. He answered at once.

"Leroy, do you have something you want to tell me?" Timmy asked.

Bobby and Glendy listened carefully. There was silence and finally Leroy said, "Can you be more specific?"

Timmy got angry at that. "Can I be more specific? What the fuck do you mean? How many things are you hiding from me, man?"

Leroy was driving and Timmy could hear traffic sounds in the background.

"Why are you mad? What happened?" Leroy asked.

"How about telling me what you were doing hanging around the Yorkshire Grand Hotel on 6th Avenue this afternoon?" Timmy asked him.

"Ah, that," Leroy responded. "I'm sorry, but I needed to make sure things are secure in this transaction."

"Oh really?" Timmy said sarcastically. "Unfortunately you have made things less secure. I don't like this one fucking bit."

"Hey, hey," Leroy said. "There's no need to get all paranoid. I was just checking things out some."

"How did you find us?" Timmy asked him.

"Tonya knows your names. It wasn't hard to find you in a nice Midtown hotel after I saw your new image. You got me thinking about the competition after you told me yesterday that someone else was bidding for your business. I needed to make sure that none of those people are staking you out. They're dangerous and I don't need the problems they could cause."

Timmy thought about that for a moment. "Okay, so you were keeping an eye out for the competition. What did you see?"

Leroy laughed. "I didn't see them. They'd have been bird dogging your woman if they were around. Either you made it up or they don't know where to find you."

Timmy looked back and forth at Glendy and Bobby. He decided that he'd have to trust Leroy and go ahead with their plans.

"Okay. So we're still on for tonight. Don't do anything to rock the boat, Leroy. Come into the lobby at the Yorkshire Grand at six-thirty in the evening and use the house phone to ask for Wade Thomas's room. I'll direct you from there. And try to keep the bulk down on the payment. Haven't you ever heard of hundred dollar bills?" He laughed then, committed and determined to make it work out, feeling that he could keep the upper hand in the deal. Leroy knew about him and now he knew about Wade. But he didn't know about the third man, Bobby. And that would be his ace in the hole if things went to hell.

Leroy agreed and they hung up. Timmy chided Glendy, "You've gotta keep your eyes open. Don't let these fuckers sneak up on you."

Chapter 39

Timmy and Glendy met Wade in the hotel lobby that night at six-fifteen.

"So this is a good restaurant we're going to, huh?" Timmy asked him.

"Yes! It's supposed to be great. American Nouvelle Cuisine. Ralph raved about it when he and Amy were here a couple of months ago. He reminded me about it on the phone today."

They started out of the hotel, the men dressed in suits and ties and Glendy in her new little black dress and heels, her jewelry on, and Wade stepped forward to hail a cab when Timmy's cell phone went off.

Timmy rolled his eyes at Wade and answered the call. As planned, it was Bobby.

"Here's your decoy, dude," he said.

"Ah, Mr. Bernstein. Thanks for calling back," Timmy said, and pretended to listen for a minute. Then he said, "Oh, yeah, I'm not sure about the proof mark on that series. I can check it out for you and call you back. No, no trouble at all. Give me ten minutes."

He flipped the phone shut and said to Wade, "Sorry, but I've got to go back to the room for a minute. This dealer is hot to buy some stamps I've got but I need to make sure it's the series he's looking for."

Wade said, "Will it take long? Our reservation's in ten minutes."

Timmy shook his head. "Tell you what, why don't you two head over there and grab the table and I'll be along in a few minutes. What's the address again?"

167

Wade told him where the restaurant was. Then he got a cab and he and Glendy got in and took off, Glendy saying, "Good luck, and don't be long!"

Timmy went back into the hotel and caught the elevator to Wade's room on the tenth floor. He let himself in with the keycard he'd stolen and sat down at the desk and pulled the phone close to him. He drummed his fingers on the desktop, working to keep his anxiety in check and looking around the room.

He spotted a Borders Books bag on the floor in a corner and got up and went over to it, wondering if Wade had bought anything interesting. He saw his three CDs inside and had a moment of confusion, trying to understand how they had gotten here. Then the room phone rang.

"Hello?" he said.

"Is Mr. Thomas there?" came Leroy's voice.

"It's me," Timmy said. "Come up to 1025."

While he waited for Leroy to get there he thought about the CDs some more. He hadn't been able to find them since they'd gotten to the Yorkshire Grand, and he'd been pissed off about it. He thought maybe they'd left them at Gail's. How had Wade gotten them? There was a knock on the door and Timmy went over and looked through the peephole. Leroy stood there alone, looking back at the peephole as if he could see Timmy on the other side of it. He grinned.

Timmy opened the door and Leroy picked up the two large sample cases from the carpet and walked into the room. Timmy looked up and down the hallway but no one else was there. He closed the door.

Leroy looked around and said, "Nice accommodations. I'll have to stay here sometime."

Timmy gestured at the cases and said, "Let's have a look."

Leroy flipped open the tops of both cases and Timmy quickly shuffled through the contents. Leroy had, indeed, heard of hundred dollar bills. Although there were some fifties and twenties, most of the money was in hundreds. It was all there, $825,000.

"Your turn," said Leroy.

"We have to relocate just a little," Timmy said, and Leroy frowned.

"What's this all about?" he asked.

"No sweat. You take precautions, I take precautions. Follow me."

Timmy put the keycard back in the envelope on Wade's desk,

picked up one of the cases, looked through the peephole again and opened the door. Leroy followed with the second case. They went down the quiet, well padded hallway to the elevator and Timmy pushed the "up" button. Leroy watched him carefully as they waited for the car to arrive, saying nothing. When they got in Timmy hit the button for the twenty-seventh floor and they went up.

"Very clever," Leroy said. "You're shaking any company I may have brought along."

"Did you bring any company along?" Timmy asked.

Leroy laughed. "No. But I can't fault your thinking."

They got out and walked down the hall to Timmy and Glendy's room and Timmy let them in. He shot the deadbolt and fixed the chain behind them, then got the suitcase out from under the bed and put it on top and opened it.

"That's a lot of stuff," Leroy observed, looking at the five kilograms. "And a really crappy looking suitcase. I can't believe they let you in here with that."

"As advertised," Timmy said. "There's maybe four or five grams gone from this one." He showed Leroy the taped corner of the open brick.

Leroy shrugged. "To be expected. You have to sample it around. I just hope you leave the consumption of it to those already committed to it." He gave him a sideways glance.

"No problem," Timmy replied. "Happy?"

Leroy nodded. "I expect so. This has been a propitious undertaking. And it's a been an agreeable transaction." He stuck out his hand.

Timmy shook with him and said, "It's a business doing pleasure with you."

He showed him to the door, undid the locks and Leroy walked out into the hallway. It was quiet and empty.

"Let me know if this comes up again," he said.

"I will, for sure," Timmy replied, and watched as Leroy turned and walked away, waited a moment for the elevator, then smiled once more at him and was gone. Timmy closed and relocked the door and opened the one into Bobby's room. Bobby was standing there with a large black automatic pistol in his hand, which Timmy had never seen before.

"All done?" Bobby asked.

"Fuckin' A," said Timmy. He let out a big breath and smiled. "I think we did it."

With Bobby hovering in his own room Timmy quickly counted out $80,000 and then locked up the two cases and slid them under the bed where the heroin had recently been. He took the money in to Bobby and handed it to him.

"Thanks, man. I appreciate it. We'll get the payments together for Sandy and for Spin's family tomorrow. Sit tight while I do dinner with Wade and Glendy and we're out of here in the morning."

Bobby counted and recounted his money after Timmy went back into his own room and closed the door. He heard him rummaging around in there for a couple of minutes and then heard him leave.

He called room service for some dinner and a couple of expensive beers and considered his situation once again. He had never had so much money in his life and he wasn't sure what he would do with it. But he was pretty sure it wouldn't be the same thing he would've done a month ago.

Chapter 40

Wade and Glendy were having cocktails in the chrome and glass restaurant. There was heavy white linen on the tables along with futuristic-looking silverware. Large floor plants, including some massive ferns and what looked like a palm tree, were strategically placed around the room. The wait staff wore Nehru jackets.

"I keep waiting for an alien to walk in," Glendy said, looking around the room. "This looks like a set from Star Wars."

In truth, the place was packed and Wade had been lucky to get a reservation. Well dressed New Yorkers were busily engaged in conversations all around them. Waiters with trays full of food hustled past and Glendy craned her neck each time, trying to see what she had gotten herself involved with. She had to admit, the food looked and smelled great.

"Do you eat those flowers they have on the plates?" she asked Wade.

He took a sip of scotch and nodded. "Yes. They're decorative, but you can eat them."

Glendy pondered that for a moment. "Weird," she finally decided.

Timmy came in the front door and spotted them. He crossed the room, maneuvering around tables and people, and pulled out a chair and joined them. He smiled broadly at Glendy.

"How'd it go, babe?" she asked.

"Outstanding," he said. "No problems at all. Done deal."

"Oh good," said Wade. "So the dealer will take the stamps?"

Timmy and Glendy snickered a little and looked at each other knowingly. Wade felt a flash of irritation. They were constantly running this inside joke thing on him and he hadn't gotten used to it.

"You mean he won't take the stamps? Or is that the wrong question?" he asked his brother.

"No, no, he's happy as can be. Everything's fine," Timmy reassured him. "I need a drink."

Wade said, "And your friend brought the Mustang back for sure?"

Timmy nodded. "Late this afternoon. It's in the hotel garage."

They had finished their cocktails and were working on appetizers when Timmy turned to Glendy and said, "Hey, have you seen my new Green Day CD? I haven't seen it since we got to this hotel."

Glendy paused with a fork full of buffalo mozzarella and tomato halfway to her mouth and looked at him. She knew the CDs had been missing and he knew she knew it, so she didn't understand why he was bringing it up now.

Wade put his fork down and gave himself a light slap on the forehead. "Dang!" he said. "I forgot to tell you."

They looked at him expectantly. "What?" Timmy asked.

Wade looked at Glendy. "Your friend Gail dropped by. She brought the CDs. She said you must have left them at her place."

"You've got them?" Glendy asked.

"When was this?" Timmy said, and he began to see the problem.

"Yesterday afternoon," Wade said. "She called my room from the lobby. I came down and got the CDs and we had coffee. Don't worry, I've got them."

Timmy and Glendy looked at each other with a look that Wade couldn't read. Timmy said, "Did you tell her we were staying there?"

Wade took another bite of his crab cake. "Man, this is really good. Would either of you like to try it?"

They both shook their heads emphatically, worried looks on their faces. "No thanks," Timmy said. "Did you mention us?"

"Uh-huh," Wade replied. "We tried reaching you on the house phone but you were out."

"Did you mention our room number?" Glendy asked.

"No. Honestly, I couldn't remember it. Sorry! It was nice of her to come by. She'd like to hear from you again while you're in town."

Timmy and Glendy were exchanging looks again and Wade

decided he would just ignore their private exchanges. He didn't know why they were avoiding Gail. It was probably some interpersonal thing and given his brother's history he wasn't surprised. Since things were going so well here, between the three of them, he'd just let external complications remain external.

"What else did she say?" Timmy asked him.

"Nothing, really. She said she might be coming to Cleveland again for work sometime soon." He decided to avoid that line of conversation since it led directly to Glendy's occupation and that could be awkward. "She liked the hotel. She'd never been there before."

Glendy said lightly, "Did you encourage her to come to Cleveland?"

Wade laughed. "Hey, I'm happily married. She's a nice girl but whether she goes to Cleveland or not is irrelevant to me."

"Excuse me a second," Timmy said. "I just remembered I need to call Bernstein again. Be right back." He jumped up and walked to the front of the room and into the lobby.

"He could have called from here," Wade said.

Glendy shrugged and smiled at him. "Too many people using cell phones in restaurants, you know? Timmy tries to be polite."

The rest of the meal felt strained somehow to Wade and he wasn't sure what had changed. Timmy almost seemed anxious to get it over with although they eventually stayed for dessert and coffee. They strolled out of the restaurant at nine thirty and Wade stuck out his arm for a cab.

"How's eight o'clock sound," he said, looking back at Timmy.

"Can you meet me in the hotel lobby then and have them get the car for me?"

Timmy nodded. "Sure, that's fine. I think you'll like driving it. It's a lot of fun." Then he remembered Wade's Porsche and said, "Depends on what you're used to, though, I imagine."

"Great. Frankly, I need to get back home and an early start is a good idea."

When they got back to the hotel they said good night to each other. Timmy seemed eager to get back to their room, Wade thought. Maybe he wanted to spend some time alone with Glendy.

Chapter 41

The valet pulled the Mustang up in front of the entrance to the hotel and hopped out. Timmy handed him a five and turned to Wade.

"Here you go. I appreciate you taking it back home for me." He reached inside his jacket and brought out an envelope with "Mrs. Harriet Thomas" written on the front.

"This is the balance I owe on it. Please give it to Mom."

Traffic was backed up in front of the hotel and Timmy figured it would take Wade forty-five minutes to work his way out of Manhattan at this time of day if everything went well. The sun was out and it would be a good day for driving. The weather reports said it was clear through Pennsylvania. Wade would be home for dinner.

Wade was dressed casually, looking forward to the trip. "It's been good seeing you, Tim. I'm glad things are going so well for you."

Timmy laughed. "Yeah, things are going good."

Wade looked down for a moment, then stepped a little closer and looked at him and said, "I've got to say that I've been surprised. I didn't think you were interested in business. I'm proud of your success."

Timmy's face went hard and he looked directly at his brother and said, "I'll never be the man, Wade. I'll never be a country club, corporate guy."

Wade was taken aback. "Nobody says success has to fit a particular mold, Tim. You can be who you are. This is America, remember?"

Timmy's face relaxed and he smirked. "Oh, I'm who I am, alright."

Wade shook his head, not sure how to take the comment. Then he said, "Well, say goodbye to Glendy for me. I'll see you back home before long, I hope."

They shook hands, Wade got into the Mustang and waited for a break in traffic. A cab let him out into the flow and he pulled out, waved and was gone.

Timmy walked back inside and Glendy got up from the couch she'd been waiting on in a corner of the lobby, keeping an eye out for trouble and staying out of sight. She walked quickly over to him, doing a quick scan as she went, seeing nothing out of the ordinary. It was a typical midweek early morning and people were lined up at the front desk, talking on their cell phones while they waited to check out.

A crowd was gathered around the coffee urns.

"I've got to go to the rest room," she said. "I don't want to wait for the elevator. I had two cups of coffee while I was waiting for you."

"I'll meet you upstairs," Timmy said. "I've got to finish packing. Bobby'll take us to LaGuardia at nine. See anything funny?"

She shook her head. "Nothing."

He headed for the elevators and she walked down a hallway off of the far end of lobby where there was a flower shop and a small art boutique and a pair of rest rooms. At this time of day the shops were still closed and the hallway was empty. She knew the restrooms closer to the front desk would probably be crowded and she didn't want to have to wait.

She went into the women's rest room and gave herself a quick once-over in front of the mirror, pleased with the slacks and silk top she was wearing. Then she let herself into one of the stalls. After a moment she heard several quick steps on the tile floor as someone else came in. The water went on in one of the sinks and one of the hand driers immediately came on. That was odd, she thought.

She finished in the stall and pulled up her slacks and opened the door. Fat Elvis from the Joey D. deal was standing there. Before she could react he punched her in the stomach and she went down onto the tile floor like a bag of cement.

The blow was substantial and she was completely immobilized by the pain. She couldn't get her breath and she went from stunned to panicked in a split second. She thought he would kill her. He reared back with one stout leg and kicked her again in the stomach with his heavy black shoe. She watched the laces coming at her. She managed to catch part of the kick on her forearms but the blunt toe of the shoe got through and she blacked out momentarily from the pain, curled up like a fetus on the cold restroom floor.

He grabbed her hair and pulled her partially up off the floor and slapped her hard across the face. Blood filled her mouth. She looked up into his nasty piggish eyes and saw that this was more than work to him, and also more than personal. He liked it. She tried to get her breath but was really having trouble. The assault was so fast and effective that she was helpless.

"Okay, tootsie," he said to her. "What room are you staying in?"

His voice was oily, a thick Jersey accent cloying his words. She felt both fear and rage, got a little air into her lungs but he didn't like the look in her eyes and slapped her again, very hard. Then he kneed her in the stomach again and dropped her back onto the floor. Her head bounced off the tiles.

Bobby rode the elevator down to the lobby. He was packed and ready to go and was feeling some nervous energy, so when Timmy told him he'd left Glendy downstairs he thought maybe he'd go get some coffee and make sure there were no problems.

He spotted the guy hanging around the hallway leading to the rest rooms as soon as he walked into the lobby. He didn't know why, out of all the people milling around, he latched onto this guy. Maybe it was the body language, or the fact that he looked like an extra from *The Sopranos*, sort of a low-grade street guy with slicked back hair and a Ban-lon shirt. The guy didn't look like an appropriate guest for the Yorkshire Grand, but then again, neither did he. But he could pass for somebody from a rock band or something. This guy just looked like a skinny New York thug. And there was the fact that he was hanging around in the vicinity of the rest rooms, and Glendy was nowhere to be seen.

Bobby hooked over toward the hallway and as he approached the guy stepped out from the wall he was holding up and said, "The johns are outta order."

Bobby took a few steps down the hallway and saw that both rest rooms, the men's and the women's, had those yellow maintenance buckets with mops sticking out of them wedged into their doorways.

He looked at the guy and said, "Yeah, I gotta piss anyway," and kept walking. And that was when he heard a loud slap, skin on skin, from the women's rest room.

The skinny guy made a quick grab for his arm but Bobby saw it coming and stepped away from him. Then the guy shot his right hand toward the back of his waistband but Bobby was faster and had the big Glock out and in his hand and pointed it into the guy's face, both of them sheltered by the hallway from the people in the lobby.

The look on the guy's face was one of complete astonishment. He'd thought he was the only one in the hallway with a gun. His hands went up and Bobby grabbed the closest one and spun him around. He reached under his shirt and came out with a snub nose .38. He stuffed it in his back pocket.

Bobby grabbed his hair and smacked his face into the plastered wall of the hallway and heard his nose pop. The guy started whining and spitting blood and Bobby pushed him forward and they lurched across the hall and around the yellow bucket and into the women's rest room.

He shoved the skinny guy forward and only then did he take the time to rack the slide on the Glock and put a round in the chamber. Standing in front of him was a fat dude who had a greasy black Elvis haircut. Lying at his feet, bleeding from her mouth and gasping for air, was Glendy. The fat dude was staring at him, pure meanness in his eyes, but he had been caught by surprise and wasn't moving. The gaping hole at the business end of the Glock had his complete attention.

"Shit," Bobby said. "Can you get up, Glendy?" He had both hands on the gun and kept it leveled at the fat guy and moved his gaze back and forth between him and the skinny guy, who has holding his nose and had tears and blood running down his face.

Glendy staggered to her feet and vomited on the floor. Then she straightened up and stumbled over to him, her arms across her midsection. She was sucking air deeply now.

"Motherfucker," she said. "Motherfucker."

"Don't do nothin' stupid, pal," said the fat guy.

177

Bobby took two steps toward him, pointing the gun into his face. His eyes were riveted on it so he didn't see the kick until it connected solidly with his groin, all two hundred fifteen pounds of Bobby behind it. The air went out of him in a rush and he collapsed onto his knees, his hands grasping his injury. Bobby closed in and put the muzzle of the Glock against his eye while he ran his hand around inside the guy's leather car coat. No gun. He stepped back.

Glendy had her purse in her hand and she reached inside and came out with the tiny silver revolver and pointed it at the fat man.

"Don't, Glendy," Bobby said.

She was enraged, her eyes wild, but the little gun was rock steady in her hand. The fat guy looked up and saw it and flinched away.

"Come on," he said. "I'm sorry. Don't do it." He was grimacing with pain and tears started down his cheeks.

She stepped closer and Bobby thought she was going to do it, but then she put the gun back in her purse and took off one of her nice new shoes and hit the guy as hard as she could on the top of his head with the blocky heel. He fell flat on his face on the tiles and she hit him hard five more times across the back of his head.

The skinny guy was blubbering and she turned to him and hit him in the forehead with the shoe. He bent forward in pain and she caught him on top of the skull, too, and he fell unconscious next to his buddy. Then she put the shoe back on and kicked each of them twice in the stomach as hard as she could.

Bobby watched her and then took her arm and said, "Let's go. We gotta go."

She looked at him, grim ferocity on her face, but she nodded and wiped her mouth on her sleeve and Bobby put his gun away and they walked out of the rest room.

They hurried across the lobby and caught the elevator to the twenty-seventh floor. Timmy was packed and waiting for them, already worried by their absence. When he saw Glendy his eyes went wide.

"What the fuck happened?"

"Get moving," Glendy said. Bobby called for his car, telling the concierge he wanted it immediately, and he really meant it. Glendy slipped on her new leather jacket to cover the blood on her clothes.

"We'll tell you on the way," she said. She dashed into the bathroom and splashed cold water on her face, washing away the blood.

They grabbed their bags and hurried out of the rooms, struggling with all their stuff but not willing to wait for a porter. In the lobby Timmy went through a quick checkout and there was some sort of disturbance down the rest room hallway and after a minute some paramedics showed up, hustling by with their equipment. Some police were on the scene, down at the end of the lobby, but nobody had gotten very organized yet.

They strolled outside, forcing themselves to move slowly, and the Firebird rolled up and they got everything inside and were gone.

Chapter 42

They were careening down the New Jersey Turnpike in the black Firebird, Bobby driving and Timmy up front with him. Glendy was in the back seat cleaning herself up with those little moist towelettes you get in restaurants; Bobby had a bunch of them in his glove compartment.

"God damn it," she kept saying, dabbing at the blood and vomit speckling her silk top. "This is ruined."

Bobby and Timmy looked at each other and Timmy finally broke a smile.

"That's typical," he said. "She's pissed about the clothes."

Glendy threw the towelette at him. She was still shaken and angry.

"Thank you, Bobby," she said. "Thank you for coming after me. He was gonna kill me."

Bobby shot a glance at her in the rearview mirror. Her face was red and swollen from the beating but she wasn't bleeding anymore.

She'd gotten her hair brushed back into place and she wouldn't attract too much attention when they stopped for food and gas.

"How do you feel?" he asked her.

"I think he cracked one of my ribs. It hurts like hell. And the inside of my mouth's all swollen. When he hit me my teeth cut my mouth. My stomach hurts."

"Do you need a doctor?"

She shook her head. "Not unless I start to feel worse. Let's not draw attention. Let's just get the hell out of this state as fast as we can.

Do we have, like, a couple of Percodan or something? That would help."

"Yeah. Timmy, get her a couple of pills from that little film canister in the glove compartment," Bobby said. "Those two pricks needed doctors, that's for sure. You beat the crap out of them."

"They should thank me for not shooting them," she replied.

Timmy looked back at her and handed her the painkillers and realized she was right. She had the nerve and the anger to kill them, and they were lucky she hadn't. "All that dancing paid off," he said.

"You're in really good shape. You've got stomach muscles you can bounce a dime off of."

They coasted on, the Jersey landscape rushing past them, the sun bright.

"Why did you decide not to shoot them?" he asked her after a while.

She shrugged. "It would have been harder to walk away from," she said simply.

Timmy got out Bobby's highway atlas and studied it while they drove in silence for a few minutes.

"I'll give you another ten grand if you take us to Florida," he said to Bobby.

Bobby thought about it. He had no job at home. The rooms had been rented in Glendy's name at the Yorkshire Grand but it was possible the hotel had a record of his license plate number, and their faces were most likely on some of the security cameras around the hotel. It probably wouldn't hurt to stay away from Cleveland for a little while longer.

"Okay," he said.

"I think this'll probably blow over pretty quickly. The New York cops aren't going to spend a lot of time trying to catch whoever beat up some Mafia guys in a ladies john," Timmy told him.

Bobby raised an eyebrow at him. "You didn't see it. She fucked those guys up. They could maybe die."

Glendy laughed shortly in the back seat. "Kicking that fat bastard was like punching a pillow. But the other guy was kind of bony."

Bobby was surprised by how violent she had been. There was no doubt that the guys deserved it, but her efficient ferocity was unexpected. He had feared she would shoot them, and realized he would have stood by and let her.

"Hey, how's your shoe?" he finally asked her.

She laughed but winced against the pain and caught her breath.

"I'd be really mad if my shoe got ruined," she said.

"We couldn't risk going to any of the airports," Timmy observed.

"I heard these guys are real Mafia. They could have people watching for us."

Bobby nodded. "You're right. So where do you want to go in Florida?"

Timmy looked at the map some more.

"Let's go to Sanibel. You know, outside of Fort Myers on the Gulf Coast. It's a nice place, lots of tourists. We can hang out and lay low. You can head home right up I-75 when you're ready to."

They all agreed.

Chapter 43

The Mustang rolled up Harriet Thomas's driveway fresh from being washed, the rich red metallic paint lustrous in the noonday sun. Wade had wanted to get all the road salt and grime off of it before he put it to bed in the garage until Tim's return.

He walked into the open garage and let himself into the kitchen, hearing the sounds of Beethoven filling the house before he was inside. His mother loved classical music and often had it on her stereo when she was home.

"Mom?" he called. "It's Wade."

Harriet came in from the living room, a large photo album in her hands, and crossed the kitchen to him. She placed the album on the table and reached up and hugged him.

"How was your trip?" she asked him, stepping back and smiling. "Did you do anything fun in New York?"

He shook his head. "No, I was actually pretty busy working and waiting around for Tim to get organized. It was a nice hotel, though."

"You weren't too hard on him, were you? I know you felt that you needed to do this, but I hope there's no rancor between the two of you."

He laughed. "Well, to tell you the truth, things went pretty well. He really surprised me." And he told her about the nice clothes and the expensive hotel accommodations and, lastly, about the lucrative stamp deal Tim had been involved with.

She looked at him for a moment, puzzlement on her face, then pulled out a chair and sat at the table. Wade joined her.

"He hasn't shown any interest in stamps for years," she said to him. "His old collections are still here, in the basement. He hasn't touched them since before Dad died."

"Well, I guess things have changed. He seemed pretty busy with the whole business. And he sent this to you."

He got out the envelope that Timmy had given him from inside his jacket and handed it to her. She neatly slit the top open with a paring knife that sat next to the small cutting board in front of her. Inside was a thick stack of hundred dollar bills.

Harriet's eyes grew wide and she said, "My goodness." She began counting out the bills and found that there were one hundred eighty of them.

"Eighteen thousand bucks," Wade observed. "That's a lot of cash. Is that what he owes on the car?"

Harriet was nodding and staring at the money. "Why didn't he use a check?"

"My guess is that he doesn't have a bank account in New York. You know, they say that the diamond business there is done almost entirely in cash. This must be the same sort of thing."

"But isn't there some IRS rule about large sums of cash?" she asked him.

"Yes, there is. Any bank deposit or transaction of over ten thousand dollars is reported to them. It's to help identify drug dealing." A small wave of apprehension washed over Wade, sitting there in his mother's tidy and pleasant kitchen. That couldn't be, could it? "So when I put this in my bank account to pay off the car, the bank will report it to the Internal Revenue?"

"Yes, they will. But I'm sure there's no problem. Tim can account for it." But he was bemused by the whole thing. By putting the money into her own account, his mother would become responsible for it. And she could have to pay taxes on it. Tim should have put it into his own bank account somehow, and paid off the car that way.

"Let me think about this a little," he said to her. "I think I'd rather do this payoff through Tim's account."

Harriet got up and went over to the little desk and came back with some deposit slips and some blank checks. Wade saw that they were from Tim's checking account.

"I have these. He left a few for me when we were paying his bills here."

Wade relaxed. "Oh, good. Then we'll run the whole thing through his account. But he'll need to sign the check."

"I've signed for him before," she said. "I'm sure that must be what he had in mind for this."

"Well, okay," said Wade. "I'll take this over to his bank and deposit it. I don't want you having this much cash around; it isn't safe."

They put the cash and the deposit slip into a large manila envelope, and Harriet opened the photo album.

"Look at you two when you were younger. Tim was so cute!"

She was looking at a picture of Wade at about the age of twelve, his arm protectively around a five-year-old Tim. They were squinting into the camera on a beach somewhere, probably along the Lake Erie shoreline. They wore shorts and were shirtless. In the background a young man was launching a kite into the summer sky.

"We were closer then," Wade said solemnly. "But I'm hoping he's growing up some more now. He's a bright guy and he can go far if he tries." He thought about Glendy, not sure what to say about her to his mother.

"Do you know his girlfriend?" he asked. "She's with him in New York."

Harriet raised her eyes from the album and something flickered there that Wade couldn't quite read.

"She's nice, I suppose," she said. "A little more outgoing than I would have expected."

Wade laughed. "Hey, Amanda's outgoing, too," he protested.

She shrugged. "There are different kinds of outgoing."

They walked out through the garage together and Wade got in the Mustang again and said, "I'll only be a few minutes. Then maybe you can run me back home. This car's kind of fun to drive; maybe you'll enjoy having it around."

She shook her head. "No, I like my little SUV. This will sit in the garage until Tim comes to get it."

Wade pulled out and drove off up the street. Harriet watched him go and then walked around and up to the front door, where someone had left a sales flier of some sort. She unrolled it and saw that it was an advertisement for a handyman service. The proprietor's name was Ruiz. The thought crossed her mind that many Hispanics were now active in the trades around the West Side. A decade ago there were hardly any. The ones she'd met were all very nice and extremely hard workers. She had friends who had cleaning ladies come in and the ones from Mexico and Central America were regarded as the most honest and diligent available.

As if to reinforce her observation, an older car cruised by the house at that moment, a young brown skinned man driving, wearing khaki work clothes. He smiled and waved to her and she returned the gesture. *Really nice people*, she thought.

Chapter 44

Cesar Obregon was sitting in the little store on Denison Avenue and he felt like General Patton. He really liked that movie and he identified with the man. Patton had a job to do and he got it done. He knocked the hell out of the Nazis and he won the war for his side. His methods got him into a little trouble, though.

Take that incident where Patton slapped the American soldier, for instance. The guy was moping and crying, a chickenshit, really, and Patton gave him a good one upside his head. Straightened the guy right out and put the fear of God in the rest of the troops, too. It was the right thing to do, showed them all who was boss, got everybody over themselves and back to taking care of business. And business was all about killing the Nazis who would surely kill them if they gave them half a chance by acting like a bunch of pussies.

But what happened? Patton's bosses, the higher-up generals and the politicians, gave him a load of crap about it and told him he couldn't do that kind of stuff. They took this warrior and made him act like a fucking social worker or something, told him he had to worry about his guys' feelings, for Christ sake. Patton wouldn't change though, not really, and he knew what had to be done, pantywaist politicians or not.

Cesar was in a war and he intended to win it. That damned Hector had really put him in a bind by losing all that product because some of the money that had paid for it had come from Cesar's bosses, the guys back in San Salvador who directed MS-13. Those were some smart guys, and they controlled the organization very efficiently. They had their fingers on the pulse of each local set, whether it was in El Salvador or L.A. or Richmond or Cleveland or wherever. Cesar grew up with some of those guys in L.A. and in San Salvador himself and he knew them well. They were no joke, and they played for keeps.

So he played for keeps, too. When Hector got ripped off he gave him a chance to get the product back but he couldn't do it. Then when Hector came up with the idea of kidnapping the mother of the guy who had stolen their stuff, it sounded like a good plan, but then he screwed that up. What the hell was a boss supposed to do? All the rest of his guys were looking at him like he was going soft, and he certainly couldn't afford that. So he put that fool Hector away for good right in front of them, showed them he was the baddest badass in the place and that his patience had its limits.

This turned out to be both bad and good. Hector's cousin Jorge in Tegucigalpa was high up in the MS-13 hierarchy and he was not pleased at all. This was not a good man to have for an enemy and Cesar would have to watch his step from now on because this dude would definitely be looking for an excuse to mess him up. But the other bosses, with no particular feelings for Hector one way or the other, thought it had been a pretty good idea.

And it had certainly put his own troops on notice that screwups on that scale were not going to be tolerated, and that everybody better get busy doing what they were supposed to be doing and no more Mr. Nice Guy.

And what they were supposed to be doing was selling heroin in Cleveland. It turned out that cracking the whip and laying down some discipline that day had been very timely because right about then several suppliers on the East Side had decided they weren't going to roll over and play dead while MS-13 took over all the business. They were a loose consortium of black gangsters with lifelong roots in Hough, Collinwood and East Cleveland and they started coming on hard with the street level dealers who had begun getting their product from Cesar's guys. Their biggest dealer, Big Allan, had been threatened, and he was complaining about the pressure.

Some people had been beaten up and a couple of bodies were found in alleys and vacant lots in the very run-down neighborhoods of the East Side. But Cesar's mareros were good at this; they'd done it in L.A. and in Central America and they had the moves down. They figured out who the main troublemaker was in all this and then Cesar had sent Jaime and Luis around. They walked right up on the guy's place one night and blew away the bodyguard out front of the house and then went in and shotgunned the guy and the two women who were with him. Frankly, they couldn't believe this guy hadn't had better security. After that, things started getting a little easier and they were meeting less resistance to their marketing program.

Perhaps not surprisingly, much of this never got into the news and the cops weren't behaving very aggressively. Drug dealers had been killing each other for generations on Cleveland's East Side and nobody tried to do very much about it. Cesar didn't have very much intelligence coming out of the law enforcement agencies yet; as the drug pipeline opened further and there was more money around he anticipated being able to buy whatever information he needed.

But at present they seemed oblivious to the fact that MS-13 was here and open for business. That was just fine with him. By the time they got wise he would have several layers of people in place, from street-level teenage gangbangers to middle management original gangsters in their twenties who the teenagers idolized to a handful of upper management people like himself with houses in the suburbs. They would be well-entrenched and insulated by loyalty and anonymity and the fear of the parent organization.

Cesar's one hangup at the moment was the supplier. This was a situation which called for tact and diplomacy because this guy was providing them with the best heroin anyone had ever seen at a very good price. But he insisted that they keep the violence at as low a level as possible because he wanted to keep doing business. He didn't want the law getting interested in what Cesar was doing if it could be avoided. And he had the support of the bosses back home in this.

This of course was tricky because it was by nature a violent business and that was how MS-13 had always done it. In L.A. and later in El Salvador and Honduras it was their utter ruthlessness that had gotten them to the top of the criminal heap. But Cesar could see the wisdom in it and was working on his finesse and his strategy so that he could anticipate problems and deal with them before he had to shoot people in order to solve them. The bosses had even provided him with articles from business school books and magazines to help him with this situation.

Cesar was the only one in the set who had actually met the supplier, and he didn't know much about him. When he had first come to Cleveland the bosses had put him in touch with the guy and they had met and discussed their general plans. He was an Italian, Cesar figured, a guy in his thirties, modestly dressed and soft spoken. He'd been in America for a while because his English was very good and colloquial. It seemed like he had limitless access to product and nobody in Cleveland but Cesar knew that their plan was to expand the heroin business out into other states. Unlimited product and millions of potential users meant that Cesar could become a very important and rich player in the MS-13 leadership, perhaps even the big boss. Then it would be Jorge in Tegucigalpa who would have a problem.

Cesar would meet the supplier himself when they agreed on a time and place and would get the product from him. Frankly, he would rather not have to do this part of it. This was what underlings were for, and Cesar did not want to get caught with hundreds of thousands of dollars or kilograms of heroin in his car trunk. But the supplier demanded anonymity and it gave Cesar greater power to be the only one who was entrusted with working directly with the man.

The supplier, who Cesar knew only as the Tailor, had just hung up the phone when Luis walked quickly into the store and sat down next to him. They had just discussed the timing of the next delivery and had tentatively decided they'd get together in four days at the garage Cesar had Hector rent near Kamm's Corners, in the far west corner of Cleveland near Fairview Hospital. They'd each drive into the garage and close the doors, make the exchange, and leave separately after a reasonable interval, as they had done before. The arrangement allowed them to keep out of sight as well as away from their homes and businesses.

Cesar looked at Luis, a little bothered that he would approach him while he was talking to someone, and saw that he was excited.

Except for them, the shabby store was empty and its miscellaneous hardware and household items were gathering dust on the shelves.

"What's the news, bato?" he asked.

Luis was grinning with excitement, almost hopping in his seat.

"You know the red Mustang? At the Thomas house? I saw it parked in the garage. Timmy Thomas must be around again."

Cesar sat back and thought about that. Even with all the other things he had going on, he wanted to get even on the theft. They could either return the heroin or pay him for it, because they were obviously some pretty slick dealers themselves to have played it the way they did. But something had to be done, that was for sure.

Chapter 45

Glendy walked in the surf along the pink sand beach of Captiva Island. It was early, the sun coming up behind her and the sound of the ocean seemed to swell with the light. Birds wheeled overhead and raced the tide back and forth.

It smelled fresh and salty. Glendy had no experience with the ocean and found that she loved it here. She knew that she was looking at the Gulf of Mexico and that somewhere far off in the distance were other countries, other people starting their day. The hurricanes of the past year had taken their toll on Captiva and Sanibel, and some of the palm trees showed damage. But it was a wonderful place, the end of the long road down from New York City, across Florida and through Fort Myers and up the narrow expanse of Sanibel Island. Captiva was the jewel on the crown.

They had rented two small cottages on the beach and settled in, shaking off the pain and the fear of their mad rush out of Manhattan.

There was nothing to do but hang out. They spent hours on the beach and wandering around the little shops. In the evenings after the gorgeous sunsets the little invisible bugs came out and they went inside and watched TV. But Captiva in the moonlight was beautiful and exotic and she went out often and listened to the water and watched the stars, enchanted, while Timmy and Bobby sat inside and drank beers.

Glendy's injuries began to improve, although her cracked rib stung with each deep breath. There was nothing to be done for it; time would heal it, she knew. Her eyes never blackened and the swelling

SIX-GUN TWO-STEP

went down in her face. Her stomach muscles ached for days from the pounding Elvis had given her, but then that receded, too. After the frantic daily pace and surging crowds of New York, Captiva was restful.

They had sent off two packages from Fort Myers the day after they arrived, going all the way back over there to cover their tracks.

She had called Sandy Polarski and Spin's sister from a public phone because Bobby didn't want them identifying his voice. She told them simply to look for a package each in the mail and got their mailing addresses. She told Sandy that it was in compensation for her recent misfortune, and Sandy seemed surprised but pleased, and said, "Tell those guys I appreciate it."

She told Spin's sister it was in compensation for the loss of her brother, and that it was a collection that had been taken up by Spin's friends. The sister seemed bewildered but thankful. Then they sent off the money from a UPS store, using the U.S. Postal Service. They all felt relieved driving back to Captiva, and their consciences were soothed.

A couple of days later Bobby checked out of his cottage, hugged them both and left for Cleveland. He seemed preoccupied to Glendy, as if he had a plan to fulfill back there and wanted to get on with it.

She had noticed that he had quit using drugs and that his alcohol use was minimal. She wondered what he was going to do but she didn't ask him. In truth, she found that she envied him a little.

At night when Bobby was in his own cottage, and then during the day after Bobby had left for Cleveland, Timmy was using heroin. He had kept several grams of it from the open kilo he sold to Leroy and now he had nothing but time on his hands. He had money and no responsibilities and they were cocooned in a comfortable and idyllic refuge and he began to descend into total self indulgence.

For the first few days it was a little annoying to Glendy but she put up with it, assuming he was just celebrating his success and didn't have enough of the smack to do much of it. Then she got a look at his stash and realized he had more than enough to keep using it steadily for days.

She warned him again about addiction and he acted like he heard her, but he was starting to nod out all the time and she knew he wasn't paying attention to her.

193

She was now spending most of her time by herself, either on the beach or wandering around the shops. She went into the little cabana-like bars in the vicinity but, like bars everywhere, she found drunks there and guys tried to hit on her. So she mostly stayed away.

She made friends with the wife of the owner of the cottages, a sunny woman in her forties who liked Glendy and mothered her a little, but she was busy most of the time with her kids and with managing the cottages.

When she tried to spend time with Timmy he was indifferent to her. They made love the first night they were there but after that Timmy was high most of the time and didn't want to. She felt rejected and lonely.

That morning when she came in from her walk on the beach she was hopeful. They had the best fresh-squeezed orange juice at the little restaurant down the street and she was sure she could get Timmy up and interested in some breakfast there. They would eat and talk and plan a nice day together and she would get him away from the room for a while and out of reach of the dope. Maybe they could catch a ride down to the wildlife preserve on Sanibel and explore. Or they could rent a car; that would get them out and active again, give them something to do.

She walked into the cottage and the blinds were still drawn and Timmy was in bed. As she came in he woke up and rolled over and he had a look of utter misery on his face. Glendy saw that he was shaking slightly and his nose was running.

"Are you sick?" she asked him.

He reached for the little balloon of heroin on the night table and said, "I'll be okay in a minute."

Glendy just looked at him and said, "Oh fuck."

Chapter 46

Luis drove quietly up Harriet Thomas's street in the rain and slowed as he approached the house. He saw that the garage door was up and the red Mustang was in there, but the little white Rav 4 was gone. He eased to the curb.

Dark clouds churned overhead and thunder thumped in the distance. The rain was pelting heavily down. It had been drizzling all day but now it was really pouring and didn't look like it was going to let up. He did a quick scan up and down the street, remembering Hector's misfortune, and saw no one at any nearby windows or out walking. There were no cars on the street.

He took a chance and pulled into the driveway, then quickly got out of the car, a thick strong figure, a rain poncho over his khaki work clothes. He dashed into the garage and up to the door that led into the house and turned the knob. It was locked. There was nothing in the garage that was of use to him. Mrs. Thomas didn't seem to be at home and he didn't want to break in and risk having her spot the damage and take off when she returned. He went over to the Mustang.

They had learned that they couldn't track people on the Internet by their license plate numbers because that information wasn't available. But there was a database of vehicle ownership based on the vehicle identification number, the VIN, which every car had on its dash board on the driver's side, where a cop could easily view it.

Luis got out a pencil and a little note pad and jotted down the Mustang's VIN and the license plate number. Now they'd be able to identify it more easily in traffic and in public if they needed to.

He decided to retreat to his car because there wasn't much else he could do at the moment and he didn't want to attract attention by hanging around. He backed out of the driveway and pulled out onto the street and drove forward a little and parked. He might as well hang around a few minutes and see what else he could learn. The neighbors all seemed to be indoors out of the weather and he felt safe, camouflaged by the sullen and persistent rain.

After a minute a car turned onto the street, its headlights flashing over Luis as he sat watching. It was one of those funny looking Volkswagen beetles, also red, but a bright shade, not racy like the Mustang. He saw it turn into the Thomas driveway. After a moment the engine was switched off, and the lights, and then he saw a girl pop out on the driver's side.

She ran quickly around the car, a rain poncho similar to his own covering her, and up onto the covered front porch. Who was this? She slipped the hood back off of her head and Luis saw that she was an attractive young woman of medium height with a shoulder length curly blond hair. She fumbled with her keys for a few seconds, rifling through them, looking for one in particular. Luis could see her clearly there on the porch, but he didn't think she noticed him sitting alone in his car with the rain streaming down.

She found the key she was looking for and inserted it into the front door's lock and let herself in, closing the door behind her. Luis was excited. This was important. He wrote down her license number and called Cesar at the store on his cell phone.

"I've found another family member, I think," he told him, the storm's interference causing bursts of static in the connection.

"Really?" Cesar said, and Luis could hear the pleasure in his voice. "Who?"

"Young woman, maybe five-four or five-five, lots of curly blond hair. She just let herself into the house."

"You think she lives there?" Cesar asked him.

"No, but I think she's family. She has a key to the front door. Also, that maricon we grabbed said Timmy Thomas has blond hair. So does Mrs. Thomas, but with gray in it. This one looks like a young Mrs. Thomas."

Cesar was decisive. "Go where she goes. Find out where she lives. Stay on her and call me when you get wherever else she goes."

"Okay," said Luis. "But I can't sit around here all day. Somebody'll notice me."

As if to ease his fears, the front door opened at that moment and the girl came back out with a handful of what looked like mail, mostly envelopes and a couple of magazines. She closed the door and checked to make sure it was locked, then covered her head with the poncho's hood again and sprinted down the steps and over to her car. She hopped in and slammed the door. The engine started up and the lights came on and she started backing out.

"Here we go," Luis said.

Chapter 47

Timmy was in front of the TV in the cottage, a nice buzz going, drifting along and nodding out every once in a while. He didn't know what was on the tube and he didn't care. They'd been there for more than week but he wasn't sure how long. He still had a lot of smack and that was what had come to matter the most to him.

Glendy came and went and ragged on him regularly, but he didn't have to pay attention to her; she was background noise. They slept in the same bed but he barely noticed her. He was happy, that was all he knew.

He didn't bother going out much except to eat now and then. In his mind, when he was coming down, he told himself that he was enjoying his success with selling the heroin and getting away with it by partying a little. No big deal. But there was an awareness back there somewhere that a line had been crossed and that he was getting sick when the drug wore off. This would have been worrisome except that he always just took a little more heroin and promptly forgot about it.

He thought about getting a syringe somewhere because he was snorting the drug and that was definitely not the best use of it. He was using up more than he wanted to that way. If he could just cook it up and inject it, he could use a lot less and it would last a really long time. But he had no experience with that, had never injected anything, and wasn't sure how to go about getting syringes at a drug store without causing himself problems.

So he sat in the cottage and floated, the sound of the Gulf breaking on the shore filtering through the windows and front screen door, birds squawking now and then as they passed by. He thought about putting on some music but it seemed like too much trouble.

Outside he heard the muffled slamming of a car door and it registered that someone had just parked in front of their cottage. Footsteps crunched on the crushed seashell path and he heard vague voices, some sort of conversation between Glendy, maybe, and someone else. He didn't care.

After a moment a form filled the doorway and someone looked in on him but he ignored it. It was darker in the cottage than it was outside in the sun and he couldn't tell who was standing there just beyond the screen. The door opened and Leroy walked in.

He stood there looking at him and instead of a suit he was wearing tropical casual, a Tommy Bahama ensemble, probably, a silk shirt with a floral design and linen pants. The guy always looked good, he had to admit it.

"Are you on vacation?" Timmy asked him, collapsed in the easy chair.

Leroy just regarded him solemnly for a moment, then shook his head slowly.

"You are a sad case, you know that?" he said. "I told you to stay out of that stuff."

He started walking around the room a little, looking things over. Then he came back and stood between Timmy and the TV so he would have to pay attention to him.

"I'm afraid you blew it, Timmy. You made it but then you blew it. You're pretty much like any other fool who gets into this business."

Timmy roused himself and straightened up in the chair. He rubbed his hands across his face and through his hair, making an attempt to focus. What the hell was he talking about? What was this about? "You lost me, Leroy," he said, slurring his words. "What are you doing here?"

A small, tight smile crossed Leroy's face and he said, "I'm the relief pitcher. You've been pulled from the game and I've been called in."

Timmy saw Glendy walk up to the door and look in at them.

"Why don't you inform the young man where we're at with this?" Leroy said to her.

She opened the door and came in and stared at Timmy, her eyes huge, and shook her head sadly.

"I'm sorry, but I can't take this anymore. I'm going back up north with Leroy. You're a junky and I'm wasting my time here."

Timmy struggled to make sense of what she was telling him. She was leaving with Leroy? "How did you find us?" he finally asked.

Leroy laughed at that, and seemed pleased with himself.

"She called me. Man, you are slow on the uptake, my friend."

But then it became clear and Timmy understood, and he knew this had been coming for a while but he hadn't seen it.

"That's why Bobby saw Leroy following you outside the hotel. You met him out there," he said to Glendy. "You were playing me."

Glendy looked down, and Timmy was gratified to see that she seemed embarrassed.

"He called me. We talked. He told me I could be with him if we didn't work out. You were getting into the smack and I didn't know what to do. You were more interested in that fucking smack than you were in me, Timmy!" And she was angry at him, and tears were starting in her eyes. "I was loyal to you but you picked that fucking drug over me!"

Timmy was shaking his head. "Meeting this dickwad behind my back wasn't loyalty, Glenda," he said.

"You snooze, you lose, slick," Leroy said.

And they were all surprised when Timmy came out of the chair at him, because Timmy was smaller and full of heroin and notoriously non-confrontational. Leroy stumbled back a step and Glendy jumped to the side as Timmy reached for him. But then Leroy's hand came out of his pants pocket and he pointed a pistol at Timmy and stopped him cold.

Timmy started laughing. "Is that a Walther PPK? I don't know much but I'm a James Bond fan and I know a Walther PPK when I see one. Figures you'd pick something like that. You really think you're the man, don't you? Clothes, manners, stealing the woman. You are too fucking much." He sat down heavily in the chair again, deflated and angry, sluggish from the drug and helpless against what they were doing to him.

"Get the money, Glendy," said Leroy, and she walked over to the closet and pulled out the two sample cases while Timmy watched her.

Leroy kept him covered while he stepped over to her and they both hoisted the cases onto the bed and opened the tops. They turned them upside down and spilled the money out and then Leroy stepped back, his face falling and his eyes widening.

"Where's all the money?" he said to him. Glendy pawed through the cash on the bed and it was obvious that there was only about $80,000 there. She looked at him in surprise.

Timmy laughed at them then, glee in his eyes, and didn't say anything for a moment, enjoying their failure.

"Too bad, so sad. You snooze, you lose, asshole," he said to Leroy, and laughed at him again.

Leroy and Glendy looked at each other and were speechless. They didn't understand how this could happen; they had planned it so well.

"He had it when we left for the plane, but then we decided to drive out of town," she said to Leroy.

He lowered the gun and shook his head, catching on at last.

"He knew he couldn't risk trying to get all that money on a plane. Too much security. He got rid of it before that morning somehow."

He looked hard at Timmy. "He's smarter than he looks."

Timmy smirked at him again. Then he turned his attention again to Glendy and said, "So you thought you could rip me off. I'm really offended."

She flared at him. "Hey, this was my deal, too. You'd probably be dead if I hadn't stopped Joey D. I'm entitled to it."

"Yeah," he answered calmly, "and you'd be dead if Bobby hadn't saved your ass. And Bobby wouldn't have been there if I hadn't called him. You didn't want him to come. Why, were you afraid he'd run off Romeo, here?"

She just stared at him, and Timmy knew he'd gotten at least part of it right, that she'd been keeping Leroy in the back of her mind as a fallback position all along. She liked his looks and she was impressed by his style and money; she'd made that clear from the first.

He looked back at Leroy and said, "So, poser, you still want her even without getting all your money back?"

Leroy smiled slowly and said, "You disrespect a beautiful woman and look what you get. No more beautiful woman. And in your case, a monkey on your back. Enjoy it, fool." He shoved the money back into one of the cases and held up a twenty.

"This is for you. So you don't starve." He put it on the bedside table. "Enjoy your smack. My guess is you'll be decomposing in here before the week's out."

Glendy walked up to him and knelt down in front of him, looking into his face as he sat in the chair.

"What did you do with it? Does Bobby have it?"

He shook his head. "Keep guessing," he said. He sat back and just looked at her, triumphant despite her leaving. "You could have asked me for a cut. You didn't have to bring this dickhead here and try to take it all."

She stood and turned away and walked to the closet and began putting her things in a bag. Timmy regarded her gravely and said nothing, just watched her getting ready to go.

"See ya, Timmy. Enjoy Florida," said Leroy as he held the door open for Glendy.

Timmy said to her, "I hope you have fun in New York with all your new clothes. I'm sure you'll be a big hit." He knew she'd feel bad, thinking about how they bought the clothes together.

"Goodbye, Timmy," she said, and looked at him sadly and went out the door.

"Blow me," he said to them both. He heard them crunching away down the path and then the car started and he heard them drive away.

Chapter 48

Bobby was in his new apartment on Clifton Avenue in Lakewood when the Mexicans contacted him again.

He had just gotten off the phone with his father. John Fallon was a rugged and even tempered man who had made a life for himself and his family with his lawn service and landscaping business in Rocky River. They had never gone hungry, although they had come close a few times, and winters presented particular problems until John bought a plow for the front of his pickup truck and began contracting snowplowing services to the businesses and private homes in the area.

Now, twenty-five years later, John Fallon's company was solvent and he had five guys with snowplows subcontracted in the winter, and five lawn crews working in the warmer weather, and even some indoor plant service accounts in the malls and retail stores and doctors' offices which paid all year round. He and Bobby's mother still lived in the small Rocky River bungalow that Bobby and his brothers had grown up in. Two of Bobby's brothers, Mike and Don, were just out of their teens and worked with their father in the business. Bobby was the oldest and had put in his share of work during his teenage years, helping his dad out and learning pretty much everything there was to know about what they did. But as his lifestyle had changed he had drifted away from the family business.

His dad was approaching sixty now and the long years of manual work had taken their toll, Bobby knew. Although he was lean and tough as leather from decades of outdoor work, his back continually gave him problems and he was slowing down. Bobby had decided to approach him about buying into the business.

John was delighted but initially skeptical. Bobby explained that he had saved some money and made some good investments and was in a position to offer a mix of cash and sweat equity in order to eventually become the primary owner and provide his dad with a more secure retirement. Since neither of the younger boys were likely to be in a position to do this in the near future, it was an attractive offer. As long as they all shared some degree of ownership, John would consider it. His vision was for it to remain a family business which could provide a future for each of them. They ended the conversation laughing and pleased with how the discussion had gone. John said he'd get the accountant to come up with a structured plan but the idea sounded great to him.

Bobby sat looking out the window and down at the evening traffic as he replayed the discussion. He felt good about this. It felt right to him. Spin's death and the crazy events in New York had moved him beyond his old preoccupation with partying and dealing and into a more mature consideration of where he was going and where he wanted to be. He realized that he wanted a home and a family, and he didn't want drugs and the threat of violence dogging his existence.

He smiled at the idea, finding it unlikely. He wouldn't have guessed this would happen to him, but there it was. He had changed, and he had decided to show his change on the outside and had had his hair cut short and stopped wearing any earrings. He knew his dad would be surprised by that, and pleased, too, when he saw him.

And then his cell phone rang.

He picked it up and glanced at the caller ID and realized that he recognized the number; he just couldn't place it at first. Then he remembered it was Allie Thomas's. He had called Timmy there a couple of times in the past year, down in Kent. He'd even been there once or twice himself.

He answered it and heard Allie's voice say, "Bobby? This is Allie. I..."

She stopped talking and Bobby said, curious, "Hi, Allie. What's going on?" He liked her, and was pleased to hear from her.

A different voice came on then, and Bobby knew it at once from that day downtown with Sandy Polarski, when the skinny little Mexican had pointed the machine gun at him from inside the van. It was a sort of instant visceral association.

"Hola, amigo," the guy said. "You got any idea who this is?"

There was humor in the voice, and malice. Bobby went cold.

"I've got a pretty good idea," he said. He sat up straight in his chair and he felt his heart rate accelerate.

"Guess who we got?" said the Mexican. "She's a cute little chica, curly blond hair. You know her, maybe?"

"Yeah, I know her," Bobby said, his mouth dry. "Where's your buddy? I thought he was the negotiator."

The guy laughed at that, and it was a grating sound in Bobby's ear.

"He got reassigned. I'm the guy you gotta talk to. You owe us some dinero, my friend."

Bobby's mind raced, trying to find some room to maneuver.

"Somebody does, maybe, yeah," was all he could think of to say.

"This girl's brother does, I think," said the guy. "And that means you. You his partner. We can't call him, so we call you."

"Did you try to call him?" Bobby asked.

"She give us a number, but nobody answer. You, we know already. So you are it."

Bobby cursed under his breath. Of course Timmy wouldn't take calls if he was high or just didn't feel like it, as usual. Not that he'd be able to do much about this from Florida, anyway. Bobby saw that he was it, after all.

"What do you want to do?" he asked the guy.

"I want you to come and bring me the money. Then this little lady gets to be okay. If not, well, I think you know."

"Christ," Bobby said. He didn't know what to do. "How much money?"

"A million," the guy replied.

Bobby was stunned. It was impossible, of course. "A million?" he asked, incredulous.

"Hey, what you think six keys of high grade smack is worth, bato?"

He was paralyzed in the chair, trying to understand what the guy had just told him. Heroin? Timmy had stolen six kilograms of heroin?

205

That didn't make sense. This was about cocaine, wasn't it? But Timmy was nodding out all the time, and acting secretive about it all. He started to get his mind around it.

"I don't have a million dollars, dude," he said firmly. "You've got to talk to her brother about that."

"No," the guy replied. "I'm talking to you. You bring me some money right fucking now or this girl is gonna get it. You can take it up with her brother later."

Bobby considered his options and knew he didn't have many.

"Okay, I will bring you every cent I can get my hands on but you've got to let the girl go. Agreed?"

"Sure," he said smoothly. "That's what we gonna do. You come see me and I give you the girl."

Bobby let his breath out. "Where do we meet?"

"Okay," said the guy. "You know Ravenna? You know that big fenced in place, Ravenna Arsenal?"

Bobby knew it. It was a huge enclosed and wooded preserve that once been a military ammunition plant. He didn't know what it was used for now, although he remembered something on the news about the army using it again. It was vast and remote, in rural Portage or Trumbull County, he wasn't sure which, southeast of Cleveland near Kent.

"Yeah, I know sort of where it is," he said.

"Write this down," said the Mexican. "Ready?"

"Yeah, I've got a pen. Go ahead."

"Take I-480 south out of Cleveland. South of the Turnpike you pick up Route 14 and it runs into Ravenna. Take Route 59 east in downtown Ravenna and it runs into Route 5. Go east on that and you'll be running along the south border of the arsenal. Look for Rock Spring Road and turn right. There'll be a gravel access road on your right soon after you turn. Go down there to the little parking area; people park their cars there when they fish in Hinckley Creek. Won't be anybody around at night. Got it?" The Mexican had read it to him, he knew. They'd written it out in advance. They'd been working on this.

Bobby read it back to him.

"See you in an hour and a half, bato. Don't be late, come alone and bring lots of money!"

"Bring the girl," Bobby told him, forcefully, but he had already hung up.

The Mexicans had planned this out and they seemed to know the area well. He thought about calling the cops. If he did he would be implicated in this entire mess and in all of Timmy's heroin deal. He decided that he just couldn't do that. He'd be willing to lose all of his money to save Allie, but he, Timmy, Glendy, Sandy and Leroy in New York would all go to jail for a very long time if the cops got involved.

He quickly got his Glock and the gym bag full of his money out of the bedroom closet, then pulled on a pair of heavy boots and his black Carhartt jacket. He considered his odds. He had to chance handling it himself. Spin's death had made him rethink the outlaw lifestyle. This phone call removed all of his lingering doubts. He told himself that if he lived through this he would stay on the other side of the abyss forever.

Chapter 49

The road outside of Ravenna heading east was largely deserted in the dark, a back country two lane blacktop leading further into the unknown. The farther he got from the lights of the small town the more Bobby's apprehension grew. He was on his own out here, far from any help, dealing with the people who had cold-bloodedly murdered Spin. He knew there were probably county sheriff's deputies and wildlife officers and maybe security guards from the arsenal who patrolled the region, but they would be few and far between and he hadn't seen any of them.

The arsenal by itself was on something like 20,000 wooded acres. Beyond it, rolling farmland and patches of woods stretched on for miles. Whatever happened out here would be between him and the Mexicans. He thought for a brief second about turning back but realized that could not be an option. He'd known Allie since she was a small child, and he realized that he had always been fond of her. He had to find a way to deal with this.

It was cold outside, about thirty-five degrees, and the trees were bare. An occasional snowflake drifted silently through his headlight beams as he raced along, the car's heater pouring out warm air. Ahead he finally saw the reflection of a street sign and as it grew into readability as he approached it he saw that it said Rock Spring Road. He slowed and turned right into it.

He drove slowly along, scanning the woods to his right for a gravel access road and then it appeared out of the dark, just as the Mexican had said it would. He would have missed it entirely if he hadn't been carefully looking for it. He turned into it and found himself in a narrow tunnel of trees, leafless and cold, and he crunched over the gravel, straining to see ahead beyond the headlights, looking for his first sign of them.

Suddenly the gravel path widened and he was driving into a clearing. It looked big enough to accommodate maybe a dozen cars. The black van was sitting at the far side, sideways to him and dark, and there were no other vehicles around, and no people in sight. He pulled up to within thirty feet of it, pinning its side with his headlight beams, and put his car in park. He chambered a round in the Glock and stuck it in the front of his pants under the open jacket. He picked up a souvenir ball cap he'd gotten in New York off the seat, and his big Mag-Lite flashlight, and opened the car door and stepped out under a cloudless, star filled sky. He put the cap on and turned on the flashlight and pointed it at the van and waited.

Jaime saw the headlights approaching and put a round into the chamber of Hector's M-16. He raised the big outdoor flashlight in his left hand and pointed the black muzzle of the rifle just outside of the open driver's side window and slouched back in his seat, his watch cap pulled low over his eyes so he'd be harder to see. He would turn on the light and shoot Bobby Fallon as soon as he got out of his vehicle, then go get the money and get out of there.

The car stopped and the headlights were pointed at the side of the van. He didn't know whether Fallon could see him inside or not. As he squinted past the lights he noticed that the car was not the gray Camaro they'd followed that day in Cleveland, which was what he'd been expecting. The car's door opened and when the inside light came on he saw a short haired man who climbed out and put on a cap with a badge-like insignia. He stood outside the car wearing a boxy-looking dark jacket with a square white tag on the left breast pocket. His pants were also dark and he had on heavy military style boots. The man pointed a long black metal flashlight at him and turned it on.

Now Jaime was pretty sure that a security guard from the arsenal or something had found him, probably on a routine patrol. Fallon was a wild looking guy with long hair, a black leather jacket and earrings. He'd have to bluff his way out of this, say he was scouting for a fishing spot or something. He didn't want to have to shoot the guy but he would if necessary. He slipped the M-16's safety on and slid it back down inside the van and dropped the big flashlight. He cursed his luck, knowing that this interruption would screw up the plan and they'd have to figure something else out.

Bobby saw the little skinny Mexican sitting back in the driver's seat of the van, a knit cap pulled down low over his eyes, looking into his flashlight's glare. He took a few steps closer, closing the distance to him. The guy didn't move. Except for the sound of his Firebird idling softly behind him, it was very quiet and cold, and the dark night surrounded them beyond their little illuminated scene.

"Hey," Bobby said. "Come out of there."

The van's door opened and the guy inside began to step out, one foot reaching down for the ground.

"Where's the girl?" Bobby asked him. He assumed she was inside the van with another Mexican, the way they had done it with Sandy.

Jaime's eyes went wide and he knew he'd made a big mistake. He reached behind him quickly, grabbing the M-16 off of the floor of the van and pulling it toward him. He began pivoting back in Bobby's direction, trying to get the gun out and bring it to bear.

Bobby saw the Mexican reach back and start to pull something toward him and realized as he caught a glimpse of it that it was a machine gun like the one they'd pointed at him before. His right hand went to the Glock while the left kept the flashlight's beam on the man. They were twenty feet apart.

As the muzzle of the M-16 rose in his direction Bobby pushed his gun forward and got off a shot and it caught Jaime in the left shoulder. The heavy expanding bullet broke his shoulder joint and he fell backwards to his left against the van's doorframe. But he had the rifle in his right hand and struggled to point it at Bobby.

Bobby rushed at him, the Glock held in front of him, and fired over and over, wanting frantically to smash him like a bug, obliterate him, before he could get the machine gun up. The slugs caught him in the center of his chest and in his lower abdomen and two missed him and hit the side of the van. The far window on the passenger side blew out.

Then the Mexican was sagging to the ground and there was blood pouring from him. He tried to say something but blood came out of his mouth and he fell flat onto the gravel. He shuddered and then seemed to deflate and stopped moving at all. Bobby stood over him pointing the Glock at him, then kicked the machine gun away out of reach. His ears were ringing.

He ran around the van and pulled the side door open, fearful that he may have hit Allie inside. The van yawned at him, empty. There was no one else there.

He walked back to the Mexican on the ground and he was without a doubt dead. He didn't understand why the Mexican had forced him to shoot him that way. He took off his cap and wiped his forehead with the back of his sleeve and realized he'd been wearing a souvenir New York Police Department ball cap. They sold them all over New York City and Bobby had thought it was amusing to have one. The Carhartt label on his chest and the badge on the cap probably misled the Mexican, and saved his life. At that moment he didn't feel bad about shooting the guy at all. But he began to shake from the shock and adrenaline of the sudden, lethal violence.

He walked around quickly with his light and picked up the shell casings from his gun and put them in his pocket. He went to the dead guy and carefully went through his pockets. He found a drivers license but the picture didn't even look like this guy. He had money in his pockets but Bobby left it alone.

He had to learn something about these people so he could find Allie. They would kill her for sure when they found out what he'd done. He went back to his car and put on gloves and then went into the van and searched it using his Mag-Lite. On the floor next to a big flashlight and two extra loaded magazines for the machine gun he found a small black day planner with a section for addresses and phone numbers, and it was full of entries. In the front was a personal information page, and it said that Jaime Sandoval owned the book, and it was full of graffiti-like scrawlings with the inscription MS-13.

Bobby had heard of MS-13. He knew they were a gang out of Central America and there had been a couple of things on TV about how they were operating in the United States. So now he knew who these guys were.

He hopped out of the van and knew he had to get as far away from the clearing as possible. He looked again at the dead man but didn't feel much of anything, which surprised him. He was just glad he had shot first, or he knew he would be lying there and there would be no chance of saving Allie.

He got in his car and turned around and drove cautiously out of the access road. This would not be a good time for a real cop to show up. He got back on Route 5 and began driving toward Ravenna. The road was still mostly empty, the stars were still overhead, but he had just killed somebody. He disliked the Mexican for forcing him to do it.

It occurred to him that they had called him from Allie's apartment; it had said so on the caller ID. If they hadn't brought her in the van they could still have her held captive there. With no other ideas presenting themselves, Bobby decided to head for Kent.

Chapter 50

Allie Thomas lay on her bed with her wrists and her ankles bound with duct tape. The lights were off but she could make out objects in the room from the thin illumination penetrating around the half open door from the hallway. It was her room but its familiarity was changed forever by what had been happening there this evening.

She had been home in her apartment studying, wearing only a long red tee shirt and furry slippers and she was snug against the cold outside. She had ordered a pizza and when there was a knock on the door a half hour later she assumed that's what it was. But it wasn't.

She opened the door and two guys were standing there, rather short and Latino looking, bundled up in work clothes and baggy pants. They walked right in the door, pushing her back into the room, and closed the door behind them. One of them pulled out a handgun and pointed it at her, holding it sideways like people did in the movies.

"Don't say a fucking word," said the guy. "Sit down over there."

She sat in a chair at the table in her small kitchen and looked at them, disbelieving, the shock of the invasion rendering her speechless. The other one pulled out a roll of gray duct tape and knelt in front of her. He pulled her hands forward and briskly taped them together. Then he did the same to her ankles. He stepped back and looked at her with satisfaction and smiled at his friend.

They spoke together for a moment, rapid Spanish that Allie couldn't follow, except that they said her last name, Thomas, several times.

One of them, the skinny little one who had bound her, said, "You a pretty cute girl. I'm glad we decided to do this." His face was tattooed with teardrops. His friend with the gun, a larger man, laughed.

The skinny guy stepped close again and reached out and felt her left breast, massaging it slowly, while a smile spread across his face.

She was helpless. She squirmed a little, trying to avoid the hand, but there was nothing she could do. He pushed her bound hands down and kept feeling her. The other one giggled and continued pointing the gun at her.

After a minute the skinny one said, "Madre! I'm getting turned on."

The other one laughed loudly at that, a braying sound. The little guy grabbed her roughly and pulled her up out of the chair. "Where's the bedroom?" he asked.

Allie was wild with fear and didn't say anything, shaking her head side to side at him.

"Oh yes, I think so, chica," he said. They both picked her up then and carried her down the short hallway and into the bedroom and threw her on the bed. She bounced on her stomach and then rolled over, not wanting them behind her where she couldn't see them. The little guy sat next to her and began feeling her bare legs, working his way up to her crotch. He was just about to investigate her panties when the doorbell rang.

"Who's that?" he asked her, suddenly grim and alert, scowling.

"P-pizza," she managed to say.

The gun guy hid his gun under his jacket and went back to the door of the apartment. The little guy put his hand over her mouth and she listened as the other one took the pizza from the delivery kid and paid him and closed the door again.

"We got pizza, Jaime," said the bigger guy.

Jaime smiled at her and said, "This is a bonus." He left her lying there and went into the kitchen. She heard them rummaging around in her refrigerator and opening beers, then talking in Spanish as they ate, laughing now and then. They seemed to be having a good time.

She lay there and waited for them to come back, fearful. She didn't think screaming would help because the apartments contained sound well and anyway college students lived here and screaming wasn't unusual.

They came back in shortly, drinking beer and licking their fingers, and the bigger one said to her, "We're gonna call your brother Timmy. What's his number?"

She told him that she had Tim's cell phone number in her address book in the kitchen. He got it and tried calling but he got no answer.

"He usually doesn't pick up," she told him. She didn't know if this was good or bad for her. They talked some more and wandered back into the kitchen and she heard them finishing the pizza and beer. She was uncomfortable tied up like this, her muscles starting to rebel and cramp a little. So far they hadn't really hurt her despite the groping. Maybe they'd let her go when they got what they came for.

After a while they came back and pulled her bedside phone over toward her. The little guy said, "You know Bobby Fallon? I'm gonna call him. You say hi."

He sat on the bed next to her and punched in a number and when somebody answered he held the phone up to her mouth. She said, "Bobby? This is Allie. I..." and the guy took the phone back and stood up and began strolling around the small bedroom, his eyes roving over the posters on her walls and looking out the window into the dark and quiet backyard below from time to time as he talked to Bobby.

She heard him talking about Tim and heroin and money and meeting someplace outside Ravenna. He pulled a slip of paper out of his pocket and read directions to him. He said they'd let her go.

They also implied that they'd kill her if Bobby didn't do what they wanted. Allie began to cry then, terrified of these guys, not knowing what was going on but sure that someone had done something to enrage them and that they were willing to take out on her.

"Okay, chica," said Jaime after he hung up. "This goes okay, you be okay." He smiled at her but it was an oily grimace and she knew he meant to harm her no matter what. She trembled with fear and despair. The two of them turned out the light and walked out of the room and she didn't see the little one, Jaime, again. They were talking in the next room and then she heard the front door open and close and it was quiet.

She had begun to think that they had both left when the TV came on and she heard the music from Jeopardy playing, then Alex Trebek was telling the contestants how the game worked and then asking them the questions. The guy in the other room was trying to guess the answers, "Toronto" and "1945" and "The Cincinnati Bengals," and she heard him groaning and cursing and it seemed he was getting them all wrong.

The final commercial came on and he came into the room and turned on the light again and looked at her lying there, tears running down her face.

"Please let me go," she said to him.

He came over to the bed and sat next to her, then reached out and pinched her nipple very hard and she cried out. Then he leaned over her and ran his tongue over her cheek and pushed it into her mouth. She tasted the beer he'd been drinking and his breath was sour. He slid over and played with her earlobe with his teeth, teasing and then biting down hard enough to hurt. He whispered to her, "I like the crying. Keep it up, baby. You taste like salt and honey."

Bobby pulled into the parking lot at Allie's apartment building in Kent. It was a cold slow weekday night and there were a few cars coming and going, nothing out of the ordinary. College was in session so most people were cocooned inside studying although downtown probably had its share of partiers in the bars. Out here, away from the center of town, things were quiet.

The two-story building was three sides of a square with a courtyard and parking lot in the middle. Bobby parked and walked to the staircase closest to Allie's second floor apartment and quickly went up, looking around for any sign of the Mexicans. He got to her front door and pressed his ear to it, listening. From inside he heard the TV, some variety show. He tried to look through the window but the drapes were closed and he could only see a tiny corner of the kitchen table and what looked like a pizza box. He very gently tried to turn the front door knob but it was locked.

He pressed his ear to the window and this time he heard a short cry, a woman's voice. *Somebody is in there with Allie*, he thought, *but I can't get in the door. It probably locks when you close it.*

Then he remembered that there was a back door, too, which led down to the garbage bins behind the building. Most people don't lock their doors and if luck was on his side Allie would have neglected to lock hers. He casually strolled around the second floor landing and down, then headed around the building. A guy was walking a cocker spaniel back there and the dog barked at him, but the guy only said, "How you doin'" and kept going.

He found Allie's stairway in the back, a couple of floodlamps on utility poles providing dim illumination, and quickly went up, the Glock in his hand, the NYPD cap backwards on his head. He tried her doorknob and it turned. He went in and closed the door behind him, locking it, and he was in a darkened back entryway where Allie had her bicycle and a couple of plastic trash containers. He eased open the door to the apartment and stepped into the hallway.

He heard a man's voice coming from what he assumed was the bedroom, murmuring and the words indistinct. Then Allie spoke, her voice high and frightened. She said, "Please stop, please."

Bobby stepped into the room and raised the Glock. He saw Allie lying on her bed in a red T-shirt that had been pulled up to expose her breasts. Her feet and hands were bound with tape and she was looking wildly at the man standing over her at the side of the bed.

He was one of the Mexicans, although Bobby hadn't seen him before. He was wearing a brownish wife beater undershirt and thin blue tattoos wound around his bulky arms. His dark brown pants were in a heap around his ankles and he was playing with his erect penis with one hand while he wormed the other between Allie's clenched thighs. A heavy winter coat lay on the floor and a pistol, it looked like a stainless steel Smith and Wesson automatic, sat on a dresser next to the door beside Bobby and just out of the man's reach.

Both of them saw him at once. Allie broke into a delighted smile, wonderment on her face, and the Mexican went pale as death. He quickly took his hand off of Allie and tried to cover his rapidly wilting erection.

"Don't move a fucking muscle and I'm not kidding," Bobby told him. He realized he sounded like the voice of doom, and he liked that. He felt his anger grow.

The sense of déjà vu was pronounced. Were all these gangster assholes rapists and perverts? He half expected Allie to leap off the

WILLIAM C. DUNCAN

bed and try to beat the man to death the way Glendy had, her restraints the only thing preventing it. But Allie was crying with relief now, and he saw that she was gentle and only interested in getting away from this guy and his probing hands.

"Oh, Bobby, thank God," she said.

The Mexican tried to talk but his mouth had gone dry and it took him a couple of tries.

"Don't shoot me, amigo," he said. "I beg you. Please." His eyes were wide and he began to reach down for his pants.

"I said not to move, compadre," said Bobby, taking a step closer and keeping the gun on his face. The guy froze.

"Are you hurt, Allie?" he asked her.

She shook her head, relief radiating from her and said, "They molested me. I think he was going to rape me. He'd been working up to it. You came just in time."

Bobby reached into his pants pocket with one hand while he covered the guy with the gun in his other and came out with his folding knife. He flicked it open.

"Step back, you fucker," he said to the guy, and he shuffled back a couple of steps, the pants restricting his movement.

"Put your hands on top of your head and sit down," Bobby told him, and he looked behind him and eased himself into the chair in the corner of Allie's bedroom. He was naked from the waist down and sitting there helplessly with his hands on his head, his eyes fixed on the Glock.

Bobby stepped close to Allie and pulled her shirt down over her breasts and then deftly cut the tape. She sat up and peeled it off of herself, and rubbed her wrists and ankles for a moment, trying to get her circulation restored. She climbed unsteadily off the bed and stood a little behind Bobby, watching the Mexican.

"There's another one," she said. "He might come back."

Bobby shook his head, looking grimly at the guy in the chair.

"He's not coming back," he said, and was pleased when the guy's mouth dropped open. "Who the fuck are you, amigo?" he asked the guy.

He shook his head slowly back and forth, defiant but wary. "It's better you don't know. Let me go and we forget about this."

Bobby reached into his jacket pocket and came out with Jaime's day planner and the other guy was clearly startled. Bobby flipped it open to the address section and said, "Maybe you're Arturo Aracambo. No? How about Jose Alvarez? I've got 'em all right here. Everybody's name, address and phone number. You MS-13 dudes are organized, I'll give you that."

The guy was still shaking his head, not saying anything, fear in his eyes.

"I know who you are now, pal. You've lost your edge."

Bobby turned and scooped up the Smith and Wesson from the dresser and put it in his belt.

"I would really like to kill you for what you did to this girl. But I don't want them finding your stinking body in her home. Stand up."

The guy stood, his hands still up, watchful and unsure of what Bobby would do.

"Pull up your damn pants, you asshole. Carefully. You are a sick fuck, you know that?"

The guy bent over slowly and pulled his pants up and buckled his belt.

"Thank God we don't have to look at your pitiful anatomy anymore," Bobby told him. He grabbed up the guy's coat and felt through it, checking for weapons. "Put this on."

With Allie backing out of the way he marched him into the kitchen and made him sit down with his hands up.

"Allie, pack up everything you need for a few days. Clothes, books, whatever."

He sat down quietly across from the guy and let him look at the muzzle of the Glock while they waited.

"Guess what?" he said in a quiet tone. "This is the last thing your little buddy ever saw." He watched the guy turn gray again, and he looked like he might vomit from the fear. "Don't you dare puke in here, you pussy," he told him. "Or I'll make you eat it."

After a few minutes Allie came in, dressed and wearing her coat, with two large and bulging soft bags.

"Let's go," Bobby said, and they stood up and walked to the door.

Allie opened it and they went outside onto the landing and nobody was around so Bobby kept the gun trained on the guy. Allie

219

pulled the door shut and made sure it was locked and then Bobby motioned the guy forward. They all headed for the stairway and went down to the parking lot.

"That's my car over there, Allie," he told her. "Get in with your stuff."

While she was occupied with that he stepped a little closer to the Mexican and said, his breath clouding in the cold air, "I advise you and your crew to leave us alone from now on. I know who you are and I can get to you. You are very, very lucky that I'm choosing not to kill you, you perverted sack of shit." And he hit the guy in the teeth quickly with the gun.

While he was staggering around holding his mouth Bobby got in the car and turned the ignition. He backed out fast, watching the Mexican the whole time, then drove out of the lot and was quickly gone in the night.

After a while the guy sat down on the curb, spitting out blood and tooth fragments, and got out his cell phone from his pants.

"Cesar," he said with difficulty. "This is Luis. Somebody has to come get me."

Chapter 51

Timmy woke up in his own sweat and reached for the drugs on the night table and was surprised to find that they were gone.

He searched his memory and tried to recall finishing them but he honestly couldn't. The small plastic bag was empty, the straw he used for snorting next to it. The sun was coming up outside and the gulls were screeching as they wheeled through the sky overhead. A morning breeze wafted through the cottage and he saw that he'd left the front door open last night, the screen banging softly when the wind hit it. The TV was still on, the volume turned down, and somebody, a beautiful blonde woman, was talking to the camera on the Fox News Channel.

He wondered if maybe somebody had come in and stolen his smack while he slept but he knew that was paranoid and stupid.

He'd simply used it up, with no thought of what he would do when he finally ran out of it. And he was feeling pretty crummy, to tell the truth.

He rolled off the bed and went into the bathroom and rummaged through his shaving kit, where he kept a little package of dope hidden, but he remembered he'd used that yesterday. Then he went through all his luggage, piece by careful piece, looking for anything he had overlooked or squirreled away or hidden for this moment, when he was out of options. It was all gone.

He sat heavily in the easy chair in front of the TV in his underpants and began to feel chilly, like he was really coming down with the flu or something, so he got out his hoody and threw it on.

His nose was running pretty good now, and the chills began to build in intensity and he shivered involuntarily against them, his body trying to stay warm. Why was it so cold in Florida? Then he remembered that he'd used up most of his money, too, over the past days. Out of the twenty Leroy had left him, a dollar bill and some change sat on top of the TV. He'd eaten every now and then, hamburgers and chips and stuff, and a couple of beers. How long had it taken to go through the money? He couldn't remember.

He had no idea how much rent he had left prepaid on the cottage. For all he knew, the landlady could show up any second and throw him out. She hadn't been too friendly since Glendy left, anyway, giving him the bad eye when he stumbled out of the cottage and down the road in search of a meal.

He suddenly realized that he wasn't very smart after all. He was starting to go through heroin withdrawal by himself, lonely in a cottage by the sea without his woman, and she was off in New York with some slick hustler who had swept her up while he was playing William Burroughs. He was out of money and could be out on the street today, and he didn't know how bad he was going to feel before this was over. Could you die from heroin withdrawal? He remembered somebody telling him once that you couldn't; you only wished that you could.

His muscles cramped then, and his stomach, too, and he bent double with the pain. He lurched to his feet and into the bathroom and vomited in the toilet. He felt a little better and raised his head and saw himself in the mirror, wasted looking, red eyes and with mucus copiously flowing out of his nose, his hair scraggly, stubble on his jaw. He looked terrible. Then he had to vomit again.

Later he was curled on the cool tile floor of the bathroom, hot and still sweating, unable to vomit anymore. His muscles alternately cramped and released, and the thought crossed his mind that it resembled the effects of an exercise device he'd seen once. You attached these little electrodes to different places on your body and an electrical current stimulated your muscles and made them contract rhythmically. It was for physical therapy or something. This was sort of like that, except that somebody had replaced the batteries with a 240 volt current and with each contraction he felt like he was being dismembered. When the cramps released he had the sensation that insects had somehow gotten under his skin and were busily creeping back and forth. Had bugs somehow crawled into him while he lay on the floor? Florida was full of bugs.

He found himself on the bed a little later, and he saw that a different blonde was on the TV but he didn't know her. It was hot in the cottage because he hadn't closed the front door and turned on the air conditioning. He'd been so cold before, and now he was really hot. He wondered how he gotten such a hideous case of the flu, and then he remembered that he was a heroin addict and was paying the price for his pleasure. What goes around comes around. How did the Chinese say that? They had some idea about yin and yang, and the balance of things. His bill had come due in a major way.

It occurred to him that he had a few drugs with him that could possibly ease this torture. He went back into the bathroom and there was vomit splattered around the toilet. He found a little box in his shaving kit and got out two Percodans and washed them down hurriedly with a glass of water. He stumbled back to the bed but before he got there he was hit with stomach convulsions again and turned back and vomited some more.

The sun was going down and he still had quite a bit of cocaine with him so he tried some of that, first blowing his nose repeatedly, trying to open it up so he could snort the stuff. It did help some, and he drifted away, delirious, fretful and cramping as he tossed on the sweat drenched bed, naked, the hoody long since discarded.

It was long after nightfall. He tested his body a little, trying to move, and was rewarded with a sense of profound illness that penetrated him to his core. He felt like death had crept inside him and crouched there, savoring its advance, contemplating where it would take him next. He raised his head slightly and saw on the bedside clock's illuminated face that it was two in the morning. A breeze flowed through the cottage and he realized that he'd been too sick to close the door and turn on the air conditioner when he was so, so hot before.

He felt deeply stupid for having done this to himself. He wanted to blame somebody, but Glendy had tried to stop him and even Leroy, the prick, had warned him. Nobody else even knew about it. So he was stuck with himself; he was responsible.

223

He carefully sat up, trembling and feverish, and picked up his cell phone. He saw that he'd remembered to keep it charged. He pushed the numbers for Glendy's cell. After a while her voice mail came on.

"I'm sorry," he said. Then he turned it off and fell back on the bed.

Chapter 52

Bobby and Allie lay together on his bed in the apartment in Lakewood, his arms around her. She had drifted off to sleep a little while ago, her face nestled on his chest. She had on another long tee shirt and he had on his sweat pants, and he had been able to comfort her after the terrible evening, talking softly to her and holding her to him until she had become calm again.

He smelled her hair, tousled and curly, against his face, and thought about how relieved he was that she was okay. She really was a special person, smart, sweet and funny. She had always wanted to hang around when he and Timmy were teenagers and she was younger, and even then he found her gentleness and humor compelling. She would not get over the emotional effects of what the MS-13 guys did to her for a long time, maybe never. But he had stopped the worst of it, and he was glad.

She had told him about what Jaime had done and described the other one's actions, too. Bobby was grimly satisfied that Jaime was dead, and that he'd messed up the other one. After Sandy, after Spin, after trying to kill him, and after this vile assault on Allie, these guys deserved whatever happened to them. He only hoped that his possession of Jaime's day planner would be enough to keep them at bay.

She had wanted to talk to him about what she had overheard when they called him. She knew this somehow involved Timmy and drugs, and she needed to hear all of it. He told her to rest, that there would be time for that, and she had accepted his word and finally drifted off to sleep. She seemed deeply soothed by his presence and his strength and he found himself inordinately pleased by that.

Before he slept he decided that he would have to talk to Wade Thomas about this. It was now clear that MS-13 knew who Timmy was and how to get to his family. Wade would have to be brought into the loop. Bobby didn't look forward to explaining it to him.

They met him in a little neighborhood family-run restaurant on Detroit Avenue near Lakewood Hospital. He came in expecting to have a short-notice breakfast with Allie and was surprised to see them both together in a booth near the front of the place. It was late on a bright Saturday morning, Amanda was with Little Wade at tae kwon do and the breakfast crowd was mostly gone, the lunch patrons not yet arrived. He was already wary when he slid in across from them, his back to the door.

"Hi, you two," he said. "This is a surprise." He quickly took in Bobby's new appearance, his neatly cut hair, sweater and blue jeans.

The discreet corner of a tattoo was visible above the edge of his collar but it was easy to miss. Wade decided it was an improvement.

Allie smiled at him and he was struck by the blend of emotions she seemed to display. She was leaning in close to Bobby, comfortable with him. Intimate? She appeared to be at ease with their physicality, even happy with it. At the same time there was a deep urgency and tension to her expression and Wade was troubled by that.

"Hi, Wade," she said to him, and reached across the table and squeezed his hand. She was clearly having a difficult time with some aspect of this meeting but it didn't seem to be in her relationship, whatever it was, with Bobby.

"If you didn't look so cozy together I'd think you had something awful to tell me," he said to them.

Bobby leaned forward and looked him in the eye and said, "I have to talk to you about something pretty serious, and I'm truly sorry about that. But it's very important that you know."

And with the waitress coming and going and bringing them juice and coffee and then bacon, eggs and oatmeal, Bobby laid it out for him. Wade saw at once why they had wanted to meet him in a public place. It was for the same reason business people went out to restaurants with employees in order to fire them, because the injured party was less likely to blow up, act out and make a scene.

He sat and ate without tasting anything as Bobby told him that Tim had been dealing cocaine and that he had been involved, too. That Tim learned of a house where drug dealers lived and had been found dead and he went there without Bobby's knowledge and found six kilograms of heroin and some cocaine and had taken it. That the drugs turned out to be the property of a gang from Central America operating in Cleveland called MS-13, and how they had tracked down a girl Tim knew, and then him and his roommate, and demanded their property back. How Bobby had gone and found Tim, who was in hiding, and told him all this and how Tim pledged to settle it with the gang but instead fled to New York with Glendy.

"Did you know they had heroin?" Wade interrupted him, keeping his voice low, nervous to be discussing something like this at all, and stunned by what he was hearing.

Bobby shook his head. "No. I thought he'd gotten some cocaine, and I'll agree that was bad enough. But I had no idea what he was really doing."

Then, somberly, he told him about the threats from the Mexicans and how they had managed to find his roommate and kill him.

Wade's mouth went dry, and Allie, who had heard this earlier, was struck by Bobby's anguish.

"I had to sell my car and get a new job and apartment. The girl they had found, the one who led them to me, had to leave town with her kids. We didn't know if they'd find us, too, and I didn't know where Timmy had gone."

Wade shook his head. "He could have stopped this as soon as it started by giving them back their drugs."

"Maybe," Bobby said. "But these are pretty bad people. I think they're insulted that they were robbed."

Then he explained about the call from Timmy that took him to New York, how he was in the hotel the whole time without Wade seeing him, and how Timmy and Glendy had narrowly avoided being robbed in Greenwich Village and how Timmy engineered the sale of the heroin in the hotel and how he used Wade's room to do it.

"So it was all a front, a charade," Wade said bitterly. "They were lying to me. They used me to do their drug deal."

"I'm afraid so. They used me, too. I didn't know what they were selling and how much they had."

Wade flared at him and raised his voice then. "You knew it was a drug deal, Fallon. How can you act like the injured party? You're in this up to your neck." They all glanced around the restaurant but no one was paying attention to them.

Bobby sadly nodded. "You're right. The whole business sickens me. I decided to give it up and I came back here. You see how I look. I haven't used anything in weeks. I am involved and I won't try to minimize it. But you see, I couldn't get free of it."

And he told him about the call from MS-13 and how they had kidnapped Allie and told him that this was about six kilograms of heroin. Wade started forward, reaching for his little sister, alarmed beyond anything he had known before. She smiled at him and tears started in her eyes as she squeezed his hands in hers.

"I'm okay. Bobby saved me," she said.

"What happened?" Wade asked him.

"They found her somehow," Bobby told him, and he was aware of how awful and terrifying this whole chain of events sounded, and tried to imagine what Wade was feeling as he listened to it.

"They tied her up and held her at her apartment and wanted to meet me out in the middle of nowhere last night to get money from me."

"You went?" Wade wanted to know.

"I had to. I couldn't think of any other way to save Allie."

"And you paid them off somehow?"

Bobby shook his head. "No. The guy was set up to kill me. They were planning to shoot me no matter what."

Wade regarded him for moment, thinking through the possible scenarios. He cautiously said, "Can you tell me what happened?"

Bobby just looked levelly back at him. "It's probably better if I don't."

Wade sat back, lightheaded and disbelieving. How could something like this be happening to his family, and to people he knew? It seemed unreal. But Bobby's and Allie's sober faces told him otherwise.

"He came and got me, Wade," Allie continued earnestly. "He

saved my life. This guy was molesting me and Bobby snuck in the back door and made him stop. We got away."

"Where's the guy now?" Wade asked.

"My guess is he's at the dentist," said Bobby, and he smiled for the first time.

"But they know who Allie is, that she's Tim's sister. They know how to find my family."

"They seem to. They didn't before but they figured it out somehow," Bobby told him.

Wade was overwhelmed by the gravity of the situation. His family, his sister and his mother and his wife and son were in mortal peril.

His brother, who had betrayed them all by his selfishness and his degeneracy, was nowhere to be found. The potential for further tragedy was enormous, and Wade felt the full weight of the responsibility for avoiding that.

"We have to go to the police," he told Bobby. "There's no other way."

"You may choose to do that. Believe me, I've thought about it. If that's what you decide, then I won't contest it and I'll cooperate. But you have to be prepared to answer for the time you spent in New York with Timmy while he was doing his deal, and the fact that he used your room, which he was paying for at that point. He has implicated you."

Wade just stared at him, unable to respond. He was right. Tim had set him up and he would be scrutinized as an accomplice.

"And I will be held accountable for what happened in those woods outside of Ravenna last night," Bobby said slowly.

Allie reached for Wade again, urgency and fear in her voice. "He saved me, Wade. They tried to kill him but he won and he came and saved me. We can't let him suffer for it."

"My God," Wade said, completely at a loss for answers. "What the hell can we do? These people will come after us and we can't let that happen."

Bobby reached under the table and came up with a small black day planner-type notebook. He handed it across to Wade, who took it from him and then looked up, questioningly.

"You have a moral dilemma. But maybe we've got a Plan B," said Bobby.

Chapter 53

Wade and Bobby sat next to each other at Bobby's kitchen table while Allie alternately sat with them and wandered into the living room to look out at the street below. She was having a hard time remaining composed even though she was relieved that Wade was involved now.

None of them were sure that a way existed to control the problem. They had tried calling Timmy's cell and gotten no answer. Then Bobby called the cottages on Captiva and was told that Mr. Willard had checked out; there was no mention of Glendy.

"I could talk to Mike Rodriguez at work," Wade said. "Maybe find out what makes these guys tick."

Bobby smiled at that. "This is not an ethnic problem. I'm sure that Mike Rodriguez, whoever he is, doesn't know any more about these people than you do. These are gangsters, and they think and act like gangsters. Black, white, yellow, latino, whatever. They're mean and they want people to be scared of them."

Wade mulled that over. "I'm sure you're right, although I don't know any gangsters myself. But they're also businessmen, right? This whole thing is about their business. I need to convince them that continuing this would be very bad for business."

Wade had looked at the day planner briefly in the restaurant and now he and Bobby went over it carefully page by page. If they hadn't known it was a criminal's records they would have probably overlooked it as just another pocket notebook. Aside from the MS-13 graffiti on the personal information page, it was a daily record of what Jaime Sandoval had done since the start of the year and what he had planned to do in the future.

Much of it was in abbreviated form, with people's initials often replacing full names and places reduced to a few letters. But when they looked at the address book they found very detailed names, addresses and phone numbers for dozens of people, and the names correlated with many of the initials in the date book portion.

Bobby quickly turned to the days around the time of Spin's disappearance and found an entry which read: Agarramos al companero de casa.

"Allie, do you know what this says?" he asked her.

She came back into the kitchen and looked over his shoulder.

"Caught roommate," she translated. They looked at each other, grim faced. Wade shuffled through the pages and they were full of day-to-day details in Spanish. They picked a few at random and Allie read them back for them.

"'H delivery with L. at Kamm's.' 'Meet with Cesar.' 'Go see Big A. at East 55th.' 'Meet with Cesar', once again." She was wide-eyed.

"This says what he was doing every day, and it's pretty easy to figure out."

"Cesar's in here a lot," said Wade. He went through the address book and found the name Cesar Obregon, an address on Denison Avenue and another in Berea, just south of Cleveland, and several phone numbers. "This guy must be the boss."

"Why in the world would this Jaime guy be driving around with the whole team roster in his car, especially if he was committing crimes?" Allie wondered.

Bobby said, "My guess is that he didn't expect to lose it, and that maybe he wanted access to all these numbers because he was operating out in the countryside in the middle of nowhere and wanted to be able to get help fast if he needed it."

Wade shook his head. "He made a serious mistake."

"Let's take advantage of it," Bobby replied.

Wade took in a deep breath and let it out. "This is terrible. But we need to get on with it before they try something else. Are you ready to do it?"

The other two nodded firmly and Wade steadied himself. He decided to think of it as another serious business negotiation with serious consequences, and he had been involved with a great many of those. He tried not to think about what those consequences could be this time around. He picked up Bobby's cell phone and punched in the first number for Cesar Obregon.

At the store on Denison Cesar was in the warehouse in back with Manuel and a couple of other mareros and they had just hosed the blood out of the black van.

Cesar himself had responded to Luis's call for assistance last night and he had taken a well-armed crew down to Kent just in case they ran into Bobby Fallon. Instead they found Luis weeping and shivering in some bushes a couple of blocks from the girl's apartment, hiding until help came and bleeding from his shattered mouth. They had hurried out to the spot Jaime had picked for the ambush and found him there, shot three times and already cold. They'd bundled him into the van and fled the scene as quickly as they could. Cesar did not want the authorities to know that this had happened; that would be bad for them all by attracting attention to their activities.

On the way back to Cleveland they had detoured to another remote patch of woods in Brecksville where they buried Jaime in a gully alongside Hector and a girl they had killed last year, a seventeen-year-old hangaround who had been bragging about MS-13 to outsiders and who Cesar suspected of stealing some cocaine from the warehouse when one of the guys had brought her around. He hated putting Jaime there with these two fuckups but it was important to keep his death quiet for now. Maybe in a year or so they could have a celebration in remembrance of him.

Then Luis had told him that Bobby Fallon had Jaime's notebook and Cesar decided that Jaime would not get a celebration after all.

He was amazed that Jaime would do something so stupid. He knew that the notebook contained the names and addresses of the entire Cleveland set, their contacts and dealers, and a record of Jaime's day-to-day activities. He had encouraged Jaime to keep these records as a backup to his own, but he had tried to impress upon him the importance of keeping them safe.

So he was not surprised when his cell phone rang and he saw Bobby Fallon's number on the caller ID. He glanced at Manuel and the others and said, "It's the guy."

He walked into the front of the store and sat behind the counter by himself before he answered.

"Hola," he said cordially.

"Is this Cesar Obregon?" Wade asked, deliberately using his full name to let him know he'd been identified.

"Who is calling, please?" Cesar replied, assuming this was Bobby but not giving anything away.

"My name is Thomas. I'm the brother of the girl you attacked last night," Wade said.

"Oh, not Bobby Fallon?" Cesar said, surprised. "Where is he?"

"He's sitting right here. Do you have a minute to talk?"

Cesar laughed. "Timmy Thomas, I will talk to you as much as you want."

Wade shook his head. "Not Timmy. I'm his brother. We have no idea where he is at all. You can believe that or not but there it is."

"Ah," said Cesar. "So, what is your first name, Mr. Thomas?"

"Mister," Wade told him. "As you see, I know who you are. A friend of yours misplaced a notebook and I used it to call you. I see that there are a lot of names here and I assume that all of you are acquainted with one another."

Cesar paused, then said, "I appreciate you calling to return the notebook. My friend will be happy to get it back."

"No, I don't think so. This notebook will not be going anywhere as long as we reach an understanding. Otherwise, it will be going to the police."

"You don't intend to return our property? You people are making a habit of this."

Wade shifted in his seat. His elbows were on the kitchen table and he was hunched over the phone. He needed to stay in control and he needed to relax to do that. He sat back and took a deep breath again, then eased it out. He reminded himself to go slow, to not let the other guy set the pace of the conversation.

"I'm sorry about whatever happened in the past. That is not my business. But I cannot allow you to harm my family. I'm sure you understand this, and that you'd feel the same way."

"True," Cesar allowed.

"I do not want to bring in the police because that could be harmful to us, as well. We know this and you do, too. But if we are put in a position of being continuously attacked by you, we will have to take the lesser of two evils and go to them."

Cesar considered that. "Surely it would be more manly if we settled our differences without bringing in the authorities. That is not an honorable way of doing things. Are you frightened of us?"

"You are targeting women. That is also not honorable. I think Bobby demonstrated our ability to deal with things in a manly way but we would prefer to have this stop now."

"What about what is owed to us?"

"I'm sorry, but that is the cost of doing business. Sometimes you have to take a loss. If I could recover what you lost I would try to, but I cannot. My brother has fled and I cannot reach him. Now I must protect my family."

"Señor, this is very distressing. We were wronged in this." Cesar was trying to find an angle for negotiation but it was clear to them both that Wade had the upper hand.

"I'm sorry," he told him again. "But I must insist that you stop looking for us or bothering us in any way. I am willing to keep your secrets as long as you agree to that. If any of your people come around any of us again, I will be forced to take this notebook to the police."

"I am not happy with this," Cesar said. "How do I know you will keep your word? Why not hunt you down now and keep you from telling anybody?" Cesar's last chance was intimidation. His voice shifted from a calm purr to a rough growl, the menace coming through. "I can make sure you never get a chance to interfere with us."

Wade faltered a little; the threat was clear and he knew this guy would carry it out if he thought he could get away with it.

"It won't work," he told him forcefully. "If anything happens to any of us a copy of these records will go to the police. You can be assured of it. I will keep my word because exposing you will make us accountable as well. I would rather avoid that but I will do it if it will keep you from trying to kill us."

Cesar saw that he had no way out of it. It was an unpleasant realization, but he would have to cut his losses and go on from here.

He sighed heavily. "Okay, señor. We will stay away. Please honor your end of this by keeping the records secure."

"You have my word," Wade said, and felt that he had made a deal with the devil. Would he forfeit his soul? They hung up and Wade slumped in his chair, drained, while Bobby and Allie patted his shoulders and smiled. With any luck, they had shut down the threat and could move on with their lives.

"You got him, Wade," Bobby told him. "I think we'll be okay."

Wade looked up at him balefully and said, "This has to be the end of it, Bobby. No more dope. I don't know what you've got going on with Allie and I'm grateful you helped her, but this has got to be on the straight and narrow. I cannot have her put in this kind of jeopardy."

Bobby nodded. "I'm out of it," he told him. Allie hugged him.

Cesar sat quietly in the store and considered what had happened. He sorely did not want to leave the records in the hands of these people but he could not figure out a way to get them back. If he seized the girl or Mrs. Thomas he could bargain for their safe return but surely this Mr. Thomas would know that giving in to him would be surrender and they would all be killed.

He hated giving up on the lost six kilos but there was nothing to be done now. He risked jeopardizing their entire operation if he continued trying to get even.

And he was particularly worried about one entry buried in Jaime's address book, which was worth protecting above all else. The last time he had met the Tailor he had made a secret note of his car's VIN number when the guy was busy unloading product from his trunk. He figured that knowing who he was could be useful insurance. So he had traced him through his VIN on the Internet and now the Tailor's real name, address and phone number were hidden in his own records, and he had had Jaime copy them, too, for safekeeping. But the Thomases wouldn't know what they were looking at. It would be a secret; nobody had to know.

Chapter 54

There was a solid knock on the door of the cottage that aroused Timmy from his torpor and he pulled himself out of the easy chair and went to answer it. The landlady stood just outside, her hands on her hips, and regarded him with distaste.

"Mr. Willard," she said. "You're paid up through tomorrow. I'm wondering if you intend to book another week with us?" Her expression clearly told him that she was hoping he wouldn't.

"No, I don't think so," he said. He felt relief wash over him because he had worried three days ago that he might be out on the street, and it turned out he had another day. "Thanks for asking."

She turned and stalked away down the path. Timmy went into the bathroom and looked at himself, wondering what she had seen. It wasn't good. His hair was awry and he hadn't shaved in a while. He'd also neglected bathing. He was wearing only baggy shorts and he was emaciated. He had sores on his body where he had scratched at a relentless itching. His eyes were red and he looked like someone who had gotten into very bad habits and let himself go. Which was exactly correct.

He still felt ill and alternated between chills and tremors and feverish heat, but it had gotten a lot better. He found he was finally a little hungry, which was a problem because he only had the dollar and some change. But at least he had that.

He threw on a shirt and some sandals and went outside into the sun and warm breeze and started walking toward the shops and restaurants up the road. He tired quickly and had to go slowly and he realized for the first time how terribly this drug and its aftermath had depleted him. He hadn't had a thing to eat in days.

He came to an ATM machine and on a whim, hoping against hope, he got his card out of his wallet and put it into the slot and keyed in his password. When the screen prompted him, he hit "balance inquiry." To his amazement it showed that he had $643 in his account. How was that possible? He remembered then that he'd given Wade $18,000 for the Mustang and that his mother must have put it into his bank and then paid off the loan. The loan balance was a little less than the deposit, and it left him with a lifesaving margin. He withdrew $200 and headed up the road to a burger shack and thankfully ordered a meal.

Nobody paid much attention to him but he was somewhat out of place here, looking bedraggled and sick. Captiva was an upscale area and he looked like vagrant. He'd have to do something about this.

When he got back to the cottage he broke out his cocaine stash and looked it over. He still had three uncut ounces and about sixty grams, and he had his electronic scale. Glendy hadn't even thought about that when she and Leroy were leaving; they were focused on the heroin money. He figured he could possibly score some manitol or something for cut and weigh out the rest of the ounces and have around a hundred fifty grams to sell, which meant over fourteen thousand bucks. Things were looking up after all.

But he'd have to leave Captiva. It was too expensive and he'd draw too much attention here while he got his act together and felt out customers. He needed cheaper accommodations and lots of young people hanging around in lots of bars. He saw a plan and a future beyond the sickness and despair and it improved his spirits.

There'd be fun and girls where he was going, and he'd have a good time again. He could still stay safely away from Cleveland and the bad guys there who were looking for him until enough time had passed for things to settle down.

Still, as he felt better, he began to miss Glendy even more. She had screwed him over, there was no doubt about that, but he had been a poor excuse for a boyfriend and she had probably wanted to teach him a lesson. He knew she felt bad about leaving. He called her cell phone a second time and got her voice mail again.

"It's me," he said. "I miss you."

The next day he packed up all of his things in several large bags and went by the office and checked out. There was no balance due on the rooms and they hadn't used the room phones for anything.

The landlady gave him a last grim look.

"Goodbye, Mr. Willard. I hope you enjoyed your stay." Clearly she didn't care how he felt about his stay. She just wanted him gone.

He couldn't guess how much she knew, but a guest who spent his whole stay indoors, vomiting much of the time and looking like a homeless person, couldn't be up to any good.

He smiled sweetly at her. "Thanks for all of your kind hostility," he said, and left her wondering if she heard him correctly.

He caught a cab down Captiva Island and across to Sanibel Island and past the wildlife refuge and then through the crowded avenues in the town. Sanibel was bigger than Captiva but still upscale and insular. He wanted more room to move around in a place where he wouldn't appear out of the ordinary. The cab crossed over the causeway and into Fort Myers and then turned down San Carlos Boulevard to Fort Myers Beach.

"So where to?" the cabby, a young guy chewing gum, asked him.

"I need a motel. Just cruise down the main drag," Timmy told him.

They drove along Estero Boulevard for a couple of blocks and Timmy saw that this was a good choice. There were quite a few bars and seaside restaurants and there were teens and twenty-somethings strolling around, the girls tanned and many wearing bikinis. Perfect.

They were approaching a small motel with a vacancy sign out and Timmy told the cabby to stop. He went in and an older guy in a Hawaiian shirt with a nose full of broken blood vessels looked up from the desk in the cramped office and said, "Can I help you?"

"Yes, how much per night for a room? And what's the weekly rate?"

"One person? Fifty dollars a night plus tax. Two fifty a week."

"I'll take it," Timmy said. "Let me pay you for two nights now and I'll be back as soon as I find an ATM to pay for the rest of the week. Okay?"

The man nodded. "Sure. Let's see your driver's license and sign the register, please."

"Let me pay the cab first," Timmy said. He went outside and settled with the cabby.

"Nice place?" the cabby asked him.

Timmy shrugged. "It'll do for now. I'll upgrade later."

Chapter 55

There were cops in Fort Myers Beach but Timmy knew what to look for and kept his head down. Up until now he'd been using in Florida and now he was dealing, which was another level of action, and Florida was a state with a lot of drug experience. There were undercover people around as well as uniformed patrols, but they didn't slow him down at all.

He got settled into the motel, in a room on the second floor which allowed an ocean view if you leaned out the window and strained your neck. But it was private and the queen-sized mattress wasn't too old and lumpy, and he could get basic cable and HBO on the TV. He carefully hung his new suits in the closet for the day when he could have a higher standard of living again.

The other residents of the place came and went on a daily basis and he seemed to be the only one staying long term except for an elderly man on the ground floor, who he suspected might be the proprietor's father. They had the same taste in shirts and the same ruddy drinker's face. The guests were mostly college aged because the place was cheap and they could afford it. This was perfect for Timmy and he made two hundred bucks the second day he was there.

He met a young guy with a lot of piercings and tattoos in the stairwell and they fell into a conversation, Timmy asking how long the guy had been around and where the fun was. The guy was happy to tell him which bars were the best in his opinion, and where you could get an affordable meal. He'd been there for three days with two buddies and they were leaving in the morning, going home to Atlanta. He was planning to do some serious partying on his last night there, and Timmy walked right into his opening and offered him some blow. They went back to Timmy's room and did a quick line each and the guy was impressed. He pulled out a roll of bills and bought two grams on the spot.

Timmy decided after that not to sell to anybody in the motel because that was probably too dangerous. He had needed a cash infusion and this guy was safe, but from now on he'd take his show on the road and not let anybody he met know where he was staying.

He hung around the bars in the evenings, sipping beers and getting into conversations with the bartenders and the waitresses. One girl was kind enough to point out an undercover cop to him the second time he was in the place. The cop was young and a little scruffy, with a couple of days' stubble on his face and an athletic build. He sat by himself at the bar and talked to whoever would talk to him. He was so obvious that Timmy kept an eye on him and, sure enough, he had a partner who looked like a real stoner, who never talked to him or went near him in the bar. Timmy found this out by following the first guy into the restroom and catching them together, both of them freezing in mid-sentence when he walked in. He went about his business but then had a good laugh about it when he went back to his seat.

The bars were generally faux-tropical, with fake palm trees and pretend cockatoos sitting on swings hanging from the ceiling. The music was Jimmy Buffett's "Margaritaville" punctuated with things people his age actually wanted to listen to, like Outkast and Foo Fighters and Avril. The places filled up at night and there were lots of unattached girls, staying together in crowded hotel rooms, hanging out on the beach during the day and partying late into the night, grabbing fun-in-the-sun vacations before heading back to the murky late-spring reality of places like Baltimore and Columbus and Chicago. And pretty much everybody was a cocaine fan.

He worked the bars sequentially, hitting them on alternating nights for a while until he got the feel for them and the people who worked there began to recognize his face. He would have used a fake name except they tended to card everyone under forty and he had to show his driver's license all the time.

He made friends with people and after some conversation he'd offer them a line of coke. They'd walk outside and find a private spot in the moonlight and Timmy would share his little tooter, a gram-sized bottle with a nozzle on the top that measured out line-sized hits. You could snort right from the tooter, which eliminated all the fooling around with razor blades and mirrors and straws and got things done in a hurry.

After he'd see the person actually use the drug he'd feel comfortable offering to sell them some, because cops weren't supposed to use the stuff, just pretend that they did. And it was hard to pretend with the tooter. Either they snorted up the contents in the end of the nozzle or they didn't. He never met anybody who didn't.

Within a week he'd sold twenty-two grams, and money was no longer a concern. He was comfortable where he was and the heroin withdrawal was past, although the memory of those awful shivering nausea filled days weighed upon him. He still had a taste for the stuff. If he'd had some more he wouldn't have had to go through all that hell in the first place. He knew this was circuitous reasoning, pretzel logic, but that's how he felt.

He even got laid. He met a girl from Fort Wayne, Indiana who was vacationing with a mixed group of friends. One of them was supposed to be her boyfriend but they were having a fight or something and the short, curvy brunette, she had an Italian name, latched onto Timmy and he shared some coke with her. They wound up on the beach together and had pretty good sex, both of them a little drunk and high. He figured it made the vacation for her; she got to have a real adventure in Florida and screwed over her dumbass jock boyfriend at the same time.

He walked her back to the bar and then it was awkward because her friends were asking where she'd been and the boyfriend, although quite uselessly drunk, began giving him the evil eye. So he left, and that was that. It had been nice, but frankly he couldn't understand the infatuation many women seemed to have for sex on the beach. It was actually pretty gritty and sand got into all the uncomfortable places.

Back in his room late at night he'd watch cable and drift on the comfortable fog of beer and the little coke he'd used while dealing. He didn't want to get too agitated so he kept it to a minimum. He'd check his cell phone's voice mail and found countless calls from Bobby and Wade and Allie and his mother and all sorts of other people but he didn't feel like talking to them. There were no messages from Glendy. He felt a little lost without her and he didn't like admitting that to himself. She always gave him purpose, and he found that he actually liked the focus she had given his life. It wasn't that he felt he needed to please her. It was more that finding things that pleased them mutually was gratifying to him.

He called her a couple of more times the first week he was there, and the last time he told the voice mail where he was. He said that he had quit the heroin and had been through withdrawal, and that she had been right all along about that, and he just wanted her to know that he knew. He hoped she was doing well and, again, that he missed her.

But she still didn't call him, and he went on with his routine and worked his way into the nightclub scene in Fort Myers Beach and fell into a smooth tempo of hanging out and dealing and meeting new people, but it felt sort of empty.

Chapter 56

Wade walked out into the parking lot of the Conlin Company's corporate headquarters and was pleased to see that the sun had come out and it was shaping up to be a nice day.

Traffic churned by out on Rockside Road and all the snow was gone. It always took Cleveland a long time to emerge from winter, and spring didn't get really nice until it was halfway to summer. He figured it was probably fifty or even fifty five degrees, which was tee shirt weather in most people's opinions. The ones he passed on his way to his car had their jackets slung over their shoulders and their greetings to him were upbeat. Everybody was happy when the weather finally turned.

He unlocked the Boxster and he was about to slide into the driver's seat when a sharp popping sound split the air and he found himself ducking into the car so fast that he dropped his briefcase on the pavement. He crouched there for a second or two, his heart pounding, but nothing else happened. A truck's load had shifted, or something had fallen off of one out on Rockside, that was all. Conlin employees, salesmen and office workers, continued heading into and out of the gray, modern building, off to lunch or coming back from it, or on various errands. Nobody but him had reacted very much to the noise.

He straightened in the seat, embarrassed, and deliberately slowed his breathing, hoping no one had noticed. He realized once again that he was on edge and he wondered if he would ever be the same again.

His sense of things being out of sorts had persisted for weeks now, since the day Bobby and Allie had come to him and he had called the gangster. The feeling of looming disaster was always there. Sometimes it was dialed down very low, but it only took a loud noise or a prolonged glance from someone he didn't know to raise his anxiety. His fight or flight response had never returned to its baseline and it sapped his energy and disturbed his sleep. He knew that psychologists called what he was feeling "hypervigilance" and he supposed he was having some post traumatic stress. But he also recalled a line from a song Allie had told him about, something about how being paranoid doesn't mean nobody's after you.

When his father had died he had a period of heart pounding emotional distress, the sense that he was ensnared in awful events which he was helpless to control. This was similar. Although he felt that he had put the gangster in a box and the threat had been contained, the knowledge that there were murderous people out there who could still do something violent to his loved ones was oppressive and frightening.

Just as bad was the moral quandary he had been put in. His natural impulse was to go to the police and tell them exactly what was going on. He had detailed information on this MS-13 group, including their membership. There was probably enough evidence to convict some of them of serious crimes, including murder and drug trafficking. He had this evidence in his hands but he could not act on it, and so he was complicit in letting them remain at large. But turning them in meant opening his brother to criminal prosecution as well, and Bobby, too, and possibly even himself. Would a prosecutor believe that he had nothing to do with the deal in New York? Certainly a circumstantial case could be made against him. Getting it sorted out would mean public exposure of the entire mess and that his world had shifted. He had hoped that reaching an agreement with this Cesar person would allow them all to move on and put this chapter of their lives behind them, but it continued to haunt him. He had told Amanda in very general terms what had happened. He said that Timmy had gotten into trouble with some bad people over drugs, that they had tried to involve Allie and that Bobby had stopped them, and that he himself had talked to the people and gotten their commitment to stop. She was duly alarmed but he worked hard to reassure her that, while it had been a nasty episode and he was very distressed with Tim over it, they had nothing to fear. He knew he was minimizing it to her, and he felt bad about that, too. She was not pleased and urged him to go to the police, but he assured her that wasn't necessary, that everything was resolved. He hoped it was true.

He told his mother a toned down variety of the same story, and predictably she minimized Tim's wrongdoing. She was sure it had to be a misunderstanding. Wade insisted that she be aware that it was not a misunderstanding, and that Tim was culpable. He asked her to also be aware of any unusual people in the neighborhood, and to call him at once if she was concerned. She was sure she wouldn't be, and he had difficulty containing his exasperation with her.

As a precaution, he helped Allie line up another apartment on the other side of Kent from her present one, and he and Bobby had gone down there and helped her move immediately. Bobby paid for her expenses, paying off the old lease and coming up with the first two months' rent on the new place and renting a trailer for the day.

The two of them spent a lot of time together that day, hooking the trailer to Amanda's Jeep and driving down to Kent together, loading and hauling boxes and Allie's minimal furniture, lurching in tandem with her couch and china cabinet and bed first down and then up stairs to get her safely relocated.

They talked quite a bit during the drive down and back, and Wade found that he liked Bobby. He was a straightforward guy, demonstrably brave and loyal, and he was fiercely committed to making a new life for himself. He was clearly intelligent as well, and his relationship with Allie was emotionally intimate but surprisingly innocent.

"We're very close," Bobby told him at one point during the drive home. "But not on all levels, if you know what I mean. I like her a lot but we're going slow." Wade hadn't expected that and was pleased by it.

Bobby had joined his father's business as a partner and he had called Wade several times since the move to ask his opinion on financial and organizational matters, which Wade had offered to advise him on if he wanted him to. This whole aspect of the situation, Bobby's growing relationship with Allie and his renewed personal and professional life, was a positive note, something good which had unexpectedly arisen from a bad situation. They saw each other for Sunday dinner at Harriet's twice in a month, and everyone in the family had come to accept Bobby and Allie as a couple.

Little Wade liked his tattoos, which Bobby kept generally covered but which caught the boy's eye anyway. Wade and Amanda were a little nervous about that, but Bobby did his part by downplaying them and redirecting the child's interest whenever it came up.

"Do you wish you hadn't gotten them?" Wade asked him once.

"No, they're me," Bobby said. "I am who I have been, and that's okay. But we grow up, too, if we're lucky." And Wade couldn't disagree with that.

The matter of what happened in the woods outside of Ravenna went unspoken in the larger scheme of things. No body had ever been reported being found in the woods near the arsenal and that was fine; it made it easier to ignore. Wade figured the gangsters had probably disposed of it and he assumed that Bobby thought so, too.

But Wade thought about the killing from time to time and he felt sure it weighed upon Bobby. The idea of actually killing someone had never seriously entered Wade's mind, and he found it an awful prospect. He and Amanda and Little Wade went to church on an irregular basis and he viewed homicide as most people would, as a terrible tragedy and a moral transgression of the highest order. He secretly looked for some tangible mark of Cain on Bobby but never really saw it. He came to accept that Bobby had really had no choice when he had killed the gangster, that it was either him or the other guy, and the other guy fully intended to kill him if he could. It was like what soldiers faced in combat. The difference was that it happened in the context of a criminal conspiracy which Bobby had participated in.

And now Wade was involved in a conspiracy of silence regarding criminal matters, and he had no compass for dealing with such a thing. Would he also kill someone if he was forced to? He was physical person, had played contact sports, but this was beyond his experience. He supposed that if he absolutely had to, he'd do whatever was necessary in order to save himself and his loved ones, as Bobby had.

He was driving into Cleveland along I-77, listening to blues on the radio and calmed finally from the noise in the parking lot. Only time would tell them all if this problem was past. Tim was still in hiding but he assumed that they would have a day of reckoning eventually and he rehearsed it in his mind many times. His life had been permanently altered by his brother's actions and he wanted to confront him about it, to tell him how wrong this was, and how hurtful.

Maybe he would feel some closure then, and the anxiety would diminish. In the meantime he was struggling a little to do his job and stay focused in his day to day life. He hoped things would get better and he could feel healthy again.

Chapter 57

Timmy walked along Estero Boulevard in the midday sun and thought about maybe changing hotels. He had quite a bit of cash now and it was probably a good idea to relocate and make his trail a little harder to follow. He considered the various places along the beach where he could go, and some of them were very nice resort-like establishments and he'd be more comfortable in one of them.

Coming to this area had been a very good plan and he congratulated himself for thinking of it. He felt much better and had put a few pounds back on. He got some Tommy Bahama clothes at a local boutique and he wanted to start dressing better again, but he'd look odd in them around the low-rent place he was in now. He had to admit, he felt pretty healthy.

At one of the bars he frequented he'd hooked up with a bartender, a young and pretty honey blond named Miranda with a lithe figure and a taste for coke. She was from Pittsburgh and had been hanging around down in Florida for a year because she liked the climate and the easy lifestyle. She noticed him when he started looking and feeling better and had gotten a haircut and she talked to him whenever she had a chance to. He'd eventually been to her place twice, a small apartment a few blocks back from the beach which she shared with two roommates, and had had sex with her each time in her tiny bedroom with its twin bed and a creaky box spring, the ceiling fan lazily rotating above them. She was nuts about him and the cocaine and he went out of his way to avoid her most of the time because he had things to do and didn't plan on being here forever.

He was scanning the street ahead as he approached the motel because he didn't want her ambushing him and demanding his time the way she had a couple of days before. She knew he was staying somewhere along the strip but he'd deftly avoided telling her where.

When he saw the big black Cadillac parked alongside the palm trees in front of his place he slowed and took notice, because nobody who was staying there had a ride like that. It was a shiny new Cadillac STS four door and he saw the Ohio plates immediately, and looked closer and saw the Cuyahoga County sticker on them, too.

Cleveland. What the hell? What did this mean, he wondered.

The driver's door opened and Glendy stepped out into the street, looking at him across the way with a solemn gaze. She was wearing white shorts and sandals and a sky blue silk blouse and Timmy thought that she looked like a wealthy young heiress or a model or something but he knew who she really was, and the thought made him smile. He walked across to her and stopped just short of touching her, searching her face for some clue as to what she intended. She smiled tentatively at him, then took his hand in hers and said, "Well, aren't you glad to see me?"

They fell into each other's embrace and he kissed her, the cars going wide around them as they stood in the street. He pulled back a little and said, "What are you doing here?"

"I came back," she told him. "Come on, let's get my bags into your room and I'll tell you all about it." And just like that, oddly, they were back together as if no time had passed at all.

He led the way up the stairs, lugging a large suitcase while she carried two bags behind him, and she grabbed his ass halfway up. He turned back to her and she was laughing, and so did he, and they went into his room together. They set down the luggage and reached for each other and landed on the bed.

Timmy thought that she was the most beautiful thing he had ever seen and realized how deeply he had missed her. They made love urgently, and then again slowly and gently, taking their time, and before long it was dark outside and they were laying naked in each others' arms, at ease and happy.

He finally asked her, "What the hell happened? Where did you get the car?"

She looked up at him, her head on his chest, and said, "I've gotta tell you this whole story. You're not gonna believe it."

She had gone back to New York with Leroy and when they got there he moved her into an apartment in Harlem, a very nice and well-furnished place, but he didn't stay there himself. He had a second apartment a block over and that's where he lived and had an office, too. Her place was where he kept his inventory, and right away she wasn't happy living in an apartment full of heroin.

"So, how was the romance?" Timmy asked, stoically, prepared for whatever she wanted to tell him about it.

She shrugged. "He was okay. He was really into himself, mostly. We had some fun but he was always rushing around doing business. He had this bunch of guys who'd come around and get product and I didn't like them coming to my place, but that's how we did it. Leroy would call me from the office and tell me what to give the guy when he showed up, and that's what I did. They weren't all stylin' like Leroy; some of them were real street-looking gangstas. But none of them bothered me because they knew I was with Leroy, even though not much was happening in that department."

"Really?" Timmy wanted to know.

"Seriously," she said, and he figured he'd probably never know the truth of it.

"So what changed?" he asked.

"After a couple of weeks I was sitting in there one day, feeling a little bit caged up, you know? But I didn't want to be out strolling around in Harlem, even though there's all kinds of people there. I kept thinking about those Mafia guys. It's probably paranoid but I was worried about them spotting me."

"Didn't you do things? You know, like go out with him and stuff?"

"We went out to dinner a couple of times, and that was nice. But I got the feeling I was like a trophy or something. He treated me good but it was starting to suck."

Timmy eased out of bed and got a bottle of Merlot off of the dresser and poured them each a glass and sat down next to her again. "Go on," he said.

"So anyway, on this particular day at about three in the afternoon I hear 'pop pop pop' from the street outside. I look out the window

251

and one of the guys I would give product to is limping away, blood all down his leg, and some really crazy looking black guys are driving off, looking back him. I was freaking, 'cause somebody did a drive-by right in front of my place. Then in a few minutes Leroy calls and wants to know if I'm alright. I say, 'What the hell, Leroy. What was that all about?' And he tells me that the Dominicans just shot up one of his guys."

"How did they get on to him?" Timmy wanted to know.

"That's what I asked him. He hemmed and hawed and then told me that Tonya got wind of him having me there and ratted him out to the Dominicans."

"Tonya? From Promises?" Timmy asked.

Glendy nodded. "Un-huh. Seems she had jealousy issues. So now I'm really freaking because she could tell the Gambinos I'm around, too, and then I'm screwed."

"So you left?"

She shook her head. "Not yet. About an hour later I'm thinking about what to do and there's a big explosion. Like, 'Blammo!' The whole frigging building shook. I look out the window and there's a bunch of smoke coming up from behind the building across the street and I know that's where Leroy lives. Then the phone rings in a few minutes and it's Andre, one of his guys, and he tells me the Dominicans just blew Leroy up. He's alive but he's going to the hospital and he's all messed up."

"Wow," Timmy said. "You're lucky you got out okay."

She smiled widely at him, her eyes full of glee, and said, "I did better than that. The place had eight kilos of heroin sitting around, including what he got from you."

Timmy sat up abruptly, spilling his wine. "You grabbed the smack?"

She turned up the grin another notch and said, "No, you dumb fuck. I flushed it all down the toilet. Each fucking one of those fucking keys. It took me forty-five minutes."

He stared at her, dumbstruck. "Are you kidding?"

She gazed steadily at him and her smile dropped off by degrees.

Finally she was looking at him firmly, not an iota of compromise in her expression. "I would not come anywhere near you with heroin. I hate that damn stuff. It kills people. I destroyed it and the world's a better place for it."

"But, Glendy," he said, anguished. "That was like one point three million dollars worth of smack."

She got up, her wine glass between her fingers, and walked naked to her bags on the floor. She picked up one of the bags and overturned it on the bed. Money spilled out, stacks of bills secured with rubber bands.

"He also had some cash there. A half million. So it wasn't a wasted trip after all."

Chapter 58

They moved up the beach a little to one of the nicer resorts, settling into a suite with a king bed and a separate sitting room. They had a nice view out over the water and watched some beautiful sunsets, and lounged by the pool in the afternoons working on their tans and sipping tropical drinks. With a half million dollars you could do this for a long time, and they didn't feel much need to do anything else.

Timmy was amused to find out that Glendy had run back to Cleveland after things went to hell in Manhattan the second time. She'd been lugging the bag full of money with her wherever she went, afraid to risk losing it by hiding it somewhere.

They were sitting in the pastel colored restaurant at the resort, enjoying a late breakfast from the buffet and watching the tourists wend their way among the palm trees to the pool area beyond the window glass. Waiters and waitresses in black pants and white shirts scurried here and there, delivering orange juice and coffee and picking up used dishes. They'd been there for a week already and were going to go shopping again this afternoon, but they'd seen most of what the area had to offer.

"How long do you want to stay here?" Timmy asked her.

She looked away from the view outside and regarded him with confusion. "Are you tired of this already?"

He shrugged. "A little, maybe. I was hanging out here for a while before you came back. It's nice being here with you but we can go wherever we want. Maybe we should move on."

"Where do you want to go?" she asked.

"Well, we probably ought to get your money put away somewhere. It doesn't make sense to haul it around; we're just setting ourselves up for getting robbed or something."

She shifted in her seat and her look was puzzled. "Yours, too, right? Shouldn't we put all of it somewhere so it's safe but we can get at it with our ATM cards or something when we want to?"

Timmy nodded. "Yeah. We need to maybe put most of it in safety deposit boxes but deposit a bunch of it into a few bank accounts so we can use it to pay bills, credit cards and that kind of thing. It'll make it easier than doing everything with cash and drawing attention to ourselves."

"And yours is in Cleveland, right?" she asked.

"Yes. I sent it to Cleveland before we left New York. It's safe but we'll need to go get it."

"So we should probably go to Cleveland and get it set up the way we want it, right?"

Timmy thought it over for a moment. "I don't want to risk running into these Mexicans who are looking for me. But you didn't have any problems when you were there, did you?"

Glendy shook her head. "I didn't see anybody except my family. I stayed away from the Pony and I sure didn't call Bobby or June or anyone."

Glendy had slipped into town in a rented car and leased a new apartment in Lakewood, moving her things with one of her brothers and shutting off her old utilities and phone service. Then she went to the Cadillac dealer on W. 117th Street and paid cash for the new black STS, an indulgence she felt she'd earned by risking death once again in the Big Apple.

"We're gonna have to declare a little of this money to the IRS, call it gambling proceeds or something and pay taxes on it," Timmy told her. "Otherwise somebody will start looking at us for paying off two cars with cash."

"Do we?" she asked him. "That doesn't seem fair."

"Oh yeah," he assured her. "That's how they got Al Capone. We'll need to send in some tax money at some point. Maybe I can talk to an accountant."

"You could talk to Wade," she suggested.

He laughed. "As long as he thinks it's about stamps, I guess I could."

"And we still have the place in the alley in Playhouse Square," she reminded him. "I checked with the landlord and paid for another couple of months' rent, just so it would be there if we need a hideout."

"I'm sure my old Lakewood apartment is gone," he said ruefully. "They probably threw out all my stuff."

She laughed. "We'll buy more."

They ate in silence for a minute as the hotel guests wandered by and a crowd gathered by the pool. There were a lot of young children splashing around and it was getting noisy out there. Timmy thought about the girl he'd met, Miranda, and how he had gone to the bar where she worked the night after Glendy arrived and told her he was leaving town. She was upset and tried to get him to promise to write to her or to call. Now he was a little concerned that they'd run into her somewhere around town and there'd be a scene with Glendy. He was ready to leave.

"Where do you want to go after Cleveland?" he finally asked her.

"We can get our money squirreled away there and keep the two places rented and only come back every few months to move the money into checking accounts so we can get at it. What about New York?"

She looked at him wide-eyed. "Are you serious? With the Mafia and maybe Leroy looking for us? It's all concrete canyons anyway. Too crowded for me. We can visit sometime in the future, but we ought to stay away from there for a while, if you ask me."

He nodded. "It doesn't seem like it right now, but we're gonna need more money someday. We've got maybe one point two million or so, but if we just spend it all we'll go through it in a few years. We should think about getting more."

She put her fork down and leaned in toward him, a grin starting on her face. "That's what I like to hear," she said. "What do you have in mind?"

"If things have cooled down with the Mexicans, we ought to think about scoring a kilo of coke and dealing it out."

A waitress was walking past and he stopped her and asked to

borrow a pen. He began jotting figures on the margin of the newspaper he'd brought to the table.

"If I can score a key for twenty thou, and sell it in hundred dollar grams, that's four hundred eighty grams so it's forty eight thousand. We clear twenty eight. If we do that two or three times a year we keep most of our money intact and still live the way we want to."

Glendy thought about it. "So we use our money to invest in coke."

"Only a little of it. Twenty thou. And we keep our cash flow going."

"We'd have to do it in Cleveland. That's where we have contacts."

"Well, there's also here and New York. We'll avoid New York. It was easy getting set up in both places because there's a market. We can do the same thing wherever we feel like going."

"So basically we'd be millionaires living wherever we feel like and dealing a little coke for fun."

He nodded. "That's about right. And we'd go back to Cleveland now and then to shuffle the money, visit, whatever."

She looked out the window for a minute and then back at him.

"I like it," she said. "When do you want to go back?"

Chapter 59

Harriet Thomas was in her kitchen rolling out cookie dough. Little Wade would be over in an hour with Amanda and they were going to make cookies together. She had Tchaikovsky on the stereo in the living room and she hummed along with the heavy melodies as she pushed the rolling pin, flattening the dough.

The doorbell rang and Harriet put down the rolling pin and rinsed her hands quickly at the sink. She walked through the kitchen and the living room to the front door and saw Tim and his girlfriend through the glass windows flanking the door, standing on the porch.

She threw the door open and embraced him.

"Hi, Mom," Timmy said, bending down to hug her, his words muffled in her shoulder.

"Tim, you've been away so long!" she exclaimed. "I've missed you so much!"

"I've missed you too, Mom. You remember Glendy, right?"

Harriet let go of him and gave Glendy a quick squeeze as well.

"Hello, Glendy. How are you?"

"We're both fine, Mom," Timmy told her.

Harriet took his arm and guided them both into the house and closed the door. She stepped back and looked at them and they did, indeed, appear to be fine. Better than that, even. Timmy was dressed in a tasteful tweed sport jacket and slacks, and Glendy wore what appeared to be a designer pantsuit in dark blue and heels.

They were tanned and healthy looking and smiling.

"It's so good to see you," she said. "How did you get here?"

Timmy pointed outside and said, "We're in Glendy's new car."

Harriet peeked back out the window and saw a gleaming black sedan in her driveway. "Is that a Cadillac?" she asked them.

"Let's sit down, Mom," Timmy suggested. Harriet turned down the stereo and settled into the easy chair and Timmy and Glendy took the couch.

"I heard that you were in Florida," she said to them.

"Yes, we were, but we're back for a while," he replied. "I thought I'd better do some fence mending and come see you. I'm sorry I've been so out of touch."

She waved her hands dismissively. "I'm just glad that you're here. Would you like something to drink?" And she hopped back up and hurried into the kitchen. "I have some pop, Coke and Sprite. Or lemonade. Or I can make some coffee."

"Coke's fine, Mom," Timmy answered.

"Me too, Mrs. Thomas," Glendy said. "Thank you."

Harriet came back in with two glasses and napkins and handed them to them. "Will you be in town long?"

"I'm not sure. We have some things we need to do."

"Well, I should tell you that your brother wants to talk with you pretty badly. Have you spoken with him lately?"

Timmy shook his head. "Not since he was in New York. Why?"

"He's told me some concerning things, Tim. I think you should talk to him right away. I don't like mentioning this but there are concerns about, well, drugs, and some bad people. Somebody went to Allie's apartment."

Timmy almost choked on his Coke but controlled it. He saw Glendy's eyes go wide but she said nothing.

"What?" Timmy said to Harriet. "I'm sure there's some sort of misunderstanding. Who went to Allie's place?"

"You'll have to ask Wade. Or Bobby. Allie and Bobby are dating each other."

Timmy shook his head in confusion. Allie and Bobby? He exchanged a glance with Glendy and he knew they'd have to find out what was going on before they went any further.

"Excuse me, I'm going to try to reach Bobby," he said, and got up and walked into the kitchen. He dialed Bobby's cell phone but got his voice mail and didn't leave a message. Next he called Wade at work, the number posted alongside Harriet's phone. He got past his secretary and Wade picked up at once.

"Where the hell are you?" Wade asked him, and he was clearly angry.

Timmy eased into one of the kitchen chairs and said, "Nice talking to you, too. I'm at Mom's."

"Tim, I know about what you were really doing in New York." His voice was low and Timmy figured he didn't want anyone overhearing this. "The people you stole the drugs from killed Bobby's roommate. Did you know that?" He was trying to control his emotions but Timmy heard that rage and despair in his voice.

"What do you know about anything?" Timmy asked him.

"I know these same people broke into Allie's apartment and almost killed her!" Wade's voice was louder. "If Bobby hadn't gotten to her they might have killed her, too! What have you done?"

Timmy deliberately kept his tone casual, knowing that his mother and Glendy would be straining to hear the conversation from the next room. "Is she okay?"

"Aside from being taped up and molested, yes, she'd pretty much okay. You can thank Bobby for that. I certainly have." Wade's breath was coming in gasps and Timmy thought maybe he could have a stroke or something.

"Calm down," he said.

"Don't you dare tell me to calm down. You've put your entire family in danger. It's been horrible."

"So, these people are still around, or what?" he asked him. "Are the cops involved?"

"I couldn't call the police. Bobby had to, uh, do something to one of these people. Also, you've got me implicated in this mess. You used my hotel room for your damned deal."

"So, what about these people?" Timmy asked him again.

"They backed off. We have some records of theirs and they don't want us going to the police. How could you do this to us? This is the most selfish and irresponsible thing I've ever heard of!"

Timmy exhaled. "Look, Wade, I'm sorry if there was a misunderstanding."

Wade raged, "You jerk! You're just saying that because Mom's probably close by. There is no misunderstanding. Everything is perfectly clear. You almost got everyone you love killed. I will not forgive you for this."

"I'm sorry," Timmy told him, his voice level and measured. "It was a mistake. I'm glad it's under control."

"We hope it's under control. Time will tell. In the meantime, maybe you ought to stay away from here. You caused us all tremendous problems."

"I won't be around for very long, I can tell you that. I'm sorry. I hope Amanda and Little Wade are doing okay."

Wade slammed down the telephone and Timmy quietly hung up. He went back into the living room and his mother and Glendy were looking at him expectantly.

"I think we got that straightened out," he said. "As I figured, there was some misunderstanding."

Harriet was nodding at him. "Oh good," she said. "I thought you two only needed to talk." But her face was strained and he knew she wasn't convinced.

He sat down and took a sip of coke and Harriet said, "Amanda and Little Wade are due here soon. I know they'll be glad to see you."

Timmy stood up again and replied, "I really need to get an oil change for my car, Mom. We need to get going. I'll bring it back in a day or so, though, if it's okay with you."

Harriet and Glendy stood, too. "Yes, yes, of course. I'm glad you'll be here for a little while. We have so much catching up to do."

They took their drinks into the kitchen and hugged goodbye.

Timmy got the Mustang's keys and they went out into the garage and he pushed the button and raised the garage door. Glendy headed for the Cadillac.

"Goodbye, Mom. See you soon," he told her. And she stood watching as they both backed out and drove off down the street, the sky overcast but the leaves coming out on the trees, spring pretty much in full bloom.

He followed Glendy out of Rocky River and into Lakewood and over to her new apartment, which was in a newer building with garage space behind it. Glendy had rented a garage and she pulled up in front of it and opened the door and Timmy pulled the Mustang inside. Glendy got a large duffle bag out of the Cadillac and went into the garage behind him and closed the door.

Timmy shut off the engine and climbed out and went back and opened the trunk. With Glendy watching he peeled back the trunk liner and she saw the bundles of money taped neatly all over the inside of the trunk. He began pulling the money loose and putting it into the duffle bag, and she helped him.

"I did this after the deal and before I joined you and Wade for dinner. Bobby thought I left it under the bed but I snuck it back out and took it to the parking garage and taped in under the liner. Hardly took me any time at all."

She was shaking her head. "That was pretty sneaky."

"Yeah," he said. "If Wade knew he transported $725,000 in drug profits back here for me, he'd really be upset." And he laughed.

Chapter 60

Luis Acevedo pulled up in front of the antique shop in Kamm's Corners and immediately noticed the car that had just backed out and was in the process of driving away. It wasn't surprising that he spotted it because he had spent plenty of time looking at it in the past. It was Timmy Thomas's red Mustang, no doubt about it. The license plate confirmed it.

Luis got out of his Chevy and stood watching the car move off into the traffic beyond the intersection of Lorain and Berea Roads, heading west in the direction of Fairview Hospital. It was a pleasant afternoon, sunny and warm, and the usual weekday traffic swirled through the area, but Luis saw only the Mustang, and he strained to catch a glimpse of the driver, his unseen enemy. There was a guy driving, for sure. The hair looked sort of curly. He knew it was him.

Luis found himself trembling and clenched all of his muscles, then released them and took a deep breath. He had never actually seen Thomas, but he thought about him all the time. This guy had stolen their property, and then Hector had died for it. He had to admit that Hector had been asking for it, you can only screw up so many times, but he had liked Hector and he was sorry about what had happened.

What happened to Jaime, though, and to himself, was another matter. That fucking Bobby Fallon was a badass motherfucker and he would love a chance to try him again, preferably when the odds were even and Fallon didn't have a .45 in his face. Then they'd see who was a tough guy. But Fallon was just working for the Thomases; it was Timmy and his brother who were headlining that operation.

They were the ones who needed killing. Timmy was a sneaky bastard and they had never even spoken to him, yet here he was, in broad daylight, driving away from an MS-13 dealer's place.

Luis hitched up his baggy pants and strolled around his car and across the sidewalk and pushed open the door to the antique shop.

It was dark inside compared to the street, and the room was rather small but it was hard to tell exactly how small because it was crammed with antiques. Tables and chairs and couches covered most of the available floor space, with dressers and cabinets filling the gaps. The smell of old wood and dust was intense. Salvaged glass display cases held hundreds of pieces of old jewelry and silverware and all of it seemed randomly organized, chaos overwhelming any sense of order. It looked to him like a huge bunch of junk, and he couldn't believe anybody would pay good money for any of it.

The owner stood there behind the little desk wedged between two old tables and he looked up quickly when Luis came in. He had a brown paper bag in his hands, a small one, and he rolled the top closed and then put it inside a desk drawer as Luis approached.

"Hi, Luis," he said, but he had a nervous grin and Luis knew right away the guy was up to something.

"Hola, Jerry," Luis replied, and he gave the guy a wide smile, showing off his new white teeth that had cost so much and had been so painfully reconstructed. The guy was thin and shabby looking, like his merchandise, with gray shaggy hair and an unsettled manner.

Luis knew he was probably using some of the product he was dealing, but he wasn't sure which varieties. He was no doubt a coke head but didn't show any signs yet that he was into the smack. They wanted to keep an eye on that, because once the guy started liking that stuff his value as a dealer would diminish and they'd have to consider phasing him out.

"Hey, I just saw a friend of mine leaving here," Luis told him, still smiling. "He doing some business with you, maybe?"

Jerry was very afraid of Luis and wished he'd never gotten involved now with MS-13. Hector had been personable and everything was fine when he was the main contact. Then he didn't come around anymore and it was Jaime, and he was at least smart and on top of things and more or less reasonable, despite all those teardrop tattoos that let you know he was a killer. But now his contact was Luis, and Luis was a stupid thug who pressured him all the time to move product and came on hard at the slightest excuse, flexing his muscles and sneering at him if he wasn't ready to buy more smack when he thought he should be. He couldn't think of any way he could get out from under them, and was considering cutting his loses, grabbing up all his cash and leaving town for good.

Now Luis had come early and seen Timmy leaving and if he knew Timmy he would know there was something going on. Jerry decided it was smarter not to lie.

"Oh, you know that guy?" Jerry asked him.

"Yes, we know him," Luis said, letting him know this was an MS-13 matter, not just a personal thing, and Jerry better be straight with him.

"What's he doing here, man? You doing some business with him?"

Jerry looked down and began to putter around with papers on his desk. "Yeah, I picked up a little blow from him, you know? He has some good stuff."

"Really?" Luis asked, and he moved up closer to the desk. "How much blow you get from him?"

Jerry regarded him solemnly for a moment and then reached inside the desk and took out the paper bag. He opened it up and held it out so Luis could lean forward and see inside. There were six grams wrapped in little paper envelopes in there. Luis stood back and laughed.

"That's nothing, man," he said. "I thought maybe you buying some quantity from the guy. Why you spending good money buying grams? I sell you a pound or a key, you get all the free blow you want."

Jerry knew this but he didn't want to do any cocaine business with Luis at all. He was already in deep enough with the heroin. "Yeah, sure Luis. Thanks. I'll do that from now on."

Luis strolled around the shop touching things and picking up jewelry boxes and letter openers and looking closely at them. "You shouldn't do business with that guy. He'll screw you over. We're not big fans of his, you know?"

Jerry was nodding vigorously. "Sure, Luis. I'm glad you told me. Thanks a lot."

Luis came back to the desk and pushed Jerry's papers aside and sat down on the edge of it. "So how's the product moving? You ready for another load?"

Jerry blanched. He'd bought a pound of heroin two weeks ago, paying cash for it. He'd been dealing it to his customers around the far West Side but he still had about half of it left. "Damn, Luis," he said nervously. "That's a little sooner than I'd planned, you know?"

Luis sniffed and gazed around at the ancient pressed tin ceiling.

"I think if you can buy coke from that guy I just saw, you can buy some smack from us. Right? How about some ecstasy or some meth? We getting more of that in, too. We can take care of you."

In the end Jerry agreed to take another pound of heroin in three days, and a thousand hits of ecstasy, too. After Luis sauntered out of his shop, grinning happily, Jerry went into the back room and drank three quick shots of bourbon and did a long line of coke and after a while he felt a little better about the whole thing.

Luis went back to his car and felt his rage growing. So now Timmy Thomas was selling to their dealers. This was too fucking much. He sat behind the steering wheel and seethed. He took out his big Colt King Cobra .357 Magnum revolver and held it, rubbing it with his hands and wanting to go find Timmy and do something to settle this. He got out his cell phone and called Cesar.

"Jefe, guess who I just saw at Kamm's? Fucking Timmy Thomas. He sold the guy some coke." Luis knew his voice was shaking and he struggled to calm himself.

"How much coke?" Cesar asked him, and his voice was calm and reasonable and that just made Luis more angry.

"Six grams," he told him, and Cesar laughed the same way he had when Jerry had shown it to him.

"Don't worry about six fucking grams, bato," Cesar said. "That's hardly doing business at all."

"It's our dealer, Cesar! When do these people stop messing with us?" Luis was shouting, and people walking past the storefronts glanced over at him.

"Calm down, man," Cesar said sharply. "It's nothing. Stay the fuck away from him. You know what the deal is. We can't afford to do anything about it right now. That's just the way it is. You got that?"

Luis took a few seconds to answer and he knew he was making Cesar angry but he was beginning not to care. "I've got that," he told him. "But I don't like it."

"Well, you know what, amigo? You don't have to like it. You just have to do it." Then Cesar hung up on him.

Luis sat there a little longer, then started his car and pulled out and headed for his next stop, further east down Lorain. He found that he was having a very hard time accepting this situation.

He made a delivery in Cleveland, five pounds of very good marijuana, and hung around with the dealer for a while and smoked a little with him. He was a homeboy like Luis and they understood each other, not like these fucking cold weather Anglos he had to do business with most of the time. When he came out of the guy's place it was dusk and the rush hour traffic was in full swing. He made a right turn instead of a left, though, pulling out of the guy's street, and found himself moving steadily westward with the commuters on Lorain. He told himself he wasn't sure why he did that, but he had a nice buzz going and he didn't feel like heading east, down to their neighborhood and the store on Denison.

He loafed along in the heavy traffic listening to the radio, music from home, until he found himself in Fairview Park. He angled north over to Center Ridge Road and continued into the setting sun for a while, then cut north a few more times and realized he was cruising into Mrs. Thomas's neighborhood in Rocky River.

He knew Cesar wouldn't like this but he was relaxed and coasting along and he didn't care too much about that. He drove past the Thomas house and saw a guy getting into a little blue Porsche there and so he eased down the street and then came back around and followed him as he pulled out and headed further west into Westlake.

Traffic was still heavy but it had eased enough that Luis could keep an eye on the car even though the guy was driving like he was in a fucking race or something. Soon it was so dark that he had to get closer to the guy in order to be sure it was him but that was okay, the guy wouldn't notice him now. They edged up Clague Road in a long parade of cars and then took off west on Hilliard and then the guy swung into a fancy subdivision, a big brick entryway in front with elaborate plants and landscaping.

The Porsche turned into the driveway of a big brick house on a large lot and the garage door started up. Luis drove slowly past, watching as the guy pulled into the garage. He continued down the street for a block and then turned around and came back. He stopped and jotted down the address. It was a very nice house, a rich man's home, and it figured that these sneaky Thomases would have a place like that. Then he took off again, headed back to Cleveland.

This was okay, he told himself. Nobody saw him, and now they had a little more information on the Thomases, just in case.

Chapter 61

Wade was trimming bushes in Harriet's front yard with her pruning shears when Timmy and Glendy drove into the driveway in the Mustang and the Cadillac. He turned to look at them and put down the shears and wiped his hands on his jeans. It was a balmy Sunday afternoon and he'd been looking forward to the pot roast his mother was making. But now his mood was soured.

Bobby and Allie were over, too, and the running joke had been that Wade would do the yard work because it was Bobby's day off. In return Bobby promised to fill in for Wade and do any financial advising anyone might ask for. So he was sipping a beer on the back porch and talking to Amanda and Allie while Harriet bustled around her kitchen with Little Wade helping her. It had been a pleasant afternoon until now.

Timmy and Glendy got out of the cars and looked at him, their faces blank. They were nicely dressed in designer sportswear, an affluent young couple out for a Sunday drive. It was the first time he had seen them since New York. Then Timmy stepped forward toward him and gave a half-hearted wave.

"Hi, Wade," he said. "How you doing?"

Wade opened his mouth to respond, not sure what would come out, when Bobby came around the side of the house. He walked up to the cars and regarded the two of them for a few seconds, then grinned a little.

"Bonnie and Clyde," he said. "Whaddaya know."

Timmy shuffled his feet sheepishly and said, "Hey, man, don't make it worse than it is already."

Glendy came forward and threw her arms around him. "Nice to see you, Bobby. You look different."

"Bad?" he asked her, leaning back against her embrace so that she could study him.

She shook her head. "No, good." She turned to Wade, releasing Bobby, and said, "It's nice to see you." Then she looked at the ground and nobody said anything, the silence hanging between them.

Bobby broke it and said, "You staying for dinner? Your mom's got something good cooking."

Timmy shook his head. "No. I'm dropping the Mustang off. We're going out of town again for a while. I didn't know all of you were here."

Wade laughed ruefully. "Awkward, huh?" he asked him. "You didn't want to see us, and I don't blame you."

Timmy and Glendy were staring at the ground and Glendy's face was red.

"I told you I'd stay away, Wade," Timmy said. "I'm trying to keep that promise."

Wade snorted derisively. "Well, I'm sure Mom wants to see you. Everybody's here so you may as well make the rounds and do your caring relative impersonation." He turned his back on him and carried the shears into the garage.

Bobby led Timmy and Glendy around the house to the back porch and they went up the steps and into the screened enclosure where Amanda regarded them grimly for a second, then relented and embraced them.

"Nice to see you," she told them, and it was clear that she was trying to be decent about it, but it felt uncomfortable anyway.

Allie hopped up and hugged Timmy hard for a while. Her eyes were wet when she let him go and said, "I know you didn't mean to hurt anybody. I just hope you get your act together."

Timmy was embarrassed and Glendy kept her head up but they looked like they would rather be a thousand miles away at that moment. Then Harriet and Little Wade came out onto the porch and they were genuinely happy to see Timmy.

Harriet hugged him and thanked him for calling her so often over the past two weeks while they were in town. Whatever the trouble had been, she was glad that he was whole, she said, and hadn't been harmed. Little Wade jumped around and pulled on his uncle's arms and began tugging him into the house.

"Uncle Tim! You've got to see the new racer Dad bought me! It's so cool!"

Timmy allowed himself to be dragged inside. Harriet hugged Glendy, too, and said, "Please have a seat, Glendy. Would you like a refreshment?"

Glendy sat down in a folding chair and the others did the same.

"No, thank you, Mrs. Thomas. We have to be going soon."

"Tim said you were traveling to Maine. Is that right?"

Glendy nodded. "We want to take advantage of the nice weather. I have a friend in Portland and we thought we'd see Bar Harbor, maybe do a whale watch, that sort of thing."

Bobby peered at her over his beer bottle and said, "Yeah, I hear they've got some active night life in those towns."

Glendy shot him a quick look of displeasure but it was gone in an instant. "Really?" she remarked. "We'll have to check that out."

Harriet leaned in close to her and lowered her voice. "Wade's in the garage, right?"

Bobby and Glendy looked around and Bobby said, "Last time I saw him."

"Well," Harriet said, smiling conspiratorially, "we're planning a surprise birthday party for him next month. I hope you and Tim will be back for it. I don't want my boys separated by bad feelings and I hope it will give everyone a chance to have a nice time together. Please tell me you'll try to come."

Glendy smiled back at her and said, "Of course. Thank you very much for asking us. If you can't reach Timmy on his cell phone, try mine." She got a note card and a pen out of her little sequined purse and jotted down the number. Handing it to her, she said, "You can count on us."

Timmy and Little Wade came back onto the porch and Timmy said, "We ought to go, Glendy. We want to cover some good distance before it gets dark."

Everyone stood again and hugged and Timmy told his mother, "Thanks for keeping the car for me again, Mom."

They all walked around the house and Wade was still out front.

He was gazing at the Cadillac and shaking his head slowly. "Nice car, Glendy," he said to her.

She looked at him evenly, not shrinking from his implied criticism, and said, "Thanks, Wade. I enjoy it."

Timmy walked up to Wade and stuck out his hand. Wade hesitated, then grasped it but there was no enthusiasm in the gesture.

"Mom's watching the Mustang for me while we're gone again. Please use it if you need it. It's just going to waste otherwise."

Wade considered a retort but then simply nodded and said, "Sure."

As they got into the Cadillac, Timmy driving, Bobby leaned against the door and said to him so no one else could hear, "Watch yourself. Being a white drunk on coke isn't all it's cracked up to be. You've made out, why not cool it and stay alive for a while?"

Timmy said, "Thanks for saving Allie. I've wanted to tell you that."

Then he laughed. "But jeez, I never thought I'd see you get so boring."

Bobby stepped back and shrugged. "Good luck," he told him.

They all stood watching as the Cadillac backed out of the driveway, and Harriet, Allie and Little Wade waved to them until they turned the corner and were gone from sight. Then they all trooped into the house and got ready for dinner.

Chapter 62

Dr. Brian Pomeroy waited for traffic to clear and pulled out of his driveway on Lake Road in Bay Village in the red Mustang and headed east toward Rocky River. He'd finished working his day shift in the emergency room, a pretty routine tour, and he was ready to take care of some errands. He thought the Mustang was fun to drive; maybe he'd consider buying one sometime. But for now, his Saab was ready to be picked up and he was happy enough with that.

It was nice of Wade and his mother to let him use the Mustang for a couple of days while he got some much needed work done on the eight-year-old Saab. They always did an outstanding job with it at Block's Automotive on Detroit in Rocky River. His car wasn't old by Swedish automotive standards, but it was always nice to get something new. Kathleen had her Jeep, just like the one Amanda Thomas had, but he agreed with Wade that it was good for a guy to have something sporty to drive around in. Erin was only three and he didn't need much seating room in his own vehicle.

It had gotten surprisingly chilly overnight, a late spring surprise, and Brian had the heater on low and was wearing his leather bomber jacket as he headed for Harriet Thomas's house to drop off the Mustang and get a lift to Block's with Wade. It was four thirty on a weekday afternoon and rush hour hadn't started yet. He was hoping to retrieve his car and then get back home before he got caught in the inevitable traffic.

Luis was cruising around Rocky River and he was drunk. He'd spent the first half of the day sleeping and when he woke up he went to the store on Denison to see what was going on. Cesar had been short with him and that made him angry.

Ever since he had given Cesar the note with the Thomas guy's address on it there had been tension between them. Cesar felt strongly that he should not have been following the guy around and should have never gone near Mrs. Thomas's house at all. Then he completely reversed himself and was chuckling gleefully when he entered the information in the records he kept at the store, pleased that he had some new intelligence on these people.

Luis said to him, "So which is it, Jefe? Are you happy I got this information or are you mad that I followed the guy?"

Cesar was a real prick and told him, "You are a fuckup and you disobeyed me. You're lucky I am having a good day." Then he showed Manuel the note and was bragging about it like he came up with it himself, for Christ's sake.

So today it was more of the same, Cesar disrespecting him, and so he went over to a friend's house and they drank mezcal and beer all afternoon and did some coke, too. The guy's wife was due home from work soon and Luis didn't want to be around for that because his friend was even drunker than he was and the old lady would probably be all unhappy about it. So he did a last shot of mezcal and grabbed a beer for the road and lurched out to his Chevy and took off.

Now he was driving around the west suburbs and it was a good thing he was a decent driver or he'd probably get arrested for drunk driving. It was like a magnetic phenomenon, the way he got pulled to the Thomas house whenever he went out cruising around. He didn't even have to think about it, he just found himself drawn there. Amazing. It was like God wanted him to go there or something.

He drove west out Detroit Road all the way to Clague and then turned north and hit Lake and turned east again, heading back into River. He was cruising along a little slowly, not wanting to attract attention from any cops who might be around, and he was listening to some cheerful music and singing, minding his own business, when the Mustang appeared in his rearview mirror.

He just couldn't believe it. He looked carefully at it, couldn't read the license number because it was reversed in his mirror but he thought it looked right. There was a guy driving, brown curly hair.

Maybe he'd dyed it. Luis felt his heart speed up. Timmy Thomas was right behind him. Heaven had maybe sent him to this place, right here and now. It was too strong a sign to be ignored. But he thought briefly about Cesar and decided he better be careful about doing anything. He was uncertain about what to do, but he didn't want to let this opportunity get past him.

He slowed down some more and the Mustang's turn signal came on and the car swung out into the other lane, no traffic coming, to pass him. As it pulled level with his car he looked over, trembling to finally see his enemy eye to eye, and the guy was wearing a brown leather bomber jacket just like that asshole they killed said he did.

The guy turned his head quickly and gave him an irritated glance and then swung past him and in front of him. Now Luis could read the license plate and it was the right number.

Luis felt immense rage boil through him as he registered the implied insult in the guy's look. This guy had just disrespected him, acting like he owned the fucking road and treating Luis like he didn't know how to drive. The arrogance of the man was beyond Luis's tolerance. He felt himself go cold as he reached into the back seat and pulled aside the blanket covering Hector's M-16. He pulled it over the seat and chambered a round, then pushed the button for the passenger side window. The glass rolled smoothly down and he rested the barrel on the bottom of the window frame, holding it with his right hand while he steered with his left.

A car passed them going in the opposite direction and then it was clear. The Mustang was slowing a little because there was traffic ahead. Luis pressed on the accelerator and swung out into the other lane and quickly pulled up alongside the Mustang and stared at the guy, hatred in his eyes, his lips tight and thin with rage. The guy glanced at him and a puzzled look crossed his face and then Luis pulled the trigger.

The M-16 spit a long burst of bullets at the Mustang and a line of small holes appeared across the driver's door. Then the car was flying off the road. Hot spent shell casings were bouncing around inside Luis's Chevy and he swerved back into his lane, the Mustang behind him screeching and bouncing into a little ditch alongside the road and then impacting a utility pole with a loud crash. Luis watched in his rearview mirror, pulling away, and the pole came down and the Mustang buckled to a halt, the front end caved in.

Luis realized he'd been lucky that the Mustang hadn't run into him. Ahead traffic had slowed way down and he shot around them, forcing two cars coming toward him in the other lane to swerve off the road. He sped up and roared through Rocky River, trying to compose his thoughts but reeling with a drunken mixture of triumph and exhilaration and foreboding. He dodged through traffic for several minutes, thinking that if he could get onto a highway and into Cleveland he could get away.

He was crossing the bridge into Lakewood and saw flashing lights behind him. He planned to take a right and work his way south onto I-90 but as he got to the end of the bridge he saw four police cars blocking his way, lights going, the Lakewood cops ready for him. He slammed on his brakes and spun out, his tires burning, and crashed into the concrete side of the bridge. He hit the steering wheel with his nose and went blank for a moment. He was stunned but floppy from being drunk and he opened the car door and fell into the street, his face bleeding. The Rocky River police screamed up behind him in three cars as he lurched to his feet and pulled out his .357 Magnum.

They shot him eight times before he could even point it at them.

Chapter 63

In his small shop on Dover Center Road in North Olmsted, Enzo Fifini looked up from his sewing machine, startled, as the early news came on the little television over his bench. The news anchor was saying something about a shootout in Rocky River, maybe six or seven miles away as the crow flies, and he heard "MS-13" mentioned.

He stopped what he was doing, which was hemming the trousers of a very nice suit, and stood and turned up the volume. Then he watched with mounting concern as the anchor described in alarming fashion a shootout between a gang member and the Rocky River police on the Lake Avenue Bridge. The criminal was dead, but he had apparently been responsible for shooting a prominent doctor in Rocky River before the police put an end to his rampage.

Enzo sat down heavily on his comfortable rolling chair and ran his fingers through his hair. Although he had anticipated MS-13 someday doing something stupid and violent enough for him to sever his ties with them, this was a catastrophe. Something this extreme would attract attention from major law enforcement agencies, certainly the FBI and possibly Homeland Security. It clearly put him in jeopardy.

He got out his disposable cell phone and put in a quick call to Malik.

"Problems with the distributors," he said simply, without identifying himself. "Watch the news. Tell the others. Normal routines but remain in high yellow."

"Yes," said Malik in his funereal voice, and hung up.

They used a color code alert system. Green was for when everything was fine, they could go about their routines with confidence. Yellow meant that something had happened to make them wary, and there were degrees of yellow. Red meant that they were in serious trouble and should be prepared to take decisive action immediately. They had never needed red.

Enzo turned off the TV and shut off the lights in his back room, where he did most of his work. He walked into the front of the shop where the fitting rooms were and sat down behind the counter. The sign on his front door said that he would always be there until six o'clock, and he forced himself to maintain discipline and sit there because several customers were supposed to pick up their tailoring today and he didn't want to do anything out of the ordinary.

A couple of people did come in during the next fifteen minutes, Mr. Vargas picking up his newly finished Hart, Schaffner and Marx Gold Trumpeter suit and Mrs. Chamberlain her Donna Karan three-piece.

Enzo went through his usual routine with them, guiding them through a final examination of the fit he had created for them, and they paid him and left quickly, neither interested in small talk tonight, for which he thanked Allah.

He closed the store and went outside. It was still light out and as he locked up his eyes roamed over his sign once more. "Tailor Shop," it read. "Italian trained tailor. Alterations for men and women." He always found that amusing. People assumed that since his name was Enzo Fifini and the sign said "Italian," that he was himself an Italian. To be sure, he carried off the charade very well.

He had spent many years in Milan working in the fashion houses and was expertly trained as a tailor. He spoke Italian like a native. The few times any real Italians came into his shop to do business, he fooled them, too, conversing about Milano and their families and such things. Nobody knew he was really Enver Fifinic and he was a Muslim from Bosnia.

He got into his three-year-old beige Ford Taurus, a medium sized, smoothly shaven, soft spoken man with nondescript Mediterranean features. He drove carefully through the busy suburban streets, taking the back way home and avoiding the congestion around the

278

sprawling Great Northern Shopping Center on Lorain. He lived in a small brick house in a side street off of Columbia Road, and he got there in a few minutes, put the car in the detached garage and let himself into the house. Everything was as it should be, the only sound the muffled ticking of the desk clock in the living room, and the hairs he had precisely left stuck across doors and desk drawers and the telephone were undisturbed. No one had been in the house.

The place was sparsely furnished but contained enough chairs, tables and such things to avoid suspicion. There were photographs of a smiling woman with small children in frames in the living room and in his bedroom, but he had no idea who they were, although he had made up a story to explain them if he needed it. It was all camouflage.

He made himself some tea in the kitchen and as he waited for the water to boil he considered his options. There were two: He could pull the plug on the entire operation and vacate the area, or he could make sure MS-13 had nothing to say when the authorities came looking for them. He did not want to close down his operation. He had developed his cover and his contacts painstakingly over six years, arriving in the United States in 2000, establishing a home and a small business in the Cleveland area, going through all the legalities as a resident alien using the identity that had been so carefully constructed for him in Italy. Nobody suspected him of anything; they weren't even looking in his direction.

He had brought in Mounir to join him two years ago, and recruited Malik and Anwar since he'd been here. Mounir was a twenty-nine-year-old brother from Algeria who had spent much time in the struggle like he himself had. They had used their contacts with MS-13 to get him into the country through Mexico, his false identity that of a Guatemalan. Malik was an American black, twenty-seven, raised in the Islamic tradition, and Anwar was an Egyptian youth of twenty-two who had come to this country with his parents as a child. All were absolutely committed to Jihad.

Enver had moved with excruciating precision as he felt out various candidates for his group, rejecting dozens before he recruited Malik and Anwar. He needed Americans because they knew the culture and blended in in ways that he and Mounir never could. It had been harder than usual because he avoided going to any mosques at all. But he met Malik at a shooting range in Broadview

Heights, and Anwar was one of many Arab Americans in North Olmsted and had come into his shop one day. Both had been surprised to learn he was a Muslim when he had finally shared it with them. Over time he had introduced them to his real purpose there, and they had become deeply immersed in the struggle and had gone off to training camps in Sudan and Pakistan to learn the skills they'd need.

Their conspiracy was going very well. They brought the heroin in from Canada, where brothers had much greater freedom of movement, using the old smuggling routes across Lake Erie. During prohibition, and then beginning in the sixties and up until the present, the water route across from Leamington in Ontario and Pelee Island and through the American islands of North Bass, Middle Bass and South Bass, and Kelley's Island were a lucrative and difficult to disrupt conduit for contraband. Thousands of pleasure boaters cruised these waters daily during the warmer months and the border there was invisible. Canadian and American boaters blended freely and it was virtually impossible to identify and interrupt transshipments on the lake or in the secluded coves or the riotous party port of Put-In-Bay on South Bass. Like the rum runners of the twenties, drug smugglers found it easy to get their products into Northern Ohio from Canada. Enver had even met Americans who rode their jet skis across the lake to Pelee Island, a distance of twenty miles or more.

They had brought in a substantial amount of heroin over the past year and a half, and had generated several million dollars for their cause. Most of the money went back to the center of the struggle in the Mideast for distribution to brothers in various regions, but Enver had two million that he had been allowed to keep and which he would use to finance an important action here, in the home of the Great Satan. He was looking forward to it.

By selling heroin into the American heartland he knew he was doing great work. He was allowing the infidels to poison themselves and assisting the decadent enemy culture in its inevitable weakening and decline. It was risky working with the erratic gangsters in MS-13, but it had paid off. But he wanted to do more, something dramatic and decisive, and so did his group. They had been running surveillance on potential targets ever since they'd gotten here, and had a sizeable hoard of intelligence.

So he found it difficult to imagine having to pull the plug and relocate all of them. They'd accomplished much but still had so much they hoped to achieve. This alliance with MS-13 had been forged at the highest level of Al Qaeda and so far had been very profitable to the cause. But Enver had full operational discretion in dealing with his local contacts. They had no idea who he actually was, their own bosses in Central America keeping them in the dark while reaping much wealth from the partnership. He, on the other hand, had thorough information on them and their local hierarchy, because he wanted to be able to handle them if needed. It looked like it might be needed now.

His water had boiled and he made himself a cup of tea and sat quietly at the kitchen table, considering what he would do. When he had formulated his plan completely he got out the cell phone and tapped in Cesar Obregon's number. He sipped the tea and waited patiently for him to pick up.

"Hola," Cesar said, and Enver could hear the stress in his voice. He already knew about the shootings.

"This is the Tailor," he said quietly. "Looks like you've had a little trouble today, my friend."

Cesar's breath exploded in Enver's ear and he said, "Trouble? You could say that, I think. But we'll be okay, don't worry."

"You were asked to avoid this sort of thing," Enver told him.

"The guy went off the reservation. I don't know what he was doing. I'd kill him but the cops beat me to it."

"This will draw a lot of heat to you."

"We're laying low, don't worry," Cesar said. "They ID'ed him from his tattoos. They didn't even know we were in town."

"You're not at your store?"

"No, no," Cesar replied. "I don't think the cops know about it but I closed it down for today. Everybody went home. I'm hanging out watching TV. I don't know nothing about no shooting rampage."

"Okay," said the Tailor, and hung up.

He finished his tea and called Anwar on the cell phone and told him to be ready in thirty minutes. Then he went upstairs to get ready for what he needed to do next.

Chapter 64

Wade waited until well past five o'clock before he began to wonder what had become of Brian. Of course there were always last-minute emergencies in Brian's line of work, people calling from the hospital to confirm his orders and things like that. So he didn't get concerned until it looked like it was almost closing time at Block's and they'd be unable to get the car if they didn't do it quickly.

Could he have misunderstood Brian's instructions, or had Brian forgotten their plan? He called Block's Automotive but no, Dr. Pomeroy hadn't shown up there, and yes, they were waiting for him to pick up his Saab.

Then the phone rang and it was Kathleen, and she was upset but steady, her nurse's training keeping her together, and she told him that the Rocky River police had called her. Brian had been in an accident on Lake Road and was on his way to West Shore Hospital. Wade said he would meet her there.

Amanda was working and she met them just inside the emergency room door as they arrived within seconds of each other. She grasped Kathleen's hands and told her calmly, sympathetically, that Brian would be okay but he was in surgery. He was injured but nothing major had been damaged.

She led them to a quiet corner of the waiting room and sat down with them and Kathleen was wide-eyed, adrenaline pumped and wild to be with Brian and see for herself how he was. It occurred to Wade that an emotional trauma like this could be very bad for her lupus.

He flashed back to the night his father was brought into this place and died, and the remembered feelings of terror and despair washed over him.

Then Amanda quietly explained that Brian's injuries consisted of a concussion from impacting his head on the door of the Mustang when it crashed, a broken wrist in his left, non-dominant hand, and three superficial gunshot wounds to his left outside thigh and left buttock. They had him in surgery in order to remove the bullet fragments but the x-rays showed minor penetration. The bones and major blood vessels were intact.

Neither Kathleen nor Wade were able to process this information for a moment. Brian had been shot? That didn't make any sense at all.

Yes, Amanda told them, the police had explained that someone shot at Brian and caused him to crash. That was all that she knew, but there were policemen in talking with the admitting physician now and she supposed they'd be out to tell them more before too long.

"What does this mean, Wade?" Kathleen asked him, alarmed and afraid.

He shook his head. "I don't know. But he's going to be alright. That's what's important."

She began crying. "My poor husband. All he does is good for people. Why would someone do this to him?"

They sat there for a while and Wade comforted her, his arm around her, and then other family members arrived, her brother and his wife and Brian's uncle. Wade got up and walked around, worried for his friend, and then stopped in front of the television perched in the corner of the room on a wall bracket. The local network anchor, a woman who lived in Wade's neighborhood, was reporting on the incident. Some sort of madman or criminal had shot Dr. Brian Pomeroy and then been apprehended and killed on the Lake Avenue Bridge by the Rocky River police. *Thank God*, Wade thought. They got the guy. He sat down by himself, giving Brian's family room to console each other.

Two River detectives walked out of the emergency room and into the waiting area. One of them was Jim Mullin, who Wade had gone to high school with. They had played football together. Mullin was big and athletic looking with short blond hair and dressed in a tan colored suit. His partner, who Wade had never seen before, was shorter and darker, wearing a blue blazer and gray slacks. Mullin spotted Wade and headed over to him.

"Jim," he said, standing and offering his hand. "How's Dr. Pomeroy? Will he be okay?"

"Hello, Wade," Mullin said, shaking his hand. "Yes, he'll be alright. This is Detective Brad Mitchell. Brad, this is Wade Thomas, a friend of Dr. Pomeroy." Wade and Mitchell exchanged greetings.

"What in the world happened?" Wade asked them.

The detectives exchanged a glance and then Mullin said, "Some guy shot at Pomeroy's car with an assault rifle. A real one, meaning fully automatic, not a semi-auto. Pomeroy took some bullet fragments in his leg and butt. It's pretty superficial. We think the guy was using hollowpoints and they tend to break up going through a car door in a small, fast caliber like this was." Wade wasn't familiar with ballistics, but he took it to mean that this was good news for Brian.

"An assault rifle? Who would do that?" Wade asked.

"A machine gun," Detective Mitchell told him. "We think the guy was a gangbanger."

Wade went cold. Just then the newswoman cut back in again with more details of the breaking story. She said that the man killed on the bridge had tentatively been identified as a member of the MS-13 gang, but details were pending.

Wade's mouth was dry and he felt his world begin to crumble around him. Mullin and Mitchell were watching the TV, listening with poorly concealed disapproval as the details of the case were aired.

"They never get it right, do they?" Mitchell said to Mullin. Mullin shook his head and gave a short laugh.

"Jim," Wade said, tentatively. "Was this MS-13?"

"Yeah, probably. Somebody seems to have told the news people, so it's not a secret. The guy had gang tattoos. MS-13 is a gang from Central America."

Wade was nodding. His heart pounding, he said, "I know who they are. Jim, you should know that Brian was driving my brother's car."

Mullin fixed him with a dead stare and said, "Yes, we know that."

Then he waited for whatever Wade wanted to say next.

"My brother had a problem with someone from MS-13." It was out, he couldn't take it back. He felt a strange blend of relief and terror.

"No kidding?" Mullin said, deadpan. "Well, we'll have to look at that, of course. Where's your brother now?"

Wade's knees felt a little weak and he sat down. Mullin and Mitchell stood looking down at him, their expressions blank.

"He's in Maine, I believe. He's been out of town for a while. That's why his car was available for Brian to use while his was in the shop."

"Huh," Mitchell said. "Do you think this guy could have been after your brother?"

"I don't know. Maybe."

Mitchell nodded. "Well, as you just saw on TV, the guy's dead. He was stopped on the Lake Avenue Bridge and shot when he pulled a gun on the patrol officers."

Wade nodded, swallowing dryly and looking at the floor.

"Do you mind if we follow up with you on this?" Mullin asked him.

Wade looked up at him and said earnestly, "I'd appreciate it, Jim. I don't want these people after my family."

"Okay. Right now we need to talk to Pomeroy's family. We'll talk to you later. Can you give me some numbers where I can reach you?"

Wade gave him his business card and jotted his home and cell numbers on the back. "Try the cell or the home phones first, please," he said to him.

Wade walked out of the hospital and got in the Boxster. It was already dark and he was surprised to find that some time had passed while they were in the emergency room. He drove home, dazed, and pulled into the garage and went inside and called his mother. She was watching Little Wade for them and he gave her a quick explanation of what had happened. She was horrified.

"Was this about that thing with Tim?" she asked him.

"I don't know," he told her. "I'll talk to the police some more about it. I won't incriminate anyone but I'll let them sort it out." She agreed to keep Little Wade overnight and get him to school in the morning.

Next he called Tim, sitting at his desk in the study, feeling a great burden lifted from him because he had told Jim Mullin about Tim and the gangsters. But the sick fear for all of their futures began to settle into him. He had no way to judge what would happen as this all unraveled.

Naturally, Tim didn't answer, so he called Glendy's cell. She picked up at once.

"This is Wade," he said. "Where are you?"

"Bar Harbor," she replied, and she picked up on the concern in his voice. "What's going on?"

He quickly began to tell her what had happened and then Tim got on, taking the phone from her.

"Maybe you should answer your own cell," Wade said to him.

"Uh-huh. What did you tell the police?"

"That you had some trouble with someone from MS-13. They want to talk to me some more. I'm not going into details with them. I will give them Cesar Obregon's name and let them go after these people. If the rest of it comes out, so be it."

"Shit," Timmy said.

"What the hell do you expect?" Wade wanted to know. "They broke the agreement. I have to stop them before they hurt anybody else."

There was silence on the other end of the line. Then Glendy took the phone back and said, "Do whatever you have to. You've got to protect yourselves. We're all the way out here and they'll have a hard time connecting us to any of it. Tell them where we are, if you want to." And she gave him the name of the bed and breakfast they were staying in. "Thanks for letting us know."

At eleven-forty-five Amanda came home from her shift and she was grim faced and unhappy. He met her in the kitchen and she wouldn't look at him when she put away her bag and slipped off her jacket.

"How is he?" Wade asked her.

"He'll be fine. Do I even have to tell you what I think about this?"

He sighed. "No, but it will probably make you feel better."

She turned to him, angry, her hands on her hips. "We could have avoided this if we'd gone to the police right away."

He shook his head. "Maybe. Maybe not. I thought I was doing the right thing. I was trying to protect our family. I told Jim Mullin that Tim was having a problem with these people. It's in the open now."

They went to bed and held each other, Amanda still blaming him but knowing, too, that they'd need each other to deal with the aftermath of this awful situation. They barely slept. At six o'clock in the morning Wade got up and threw on a warmup suit and his cross trainers and went out for a run. The sun was coming up and it looked like it would be a beautiful day. He pounded through the neighborhood and tried to work the anguish out of his body and mind.

When he got back home, sweating and some of his tension dissipated, Amanda was standing in the upstairs hallway in her nightgown. She told him, "Jim Mullin called. He's coming over."

Wade made a pot of coffee and was sitting in the living room looking out over his lawn at the quiet street when the black sedan rolled up his driveway. Two men got out, Jim Mullin driving and a large black man in a conservative suit with him, and they walked up onto the front porch. Wade met them at the door.

"Please come in," he said.

The policemen entered and Jim said to him, "Wade Thomas, this is Special Agent Warren Cuthbert of the FBI."

Cuthbert showed him his FBI credentials and Wade's heart sank.

He could see it all unfolding now. MS-13 would be derailed and his family would be safe, but the tradeoff would be criminal charges for Tim, Glendy, Bobby and possibly himself. The irony was terrible, but he could see no other way to settle it. He reached out and shook Cuthbert's hand and said, "Please have a seat, gentlemen."

Amanda came downstairs, dressed now, her expression saddened but resolved. "Would anyone like coffee?" she asked them after introductions were made. They both did, and Amanda went to get it while Wade sat with them in the living room.

"Nice home, Mr. Thomas," Agent Cuthbert said, looking around at the furniture and paintings. Wade could envision losing it all.

"Thanks," he said. "You guys start work early."

"This case is pretty high profile, as you probably know," Jim Mullin told him.

Amanda came back in with the coffee and passed it around, each man thanking her and helping himself to sugar and cream. Then they sat back and Cuthbert looked steadily at Wade and said, "What can you tell us about your brother's problem with MS-13?"

Amanda was sitting next to him and Wade felt her grow rigid, as if anticipating a blow. He took a deep breath and noticed that his hands were steady as they grasped his coffee cup.

"A man named Cesar Obregon was upset with him," he said, and the two policemen were as still as rocks, watching him evenly, the coffee untouched. "He made threats."

Mullin looked at Cuthbert who said, "And where is your brother now?"

"He's in Bar Harbor, Maine, with his girlfriend. I spoke with them last night. I have his address and phone number."

The men exchanged a look that Wade couldn't interpret. Cuthbert said, "How long has he been there?"

Wade glanced at Amanda, uncertain. She said, "We were all at your mother's eight days ago. They dropped off the Mustang while we were there and left that afternoon. They were going directly to Maine."

Wade looked back at the policemen, expectantly. They exchanged another look. Then Mullin exhaled and leaned forward and looked Wade in the eye.

"We'll need to confirm that. We'll also need to confirm the whereabouts of any other family members last evening."

Wade thought of Bobby, but said, "I don't understand."

Cuthbert leaned in, too. "Mr. Thomas, we are uncertain why this particular individual shot at Dr. Pomeroy yesterday. His identity isn't clear but we suspect he was an illegal alien. He may have been after your brother and we will want to speak with your brother about that."

Then Mullin and Cuthbert exchanged another look and Cuthbert continued. "However, we can tell you that this MS-13 group is most likely no longer a threat to you or your family. Cesar Obregon and two other apparent MS-13 officers were killed in a shootout on the East Side last night in which a well-known drug dealer was also killed. We do not know what the correlation is in the timing of the attack on Dr. Pomeroy and the events on the East Side, but the building MS-13 was using as its headquarters was burned to the ground and as far as we know there are no longer any major players at large."

Chapter 65

Enver sat at his kitchen table sipping tea in the early morning light and mentally reviewing the action they had carried out yesterday evening. He was due at his shop at 8:30 and he had just finished a two mile run around the neighborhood, nodding at his neighbors and smiling as they passed each other, hardy dawn fitness enthusiasts all. He had some time to spend before work and he had some things he wanted to do.

It had been a pretty flawless operation, really, as he had hoped it would be. The key to these things was to always do one's homework, get your ducks in a row as they say, and then shoot them down effortlessly. And that's pretty much how it had gone.

The big trick, the element upon which the entire operation depended, was getting Malik into Big Allan's house so he could call Cesar from there. But Enver had a rough working plan for eliminating the MS-13 hierarchy ever since he had started doing business with them, and so they had thoroughly researched this aspect of the situation. Malik had actually met Big Allan under innocuous circumstances six months ago and had gotten into a conversation with him and secretly recorded his voice, and Malik had an ear for mimicry, so they were well prepared.

Last night he had given Malik the go ahead and Malik had called Big Allan's club and made sure that he was actually there, then had driven down to the Big Allan's house off of Chester Avenue and adeptly let himself in.

It was not a difficult thing to do for someone trained overseas in Al Qaeda's excellent camps, as Malik had been. If these people had any notion that they had been compromised, that trained foreign agents were stalking them, perhaps they would have been using better security. Or picked another line of work. But of course they had no idea. He had slipped into the poor, black neighborhood in the dark and parked down the street, then walked casually up to the front door of the big old house and had the lock open in moments. Once inside he was careful to disturb nothing except the telephone.

He called Cesar on his cell phone and pretended to be Big Allan, his sonorous voice almost the same, and told him how alarmed he was about the Rocky River shooting and what that could do to their business, and that he would like to see him right away.

Enver knew that Cesar would be concerned about keeping his primary East Side dealer under control and happy, but naturally he would be wary as well. They knew he didn't talk to Big Allan very often himself because they had the store on Denison wired for sound. But he would double check the phone number on his caller ID and be reassured that the call had come from Big Allan's house. And then they agreed to meet at Big Allan's private club, an unlicensed bar in an old two-story storefront in a rundown mixed residential and commercial street off of Central Avenue.

The rest was a textbook ambush. Malik and Mounir, who would attract the least attention by their appearance in the black East Side, set up outside of Big Allan's club among the many parked vehicles in two nondescript vans with sunroofs. They bracketed the street forming a triangulated kill zone with the front door of the club at the apex. When Anwar, who was tailing Cesar and two of his men from Berea, called them to let them know they were a minute away, Malik called the club and told whoever answered that an MS-13 hit crew was coming to see them.

Almost unbelievably, Big Allan himself walked outside flanked by five bodyguards, all of them openly carrying guns, and they stood around waiting to see what was going to happen. Malik and Mounir watched them through the generation III night vision scopes on their suppressed Hechler & Koch nine millimeter MP5 submachine guns, coordinating their actions by way of headset walkie talkies. Then Cesar and his boys pulled up across the street near Mounir and got out of their car, their movements relaxed and unsuspecting, and began walking toward the men in front of the club, the streetlights probably insufficient for them to make out the firepower waiting for them.

Mounir fired a subsonic 147 grain nine millimeter hollowpoint bullet into Big Allan Comstock's heart and the three hundred fifty pound drug dealer fell face down on the sidewalk. Nobody had heard the shot but of one of Big Allan's guys saw the brief flame spit from the silencer in the dark beyond Cesar and shouted a warning. And that was all it took. Mounir and Malik dropped back down into the vans from their perches above the sunroofs and waited for the shooting to stop. Then they did a quick scan through the nightscopes and ascertained that Cesar was bleeding in the street, his head heavily damaged, and the other two MS-13 guys were down as well. The bodyguards were scattered along the sidewalk looking for something else to shoot and hadn't spotted them yet so Mounir and Malik started their vans and drove off the street in opposite directions, headed for home.

Meanwhile, Enver had burgled Cesar's house in Berea and found all of the MS-13 records and files. He bundled them up along with two cell phones and quietly slipped away. He met Anwar twenty minutes later outside the MS-13 headquarters on Denison Avenue.

As Cesar had told him, the place appeared dark and deserted but they spotted a guy dressed in baggy blue and white athletic clothes, the signature MS-13 look, hanging around at the end of the block in the dark, a sentinel, and Anwar had snuck up behind him. When Anwar was in position Enver drove up to the kid and rolled down his window but the guy hung back, suspicious. But he was distracted enough for Anwar to come up on him and put a gun in his ear. They took a pistol off of him and then they all went down to the store, the street quiet in the cool night, and got the kid to unlock the place and let them inside.

It only took them a couple of minutes to get him to tell them his name was Manuel, that Cesar was with the only other two original gangsters in town, Fernando and Jorge, and that while there were a couple of dozen street gangbangers in their crew they were nobodies and didn't know anything about high level MS-13 operations. By then the kid was crying and bleeding from his torn fingernails so they shot him in the back of the head with his own gun and searched the place quickly.

There were no records there, Cesar had apparently moved them all to Berea. There were two kilograms of heroin, forty pounds of marijuana, three kilos of cocaine and three boxes filled with thousands of pills and tablets which they couldn't identify, probably ecstasy. They took the heroin with them and set fire to the place using crude gasoline bombs because they wanted to make it look like Big Allan's people were responsible. Then they snuck out again, got in their vehicles and went home. It had been a big risk, going to the store that way. It was possible that the authorities had already identified it. But they had to make sure they had thoroughly eradicated MS-13. Their boldness and daring had paid off and now the slate was completely clean.

Enver enjoyed his tea and looked forward to his day in the shop. He actually liked being a tailor quite a bit and he was good at it. It was both creative and precise and required technical knowledge and he felt that it kept his mind sharp. Of course, there was nothing like a real operation to get the blood flowing and let them all stretch their legs. They trained so much with surveillance and physical fitness and firearms that they were always ready to go, and it was good to put it all to the test once in a while. He felt that the takedown of MS-13 had been very well done and they could all be proud. They were still intact and undetected. They would have to develop new avenues for their heroin trade, of course, and Enver made a mental note to have Malik begin feeling out the remains of Big Allan's crew after the police were done with them and the dust settled.

He paged through Cesar's records, noting names and times and places, a routine intelligence debriefing of the artifacts of a man and an organization now completely erased. And he came across his own name and address.

He put the tea down and sat there quietly, somewhat surprised.

Cesar had been smarter and more dangerous than he'd imagined, and had somehow learned his identity, at least as Enzo Fifini. His home address was right there. He had underestimated the man, and that was dangerous. Praise Allah, he had nipped it in the bud.

Chapter 66

They were all sitting in Harriet Thomas's living room, Wade and Amanda and Bobby and Allie and Harriet herself. Five days had passed since Wade had sat with Mullin and Cuthbert in his own home and learned that MS-13 was gone from their lives.

They had finished a nice dinner, roast chicken and mashed potatoes, which the three women had jointly made that afternoon, and now they were looking at each other over their wine glasses as the sun went down outside beyond the picture window and Little Wade ran around the front yard chasing Benny the cat. Benny would dart out of his reach and sit waiting for his renewed approach and then do it again. Neither of them seemed to tire of it. Fireflies began drifting through the yard and across the street they could see neighbors, the two elderly sisters in their exercise clothes talking to Mrs. Larson as she played her garden hose over her shrubbery.

Bucolic, Wade thought. This is what they call a bucolic scene, like those paintings from the Middle Ages with the peasants going about their chores with all of God's beautiful creation as a backdrop. Now he hoped that he could get used to it again.

"I want to say some things about what has happened to us," he told them, and they all regarded him raptly, knowing this was the reason they had gathered this evening. They needed to conclude this chapter of their lives, define it and put it to bed and move on from there.

"The police did ask me if I knew what may have caused that man to shoot Dr. Pomeroy, what they may have had against Tim. I told them that I had no firsthand knowledge of what may have caused it. They asked me to take a guess and I said that I'd rather not speculate and that they needed to talk to Tim about it. Jim Mullin isn't completely happy with me but I think he understands my position; he has a family, too."

He took a sip of wine and, as if on cue, so did Allie and Amanda and his mother. Bobby just sat watching him.

"I know that an FBI agent went to see Tim in Bar Harbor from their local office because Glendy told me so on the phone yesterday. Apparently Tim told him that he had had an argument with the guy at a night club in Cleveland a couple of months ago over a woman. That's where it stands; the FBI has no one to talk to who can either confirm or deny it. With all of the MS-13 leadership apparently dead, there doesn't seem to be much need to pursue it further."

Harriet shuddered and put down her glass, and Allie, who was sitting next to her, put her arm around her and hugged her. "It's okay, Mom," she told her.

Amanda said, "Wade and I have talked to Brian and Kathleen Pomeroy. He's recuperating at home and is up and around. The biggest problem is the broken wrist, which will take awhile to heal. He's going back to work next week. The gunshot wounds, thank heavens, were minor, and that's a miracle." They all nodded in agreement, their guilt pulling on their faces.

"We told them that we think this happened because of a problem Tim had with this gang, and that our entire family is deeply sorry for what Brian has been through. We would have done anything to avoid this, but we had no idea that they knew about Tim's car and would do something like this. I still feel very guilty, and believe we could perhaps have kept this from happening if we had gone to the police earlier, but I understand what was at stake." She looked back and forth from Wade to Bobby and they met her gaze.

Wade continued, "Somehow these criminals have managed to get themselves killed in a drug war with other gangsters from the East Side. Jim Mullin told me yesterday that their investigation has turned up no surviving members of the MS-13 hierarchy. They found the remains of one yesterday in the burned down store on Denison

Avenue where they had their headquarters. Jim says that the only ones left are a handful of street teenagers hanging around in the Hispanic neighborhoods, and the police are all over them. They'll either go back to stealing hubcaps and wind up in jail quickly or find a better way to live." He noticed that Bobby smiled at that.

"The threat to our family and friends looks like it's over. I can't tell you how relieved that makes me. I still feel like I'm walking away from a train wreck and can't believe it wasn't any worse."

Allie sat forward and said, "What about Tim? What will happen to him?"

"Well, I think he's clear of the authorities unless he continues to do stupid things," Wade replied. Bobby looked down and shook his head, and Wade understood that was not a good sign.

"It's his drug use," Allie continued. "Maybe we can do an intervention or something."

Amanda told them, "That's a real possibility. I can look into it. The difficulty will be getting him into town long enough to do it."

"Great idea," Wade said, although Bobby looked dubious. "Let's see what we can do. We've had the great good fortune to survive a disaster and we owe it to ourselves to make the most of it."

Harriet looked back and forth between all of them and said, "I just want my son to have a happy life. Why did this have to happen?"

She began to sniffle and Allie got to her feet.

"Come on, Mom. Let's get the dessert."

The three women went into the kitchen and Bobby reached into his pocket and came out with two sizeable cigars.

"Care to indulge, Wade?"

Wade laughed a little. "I usually don't, but I think tonight could be an exception."

The two of them got up and walked back through the kitchen and over to the sliding door to the back porch and went out. Bobby slid it closed behind them. "Your mom won't want the smoke getting into the house," he said.

They sat in the folding chairs and carefully got the cigars burning, savoring the flavor as they watched darkness creep over the neighborhood. The last sounds of a lawnmower a few doors down faded away.

"Good cigar," Wade told him.

"Cuban leaf, but from South America," Bobby replied. "Not cheap, but not ridiculous, either."

As Wade examined his cigar, rotating the burning end, Bobby watched him and seemed to reach a decision. He stuck his right hand into the cargo pocket of his pants.

"Wade, I would like to give you something. If you really don't want it, just say so. But I've been thinking about it and in my opinion it's not a bad idea." His hand came out and there was a squat, shiny, dark blue revolver in it.

Wade looked at him questioningly. "What's this?"

"You may want to think about holding on to this. Having one saved my ass and Allie's, too, and you can't be absolutely sure this is all over."

Wade looked at the gun, perplexed. He had fired guns before, mostly skeet shooting and a couple of handguns at a range with friends. But he didn't own any and hadn't ever thought much about it.

"What am I going to do with this?"

Bobby leaned closer and said, "You could keep it with you. There's a saying: It's better to have a gun and not need it than to need a gun and not have it. Those guys would have killed me if I hadn't had one, and I would have had a hard time helping Allie without it."

"Is this your gun? You know, the one you, uh…"

Bobby shook his head. "No. This is a different one." In fact, it was the one he had taken from the waistband of the Mafia guy at the Yorkshire Grand. He had gotten a new barrel for his Glock 21 just in case Jaime's body with his bullets in it ever turned up, so it couldn't be matched by a ballistics expert. And he had thrown the stainless Smith and Wesson automatic he had taken from the other guy at Allie's into a lake at his first opportunity. He figured the Mafia hood was probably smart enough not to carry around a gun that could be matched to crimes, but he didn't think the MS-13 guy was. "I took it off that guy that was after Glendy, but that was in New York. It's a good gun, a Colt Detective Special."

Wade asked, "Is it loaded?"

Bobby said, "No. Here's the six that were in it." He handed Wade the bullets and Wade looked at them curiously. "It's a snub nose .38. You need .38 Special ammunition for it. These are kind of mild, wadcutters, target loads. Go to a gun shop and get some good hollowpoints."

Wade said, "I'm not sure I want something like this around. Amanda won't be too thrilled, that's for sure."

Bobby shrugged. "What you tell her is up to you. But I've got to say," and he looked at him intently, "you don't want to be waiting for Jim Mullin to answer the phone if these assholes show up in your bedroom at two a.m."

Wade thought about what that would be like. Bumps in the night, a frantic phone call to the police, then sitting in the dark, helpless, hoping help would arrive before some murderous creep came into the room and gunned them down or hacked them to death. "I figured it was all over," he said. "Don't you think so?"

"I hope so," Bobby said. "Believe me, nobody wants it more than I do. But we don't know. You can't be too careful, I figure."

Wade sighed. "Our lives will never completely be the same," he said.

"You're right. We're all dancing to a different tune now," Bobby observed.

Wade smiled. "I don't mind dancing. I just never thought I'd be dancing to the six-gun two-step." And he took the gun from Bobby.

Chapter 67

In the evenings Enver worked on his plan.

He would sit at his kitchen table in his small suburban house, a cup of tea beside him, and go over his data meticulously, time and time again, teasing nuances of the facilities and their security from the reams of documents and photographs he had accumulated. He had been doing this for five years.

The great success of the brothers on September 11, 2001, had convinced them all of the potential for victory. Smashing two planes into the World Trade Towers and one into the Pentagon had completely disrupted the United States. Financial institutions had been unstable for a year or more afterward. Something equally destructive, or more so, on a larger scale would surely stagger the Great Satan, demoralize its people, and advance the cause of Islam.

They lacked the manpower on the ground to wage a persistent low grade war of the sort Hamas had pursued in Palestine. Many brothers would happily assault the vast shopping malls with guns and bombs and wreak havoc among the smug Americans but such a plan was not sustainable. They would all surely be eliminated during and immediately after any large scale attempt to do this. And their ranks were too well trained, scarce and valuable to squander this way. So they had something bigger and better in mind.

Enver passed his magnifying glass once again over his aerial photographs of the Davis Besse Nuclear Power Plant in Oak Harbor. Sitting alone in a national wildlife refuge on the shore of Lake Erie to the west of Cleveland, it had gone online in 1977. To the east, on the opposite edge of the great southern bowl of the lake's shoreline along which stretched the giant urban sprawl of Cleveland, was its cousin. The Perry Nuclear Plant sat on an eleven hundred acre site and was the most expensive nuclear power plant ever constructed when it went online in 1986. The two facilities were separated by one hundred twenty miles of water. These two plants bracketed the shoreline of central northern Ohio, two hands with a precious cargo suspended between them, the cities of Sandusky and Lorain and Cleveland and all of their attendant suburbs. Millions of people lived there and depended on the plants for much of their electricity.

Enver was going to attack both of the plants simultaneously, opening their containment vessels and spewing radiation into the lake and the atmosphere, where it would drift along the shoreline on the currents and prevailing west-to-east winds from Davis Besse into Cleveland and from Perry further along the lake eastward into Buffalo. The resulting air and water-borne contamination would render a substantial portion of Northeast Ohio unusable for quite while, would poison the lake and its wildlife and fishing, and would ruin the economy of the region. It would be like Chernobyl one hundred times over or more. Quite a few people would probably die, too, but that was just an additional benefit. It was the ruination of a functioning major urban center that was most attractive to them.

Take out a block from the base of the child's toy tower and the tower falls. If similar plans came off well in other parts of the country at the same moment, the results could be staggering. Enver had never been told that others like himself where pursuing similar and congruent plans, but he knew it was the best way to achieve their goal and so he assumed that was what was going on.

They had done quite a bit of their reconnaissance from the water, using their two four hundred horsepower, thirty foot long Wellcraft cabin cruisers. They kept the boats docked in Edgewater Marina in Cleveland and in Port Clinton near Sandusky, and used them alternately to rendezvous with their contacts from Canada to tranship their heroin and profits. So they were making the most of their resources, doing surveillance and smuggling with the boats, and they had all become very competent at handling the vessels and navigating around the vast lake, the thirteenth largest in the world.

Enver foresaw a joint land-water-air attack on both plants at some future time, and that time was coming nearer. After all of their years of planning, brothers from other locations and from overseas would converge on the targets to perform the actual attack. They would be relying primarily on small aircraft with explosives on board, and it would be no problem finding pilots. Young Jihadists were lining up for this kind of mission. They'd love to reorient the fight from Iraq and Afghanistan to the beating heart of the enemy's homeland.

There were thousands of small airstrips in America. In addition to the usual and plentiful single engine propeller driven planes, tiny microjets were also expected to begin to operate from them before too long and would provide much faster attack platforms. Seven or eight of them laden with high explosives and aimed at each containment building at the power plants would certainly blow them open and release the radiation; their planners and engineers had told them so. But bomb laden trucks on the ground and boats equipped with portable rockets on the lake would ensure that the buildings would fall in a coordinated barrage of destruction. Most of the attackers would die, but that was the way of such things, and the martyrs would have their reward in Paradise. It was a good plan, and it would be impossible to stop completely once it was in motion.

So Enver spent quite a lot of time in the evenings going over his information, scrutinizing the roads and the facilities of the plants and the locations of nearby police stations and National Guard headquarters, all with an eye for timing and coordination and deadly precision in the attack. He didn't devote himself too much to other matters because this was his primary mission, although his men, the other three in the cell, had never been told specifically what he was doing, although his interest in the power plants was apparent. It was strictly need-to-know information at this point. He often had one or more of them, although never all of them at once, at his home in the evening to work on other research, small parts of the puzzle that were necessary for the success of the whole plan.

Tonight Anwar was over, sitting in the living room so that he wouldn't see what Enver was doing. He had his iPod in his shirt pocket and his earpieces in place and was bouncing a little as he sat on the couch reviewing papers, listening to some American pop music that Enver was happy he couldn't hear. Anwar could read Spanish much better that Enver could, so he had tasked him with reviewing all of the MS-13 documents he had taken from Cesar's home in Berea, a sizeable pile of papers, really. Anwar probably thought that it was busywork, unnecessary. After all, the MS-13 people were all dead. But Enver knew that secret work such as theirs required meticulous attention to details. Having found his own name and address in Cesar's possession, he was determined to have Anwar look at every scrap of paper, every offhand note, to see if there was anything else there that was of interest to them.

At nine-thirty in the evening he heard Anwar exclaim, "Wow." He got up from his kitchen chair and closed his folders of research materials on the power plants so that their contents were hidden.

Then he went in to see what Anwar had found.

"What do you have?" Enver asked him.

Anwar looked up at him, his large brown eyes wide. He took the earpieces out and turned off the iPod. "Do you see what this says?" he asked him, offering a sheet of lined notebook paper to him.

Enver took the page and saw that it had a number of names and phone numbers and some addresses jotted down on it, scribbles and half-completed thoughts trailing across it. He saw the name "Thomas" several times, and "Fallon." There were notations of times and dates as well.

"What do you think this is?" he asked Anwar.

"They were surveilling these people, whoever they are. Lots of urgency. The writer was keeping a record of his attempts to investigate them. He has several addresses here, in Rocky River and in Kent. What first caught my eye is this phrase, where he says 'Como llegera alos?' It means 'How to get to them?' So I wondered what the problem was, why they were after these people."

"Okay," Enver said, sitting on the couch next to him. "What did you come up with?"

"This," replied Anwar. He produced another slip of paper, with a recent date and a name on it. It was one of the names from the first paper, W. Thomas. Enver took it and read the words on it.

"I'm not sure what 'Este hombre tiene nuestros registros del nombre y la direccion' means," he said to Anwar, but he had a suspicion.

"It says, 'This man has our name and address records.'"

They looked at the paper together for a moment and then Anwar pointed out, "Your name and address was in their records."

Enver nodded slowly. "I'm aware of that," he said. He looked through the stack of papers and documents and found Cesar's address book, where he'd discovered his own name. He flipped to the "T" section and found the name Wade Thomas and a Westlake address and phone number.

"More cleaning up to do," he told Anwar.

Chapter 68

The black Cadillac cruised along Route 6A toward Route 6 and began heading out of the Provincetown area. Cape Cod stretched ahead of them as Timmy and Glendy headed into a warm and rainy morning. With any luck they'd be in Buffalo by nightfall, or maybe further.

"That was the gayest place I ever saw," Timmy said as he eased the car through the tourist traffic.

Glendy laughed, watching people scuttling along under umbrellas as they dodged into and out of the quaint shops and boutiques they were passing. "You knew that before we came here," she reminded him. "Don't complain. You got more attention from the waiters than I did. It was an interesting change. Everybody was nice."

They'd bailed out of Bar Harbor right after the FBI agent dropped in on them. They'd stashed all of their product in a rental locker because they knew somebody would show up, so they were clean when the knock came on the door of their room at the bed and breakfast.

The agent had been very professional, a youngish white guy in halfway decent suit, and Timmy knew he'd pegged them as dopers in the first couple of minutes. But the questions were predictable with no unpleasant surprises, and they'd been able to give him a simple and consistent explanation for why a gangbanger from Central America might want to shoot him with a machine gun in broad daylight in a middle class suburb in Ohio. There was a small sitting room in their suite, the decor antiquey and vaguely nautical, and they'd sat talking civilly for a half-hour before the guy thanked them and departed. Neither of them thought he'd bought the story, but he had nowhere to go with his suspicions because the other guys were all dead. The only option he might want to exercise would be to keep an eye on them and find out what they were really up to. So they left town.

They'd had a good time first in Portland, with its night spots along the waterfront, and then in Bar Harbor. They'd actually gone out into the Atlantic on a whale watch one day, amazed to see the giant creatures diving from their vantage point on the big ship they'd gone out in, then snuggling together in the cold wind as they cut through the miles of waves heading back to port. And they'd sold a pretty good amount of coke in the bars in the evenings, hanging around and getting to know some of the locals and the tourists. Timmy did his usual routine with the tooter, inviting the customer outside for a quick sample, and pretty soon they had made a couple of thousand dollars in each town, easily enough to cover their expenses. They stayed in nice places and ate in good restaurants. They knew they could cycle back through here again in a few months and do it again if they felt like it.

After the visit with the FBI man, they decided they'd try another resort area and headed for Cape Cod and all the way to the end to P-town. This time they found that there was a bustling market for the ecstasy they had with them, as well as the coke, and they sold even more product than they had in Maine. It was a different environment, a predominantly gay crowd of both residents and tourists, but their taste in illegal substances was the same as anybody else's, and their money was just as green.

"I'd like to maybe check out Newport next," Timmy said as he drove through the rain. "They've got these great old mansions there, I hear."

"Where's Newport?" Glendy asked him, looking at herself in her visor mirror and putting on some lipstick.

"Rhode Island. It's not too far from here."

"Maybe later. We can come back. We've got to go to your brother's surprise party. I promised your mom."

"Yeah, fine," he told her. "We should maybe get a little more ex when we're there. I'm betting we can move a lot of that."

"Where'd you get that from?"

"That guy, Jerry, over at Kamm's Corners. I'll swing by when we get in, see if I can score maybe a thousand hits off him."

Glendy shrugged. "Sure, whatever," she said.

Timmy knew that Glendy didn't know Jerry and so she didn't know that he had a lot of stuff for sale in that crowded junk shop on Lorain.

Timmy had scored a little smack when he got the ex, just a small amount, and he had used it just a couple of times, chipping a little, while they were in Maine and Massachusetts. She never caught on, as far as he could tell. Of course, he was being really discrete, just tasting it, not getting all nodded out and everything. So there was no reason for her to get all uptight about it. If she found out, he could just say, *Hey, I've been tasting it for a while and you didn't even know. So what's the problem? I can handle it.*

Maybe Wade would be a little cooler when he saw him. After all, this thing with the Mexicans was all over and there was no reason to still be so uptight. Maybe they'd have a good time at the surprise party. His mother had told Glendy that they'd set up for the party at Wade and Amanda's house while they were out with friends and then would do the whole routine when they came in, jumping out from behind furniture and everything, giving Wade a jolt. However it went, he and Glendy could blast off again in a day or so if they felt like it; there was no reason to stick around, especially if he was still getting a bunch of static from everyone. Bobby wasn't too much fun anymore, so what was the point of hanging around? The sky was clearing as they headed west out of Massachusetts and Timmy was thinking about how soon he could get in front of Jerry again.

Chapter 69

Wade pushed the starter button and the Bayliner's small block V-8 rumbled to life. He glanced over to the dock and smiled widely at Amanda, Ralph and Amy.

"We've got power! Bring the cooler."

Ralph and Amy hauled the cooler between them down into the boat and secured it in its niche behind the bridge. Amanda hoisted the fishing tackle in two large containers to Ralph and then climbed aboard with two of the fishing rods. While Ralph stowed them she turned back to Nate, the dockmaster, and he handed her the other two rods.

"*Mudpuppy's* topped off, Mr. Thomas," Nate reported. "We put in fifty gallons."

Ralph nudged Wade and remarked, "Guess it's a good thing we closed the deal at University Hospitals. You could go broke running this thing."

Wade laughed. "Yeah, I need to get underlings who have boats so I don't have to. Like you do."

Ralph laughed back. "Just keep inviting us and we'll bring the food and drinks. We like to do our share!"

Amanda shoved him, laughing, and said, "You do your share of eating and drinking, that's for sure."

They were all excited and having a good time as they checked out the galley and forecabin, Amanda double checking that the head was stocked with necessities and that all the compartments were water tight. Wade checked his instrumentation while the exhaust burbled cheerfully in the water off the stern.

"Looks good. Cast off, please, Nate," Wade said, and Nate untied the bow and stern lines and tossed them into the boat where Ralph furled them as Amanda and Amy slipped the bumpers over the bulkhead and tucked them away. Wade took a last look around, saw that no other boats were approaching, and eased away from the yacht club dock and into the channel. Nate waved to them as they glided away.

Amanda came forward and stood beside him as he carefully steered the boat north up the Rocky River to its mouth at Lake Erie. She wrapped her arm through his as they both scanned the water ahead.

"Looks like a wonderful day," she remarked. She checked her watch and saw that it was ten o'clock.

"Not a cloud in the sky," Wade said. "The weather reports are all favorable. It should be a perfect day."

They cruised out into the lake, skirting the breakwall to their right, and angled left, heading west. There were other boats out, quite a few in fact, but the lake was vast and they had huge stretches of water to themselves. The sun was heating up and Wade slipped off his windbreaker, down to a polo shirt and shorts and his docksiders, and stuck his Indians ball cap on his head.

"Better get out the sunscreen," he said to Amanda. "It's going to be toasty out here."

"Should we put up the canvas cover?" she asked.

"Let's enjoy the weather. If it gets too intense we can think about it."

As he motored steadily westward at an easy ten knots Amanda and Amy shed their jeans and shirts and soon were lounging in their bathing suits in the chairs behind him, working on their tans. Ralph came out of the cabin and stood next to the captain's chair and opened a beer.

"I know you don't want one of these yet, right?"

"Not for me. I'll fall asleep at the wheel if I start drinking beer in the morning."

Ralph sipped the beer and gazed out over the lake through his sunglasses. "I thought you were thinking about getting a bigger boat."

"Yeah, I was. But I'm putting it off. I like this one, but it would be nice to have a little more room for more people. Then I can take out some of the sales teams, sort of reward them, you know? Do a cruise a year up to Put-in-Bay or something."

Ralph nodded. "Good idea. Can you write some of that off?"

"I think so. Also, Brian is interested in possibly taking this one off of my hands, but his accident put that on hold."

"Is he doing okay?" Ralph asked.

"Yes, thank God, he gets the wrist cast off next week. He was pretty shaken by the whole thing, though."

"I'll bet. Hey, if you do get that Sea Ray, we can see about having the company fund an outing for the sales people."

"Sounds great. You're trying to tempt me into it, aren't you?"

"Sure!" Ralph said. "I'll be sure to go with you guys. Or maybe we can do an upper management excursion, too. What do you think?"

"Any excuse," Wade observed, and they both laughed.

They cruised for the better part of an hour until they were north of Avon Lake somewhere, the shoreline only barely visible a few miles distant. Wade shut down the engine and they drifted a little, soaking up the sun and talking about their kids and work, and they got out the tackle and bait and rigged their fishing rods and leisurely cast their lines from the stern of the boat. There was no need to drop anchor, they were in deep water and they weren't in danger of drifting into anything.

They bobbed gently along on the lake's swells, the water lapping at their hull, and fell into comfortable monotony as they fished and chatted. The sun was warm but not uncomfortably so and they were all down to minimal clothing and lathered with sunscreen. Every so often their relaxed conversation was interrupted by someone actually hooking a fish, and then they'd all jump up and watch excitedly as the fight played out, one of them eventually landing a perch, which they'd then toss back as soon as they freed it. They all drank a little beer and had sandwiches and the day slid by quickly. Wade would fire up the boat from time to time as they drifted and coax it back to where he wanted it. They had some music on the CD player, relaxed jazz, and several times during the day Amanda and

Amy jumped into the water to cool off, Wade and Ralph content to watch them and talk about work and the Indians and boats.

At three in the afternoon Wade said, "Everybody had enough?"

They all laughed, sunburned and happy and began to stow the fishing gear once again in preparation for the ride back to port.

As Wade bent over his instruments he caught a glint of reflection in the water beyond his bow. He looked up and saw that a boat was approaching at a moderate pace, a little at an angle to them, but its present course would carry it within a hundred feet of them.

"That's closest we been to anybody all day," Wade remarked to Amanda, who looked up and saw the boat, too.

Then, too their surprise, as the boat reached its closest approach to them, they heard its engines roar and it swung sharply in their direction and quickly began to close with them. It was a good sized red Wellcraft and as it got closer Wade saw two men, one quite dark skinned, standing at the bridge and looking at them.

Chapter 70

Kathleen Pomeroy's Jeep Grand Cherokee turned into Wade and Amanda's subdivision and crept up their street. Kathleen and Harriet were wide-eyed, looking furtively around for any sign that they had come home early from the boating excursion.

"They're not here, Grandma!" Little Wade told them firmly, for the third time. "Don't worry!"

"We want it to be a surprise," Harriet said to him. "We don't want them to see us if they came home early."

As they approached the house they saw no sign of activity, no evidence that anyone had been there since this morning. If they'd come back, Ralph and Amy's BMW should be here, since they had driven. But it wasn't.

"I think we're okay," Kathleen observed, and she turned into the driveway, up the slight incline and stopped in front of the side-facing garage door.

"This is like being the Easter Bunny or Santa Claus," Little Wade remarked, excited. "It's like a stealth mission!"

"Or the Tooth Fairy," said Kathleen, laughing.

"The Tooth Fairy's not real," said Little Wade seriously, looking at her as if she had lost her senses.

They got out of the SUV and Harriet went up to the front door and unlocked it with the key Amanda had given her. When she opened the door she heard a beeping sound start up from somewhere inside. She went in, Kathleen right behind her, and they quickly shut down the alarm system at the keyboard by the back door.

"Whew!" Harriet said. "I was afraid I'd mess that up and we'd have the Westlake police here!"

They went back out and opened the Jeep's tailgate and began unloading bags full of party decorations, food and gifts and carrying them into the house. Little Wade helped, struggling with a heavy bag of food until Kathleen relieved him.

"Here, you can carry this one. It's got the hats and noisemakers," she said.

In a few minutes they had arranged all the bags in the kitchen and began unpacking them.

"Let's get this food in the refrigerator. Amanda cleaned out the one in the garage so we can put most of it out there," Harriet suggested. "This potato salad needs to stay cool."

They hurried back and forth, excited and gleeful about their plot.

"What time do you think they'll get back?" Kathleen asked her.

"I'm guessing probably four-thirty or five. I told everyone to be here by four just to be sure." She laughed. "Wade's going to come in here sweaty and sunburned from boating. He'll never be expecting this!"

"And Ralph and Amy are driving them, right? So they'll be here when we surprise him."

Harriet nodded. "Exactly. They can call us if there's any change in plans or if they'll be late or early. I think we've planned for every eventuality!"

When they got the food put away, carefully arranged so that they could deploy it quickly when the time came, they set up disposable plates and cups and silverware on the kitchen counter.

"You have candles for the cake, right?" Kathleen asked.

"Yes. I can't believe he'll be thirty-six. Where does the time go?"

They began unrolling crepe paper streamers and Kathleen, who was taller, stood on a chair as she taped them around the kitchen, Harriet feeding it up to her and Little Wade standing by with scissors and extra tape.

"When can Brian get here?" Harriet asked.

"Well, he's supposed to be done with work at three-thirty, but that's always iffy. My brother and sister-in-law are at our house with Erin. I'm planning to meet Brian at the hospital at three-thirty and then come right back here. If we can't make it by four fifteen or so I'll call you and you can tell us whether to wait or come ahead. We don't want to show up at the same time Wade and Amanda do."

Before long they had decorated the house the way they wanted it. You couldn't see the streamers when you came in the front door. Everyone would hide in the back margins of the kitchen and ambush Wade when he excited the hallway from the entryway and came into the kitchen. It would be up to Amanda to get him to do that.

"Are we all set?" Kathleen asked. "Do you need me for anything else at the moment?"

Harriet glanced at the kitchen clock and saw that it was three o'clock.

"No, you go on and do whatever you need to do. Thank you so much for helping! We'll see you back here soon."

Kathleen laughed. "This is fun. I'll go, then. See you in a little bit."

She hurried outside and Harriet watched her drive off down the street.

"Do you know if your mom has a cake knife?" she asked Little Wade. "This is so exciting!"

Chapter 71

The black Cadillac pulled up in front of Bobby's apartment building on Clifton Avenue in Lakewood. It was a nice afternoon, sunny and balmy.

Timmy and Glendy had gotten into town two days before and were staying in her new apartment on Lake Avenue on the Gold Coast. It was a newer high rise building, the apartment equipped with new appliances and nice fresh paint and carpeting, and they had decent view between the buildings across the street and could see the lake.

Their habit was to sleep late and lounge around, then get moving in the afternoon and shop or go out to eat. Timmy had scored some more coke and had gotten the ecstasy from Jerry in Kamm's Corners so they had a good inventory.

Their new coke source was a guy he'd known for a while, a roady for a well known rock band. He lived in Lakewood too, although he was often out of town for long periods when the band toured. He didn't have the kind of connections that Bam and Susie had, but Timmy scored a half pound from him and that was a nice start.

Jerry was another matter. It seemed like he was scrambling for sources, too. Timmy suspected he'd been hooked into MS-13 and so his supplier was no longer in business. The smack he'd gotten from him seemed identical to what he'd gotten from the garage, the six kilos that had started this whole adventure. But Jerry still had some so Timmy bought a few grams of it from him, just to keep life on the road more interesting. He also got five hundred hits of ex. He'd wanted more, but Jerry was running low on that, too.

They kept a handy supply with them but Timmy stashed most of his inventory in the hideout downtown. He also built a little secret storage bin into the center console of the Cadillac, so that they could hide the drugs in there and not get caught with them on their persons if something went wrong. It was a good system, and for the past two evenings they'd visited the bars around the Detroit Road curve, where the bridge connected Lakewood to River, and sold ten grams of coke and thirty hits of ex to people they knew.

They parked the car in front of Bobby's and Timmy spotted his sister's red Volkswagen a few spaces up.

"Allie's here already," he said.

"They're really cute together," Glendy remarked.

"He's a serious dude. I think he's too much for her."

"In what way?" she asked, looking at him.

"I've known the guy forever. We've done a lot of crazy things together," Timmy told her.

"In case you haven't noticed, he's gone straight," she said. "And he saved her life. I think you can trust him with her."

Timmy shrugged. "He's a solid guy. I guess she could do worse. I just see him as, you know, sort of a criminal."

"Like us, you mean," Glendy responded.

"Yeah, sort of like us."

They sat quietly for a moment, both struck by a sense of having been left behind somehow despite having gotten rich. Then Timmy sighed and said, "Well, let's go in."

Bobby buzzed them into the building and they trudged up the stairs to his apartment. Timmy felt odd because he had been used to living in a place just like this until recently, but now found it beneath his standards. Yet he resented Bobby and he wasn't sure why. It was as if Bobby thought he was better than him, or something. He didn't understand the feelings.

But when the door opened it was the same old Bobby, despite the short hair.

"Hey, man!" he said. "It's really good to see you."

He hugged them both and Allie got up from the sofa smiling broadly and embraced them, too.

"What did you get for Wade?" she asked Timmy. She was excited about the party plans.

"A book about single malt scotches," Glendy told her. "We found it at Borders."

"We got him some kind of golf club. Amanda told us he wanted it. Boy, are those things expensive!" Allie shook her head in disbelief.

They all laughed.

"Sit down, you guys," Bobby said. "Want a beer or some wine or anything? We don't have to leave for a few minutes. Your mom wants us there by four."

"Nothing for me," Glendy said.

"I'll have a beer. What have you got?" Timmy asked.

"Heineken, Dos Equis, Bud," Bobby replied.

"Dos Equis."

They sat down in the living room and Bobby went into the kitchen. Timmy looked around the room and said, "Hey. Is that my TV?"

Bobby came in with his beer and handed it to him. "It used to be."

Timmy looked at him for a moment, then laughed and shook his head. "Okay," he said. "I don't blame you."

A little while later they all went down to the Cadillac and put the golf club in the trunk alongside the gift wrapped book. Then they all got in and drove off, heading west on Clifton toward Westlake in the pleasant afternoon sunshine.

Chapter 72

The red Wellcraft loomed up alongside, only a couple of dozen feet separating it from Wade's boat, and its wake rocked them back and forth vigorously.

"Ahoy! *Mudpuppy!*" called the lighter-skinned man on board.

Wade stepped to the port side of his boat to get a better look at them and said, "Ahoy!" He craned his neck, trying to get a good look at the two men, but the western sky was behind them and the sun in its three o'clock position obscured his view a little. It looked like about a thirty foot craft, and Wade knew it to be more powerful than his own. The Wellcraft's engines were idling and the helmsman, the darker man, nudged it in closer to them.

"Is Paul Johnson aboard?" called the other man.

Wade and Ralph and Amanda and Amy exchanged glances.

They were all on their feet, watching the Wellcraft move in. This was very unusual, to have another boat approach unexpectedly on the open water. Was this a case of mistaken identity, or was someone in trouble or something? "We have no Paul Johnson here," Wade called back.

"Oh, we thought you were Paul's party," came the reply. "Our friend has a Bayliner with the same name as yours."

The boat had drifted closer and only a dozen feet separated them now. Wade was struck by two things at once: nobody on Lake Erie besides him had a Bayliner named *Mudpuppy* and he knew it, and the man seemed to have a foreign accent. Then, unbelievably, the man raised a large grappling hook, swung it once and adroitly cast it across the space between them. It sailed through the air and connected with the topside bow and a cracking sound rang out.

Instantly the man pulled it tight with a heavy line as it caught on the upright portion of the bow rail. He began pulling the two boats together as the second man laid on a little power from the engines and motored in closer.

"Hey!" Wade shouted. "What the hell are you doing?"

The man launched two more grapples at them, one at the bow which missed and landed in the water, and the other at their stern. They all stepped back to avoid being struck by it as it landed in front of them, and then the man hauled on it and it caught the handrail. The boats were within seconds of being lashed together and Wade jumped forward again to try to pull the rear hook off.

"Step back!" commanded the man who was piloting the other boat in a deep bass voice. Wade looked at him and saw a large black handgun being pointed in his direction. He froze where he stood.

The first man stuck a couple of bumpers between the boats and finished lashing them together. On the *Mudpuppy* everyone was stunned and immobile, trying to make sense of what was going on. The first man pulled out a gun as well and the pilot shut down the Wellcraft's engines. For a silent moment they all regarded each other as they floated together, bobbing gently on the swells in the afternoon sunshine. Then both men stepped forward together and quickly boarded Wade's craft.

"What the hell is this?" Wade asked them, his mouth dry. Were there pirates now on Lake Erie? "You damaged my boat with that hook."

"Please raise your hands, everyone," said the black man in his sonorous voice. "Mr. Thomas, I'll ask you to please cooperate so that we can get this over with quickly and all go home."

Wade studied the two men for a few seconds. They were both in their late twenties, he thought. The black man was tall and heavily built and looked like he would be formidable even without the gun. The other was lighter skinned but still a little dark, an Arab perhaps, and had a neatly trimmed goatee. They both were dressed like Wade and Ralph were, in shorts and boat shoes and short sleeved shirts. They looked pretty much like any other boaters.

"What do you want from us? How do you know me?" Wade asked him, raising his hands. The others did the same.

The Arab stepped up to him and pulled a set of handcuffs out of the cargo pocket of his shorts. He stuck his gun in the back of his pants and quickly brought Wade's hands down one at a time and cuffed them in front of him. With the black man covering them, he did the same to Ralph and then to Amanda and Amy, but he secured theirs so that Amy's chain was inside of Amanda's. The women were effectively chained to each other.

"Please sit down," said the black man. They all slumped down together in the stern of the boat. While the black man pointed the gun steadily at them the Arab climbed down on the swim platform at the stern and began feeling around in the water below it. After a minute he pulled a white box the size of a pack of cigarettes out of the water. Wade saw that it had a black magnet on one side.

"Got it," said the Arab as he came forward again. He put the box in his cargo pocket, where the handcuffs had been.

"Okay," said the other one, and he seemed to relax. He looked at Wade. "That allowed us to find you, but since we are all together now we don't need it anymore." He smiled then, and it was not a reassuring expression.

Wade glanced at Ralph and he was pale, his eyes wide behind his Ray Bans. Amanda was slack faced and trembling a little, and Amy was, too. Whatever was happening was frightening and they were all feeling shock and fear. Wade felt terror grip the pit of his stomach.

"What do you need?" he asked the black man. "Please don't point that gun at us. You're scaring everyone." His voice was steady and he was surprised by that.

But instead of replying to him, the man said to his companion, "Get the anchors."

The Arab climbed back on board the Wellcraft and began lifting large anchors over the side and into the Bayliner. Wade recognized them as 25-pound Danforth anchors, which were heavy and expensive. There were eight of them. Once they were resting in the stern of the *Mudpuppy* he lifted two heavy canvas bags over, too. Wade could hear chains clanking inside.

"Okay," said the black man. "I think we're ready to begin." He was still grinning at Wade.

Now Wade was having trouble getting the words out. "Look," he said. "Whatever you're planning, you don't have to do it. We'll give you what you want, whatever it is. You don't have to hurt anybody."

Ralph said, "We...we can give you money. Tell us what you want."

Amy began weeping, and but Amanda started snarling at them, rage radiating from her eyes.

"You fuckers," she said. "We all have children at home. What's wrong with you?"

The black man laughed and the Arab smiled grimly at them, a tight, merciless, cold blooded look.

"Oh, you'll give us what we want, alright," said the black man.

"Take these two into the cabin," he said to the Arab, and he nodded at the women.

The Arab pulled out his gun again and motioned for Amanda and Amy to stand up. Then he herded them down the narrow steps and into the cabin below with them awkwardly shackled together.

"Don't hurt them," Ralph said, his voice pleading. "Please don't hurt my wife." Amy was crying and looking beseechingly at him as she disappeared below. The Arab pulled the hatch shut hard, the slamming sound echoing off the water.

"Now then, gentlemen," said the black man. "Let's get down to business."

He reached into one of the canvas bags and pulled out a length of heavy chain which he looped through Ralph's handcuffs, keeping his gun on them. Then he stepped back and threaded the chain through the loops of two of the anchors and snapped a padlock through the links. Ralph watched, horrified. He was connected to fifty pounds of anchors on a six foot chain. The man sat back against the side of the boat and looked at them.

"Okay," he said, his voice like a church organ. "This gun is a Beretta nine millimeter, just like American troops use." He waved the gun at them a little. "But I don't have it loaded with military bullets. They just make a neat hole through you. I use these." He took a bullet out of his pocket and showed it to them. It looked like a regular bullet except that it had a blue tip. "This is a Glaser Safety Slug. It goes very fast and then it explodes when it hits you. It's a mechanical explosion, but I'll spare you the details. Suffice it to say that if I shoot you in the knee, your knee will turn to soup. If I shoot you in the wrist, your hand may blow off. You get the picture." He smiled companionably. "Believe me, you want to avoid that."

Wade and Ralph just sat there, unable to move, fear on their faces.

"What do you want, for Christ sake? Just tell us!" Wade said to him. He strained to hear any sound from the cabin, to let him know what the Arab was doing with Amanda and Amy, but he only heard the water lapping at the boat's hull.

"You have some information that we need, Mr. Thomas," he said to him. "We've been tracking you for some time in order to put you in a position in which you'll feel compelled to tell us where that information is."

"Information?" Wade said, incredulously. "What information?"

"Some records you obtained from a man named Cesar Obregon," the man explained to him, and Wade sat back, dizzy, trying to understand.

"The MS-13 records?" he finally asked.

"That's right. The MS-13 records." The man looked hard at him.

Wade shook his head, confused. "You're not MS-13," he told him. "I don't get it."

The man sighed and shook the gun at him, a teacher emphasizing a point to a dim student. "No, we're not MS-13. We're the people they got their merchandise from. And it's possible those records are dangerous to us."

Then Wade got it. The high tech capture, the Arab, the professionalism. And he knew they were in the worst trouble imaginable, and despair ran through him like a wave. Heroin often came from Afghanistan, he knew. It was said to finance terror groups.

"Okay," he said. "Okay. This is not a problem. You can have the damn records." He suspected who these men might be, and he couldn't let them know that he knew. "I'll get them for you."

The man shook his head, smiling, and said, "No, we can do it more simply than that. Just tell me where the records are."

Wade thought wildly, looking for an out. "I need to get them for you. You can't get them yourselves. Let's go in and I'll do whatever you want."

Again the man shook his head. "No, Mr. Thomas. You tell me right now, or your friend here will be swimming in a moment."

Ralph started forward. "My God, Wade. What the hell is this about? Give him what he wants."

Wade looked steadily at the man. "You'll let us go? You promise?"

"Mr. Thomas, we have colleagues standing by. You tell us how to get the records and we'll call them. Then you can all go home. You don't know who we are, and I don't think you'll be informing on us."

He smiled reassuringly, and Wade didn't believe him at all. But he had no choice.

"It's a black notebook, a day planner. It's in the top drawer of my desk in my office at home."

"Really?" the man asked, surprised. "We thought maybe you had it in a safe deposit box or something."

"No. I didn't know it was still important. There's nobody there now, you can get it without a problem."

The man flipped out a cell phone and quickly tapped in a number.

"It's me," he said. "It's in his house, in the top drawer of his desk in his office and nobody's home." He listened for a moment and turned back to Wade. "What's your alarm code?" he asked. Wade told him.

The man repeated the code and snapped shut the phone and put it away. "Good," he said. "He's going there right now." He turned to the helm and looked it over quickly. Then he grabbed the radio handset, pulled out a pocket knife and sliced the cord cleanly in two. He tossed the handset overboard and closed and pocketed the knife.

Ralph lurched to his feet. "No! You can't!" he shouted.

The man was taken off guard but stepped aside to avoid Ralph's approach. "Hey, man, cut that shit out," he said. He raised the gun and hit Ralph solidly across the back of the head with it and Ralph slumped forward but stayed on his feet.

"Ahhh," Ralph said in pain, soft and middle-aged but intent on going after him. "You can't do this!" He staggered toward the man in the close quarters of the boat's stern. Wade levered himself upright off the deck. His green nylon fanny pack, in which he carried his valuables while on the boat, lay in the cubbyhole next to the helm and he made a grab for it.

The man caught Ralph's shackled hands as he reached for him and turned him aside and propelled him over the side. Ralph hit the water as Wade fumbled with cuffed hands to unzip the pouch. Then the man knelt quickly, grabbed an anchor in each hand, and dropped them over the side.

Wade got his fingers on the .38 in the fanny pack's recesses, the pouch covering his hands, and struggled to free the gun but the man had already turned away from Ralph and was aiming his Beretta at Wade. He leaped to starboard and up around the helm, grasping madly at the windshield with the pouch on his shackled hands, and up onto the bow. A shot rang out and Wade felt it zip through the air an inch from his ear, a lethal flying insect sound, and he crouched below the windshield and dodged forward and flung himself over the rail and off the bow and into the water below.

Chapter 73

Anwar drove Enver's beige Ford Taurus smoothly along Hilliard toward Wade Thomas's house. Traffic was moderate, about what you'd expect on a sunny and warm weekend afternoon. People here loved it when the weather improved. It was overcast more often than not even in the summer and Cleveland was actually windier than Chicago, the notorious Windy City.

"It's warmed up nicely," he said to Enver, who sat beside him looking out the window.

"Ask your parents about Egypt," Enver replied. "It's very warm there. People would be wearing heavy coats in this weather."

Anwar nodded. "I've been there a couple of times. Also Pakistan, for my training. So I know."

Enver glanced at him. "Your blood has thinned from growing up in this cold climate. Mine has, too, although where I come from it's colder than Egypt."

Anwar knew he was from Bosnia, but very little else about him.

"You were in Chechnya, right?" he asked.

"I was there for a couple of months three years ago. They asked me to go there to help out, and I went. It gets cold there, too. It's the Russians there, just like in Afghanistan many years ago. Islam has no shortage of enemies, my friend."

He had an interesting little gun which he had taken from a captured Russian special operations officer in Chechnya, right before they cut his head off. It was called a PSS silent pistol, and it fired steel

323

bullets from piston-like cartridges which made no sound. It was basically like a gun with a silencer but without the bulk of the silencer itself. The Russians used them for assassinations and other covert work.

Enver had his in his pants pocket and he took it out and double checked it to make sure he had a round in the chamber, then slipped the safety back on. He didn't know if he would run into a dog in the house. They were approaching the turnoff for the Thomases' subdivision.

They had surveilled it repeatedly in the past weeks and they knew exactly what to look for, and more importantly, when to decide that things were out of place. They watched for any unusual activity as they drove up the street, passing people cutting lawns, a dog here and there in its yard, a soccer mom with a vanload of small children talking on a cell phone as she hurried to some arcane suburban American activity.

"It looks okay," Enver told him. "Pull right into the driveway. I'll get out. Then circle the area and be back in exactly ten minutes."

They made sure their watches were in sync. "If I don't come out in thirty seconds do another drive-around and come back in three minutes. If all else fails, call my cell, or I'll call yours. Got it?"

Anwar nodded. "Got it. Good luck. And be careful."

Enver smiled at him. "We've watched these people for some time. Malik and Mounir took them easily on the lake. They are soft Americans, enjoying their comforts and indulgences. Don't worry."

They pulled into the driveway and Anwar stopped in front of the closed triple garage doors, which faced sideways. Enver hopped out and quietly closed his door and quickly walked around the back of the garage and was gone as Anwar eased the car back down the driveway again and headed smoothly down the street and out of the subdivision. They were like ghosts; it had only taken them seconds to make the dropoff.

Enver paused behind the attached garage and surveyed his surroundings. He was behind the house and screened from curious neighbors by a row of tall pine trees bordering the yard, but he didn't want to linger outside for long. He took his lock pick out and went to work on the door from the backyard into the garage. It surrendered in a few seconds, and he quietly turned the knob and pushed it open, hoping the door wasn't on the house alarm system. He stepped into the garage and closed the door behind him.

He heard no alarm beeping its ominous countdown, but he wanted to get into the house quickly and shut it off just in case. He moved swiftly through the spacious garage, noting the Jeep Grand Cherokee and Porsche Boxster and the sizeable accumulation of bicycles and boating and golf equipment. Typical American excess, he thought dismissively. He went up the steps to the door into the house and quickly went in. He found himself in an anteroom of sorts, with boots and shoes arranged along the wall, and jackets hanging on hooks. To his surprise he still heard no alarm noises. Had they forgotten to set it? Many people did, he knew. He turned the knob and walked into the quiet kitchen.

The room was large, with a hardwood floor and extensive cherry cabinetry. There was a large center island with a butcher's block top and stainless steel cookware hanging from ceiling hooks above it. An enormous white refrigerator with an ice cube dispenser occupied one corner. And the entire room was festooned with colored streamers and a sweeping banner which said, "Happy Birthday!"

Enver was taken aback, uncertain what this meant. Then he noticed that the counter was filled with stacks of paper plates and cups and bags of chips and snacks. Somebody was about to have a party.

At that moment a woman and a small boy walked into the room from the hallway leading to the front of the house. They saw him immediately and their eyes went wide as they stopped in their tracks.

"Hello," said the woman. "You're a little early." She looked vaguely uneasy, as if she were trying to figure out how he had gotten into the house. The boy was regarding him gravely.

"Hi," Enver said. "What time is it?"

The woman turned to look at the wall clock across the room, the boy doing the same, and Enver closed with them in that moment. He took out the gun and showed it to the woman, not threatening her exactly, but letting her know he had it.

"Do what I say," he told her. "Do not cause a disturbance or I will hurt the child."

To his surprise, the boy quickly and adeptly kicked him in the groin. It was completely unexpected and painful and Enver doubled over in agony. The boy grabbed the woman's hand and said, "Run, Grandma!"

The woman hesitated, though, and Enver straightened back up as the boy pulled at her.

"Don't!" Enver commanded them. Gritting his teeth through the surging nausea, he reached out and caught her hair and pulled her to him. "Stand still, boy, or I'll shoot your grandmother."

The woman turned to him, white faced. She was attractive but older, with graying curly blond hair. Tears started in her eyes from the pain of his grip.

"Don't hurt us, please," she said.

The boy had stopped moving and was glaring at Enver. He looked like he might kick him again if he had a chance to. Enver pushed them both away from the hallway and into a corner so they would have less chance of fleeing. He pointed the pistol at them, intimidating them into compliance.

He let go of the woman then and reached into the cargo pocket of his pants and brought out a roll of duct tape. Praise Allah he had thought to bring it, just in case. He turned the woman around and pushed her up against the counter and grabbed the boy, careful to avoid his hands and feet.

"Turn around," he told him.

The boy reluctantly turned and Enver quickly taped his hands together behind his back. Then he eased him to the floor and bound his feet. Now he didn't have to worry about him, and he took his time doing the same to the woman, making sure she couldn't work her way free. He stood over them, considering his options, while they looked up at him fearfully. The fight was out of the boy now that he was restrained.

"You almost had me there, little one," Enver told him, admiration in his voice. The boy just stared back. Enver leaned over each of them and pressed pieces of tape across their mouths.

"Just stay still and I'll get what I've come for and leave. You won't be harmed," he told them, but of course they would; he was simply interested in keeping them calm.

He grabbed each of them and dragged them into the back hallway or anteroom or whatever it was and closed the door. He would keep them alive in case he needed help finding the MS-13 records and then deal with them on his way out.

He walked quickly through the house and located the office on the first floor. He pulled open the desk drawer and found the notebook at once. He flipped through the address section and there his name was, just as he had suspected it would be. So all of this was necessary after all. He looked around the room for a moment, admiring the wood paneling and furniture. It was unfortunate that this family's existence would be erased, but that was what this war was all about. He regarded it as a blow against Western culture at the most fundamental level, so it was good. Everything else they planned and did was the same as this action only multiplied many times over, with thousands of individual Americans and American families as the targets.

He went purposefully out into the kitchen again. Finding the woman and the boy here complicated their plans. They had intended that this burglary would never be detected, and that the loss of the Thomases and their friends would look like a misadventure on the lake. Now he would have to dispose of these two. He decided that suffocation followed by a fire was the best scenario, and he would untape them after they were dead and before he lit the fire. It would look very strange to investigators, especially with the boating deaths at the same time, but they'd have little to go on. He felt that he'd be able to continue operating. There was simply nothing to link the events to a terrorist cell, nothing to raise suspicions that they existed at all.

He opened the door to the back hallway and they looked up at him from where they lay bound on the floor, terror in their eyes. At that moment he heard a car door slam in the driveway.

Chapter 74

Wade plunged deeply into the water, the cold shock of it jarring him to the core. Still desperately gripping the .38 in his right hand, he began paddling and kicking his way back to the surface, the handcuffs restricting his hand movements to barely effective flailing. The fanny pack dropped away. He felt water fill up his boat shoes and they fell off as he kicked and then he moved more quickly, his lungs starting to burn. He knew the gunman waited above, the Beretta with its explosive bullets pointed at the lake's surface.

As he burst up into the air again, water filling his eyes and streaming from his mouth, a terrific explosion rocked his head and he felt like he'd been slapped hard across the face and throat. He gulped air and went under again, a second explosion following him down and the back of his head and upper back registering a massive bee sting. He dove down, trying to get away from the bullets, knowing he'd been hurt but unsure how badly. He leveled off and swam at an angle away from his boat, not knowing how deeply bullets would go in water.

He ran into a heavy rope and opened his eyes to see what it was. Had someone dropped an anchor off of the bow of either boat? In a flash he remembered the second grappling hook, which had missed the *Mudpuppy* and presumably was tied off up on the Wellcraft. He grabbed it and began pulling himself up and the fear of drowning subsided, the rope giving him something to hang onto to compensate for his shackled hands.

He angled away toward the Wellcraft, the grapple trailing off below him somewhere in the depths. Maybe he could get around its bow and catch some air before the gunman jumped over from the *Mudpuppy* and got a shot at him again. Overhead he heard two more explosions ripping the water, the man trying to hit him as he swam, but curiously he didn't feel any pain, only a slight overpressure in the water as the blast wave struck him. He realized that the bullets were exploding on impact with the water.

He got around the Wellcraft's bow and pulled his head up into the air again, gasping for breath, and heard shouting. He peeked around the bow, expecting another shot, and saw the man leap across from his boat to the other. He knew he'd come forward and shoot down at him again. He took a deep gulp of air and sank below the surface and an instant later more explosions pummeled the water and this time he felt a little stinging on his face. He wasn't deep enough to avoid the metallic spray of the bullets, but it wasn't lethal. Time was running out; the man would eventually get him in this terrible game of cat and mouse. Sooner or later he'd score a direct head shot when Wade came up for air.

He feinted underwater back in the direction of the *Mudpuppy*, guessing the man would step over to that side of the Wellcraft, then quickly angled back to port and under the overhang of the bow with a powerful kick and thrust himself to the surface, hoping he hadn't miscalculated. As he sucked in air he looked up and the man wasn't there. He raised the .38 out of the water, holding on to the rope with his left hand, and waited as his heart thudded once, twice, for the man to look down at him again.

Then his face appeared, rage in his eyes, his teeth clenched and his lips back, peering over the edge and seeing Wade there under the overhang of the bow. The gun came forward, reaching for him.

"Ha!" said the man. "Now I've got you!" His face was eight feet away and he hadn't noticed the .38's snout protruding straight up at him from Wade's clenched hands, wasn't expecting it.

Wade pulled the trigger and hoped Bobby was wrong about the wadcutters, because he hadn't bothered to replace them with anything else. The soft lead slug caught the man under the chin and his head snapped back and blood began streaming down. He collapsed on the bow deck, his head and arms hanging over, and then slowly, with increasing momentum, began sliding over the edge. He hit the water awkwardly on the starboard side, just ahead of the *Mudpuppy*, and floated there like a broken doll.

In the cabin of the *Mudpuppy* Amanda and Amy sat huddled on the couch, watching the man with the gun fearfully. He kept it pointed at them as he sat across from them and regarded them balefully.

"Don't worry. We won't hurt you," he said in some sort of foreign accent. He was an Arab, Amanda thought. None of this made any sense to her at all. And she didn't believe his reassurance for a moment.

Then they heard a loud splash from outside, followed by a series of thumps as someone scrambled up onto the bow above them, and then a shot rang out.

"Oh, my God," said Amy.

The Arab leaped to his feet and quickly scrambled up the hatchway and threw open the door. He rushed out onto the deck.

Amanda and Amy stood indecisively, their hands chained together.

"We have to go and try to help," Amanda said, and Amy nodded through her tears. They began to cautiously climb the steps and peered outside.

The Arab was dodging back and forth on the stern deck, watching whatever was happening at the bow. A series of shots rang out, again and again, and they heard the black man cursing in his deep bass voice.

"Get his head, Malik," the Arab said. Then he moved out of their line of sight, going forward on the port side, and they edged carefully out into the stern, crouching low.

The Arab was out on the bow next to the other man, who was crouching and aiming and kept shooting into the water. There was no sign of Wade and Ralph.

Then, while the Arab knelt on the bow with his back to them, the other man leaped across to the boat they had come in and walked forward and began shooting into the water around the bow.

"We have to do something," said Amy.

"We have to get this guy before he comes back here and shoots us,"

Amanda replied. They crept up around the helm, carefully holding on to each other and the windshield, hanging onto the starboard side of the *Mudpuppy*, their bodies hanging precariously out over the lake as they moved. The black man was preoccupied on the other boat and the Arab was watching him with his back to them a few feet away, his gun in his hand.

Suddenly another shot sounded and they saw the black man fall flat onto the bow of the other boat.

"Malik!" cried the Arab man, and he stood up, staring across at his companion.

In that instant Amanda knew they had to move; it was probably the only chance they would get. She started forward, pulling Amy with her, and they leaped up onto the bow. They rushed forward in a crouch, Amanda compact and athletic, Amy with a model's agile lankiness.

The Arab man turned slightly, hearing them coming, and his eyes went wide and his mouth dropped open to say something. Then they hit him together, their shoulders into his chest, and his feet left the deck as his legs hit the rail behind him and he sailed out over the water, the gun flying away from him. He landed with a splash ten feet out beyond the *Mudpuppy*. Amanda fell to the deck to halt their forward charge and Amy landed on top of her. They slid to a stop at the edge of the deck against the rail.

While the Arab broke the surface and gasped for air, Amanda and Amy slowly stood up.

"Where's Ralph?" Amy asked nobody in particular.

"Wade!" Amanda called. "Where are you?"

They heard splashing and then saw Wade drift around the front of the other boat, blood streaming from his face, holding on to a rope which trailed down from above him and with a revolver in his hand.

"Get me out of here," he said to them. He looked over and saw the Arab man treading water a couple of dozen feet away and pointed the gun at him. "Stay right there," he said to him. The Arab floated and looked back and forth at each of them, and at the body of the other man bobbing on the swells, face down in the water and the back of his head bloody.

The two women hurried over to the other boat and tossed a loose rope to Wade, then hauled him around the port side to the stern and helped him climb up the transom ladder. Wade still had the gun in his hand as he climbed onto the deck.

"I didn't know you had that with you," Amanda said.

"Where's Ralph?" Amy shouted, desperation in her voice. Wade turned to her and they both saw that his face and upper back were peppered with tiny holes and blood was leaking steadily down his face. He reached forward and grasped Amy's hands in his.

"The black guy threw him into the lake with anchors chained to him," he told her, looking into her eyes. She looked back disbelieving at first, then overwhelmed.

"Oh, my God!" she cried. "Oh, my God! Can we get him? We have to get him!"

Wade hugged her closely. "We're in probably sixty feet of water. He went over a couple of minutes ago. There's no way we can reach him."

Amy was wild with anguish and tried to jump into the water to save him, but Wade and Amanda restrained her.

"We're handcuffed together, Amy," Amanda told her firmly, calmly.

"You'll drown us both."

"I'm so sorry, Amy," Wade told her, hugging her again. Amanda comforted her, too. "He's gone. I'm so sorry," he whispered to her, his face to her ear. She collapsed against them, sobbing, Wade's blood in her hair.

They climbed together back onto the *Mudpuppy* and Amanda sat with Amy in the stern, holding her closely to her and speaking in her soothing nurse's voice. Amy began shaking and her tears gradually stopped, her expression tortured as she leaned against Amanda.

"I'm afraid she's going into shock," she said to Wade. "You're bleeding. It looks superficial but there's a lot of it. We need help."

He turned to the radio but the black man had cut off the handset. He scrambled back over to the Wellcraft and found that they'd unplugged the handset on its radio, and it was missing. They had been taking no chances. Ralph had a cell phone so neither he nor Amanda had brought theirs. It was no doubt at the bottom of the lake.

He looked out over the water, the sun lower on the horizon now, and saw that the black man's body had drifted some distance off. He couldn't think of a quick way to get the phone he knew the man had in his pocket. After he untied the two boats from each other he could go after it, but that would take some minutes. He found the Arab still treading water out beyond his bow. The man stared impassively back at him as he bobbed around.

"Do you have a cell phone?" Wade called to him. He saw the man smile at him.

"Yes, I do," he said.

"Swim around to my stern and I'll help you on board. We need to call for help."

The man just looked at him for a moment, then said, "I don't think so." The he turned and began swimming away from the boats, out into the open lake and away from shore.

"Hey!" Wade called. "What the hell are you doing?"

The man stopped and glanced back at him and cried out, "Allah Ahkbar!" And then he slipped beneath the waves and Wade didn't see him anymore.

Shaken, he went to the stern and began trying to get the grappling hook off and saw that it was set into his handrail tightly. He'd have to go over to the Wellcraft and untie the rope from its stanchion there, or cut it.

"What did they want?" Amanda asked him, rocking Amy gently as they sat together. "What in the world did those men want from us?"

Wade broke open his tool chest and rummaged through it looking for his heavy serrated folding knife with its marlin spike for working knots loose, the handcuffs restricting his movements.

"It was the notebook from MS-13," he said to her over his shoulder. "These guys were their drug suppliers. They thought the notebook could incriminate them."

"Did you tell them where it is?" she asked.

"Yeah. They called somebody to go get it from our house. They're probably burglarizing us now."

"My God, Wade," Amanda said, and he heard the terror in her voice. He turned and looked at her, puzzled. "Your mother and Little Wade are there. We were planning a surprise party for you."

Chapter 75

Timmy drove the Cadillac up into Wade and Amanda's driveway, "Yeah" by Usher throbbing on the stereo. He put it into park and turned to look back at Bobby and Allie.

"Isn't that a nice sound system?" he asked. Glendy was beaming proudly next to him.

Bobby and Allie bobbed their heads up and down in agreement.

"It's a very cool car. Unbelievably smooth and comfortable. Can I move in back here? It's nicer than my apartment," Bobby said.

Timmy turned off the car and hopped out and eased the door closed behind him. Bobby got out on the passenger's side and slammed his. He noted Timmy's wince and remarked, "Built like bank vault. Don't worry about it." Glendy and Allie were rummaging around inside, getting their assorted birthday cards and cameras organized.

"I'm gonna check the back door. If it's unlocked, it's the shorter way," Timmy said, and headed around the garage.

Bobby loped up the walkway, past the front windows and up onto the porch. He opened the front door and walked in, announcing, "Hi! It's Bobby!"

Enver edged up the hallway to the vestibule and caught sight of a large man walking quickly past the front windows of the dining room toward the front porch. One car door had slammed, one person was here. He didn't know if the front door was locked or not. He eased quietly back down the hallway and just into the kitchen, twenty feet from the door, and waited, aiming his gun.

The door swung open and the man walked in, tall and broad chested, wearing one of those pink polo shirts with a little crocodile on it. Colorful tattoos decorated his muscular arms. The man announced himself loudly and in that instant saw Enver pointing the gun at him from the end of the hallway in front of him.

He reacted remarkably quickly, faster than Enver had expected, dodging to his right in the direction of the living room, where Enver could just make out a very nice oriental rug on the floor. But Enver was quicker and fired twice and he heard the bullets smack the man in his center of mass and he yelped and fell heavily to the floor.

Timmy tried the back door to the garage and found that it was open. He went in and walked through the garage, admiring the Boxster as he passed it. He went up the three steps and opened the door to the back hallway.

His mother and Little Wade were on the floor in front of him. They had duct tape around their wrists and ankles and across their faces but the recognition was instant. His mother's eyes were full of tears and she was surprised by his sudden appearance. Little Wade just looked scared.

He looked up past them through the open door and into the kitchen. Across the room from him, at the edge of the hallway, an average sized man he didn't know wearing tan cargo pants and a black polo shirt was aiming a short barreled pistol down the hallway.

Timmy saw him pull the trigger twice but the gun didn't make a bang, only soft metallic tapping sounds. Each time it spit a spent cartridge into the air and Timmy heard the bullets slap into something and Bobby cried out.

Timmy was a little mellowed out because he'd tasted just a tiny amount of smack a couple of hours ago. But it was strange because he felt that same instant rage he'd experienced the day Leroy had mocked him when he had shown up and taken Glendy away from him. It was overwhelming, and Timmy in that moment understood with perfect clarity that it had to do with losing love, losing people who loved him. He reaction was ferocious resistance.

He leaped into the kitchen to the nice, expensive set of Wusthoff knives in its wooden block on the counter and grabbed the biggest knife he saw, a ten-inch chef's knife. He turned to the man with gun, who by now was aware that he had come in behind him and was turning away from the hallway. Timmy sprang at him.

The man was very fast and brought the pistol to bear at once and shot Timmy. He felt the bullet hit him in the upper chest but the sensation was like a punch and he kept coming. He closed in on the man, slashing at the gun, but the man pulled back away from him and shot him again. The rage became a blind adrenaline assault and he grabbed the man's shirt with his left hand and plunged the knife down in a stabbing motion. The tempered steel blade bit down through the man's thigh to the hilt and the man staggered and screamed. Blood gushed up and ran onto the hardwood floor. They stumbled back, locked together, and Timmy yanked the knife free and raised it to stab him again. The man was still screaming, fear in his eyes, but he got the gun between them and fired again and then again. Suddenly Timmy felt his strength wash away and pain seized him. He released the man and sat down on the floor. He put his hands on his chest and they came away covered in blood. His vision seemed to dim a little as he looked up at the man, who was hobbling around clutching his thigh, blood surging through his fingers. Then Timmy fell over on his side. He was having a hard time getting his breath. He saw his mother looking at him from the floor of the back hall and their eyes held each other as he slipped into darkness.

Enver staggered around the room, cursing and trying to close the wound with his free hand. He set down the gun and yanked his belt out of his pants and quickly cinched it tightly around his thigh and the bleeding slowed down. He was in a lot of pain, but he forced himself to focus. He had the notebook in his pocket and if he could get rid of the witnesses he could still get away with this. He picked up the silent pistol again and went up the hall to check out the first man he'd shot.

Bobby lay on his side with his eyes closed in a puddle of blood. The blood was foamy and Enver knew he'd hit him in a lung. The man was breathing with difficulty. Enver stepped to within six feet of him cautiously and raised the gun. He saw that it was locked opened and was empty; he must have fired all six bullets. He reached into a pocket and pulled out his spare magazine. He released the catch at the bottom of the gun's grip and pulled out the empty, then slid home the spare. He released the stop and the gun chambered a new round. Through his pain he pointed his gun toward the man's head just as he rolled over a little onto his back and opened his eyes.

"Allah Ahkbar," Enver said softly as he began to aim at the man.

"My ass," gasped Bobby, and Enver saw a big Glock pointing at him which the man had been concealing underneath him. His eyes went wide and Bobby shot him in the heart.

Glendy and Allie were halfway between the car and the front door when they heard the muffled boom of Bobby's .45 going off. They stopped dead and looked at each other, then broke for the house at a full run. They threw open the door and saw Bobby lying halfway into the living room, blood soaking his shirt. A man they didn't know was lying across the hallway from him, his head in the dining room. He was flat on his back, his eyes open. His pant leg was bloody and there was a noticeable hole in his shirtfront and blood was spurting out as his heart struggled to pump. Then it faltered and stopped, the blood subsided and the man's eyes closed.

Allie was kneeling over Bobby, cradling his head in her arms.

"Oh, God, oh, God," she said. Bobby smiled at her.

"I nailed the fucker," he said. Blood began bubbling out of his mouth.

Glendy saw Timmy lying at the end of the hall in the kitchen. She ran to him and saw he was covered in gore. As she knelt to him she noticed Harriet and Little Wade lying bound in the back hall, watching her. She lifted his head, terrified at how limp and heavy he was, and his eyes fluttered open for a moment. He saw her and smiled.

"Beautiful," he whispered. And his eyes closed again.

Suddenly a figure appeared in the front doorway, and Allie and Glendy both looked at him together. It was a young man, dark featured, and they didn't know him. He looked at the dead man and anguish flooded his face. He pulled out a big black automatic pistol and pointed it at Allie.

Glendy had her tiny .22 in her hand. She'd pulled it out as soon as she heard Bobby's gun go off. She aimed carefully at the young man's chest from twenty feet away and pulled the trigger and the bullet caught him squarely in the groin. He shrieked and doubled up and dropped to the front hallway floor, his gun falling away, and he writhed and cried while Glendy and Allie held Timmy and Bobby, rocking them and trying to comfort them while they pressed their hands to their wounds.

The next people through the door, thirty seconds later, were Brian and Kathleen Pomeroy, and that's what saved Bobby's life. But they couldn't save Timmy.

Epilogue

Wade sat on the outdoor patio of a restaurant in the Flats and watched an enormous freighter edging into the bend in the Cuyahoga River. Frankly, as a boater he couldn't see how the captain was going to be able to do it; the ship was too large and the angle too sharp. But as he looked on, the vessel carefully shoehorned itself into the curve, narrowly missing the banks on either side, and then straightened for its run up into the mouth of the river and Lake Erie beyond it.

It was a sunny fall day and the Flats weren't busy in the afternoon. Tonight the weekend crowds would be there, but now only a scattering of patrons sat with their drinks and watched the river traffic coasting by. The leaves had changed on the trees and were close to falling. Summer lingered in the air but the crispness of autumn was making itself felt, too. Wade was nondescript in his sunglasses and jeans and lightweight blue jacket, and he didn't know anyone there, which was fine with him. He had been answering questions for dozens of people for months and he was tired of it. He had picked the restaurant for his meetings because he wouldn't be likely to run across any acquaintances there.

Bobby came out of the door and onto the patio, looking around for him, and Wade raised his hand and waved. He noted the gauntness in Bobby's appearance as he approached, the effects of the gunshot wounds lingering in his face and in his gait. The doctors and the police had told them that the bullets had passed right through him, damaging a lung, and had not expanded because they were some special sort of solid steel slugs specifically made for the terrorist's silent pistol. So that was a good thing.

Bobby reached the table and pulled out a chair and eased himself into it.

"How you doing?" Wade asked him, and they shook hands.

"It still sort of feels like I was hit by a truck. But all in all, what the hell. It could have been worse. I'm doing better all the time."

The waitress came out the door, following Bobby, and approached them.

"Make mine a Corona," Bobby told her. "Wade?"

"I'm good," Wade told her, raising his half-full Heineken. She looked at Bobby speculatively, smiling as she walked away, looking back at him.

"How's Allie?" Wade asked.

Bobby laughed. "Great. We're doing fine. We went through all this together and we're still feeling really good about where we're at. The business is doing well and she's busy with her studies, as you know. But we're together as much as possible."

Wade nodded and smiled. "Cuthbert from the FBI just left," he said.

"Glad I missed him. What did he have to say?"

"We're all going to get something out of the Rewards for Justice Program. Soon, he thinks. They want to buy some cooperation, I figure, and we'll have to sign non-disclosure agreements before we see any money."

Bobby snorted disdainfully. "Shit, we killed three Al Qaeda for them and handed over another one, thoughtfully neutered for docility. They should give us fucking federal pensions."

"Yeah. Or they could have prosecuted me for withholding the MS-13 book. This could have gone either way, but I think they want to keep us happy and off the public radar so they can pursue all the leads they got out of Fifini's house. Cuthbert told me this is all considered a matter of the highest national security, and that trumps anything the local authorities might want to do about it."

"They don't know how long you had the book or whether you knew what it meant."

"Fifini had MS-13 notes saying I had it. My lawyer's position is that it came from Tim and I didn't know its significance. I sure as hell didn't know it meant anything about terrorism. Jim Mullin probably isn't too happy with me, but it's a closed matter. They want to get on with running down more of the bad guys. They've got the heroin angle figured out and that means trails back to Canada and to MS-13 in Central America. And to Afghanistan. This'll keep them busy for a while, and get more of these people out of circulation."

They sat and watched a couple of small cabin cruisers glide by, the owners getting in a little more water time before the cold weather closed in. The waitress came back with Bobby's beer and he paid her. She smiled at him but his mind was elsewhere and she drifted over to the other tables.

"How's the job?" Bobby finally asked.

"Good, really. I'm in a partnership with two other ex-Conlin guys and we're moving ahead. It's going well. I couldn't stay at Conlin after what happened to Ralph. We're settling into the new house, Little Wade's seeing the psychologist every week, and my mother's doing as well as can be expected."

"We got lucky," Bobby said. "You've got Amanda and Little Wade and your mom, I've got Allie and my family, we're self-employed and doing well. We survived those bastards."

"Amanda's still unhappy with it," Wade said, gazing out at the boats going by and the gulls wheeling overhead. "She thinks I could have avoided a lot of this if I'd gone right to the police when you first came to me."

Bobby nodded and sipped his beer. "Yeah, and then we'd have been in a different kind of trouble. There was no easy way to deal with all of this. Who the hell knew you were being stalked by Al Qaeda, for God's sake? Who could have known? We're lucky we survived. Most of us, anyway."

They were quiet for a while, thinking about Timmy and about Ralph.

"Have you seen Glendy?" Wade finally asked.

"Deadeye?" Bobby laughed. "Yeah, I saw her last night. She's still living in the apartment on Lake. If she gets money from the Feds, and she ought to, she'll probably be pretty well situated. But she's sad. She really misses him."

Wade nodded. "Everybody misses him. I miss him. I couldn't save him."

Bobby leaned over to him and said, "Hey. He saved us. He saved everyone who was at your house that day, and he probably saved Brian and Kathleen, too. He knew exactly what he was doing when he went after that guy. He saved your mother and your son. He had very little chance of winning, but he went after him anyway. It was amazing, considering. I didn't know he'd do something like that."

Wade nodded, watching clouds moving in from the east, autumn coming on relentlessly. He smiled and said, "I know." His mind drifted over the events of the past months, the terrible flaws in Tim's makeup that had led them to that awful sunny afternoon. He considered all the treachery and selfishness that had contributed to what had happened, and to that last, shining act of selflessness. Thinking about his brother in that moment, Wade realized that he was more proud of him than anything else.

Author's Note

As of this writing, 85% of the heroin in America comes from Afghanistan. The quality varies.

The Lake Erie region has historically been a smuggling route for contraband coming into the United States from Canada. Whiskey Island, in the mouth of the Cuyahoga River in Cleveland, got its name during Prohibition as a transit point for liquor smuggling. Authorities have long recognized that drug smugglers make use of the very porous border in the lake and the many small islands there.

In May of 2004, Saudi Arabian native and Al Qaeda leader Adnan G. El Shukrijumah was reportedly spotted in an Internet café in Tegucigalpa, Honduras. He had previously spent ten days in Panama in April of 2001. Honduran Security Minister Oscar Alvarez reported that three government informants had claimed that four individuals from "somewhere in the Middle East" had smuggled $1 million in cash into Honduras to finance a migrant-smuggling operation controlled by the MS-13 gang.

MS-13 is operating throughout the United States at present and is heavily involved in drug trafficking.

Printed in the United States
95606LV00005B/97/A